Five Days in May

Five Days in May

by

NINIE HAMMON

Bay Forest Books

Five Days in May
Copyright © 2011
Ninie Hammon

Cover Illustration by Mona Roman Advertising
Interior Design by BookMasters

Published by Bay Forest Books
An Imprint of Kingstone Media Group
P.O. Box 491600
Leesburg, FL 34749-1600
www.bayforestbooks.com

Printed in the United States of America by
Bay Forest Books

Library of Congress Cataloging-in-Publication information is on file.

ISBN 978-1-936164-31-8

Prologue

It dropped out of the sky at 3:41 p.m. central daylight time on Friday, May 10, 1963, into a field in southeastern Oklahoma eight miles west of Tishomingo. It was so big you could have seen it from Tishomingo if it hadn't been dark as midnight there, hailing hunks of ice the size of hockey pucks. But you could see it from Madill, eleven miles away. Well, the top of it anyway. And the monster super-cell thunderstorm that birthed it, you could see that for more than a hundred miles in every direction.

It didn't look like a tornado, though. At well over a mile wide, it looked like a bubbling black wall, like a curtain coming down onto the stage after the last act of a play.

If there'd been anybody nearby to see the behemoth descend out of clouds the greenish-purple of a day-old bruise, they'd have stood there gawking, wondering *what in the world ...?* But there was nobody around to see it touch down and chances are they wouldn't have lived to tell the tale if there had been.

The field it landed in was full of old corn stalks from last summer, dry and brittle. Farmer died and nobody'd got around to plowing them under. The twister sucked the stalks up, thousands of them, and the top ten inches of the dirt they'd been growing in. Turned the wall a rusty brown color as it rumbled across the prairie toward the stampeding herd of Black Angus cattle in the next field.

It gobbled up the cattle, too, all eighty-eight head of them. Lifted them up and slammed them into the ground over and over before it finally spewed their mangled corpses over the next two and a half miles of prairie—tangled up bodies impaled with dry corn stalks. Bloody porcupines.

Skinned porcupines. The hide had been sucked clean off every last one of them.

The brownish-black wall turned then, headed northeast toward Graham.

Monday

May 6, 1963
Graham, Oklahoma

1

Her heart banged away in her chest like a fist pounding on a locked door. Princess lay in the dark and listened to it, looked at the little piece of sky she could see out the tiny square window high up on the wall above her, and felt each individual heartbeat in that big vein in her neck.

And she wondered if that was being scared. If what she was feeling was fear. She had trouble with that, knowing the names of the things she felt. That feeling of her heart in her throat, and the empty, airy-feeling just under her ribs, like there was nothing there at all, like her body had a big rip and the wind was blowing through it. She was pretty sure that was fear.

But maybe other folks didn't feel that at all when they were scared. Maybe that feeling was something else altogether. If it wasn't fear, though, what was it? And how awful must fear be, if that wasn't even it?

She made a *humph* sound in her throat. Well, one way or the other, she'd find out pretty da-gone soon. She'd find out what *real* scared was when they strapped her into Ole Suzie and turned on the juice!

She breathed in and out carefully, tried to slow her heart down, make it stop racing. It was hard to think with her heart pounding, and she wanted to think. Most times, she expended considerable effort *not* to think. Today was different. Today, she could let go and savor the memories.

Princess had taken such good care of the memories all these years: little gemstones, each one different and perfect and with its own light, its own glow like a firefly on a summer night. Green ones and red ones and bright white ones. Golden ones, too—they were the best. But she'd always understood that the light wouldn't last, that there was just so much of it and then it would start to go out. That's what happened to a candle. Keep it lit all the time and after awhile there wasn't no candle left. So she saved the light. Didn't just haul the stones out and look at them any old time, using up the precious light, wasting it. She limited herself, like somebody lost in the desert saved the water in the canteen. Just a few drops now and then. Just barely enough to stay alive.

But it didn't matter anymore now. No reason to save the light. She could turn up the canteen and drink deep from it, swallow great gulping mouthfuls of the cool liquid, even let some of it run down her chin and drip off onto her dress.

She planned to fill up every second she possibly could with the glow of her precious stones, stare into the twinkling light of each one of them.

If only her heart would stop pounding so.

She threw back the moldy-smelling blanket and sat up on the side of her bunk in the chilly pre-dawn air. Then she reached over and pulled the blanket back around her shoulders, scratchy wool, an old army blanket. And wondered as she'd wondered so many times before if some soldier had wrapped up in that blanket once. If it'd kept some young man warm on some battlefield somewhere. She'd sniffed it when she first got it, tried hard to find the faint scent of sweat, fear-sweat, maybe. But it just smelled old and moldy, like it'd been stored away in a musty attic.

She sat with her bare feet on the cold concrete floor, shivering, watching the little piece of sky turn from gray to pink, then a pink/yellow combination that slid through yellow into blue. It did that every day it didn't rain. This morning the sky'd be blue. She knew it would be. Blue and sunshine. It was May, after all, and on a May morning in Oklahoma, there'd be sunshine.

That's not why she knew, of course. She knew the sun would shine the way she just *knew* other things, things she couldn't possibly know, but she did.

Like she was going to see Jackson soon. Of course, he'd come. Her last week, he'd come. And she was even, just a little bit, looking forward to seeing him this time, the last time. But she also knew the other one would come, the good man, the father man, the one with the smile on his face and the tears on his cheeks, the one she'd seen with eyes that weren't hers. She knew he'd be here *today*. There was no possible way it could happen, but she knew it would.

And she knew something else, too. Something that caused that open, airy feeling below her ribs, made her heart pound hard in the vein in her neck. Something that stabbed her deep down in the guts with a feeling she knew had to be fear.

Something was wrong with the child, the father man's girl. The knowing of it had been growing on her for weeks. There were dark, bat-like creatures in her head that fluttered around frantic when she closed her eyes. They made a low hum in her ears, like a generator.

The whole knowing would come eventually; it always did.

But what if there wasn't enough time left to do anything about it once she found out what it was?

◆ ◆ ◆ ◆ ◆

Joy McIntosh woke up, sat up, and threw up. One, two, three. Happened every morning.

She didn't run to the bathroom, though. Daddy'd already heard her twice. She couldn't chance waking him again. So she'd sneaked Grandma Maggie's old chamber pot out of the attic and slipped it under her bed about a week ago; she'd been using that.

She leapt out of the bed, dropped to her knees on the cold hardwood floor, and dragged the porcelain pot out from under her bed. She slid the lid off and leaned over it just in time to spew out a foul spray of bile and stomach acid that burned the back of her throat and the roof of her mouth on the way out. She heaved two or three more times reflexively, then sat back panting, tears running down her cheeks.

Slowly, the nausea passed. She slid the lid back onto the pot and pushed it under her bed and climbed back between the sheets. They were still warm.

Then she lay there, staring at the dappled dawn light that shone on the pale blue ceiling in her room through the mulberry tree outside her window. She tried to cry. She thought it would make her feel better, the way you feel better after you throw up when you're nauseous. But she was cried out.

How do you know it's mine? Gary had said.

Had *said* that!

Like she was some floozy. Like she'd done *that* with somebody else. Like she wasn't a good girl at all but some *tramp*.

Well, she was a tramp, wasn't she? Come on, look it in the eye, Joy, face reality. Tramps did it with boys and got in a family way— right? Hard to find a way around that.

No, you weren't a tramp if you got married right quick—*at sixteen?*—and everybody who knew you pretended they'd suddenly lost the ability to count to nine.

You weren't a tramp if nobody knew, if nobody found out.

And you weren't a tramp if you *fixed* it, if you did something about it.

She balled her hands into fists and pounded them into the feather mattress on both sides of her, over and over again. Tears squirted out of her eyes and flowed down the sides of her face and into her hair, and she'd honestly believed she didn't have a tear left to cry.

She wanted to scream, wail, do something to make that awful feeling in her gut go away, make it …

"Oh!" It was just a little sound, but she spoke it aloud into the silent room. Surprise and wonder.

What was that? That fluttering? That feeling right *there,* in the same place that was tied in a knot all the time.

Again! She felt it again. She hadn't imagined it! Like something had … No. Couldn't be. Couldn't *possibly* be.

But it was. Something had *moved* inside her.

She cried then. Oh, my yes, she cried then! Sobbed. Curled up in a ball, buried her face in her pillow and sobbed.

◆ ◆ ◆ ◆ ◆

Mac thought he heard a sound in Joy's room. A scraping sound, then a little later a voice, a word. He lay still and listened. Yeah, she was crying. Muffled, but he could hear it.

And?

Did he go to her? Tap on his daughter's door, slip quietly into her room and comfort her, put his arms around her and say … Yeah, say what?

Oh, he knew what to say. Knew exactly what to say. Not many people had actually taken courses on what to say in difficult situations. But he had. Seminary was all about comforting the hurting.

The stages of grief. Knew them all. Started with denial and ended with acceptance and had anger and bargaining and other things in between.

He'd only made it as far as anger. He didn't want to go any further. What was the point? The absolutely proper response to certain life situations was rage: pure, unadulterated rage. Any other reaction was ludicrous—or phony. And he'd tried phony. He'd lived phony. He'd pretended until …

So, should he pretend just a little longer? Jump into a phone booth and hop out with a big M on his chest, the mighty Minister, able to leap tall buildings at a single bound?

Tell Joy, "It's okay, sweetheart. Your mother's in a better place."

Or maybe, "You'll see her again, someday, honey."

Perhaps throw in a little, "Pray about it and you'll feel better."

Nope, not a chance. No. Can. Do.

She'd see through it if he tried. Joy was a smart girl. She'd see through the flimflam game. Probably already had.

It might just be that his daughter was the only person in the whole town of Graham who wouldn't be surprised by what he was going to tell the board of elders Friday night and the congregation on Sunday. She'd understand. He was sure that deep down, she felt the same way.

◆ ◆ ◆ ◆ ◆

Jonas rubbed lotion all over her that morning, first thing, wasn't even light outside yet. Maggie always did wake up early. She used to have breakfast ready—eggs and bacon and home-made biscuits and gravy—'fore he ever even knew she was out of the bed. He'd smell the coffee and bacon and he'd roll over and reach for her, but there was just the warm spot in the sheets where she'd been.

She'd stand at the foot of the stairs and holler up, "Jonas, are you going to sleep all day?"

All day? Shoot, the rooster hadn't even crowed yet!

He'd come staggering down the stairs, hair all upside down with bed-head, a big ole sheet crease across his cheek, and she'd look … oh my. She'd take your breath away. When she was young, folks said she favored the actress Greta Garbo. But Maggie was way prettier than Greta Garbo.

She hollered out, "Jonas!" that morning, too. But she was just talking in her sleep. Made him think maybe she dreamed about him, though, so he didn't want to wake her up.

But she was wiggling around, just couldn't seem to get situated, and he figured the lotion would help. Her skin had got so dry it looked like a creek bed during a drought, all cracked and peeling. Had to itch.

What must it be like to itch and not know that's what's wrong with you? Or what to do about it? Something as simple as an itch, and you don't know to scratch it. Which of course, begged the question: how do you know what you don't know? What is there to think "I've lost my mind" when you've lost your mind?

He got out the green bottle of hand lotion that said it had aloe and herbal extracts mixed in. Started on her right foot with a big handful of it, smeared it on every toe and in between them. Around the callus on her big toe and the bunion just down from it, up on the top of her foot, to her ankle, her calf, her knee and her thigh.

Smoothing it, rubbing it in, stroking gently in the dark with his big, rough hands.

He did it with his eyes closed. Remembering.

And yeah, he felt a stirring, 'course he did. He was old; he wasn't dead! All those years he touched her, felt her lean into him and melt like warm butter.

Then he got to the diaper she slept in and he squirted another handful of lotion into his hand and started on her left foot.

Soon as he'd smeared lotion all over her, she stopped wiggling. Didn't itch anymore and she could sleep then. He lay beside her, staring into the darkness, listening to her breathe, wondering if he could do it and knowing he had to. Tears streamed out of his eyes and ran down the sides of his head into his big ears as the sun came up. There were only a handful of sunrises left to spend in bed beside his Maggie before he killed her.

2

*T*HERE ARE BLINKING LIGHTS ON THE *marquee above the big gate where the crowd of people is pushing and shoving its way through. Princess sees the lights and she wants to look at 'em, her eyes are drawn to 'em. But she looks away quick, turns her back.*

Can't look at them lights. If she looks, they'll give her a fit, sure. She found that out the day that little bitty carnival set up in the vacant lot across from the sawmill on the edge of town right after Angel learned to walk. They passed by it on the way to get Jackson's check that time. There was flashing lights there, too, and she threw a big fit, woke up all soiled and Jackson mad, people standin' around staring at her like she was a freak.

This is it. She has finally found the right place. She knows it's time, too, and a deathly cold shiver runs down her spine. But there are still precious moments left and she's gotta hold tight to 'em, squeeze every last drop of joy out of each one.

She looks at Angel. Angel is light, too, but not like the marquee. She is light from the inside. A pure white glow shines around the little girl and when she smiles, the light's so bright it 'bout puts your eyes out. Sometimes, when Angel was a baby and Princess was feeding her in the middle of the night, she'd look up with them big brown eyes of hers and smile so big the glow from her lit up the room bright enough you could see the furniture, like in them people's houses who had electricity and could flip a switch and it'd be light at midnight.

She gets down on her knees beside Angel and re-rolls the legs of the little girl's pants, the ones Princess stole off a clothesline. They're too long for the child, but the little cotton shirt that was hangin' beside them is just the right size. Only has two of four buttons but it fits fine. Princess had time, she'd cut off them pants legs and sew 'em up so they'd fit, find some buttons to sew on that shirt, too.

But there is no time left.

She makes fat rolls on both pant legs. Then she straightens up and takes Angel's hand, so little and warm in hers, as they cross the field where the grass has been crushed by people walkin' on it. So many people, more than Princess has ever seen in one place. All of 'em talkin' and laughin', excited, like they'd come special invited to a big party. Princess listens, catches pieces of conversations,

"... a feller whose whole body—well, all you could see of it and that was more'n was decent—was covered in tattoos he got in the jungles of Borneo where—

"And you b'lieve that? I bet they painted them tattoos on him this afternoon; paint's pro'ly still wet."

"... I have a bag of peanuts? Mary Lou got peanuts!"

"... a lady snake charmer with snakes wrapped all ..."

"... ain't gonna win nothin'. Them game's rigged sure as ..."

Music from a calliope at the far end of the field mixes with the laughter, applause, and squeals of kids inside the big tent where the show's already started. It costs another twenty-five cents to go into the big tent and Princess has only a little money left. When the money runs out, so does the time. Besides, Princess is just fine with the sights and smells and sounds all around her—that's show enough.

She wanders down the midway past wagons painted purple with gold trim and sunburst wheels. Each has got the same words printed on it that hung above the gate where the man took her dime and handed her a ticket: Trimboli Brothers Circus, The Greatest Show on Earth. Says the same thing on the ticket stub and she kept it. Just the one ticket. Angel got in free, her being so little.

Princess and Angel stroll by red-and-white-striped concession stands with glasses of lemonade stacked in pyramids, banners with pictures of gigantic snakes, roaring lions, clowns, and one of an enormously fat woman *dressed in nothing a'tall but colored feathers. One banner promises Wonders Gathered From the Four Corners of the Globe. Another proclaims See The Amazing Oddities And Freaks of Nature.*

Princess turns and leads Angel away from that one, the one that talks about freaks.

A barker hollers, "Step right up, right this way. C'mon, c'mon, c'mon! Ring the bell and win a teddy bear!"

They stop to watch. A young farm boy takes his shirt off and hands it to his girlfriend, who stands there giggling, holding the shirt out from her like you'd hold a dead mouse by the tail. The boy spits in the palm of one hand, then the other, takes the sledgehammer and waggles it around, gettin' the feel of it. Then he raises it high in the air and slams it down on a beat-up metal plate with a thunderous Bam!

The impact fires a red metal circle up the pole. It flies up toward the bell … then slows, stops, and settles back down. The boy groans, the girl sighs, the barker takes the hammer and says, "C'mon, son, you can do it. Win your girl a bear." He lowers his voice. "I'll make you a special deal. One try for a nickel; three tries for ten cents."

Princess and Angel move on as the boy deposits a dime in the barker's palm and a gob of spit in his own.

Every breath draws in a different smell carried on the evening breeze. Corn popping. Peanuts roasting. Crushed grass and crushed lemons. Dust. And the underlying stink of warm piles of manure.

"You hungry, honey?" she asks Angel.

When the child nods her head, her rust-colored curls dance on her shoulders.

"You want some ice cream? It's real good!"

"Ice ceem!" The child fairly sings the word, dancing up and down with excitement.

Princess lets go of Angel's hand, checks to make sure no one's standing nearby, and digs down into the pocket on her flour-sack shift, the right front pocket. She made sure to put the key to the car in her left pocket and the money in her right. She is being very careful. She pulls the zippered change purse out and opens it just wide enough to see the money stuffed down in it. She counted it this morning, soon's she woke up, curled around Angel in the backseat of the big Ford car she'd covered with brush down a dirt road a couple of miles from town.

She'd sneaked $20 out of Jackson's front overalls pocket. A whole week's wages at the sawmill 'cept what he'd drunk up at Shakey's Tavern that night. And when he found out what she'd done ... no, she couldn't think about that now or she'd start to tremblin' and have a fit sure.

What she has left after almost two weeks on the run is $2.05—a one-dollar bill, a fifty-cent piece, a quarter and three dimes. She'd brought food along with a few belongings in the knapsack she made out of a flour sack: apples, cheese, some vegetables and cold cornbread, and they'd eaten that for two days in the boxcar. Then she'd had to buy what they ate: bread and milk, some lunchmeat, and other necessities. And one day they'd even had two bowls of soup and sodas in a diner.

She selects the quarter, zips the purse shut, and shoves it down deep into her pocket. Then she leads Angel to the booth where a man is selling pink and blue globs of cotton candy rolled up on the end of paper sticks, big sacks of popcorn, and ice cream cones.

"What'll you have, little missy?" the man asks Angel. Adults always talk to her, always stare at her.

"Ice cream," Princess answers for her. "Hon, what flavor you want, the chocolate or vanilla?"

"Ice ceeem!" Angel squeals, all smiles, glowing bright as a coal in a wood stove.

"She'll have chocolate. How much?"

"They're fifteen cents apiece, two for a quarter. Sure you don't want two of 'em?" The man's old, with greasy gray hair, and he doesn't smell good. He has that look in his eyes that people get when they're looking at you but not really. Like they're worn out and just starin' and you happen to be standin' where they're starin'.

"No thanks, just the chocolate."

She drops the quarter into the man's dirty, outstretched palm and takes the ice cream cone he hands to her with the dime change. She gives Angel the cone, and while she puts the dime back into her coin purse the child takes a big bite, gets a ring of chocolate around her mouth and a gob of it on the end of her nose.

"Ice ceem!" she says, her tongue all chocolatey, and takes another bite.

"Don't eat it too fast or it'll make your head hurt."

Angel feels the piece of ice cream on her nose, reaches up to pluck it off, and ends up smearing it on her cheek instead.

Inside ten seconds, the child's face is coated in chocolate.

Princess throws her head back and laughs out loud at the sight. That's when she spots the photo booth, up next to a telephone pole beside the fat-lady banner. There was a booth just like it in the Woolworth's store where she and Mama used to live in Texas. Four pictures for fifty cents. That's a lot of money, but ... Then it occurs to her that she must get a picture, no matter how much it costs, that nothing is as important as a photo—even if she has to spend all the money she has left.

"Come on, Angel, we're gonna get our pictures took!"

Three teenage girls stand outside the booth, holding a strip of pictures, giggling over it, as they approach.

"Your eyes are shut in all four of 'em," the pretty blonde tells the pudgy brunette.

"I can't help it, I always blink in pictures."

They see Princess coming and step out of her way, looking at her. She reads in their eyes what they see—a girl with her lanky hair all tangled, wearing a patched flour-sack dress and no shoes, holding onto a sticky-faced, barefoot toddler wearin' worn-out pants rolled up 'cause they're too long.

She knows they've branded her and Angel white trash. The teenagers move out of the way like maybe it's catching.

Princess steps into the booth and pulls the ragged black curtain closed, sets Angel on her lap, and carefully reads the instructions. She pulls the fifty-cent piece from her coin purse, focuses on the spot that says "Look right here," and drops the coin into the slot.

"Smile, Angel!"

A buzzer sounds, followed by a flashing light. The combination sur-prises Angel and she turns away and buries her head in Princess's chest.

"It's okay, honey." The buzzer again and the light. Angel tunes up to cry.

"No, sugar ..." Princess lifts the child so their faces are side-by-side. "Now, sm—"

The buzzer and the flashing light fire again and Angel wails and drops her ice cream cone.

She reaches down for it as the buzzer and light go off a final time.

"Aw, sugar, you can't eat it now, it's dirty."

"Ice ceeeem!" She's crying hard now, squirming to reach the ice cream cone stuck ice-cream-side-down on the floor of the booth.

"I'll get you another one, a clean one. You can't eat that dirty ole thing; it'll make you sick."

She pushes the curtain back and lifts the crying, wiggling child up into her arms. The teenagers are still standing there, just looking at her as Angel wails and she tries to comfort her.

"Hush now, sweetie pie. I'll get you another one."

She heads off toward the ice cream booth and gets almost there when somebody taps her on the shoulder from behind. She turns—Angel's screaming—and one of the teenagers is standing behind her.

"You forgot your pictures." The chubby, dark-haired girl holds out a strip of paper with four photos on it. "Just came out of the machine." She offers a little half smile.

"Thank you," Princess mumbles, and looks into the girl's eyes for a moment. The girl's not pretty like the others so she knows. Then Princess rushes off to get Angel some more ice cream.

She doesn't even look at the pictures until much later.

PRINCESS HELD THE WORN STRIP OF photographic paper bearing the four pictures and stroked it lovingly. It was the only possession she had that mattered to her, and she stared at the pictures every day. She could see them crisp and clear as the day they were taken, but only with her heart.

The first picture showed the hollow-eyed face of a teenage girl with horrible bumps and yellow pimples on her sallow skin and stringy, tangled, straight blond hair. Mama always called the color "dishwater blonde." The girl was holding an angel in her arms. The little girl had dark curls and chocolate ice cream smeared around her mouth and on her chubby cheeks. Her little tongue was stuck out, ready to lick the ice cream cone in her hand.

The second picture showed the same teenage girl, her face surprised and full of concern, and the back of the little girl's head, her curls hanging all the way down to her waist.

But the third picture! Ah, the third picture was the one Princess treasured. Two faces, side by side. The angel and the teenager. Sticky beauty and adoring love.

The fourth image was blurred by movement.

Didn't matter anymore if it was blurred or not. All the images were gone, had long since faded away. Nothing remained on the strip of paper but the dark background and the ghosts of two people. Her face was a blank smudge with dark spots where her eyes should have been; Angel was completely invisible.

That was as it should be. Angel—completely invisible. She touched the third empty frame with her finger, stroked it gently.

And that's when the darkness came. Her memories, the precious ones, were balls of light. But there were other ones that were balls of darkness. As the precious memories could light up a room, the dark memories could suck the light out of it. Dark memories could open up at noon on a sunshiny day and darkness would flow out of them, eat up all the light until it was just like being blind.

Dark and cold—freezing cold.

When that happened, Princess usually had a fit. The darkness and the cold were part of the fit. She'd wake up later and she'd wet herself—messed her pants, sometimes, too—and it'd be over and she didn't remember much of it.

But this time, the dark memory came and she didn't have a fit. She sat there in the blackness as the first shaft of morning sunshine streamed through the window. She shivered in the freezing cold of her memory on a May morning and saw herself back at the circus.

The calliope's playing, kids are squealing inside the big tent, and there's music coming from one of the side tents, the one with the fat lady banner on it. It's Perry Como singing "A: You're Adorable." But it's all muted, sounds like she's got her fingers in her ears. She can't smell the popcorn or the roasted peanuts or the dust and manure, either.

She feels empty, all airy inside. Just walking all alone through the crowd toward the flashing lights on the top of the marquee over the gate.

People look at her funny. They glance, then they stare and back away. Some of them point. But she just keeps walking toward the lights. Staring up at them, flashing red and yellow and green, waiting for the lights to work their magic. When they do, the world goes dark.

After that, there are just still images. In black and white, like the frames on the photographic paper that she'd paid fifty cents for in that photo booth the day before.

Flash! She's lying on the ground looking up at the crowd of people staring down at her. There's a policeman there. The one who wanted to know her name, where she was from. And how she got all that blood all over her dress.

Flash! She's in a room with policemen all around her. There's a table in the room, and on the table is Angel's dress, the pretty, lacy one Jackson brought home in the box, the store-bought dress. It's torn and dirty and there's blood all over it. There's a bloody ax on the table, too, and stuck to it is a big hunk of hair. Long hair. Auburn curls.

Flash! Jackson's face. Just his face, contorted in a wild-eyed cramp of rage. Like a monster, a devil, Satan himself. But there are bars between her and the face. Bars that keep him out. And her in.

THERE WAS A SUDDEN CLUNKING SOUND. The darkness leapt back and the room was instantly flooded with light so bright Princess had to squint her eyes from the glare.

"Prentiss?" It was the guard. Lucille Talbot, the nice guard with the soft voice.

"Yes ma'am." Princess rubbed her eyes, but she still couldn't see good yet.

"I come to find out what you're gonna want to eat Friday evenin'."

The big black woman was standing outside Princess's cell, holding the food slot open and talking through it.

"Your last meal. What'll it be? Anything you want. Well, it can't cost mor'n five dollars 'cause that's all the state'll pay." She stopped, then added, "You know what, you just order whatever you want. I'll see you get anything you ask for."

"I want me a hamburger."

"Aw, you don't want—"

"I do! I want a hamburger and French fries. With catsup. I seen the pictures in that magazine you give me."

"You want one of those McDonald's hamburgers? I'm going to McAlester on Thursday. I could pick you up one. 'Course it'd be cold by the time—"

"I don't care if it's cold, I want me one of those," Princess said. She had no idea what a McDonald's hamburger might be.

"Anything else?"

"Uh huh. I want a great big chocolate ice cream cone."

3

Maggie was sitting up in bed, rocking back and forth, talking to her own reflection in the big mirror on the dresser across from the bed. Jonas had cleaned her up, changed her diaper and got her into a fresh nightgown, then propped her up on pillows. He could hear her as he made himself a pot of coffee.

"Salad … Salad … Salad …" she droned, her voice lifeless.

He shook his head. "Where did she come up with—?"

And then it started, harsh and rasping, like she was possessed. His beautiful Maggie let fly a string of expletives, filthy, disgusting obscenities. Jonas squeezed his eyes shut; tears leaked down his cheeks. He wanted to stick his fingers in his ears and chant like a little kid, "I can't hear you! I can't hear you!" But, of course, he could hear her. Had been listening to the gutter-talk day and night for months. He couldn't take her anywhere anymore because of it.

When they were first married, she'd refused to speak to him for a whole day after he smashed his thumb with a hammer hanging a picture and muttered "dammit" under his breath. Now, there wasn't nothing she wouldn't say, cursed worse than any man he'd *ever* heard. Tossed the F word around like she was throwing feed to chickens.

"I planted a rosebush by the front gate. Salad. Salad."

Jonas let out a breath he hadn't even realized he was holding. Even smiled a little bit. Shoot, they'd never had a flower garden. And even if they had, Maggie wouldn't have planted nothing in it. She didn't like to get her hands dirty, always told him she'd let him do the planting and growing and she'd take what the good Lord provided in his bounty and make soup out of it.

He didn't know who she was talking to, either. Sometimes she talked to a woman she called Susan. Far as he knew, Maggie didn't know anybody named Susan.

"Don't you shake that rug out—you hear me, Becky!"

Apparently somebody else had come to call today.

"Shake it out and I'll ..." And more expletives.

Jonas took a mug out of the cabinet, set it on the countertop and began to pour coffee into it, hearing the sound of her voice but trying to block out the ugliness and vulgarity. Some days she cursed almost non-stop the whole time she was awake. Other days, she was quiet and morose and wouldn't utter a word, just weird sounds, grunts, and moans.

In the beginning, there was a kind of internal logic to what she said when she babbled. She might be talking to people who weren't really there or about things that happened half a century ago, but a person overhearing it wouldn't necessarily think there was anything wrong.

Anymore, most of what she said was filthy, foul-mouthed nonsense.

Jonas stared out the kitchen window at the fields and the hills beyond. He was a tall man—6 feet 3 when he was young, but he'd shrunk since then—big-boned and lanky, wearing well worn bib overalls, a chambray shirt, and clunky work boots.

He had to lean over just a little to see through the red-checked curtains over the sink—the black dirt, the thistles purple in the fence rows, and the powdered sugar dusting of Queen Anne's lace in the ditch beside the road. He'd looked at that view every day of his life, had been born in the big bedroom on the front of the house upstairs, the one he and Maggie used to share before she got where she couldn't climb stairs, and he'd always aimed to die in this house.

But he didn't love it anymore. There'd been a time when he could get all dewy-eyed just looking at the cows grazing in the field he and his daddy'd cleared with a team of mules. Or watching the chickens peck at nothing on the dirt mound over the storm cellar in the back corner of the yard. He and Daddy'd dug it with pick axes and shovels, broke through into a cave that had been cut through the limestone bedrock by an underground river, the bottom and walls polished as smooth as glass by the rushing water. Mama wouldn't let him play in the cave, said he'd get lost in it like Tom Sawyer and nobody'd ever find him. But he'd sneaked down there often and explored the dark caverns with a coal-oil lantern.

He leaned over a little farther and stared at the double wooden doors on the cellar and the rusty padlock that fastened them together. He shook his head and straightened up. He didn't feel anything at all when he looked out the window now.

It was like his whole body, his whole self, was the thumb he'd hit that day with a hammer. When he did it, it hurt so bad tears'd stung his eyes and he'd shaken his hand and hopped around, sick to his stomach. Then it'd just throbbed, ached with every heartbeat. After awhile, though, it'd gone completely numb. The nail eventually turned black and fell off. Never did grow back.

His whole life was numb like that now. Something down deep had been damaged beyond repair. It never would grow back, neither.

"Didn't that fellow play the piano well!" Maggie gushed from the other room.

Jonas froze.

"Why, I didn't want to leave, it was so pretty. Just wanted to sit there and listen to him play. I could have sat there …"

"'Til it started rainin' frogs—" Jonas whispered raggedly.

"Until it started raining frogs and—"

"And the trumpets started blowin' for the Second Coming," he finished for her.

He set the coffee pot down with trembling hands. That's what she'd said, *exactly* what she'd said, the first time they all realized something was very, very wrong with Maggie.

They're attending the graduation ceremony at the high school. Maggie's all dressed up in her favorite red dress, her white hair piled on top of her head like she's an opera star. She's wearing high-heeled shoes and the pearls Jonas gave her for their thirty-fifth wedding anniversary. Since she retired from teaching she seldom wears high heels, says they make the bunion on her foot ache for days afterwards.

Jonas is wearing the only suit he owns, the black one he's had since ... well, he doesn't remember how long. A good suit should last at least twenty years and his black one has likely been looking at a quarter of a century in the rear-view mirror for quite some time. While he's shaving, she comes into the bathroom and stands there, watching.

"You're a good-looking man, Jonas Cunningham," she says, "even if you don't have any butt whatsoever."

She probably would have pinched him where he didn't have a butt if he hadn't been shaving.

Truth is, Jonas isn't good looking. He is average. His thick shock of sandy brown hair has gone the color of a ten-penny nail, not pure white like Maggie's. His long, weathered face has sprouted jowls, his big ears have sprouted a forest of bristly hairs, and his bushy black eyebrows have just become bushy gray ones.

The bags under his droopy, hound-dog eyes are so big Maggie teases that he needs a porter to carry them, but he still has all his own teeth and can hear just fine and read just fine. In good light. With cheaters.

In the old-age department he has made out fairly well.

But Maggie. Why, she just gets prettier every year. Pale blond hair has turned the purest white. Her thin face, with its delicate features, is hardly wrinkled at all, just looks like fine porcelain with tiny, hairline cracks. Men still turn to look at her when she enters a room. And even after all these years, Jonas is still hesitant to touch her with his big, rough farmer's hands, still afraid he'll break her.

They meet their daughter and son-in-law, Melanie and Mac McIntosh, and their granddaughter, Joy, at the school. Joy will be going into junior high in the fall and she's looking around at the big auditorium the high school building shares with the junior high. Has her long red hair pulled back in a ponytail instead of braids. Jonas loves Joy's braids, told her stories when she was a little girl about how the fairies used them as rope ladders to climb up to her shoulder so they could whisper secrets in her ears when she was sleeping.

But she's growing up now. He figures her days of braids and his days of telling her stories about them are drawing to a close—if indeed, the door hasn't already eased shut without his even noticing.

The son of one of Mac's elders is the valedictorian of the graduating class. Maggie'd had him in her freshman literature class. She leans over to Jonas during the boy's address and whispers, "I wonder who wrote his speech for him."

And she squeezes his hand and winks at him. Oh, how that woman could get his motor running, just with a wink and a squeeze.

They all come back to the house after the ceremony. Maggie'd left a big pot of chili simmering on the stove and they have just sat down to supper when she says it.

"Didn't that fellow play the piano well?"

Joy looks at her quizzically. "What fella, Grandma?"

"Why the pianist at the graduation ceremony, honey," Maggie says. She cocks her head to one side and looks at Joy. "Did you sleep through the whole thing?"

"No, I didn't sleep through it! But it was so borrring." The little girl rolls her eyes, "I thought my hair would be as white as yours before it was over!" Joy always had a flare for the dramatic. "I was awake, though, and there wasn't anybody there playing the piano."

"Well, I'm sorry you missed it, sugar." Maggie laughs. She turns to Jonas. "Pass me the crackers, the pack that's already open. I don't mind if they're crumbled, I'm just going to crush them in the bowl, anyway. What did you think of the piano player?"

The room falls silent. Jonas hands her the crackers and shoots a glance at Melanie, who looks a question right back at him. Mac just shrugs his shoulders. Maggie misses the silent exchange, intent on crumbling her crackers into her chili bowl.

"Grandma, there wasn't a—" Joy begins, then her father elbows her. "What—?" She catches his look and doesn't finish.

Maggie looks up then, sees everyone is staring at her.

"What's everybody looking at? Did I spill something on my ..." She glances down at the front of her dress. "No, I didn't ..." She looks up and the good humor drains out of her face. "What is it? What's wrong?"

Jonas paints a smile on his face, though his heart is thumping so loud it's a wonder she doesn't hear it, even sitting all the way at the other end of the table.

"We want to know what you thought about it is all," he says, and manages to keep his voice light and even. "You liked him so much, you tell us about the piano player."

Maggie buys it.

"Well, he was just about the best I ever heard in my life, that's what!" she says, and Jonas swallows hard, trying not to be sick.

This isn't the first time something wasn't right. They'd all noticed it, though nobody'd said anything about it out loud.

The time Mac came by to get some fresh tomatoes out of the garden and when he was ready to leave, he couldn't locate his car keys. They tore that whole house up looking for them. Nothing. Mac finally borrowed some wire-cutters and went out to the car to hotwire the ignition. Jonas figured to make him a cold drink while he worked, opened up the freezer and there were Mac's car keys—frozen in an ice tray. Maggie just laughed, blamed it on Jonas, said he did it as a joke.

And the time she called him from the grocery store to come downtown and pick her up. He told her she had the car, but she swore she didn't. He caught a ride with a neighbor; the car was parked right there in the grocery store lot.

All the times she forgot to tell him somebody'd called for him, the times she got people's names wrong, the day she was all ready to leave the house for church, but she still just had her slip on, had forgot to put on her skirt.

All those times he'd just let it slide, didn't say anything, wouldn't let himself worry about it. People got forgetful as they aged. It happened. But this …

"… the Moonlight Sonata. *That was the best thing he played. Why, I didn't want to leave, it was so pretty. I could have sat there until it started raining frogs and the trumpets started blowing for the Second Coming."*

Maggie finally tunes in to the looks on everybody's faces. And what she sees makes her angry. That's even scarier than the imaginary piano player.

"What in the world are you all gawking at?" she says and slams her spoon down on the table with a loud whap!

The motion upsets her ice tea glass. It starts over and Joy reaches out to keep it from toppling. But she's too late, merely succeeds in tipping the glass so it dumps its contents into Maggie's chili bowl.

"Look what you did!" Maggie screeches. "So clumsy, you're always knocking things over and spilling things and making a mess!"

All the color drains out of Joy's face. Her grandmother has never said an unkind word to her in her life.

"Just a little slob."

"Mama!" Melanie bleats.

"Somebody's always having to clean up after you, you're such a—"

"Maggie, that's enough!" Jonas didn't mean for it to come out harsh, but he supposes it did. Can't do nothing 'bout that.

Joy leaps up from the table and races out of the room, crying. Melanie jumps up and follows her.

It is quiet in the dining room. Mac and Jonas sit staring at Maggie; her face is completely blank.

Then she suddenly relaxes and smiles.

"Anybody want some more ice tea?" she asks. "I sure do like ice tea on a hot evening, don't you?"

Then she picks up her spoon and starts eating her chili, all full of tea and chunks of ice, while the rest of the tea that'd been in her glass drips off the table into her lap.

THAT WAS FOUR YEARS AGO. JONAS had taken her to Dr. Clements in town, who sent her to a bunch of specialists in Oklahoma City. The doctors had poked and prodded her, run all sorts of tests. At the end of it, they didn't seem to know a whole lot more than they did going in.

Couple of them seemed to think she'd had a stroke, though at the time she could still get around fine, could read and feed herself. Senile dementia was what most of the doctors called it. But one of them, a skinny neurologist with one of those square little mustaches that made him look like Adolph Hitler, believed Maggie had something he called Alzheimer's Disease. Jonas thought he was saying old-timer's disease until he spelled it.

But as time went by, it mattered less and less what name the doctors chose to give her condition. The reality was simple and stark. Maggie was losing her mind.

She quickly got where she wouldn't walk across the grass anymore, said them pointed little blades was sharp and would stick up through her shoes into her feet. She'd get lost in the house; he found her once in the closet, fighting the clothes, struggling like they were attacking her.

The first time she didn't recognize him, snatched the sheet up to her chest and asked him indignantly, "Who are you and what are you doing in my bedroom?" he'd gone out and sat in the swing on the front porch and cried like a baby.

In the beginning, there were times when she seemed to know what was happening to her.

"I can't find *me* anymore," she told him once, whispering in the dark like they used to do when they were young and they'd just made love.

He'd reached over and patted her hand. "You're not lost, sweetie pie. Long as I know where you are, I'll keep you safe."

But he didn't know where she was anymore. The woman he loved had gone somewhere he couldn't find her.

For most of his life, he'd prayed, "Lord, please let me live one day longer than Maggie, so I can take care of her."

Now, he prayed—when he talked to God at all and that wasn't very often—"Lord, give me the strength to do what I have to do, while I still can."

4

He TUGGED THE SHOELACES ON HIS tennis shoes tight and tied the strings in a bow knot so they wouldn't come undone and trip him. Even after only a few stretching exercises, the sleeveless gray t-shirt Mac wore over his sweatpants had sprouted a wet spot in the center of the back by the time he made it to the end of the driveway. When he got home, it would be soaked with sweat, like he'd stood under a shower.

The Oklahoma plains really only had two seasons—summertime and everything else. The temperature didn't gently crank down from triple digits as trees dressed up in autumn finery or slowly warm up again when crocus noses began to peek out of the soil in the spring. September and October were hot, but a blue norther could blow through around Thanksgiving and dump six inches of snow on the ground. What few trees could be found didn't do much turning, either. Oh, the cottonwoods painted golden splotches on the blue sky, but the mesquites pretty much stayed green until one day all the leaves dropped off and they were naked, and the cedar stayed green year round. And spring roared in with a wild yell in April, trailing thunderstorms, hail, and twisters behind it like the twitching tail on a lizard.

Mac could see clouds beginning to build in the west when he turned out of the driveway into the street.

Even at forty-three, he made running look easy. Tall and slender, he had broad shoulders that tapered down to a slim waist and long legs that propelled him fluidly forward, almost like his feet never made solid contact with the ground at all. He no longer had the spring in his step he once had, or the speed, but Mac was all about stamina, endurance. And in that department, he was stronger than he'd ever been. Looked it, too, unless you got up close, saw the streaks of white in his flaming red hair and the despair in eyes the color of faded jeans.

He was a good-looking man in a rugged, lumberjack kind of way; had a high, wide forehead, straight nose, and square, Kirk Douglas chin. Even had a dimple in it that was a pain to shave around. And if he'd had one more freckle, he'd have had to put it in his pocket. There was a time when he'd also had a quick smile and a rumbling, infectious laugh, but that was a long time ago.

Every now and then Mac wondered just how many miles he'd run over the years. The total of them. If you started counting when he joined the track team in high school—what five, six miles a day and ten sometimes on the weekend?—and then on a scholarship for the Razorbacks in college. Take off two years for seminary in Louisville—he hardly ran at all then—and the only running he did when he was in the military was chasing the Japanese in the South Pacific and the Commies in Korea. But since then, as a minister, up and down the streets of Graham, day in and day out, how many miles?

He got to the stop sign at the end of the block and turned left on Thurlock Street, committing to a five-mile run instead of three. The three-mile route was a right turn. It wound around the county high school, down past one of the two elementary schools, and back to the house. The five-miler took him through the heart of Graham, down Main Street, past the courthouse, up toward the park and the baseball fields, and back down Buena Vista to the back side of his neighborhood on the northeast side of town.

His tennis shoes slap, slap, slapped a sidewalk that was "plum broke out with cracks." That's what his father-in-law, Jonas Cunningham, had said after Joy hit one on her bike when she was seven, fell off, and broke her arm. Like everything else in town, the sidewalks were well worn and scruffy. They'd needed repair when he'd run on them as a kid, and when he ran on them again after he came back from the army, it had somehow been comforting to see the same old cracks in the same old places. The world and everything he understood and believed had changed, exploded in a rumbling roar of dirt and shrapnel, blood and body parts and wailing screeches of agony, but the sidewalks in Graham, Oklahoma, were exactly as he had left them.

Most everything else in Graham was just as he'd left it, too. When he was a boy, he'd become obsessed with figuring out why Graham had been built on that particular spot. One piece of dirt was as good as another on featureless plains devoid of hills, valleys or rivers, where you could see the towering white grain elevator in Taylorsville eleven miles west—through an undulating shimmer of heat waves that set it dancing in the fierce sun. So why here? His minister father didn't often indulge in tall tales, but he finally tired of Mac's endless questions and told him that one of the prairie schooners in a wagon train bound for California had broken a wheel and the family'd had no choice but to settle down right there and build a town. He explained that all the small towns in Oklahoma had sprouted among the yucca plants and prairie dog holes the same way, said that was why there were broken wagon wheels in fence lines all across the state. Mac had believed that story for years.

Reality wasn't as entertaining. The town that by 1963 was home to about 5,000 people had grown up around a railhead where ranchers loaded their livestock into cattle cars for transport to the huge stockyards facilities in Oklahoma City and Amarillo. The incorporated township of Graham was tethered to the rest of the world by US 270. The highway divided the town down the middle from east to west as it reached out from Arkansas to grab Kansas. Main Street was therefore laid out north/south, splitting the town neatly into equal quarters. Seen from the air, Graham's unimaginative grid of straight streets looked like the business end of a giant wire fly-swatter lying on the empty prairie.

Lining those streets beneath a prickly forest of television antennas were simple ranch houses with big yards of grass that'd likely be brown by the end of August and more carports than garages. There was a sprinkling of fancy brick homes, too, of course. Doctors, dentists, and lawyers mostly; oil money didn't settle in a place like Graham. Big, leafy dogwoods, sugar maples, and pin oaks that had been planted on purpose and watered faithfully dangled tire swings beneath limbs extended upward toward the sun like cold fingers stretching out to a fire.

There was also a boring network of cracked sidewalks. The cracks no longer seemed comforting to Mac, just annoying; had to watch your step where tree roots had bowed up the concrete or you'd trip and go sprawling.

"'Lo, Preach! Howya doin'?"

The carpenter who'd built the addition on the church tipped his John Deere cap as he got into his pickup truck across the street. Hats and footwear were the Southwest version of clan tartans. Ranchers and cowboys wore Stetson hats and Tony Lama boots; farmers and everybody else wore square-toed, leather work boots and broad-billed caps advertising the tractor they drove or the ball team they cheered for.

"Fine. You?" Mac called back breathlessly and kept running. Over the years, the folks in town had gotten used to the preacher's odd hobby, what Jonas called "running when wasn't even nothin' chasin' you."

He crossed the street in front of the library, dodged around the Book Mobile bound for an isolated crossroads somewhere in Durango County, and headed toward the town square.

In the center of the square sat the courthouse, an imposing, three-story, granite structure with four white columns on a wide porch, a domed roof, and an ornate belfry—sans bells. Loudspeakers there blasted non-stop Christmas carols as soon as the live nativity scene was erected out front the first week of December every year. They also shrieked an occasional tornado or air raid warning siren— just as a test, of course. Graham had never actually been in the path of a twister or a nuclear warhead, at least as far as anybody knew. On the expansive courthouse lawn, massive cottonwood trees drizzled sticky white fluff on benches where old timers whiled away their days chewing tobacco, spitting, whittling, and telling lies.

Mac had gotten a late start this morning, which was good because it was going on nine o'clock now, so he'd miss all the school bus traffic and the parade of moms dropping their kids off. But he'd also missed Joy. Up half the night doing the two-step with chronic insomnia, he'd finally dozed off and then overslept. By the time he made it out of bed, she'd already left for school. He couldn't keep doing that, couldn't keep missing connections with her. She needed him. He had to get some routine back into their lives. She was just a kid and she needed that, too. So did he. Oh, how he longed for the return of the ordinary: days melting into nights and blooming into days again, over and over until he felt snug and safe in their endlessness.

He hit Main Street and turned down it toward the square, past the Trim Your Rim Barber Shop, smelled the aroma of lilac vegetal in old men's hair and talcum powder on their shaved necks. He swerved around one of the church deacons as he crossed in front of Simpson's Grocery.

"Hey, Mac. I need to talk to you 'bout—" the deacon began.

"The office. Later," Mac panted over his shoulder. "Try me. After ten."

"But I need—"

Mac kept running.

Yeah, the deacon needed him. They all did.

He picked up his pace. With no hills to train on—the state road department had graciously bulldozed a big mound of dirt so Graham could hold a soapbox derby—he varied his speed to change the rhythm of his workout. Around the square. Past the police station and the fire station and the newspaper office. A couple of cops waved and Mac waved back. The newspaper editor was getting out of his car as Mac ran by and he stood with his arm resting on the top of the car door, nodded his head but didn't speak.

Mac nodded back and kept running.

He turned it up another notch, determined not to slow his pace until he made it to the post office at the end of the block.

How many miles, altogether?

Melanie had tried to calculate it once.

Her face burst so perfectly into his consciousness it was like taking a fist in the belly. The blow staggered him, knocked him off his stride, and he gave in—not to the stitch in his side, but to the pain in his heart—stumbled to a stop, put his hands on his knees, and gasped.

Then, with a little inward groan that was probably audible, he let go, allowed himself to topple over the precipice into memory. He'd tried hard not to live in the past, to stay in the day, focus on reality, but as he walked slowly to the stop sign in front of the post office, he let himself wallow in the beauty of her face and the sound of her voice and the smell of her hair—like strawberries. Melanie's hair had always smelled like strawberries.

"I figured it all out, if you want to know."

Melanie is sitting in the swing on the porch of that little house behind the church in Arkansas, rocking slowly back and forth, a pad and pencil on her lap. "Calculated how many miles you've run altogether."

Mac is sprawled on the porch steps, catching his breath after a six-miler, listening to the eech-eech, eech-eech of the swing and watching the fireflies flicker under the willow tree in the front yard. He is wiping his face with a dish towel.

"How far?"

"Almost 10,000 miles."

He turns to look at her.

"How do you figure that?"

"I took an average of three miles a day and multiplied it—"

"But I ran more than that in high school, and I didn't run at all when—"

"I know that, let me finish. I added the miles from—"

"And what about the summer before seminary?"

"I counted that."

"'Cause I ran a lot—"

"I started today."

"What?"

"Started my period. I'm not pregnant."

Melanie is like that. She'll be talking about one thing and right in the middle she'll switch subjects to something else entirely.

Her lower lip starts to tremble.

"Oh, Mel, I'm sorry." He gets up and goes to her, sits down on the porch swing beside her. He wants to put his arm around her, draw her close, but he's sweaty from the run so he just takes her hand. "Maybe next month. We'll try again." He tries to lighten it up, leans close and whispers in her ear. "You know how much I like to try! In fact, my favorite thing in the whole wo—"

"Why won't God give us a baby, David?"

She calls him David. Every other human being in the world, including his own parents, calls him Mac, but Melanie calls him David.

"Is that what you think, that God's punishing us?"

"Well . . . is he?" She drops her chin to her chest and the tears that have been sliding down her cheeks begin to fall into her lap.

Mac reaches over, lifts her chin, and turns her face toward him.

"God is not denying us a baby because we ticked him off about something. That's not how he operates."

"Then why?"

"I don't know why. But I do know—"

"Oh, I do, too! I just . . ."

She bursts out sobbing then. That's another thing about Melanie. She doesn't ratchet up from sniffling to crying to sobbing. It's usually all or nothing.

He wraps his arms around her, sweaty or not, and pulls her to him, patting her on the back, his face buried in her hair—curls the color of honey with the sweet scent of strawberries.

"Hey now, it's okay. I love you. Shhhh."

He holds her, crooning her name, pushing the swing gently back and forth until she's cried herself out. It doesn't take long. Melanie's emotions are like spring storms—sudden, sometimes violent, and over quickly.

And like the sky after a storm, the sun is soon shining again.

"That's how I got to calculating how far you'd run," she says into his shoulder when the sobbing subsides.

"What's how?"

"I was adding it up, you know, calculating when I was supposed to start and I ... oh, never mind, it doesn't matter because I'm not late." She heaves a sigh, takes a deep breath and lets it out slowly. "And my math was all wrong about your running, too. You want spaghetti for supper or tacos?"

Spaghetti or tacos. That's Melanie.

"How about a grilled-cheese sandwich?"

She takes the dish towel out of his hand and starts to wipe away her tears. "You serious? Do you really—ugh!" She chucks the towel back into his lap. "Phew, that stinks!" She sits up. "And so do you!" She playfully shoves at him. "Get away from me."

"That's not what you say when you're trying to have a baby!"

He is instantly sorry. Mr. Sensitivity!

"I shouldn't have said that. I'm sorry."

"You think maybe I should go to another doctor?"

He's lost count of how many they've been to already. They'd stopped "using protection" on their second anniversary—five years ago.

"If it'll make you feel better, sure, go ahead."

"I'm glad you feel that way because I already called a specialist in Little Rock and made an appointment for Friday."

She hops down out of the swing and starts for the door. "A grilled-cheese taco with spaghetti sauce—right? Or I could grill the spaghetti ..." And she is gone.

He bows his head and prays, as he'd done hundreds of times before, "Lord, please, give us a child."

And just a few weeks later, he's out telling anybody who'll listen how God answered that prayer, not when they wanted or how they expected, but he had given them joy. Joy!

Honk! Honk!

MAC JUMPED BACK ON THE CURB as a pickup truck sped by and the farmer behind the wheel gave him a dirty look and flipped him the bird. Couldn't blame the man, Mac had stepped right out in front of him. Wasn't looking where he was going.

He took a deep breath, shook himself like a dog climbing out of a creek, and tried to rid himself of the gloom that clung to him like a swarm of gnats all the time.

No way to live, all hunkered down, just toughing it out.

He started running again and the five miles seemed to last forever. Was he that seriously out of shape? No, it was carrying the dead weight of grief and despair around with him that slowed him down, that made every effort at anything in life twice as difficult.

Home, quick shower, and into his office behind the sanctuary of New Hope Community Church by 10 o'clock. He was grateful Lillian wasn't in yet; she'd said on Friday she had a doctor's appointment this morning. No matter what time he got in, if she'd been sitting at her desk a minute longer, she gave him the scolding, third-grade teacher look that pronounced him guilty on the spot—no judge or jury needed, thank you very much—of the sins of slovenliness and laziness.

Oh, how he longed for the day he wouldn't have to greet that look every morning.

And what would he greet? What would his mornings look like after Sunday?

Don't know, don't care. Just know they'll be different. And right now, different is good enough.

The phone rang before he got settled behind his desk. The voice sounded familiar, but it was a moment before Mac could place it. The caller was Oran Blackburn, the warden of the Oklahoma State Women's Penitentiary, the ugly stone structure that sat isolated out on the prairie northeast of town.

"I need your help, Mac," Blackburn said.

"What can I do for you?"

"You can take Ralph Beecher's place this afternoon at 2:30."

Beecher was the pastor of the Assembly of God Church and the chaplain at the prison. He was a weird little man who'd come to Oklahoma from eastern Kentucky two years before with what the old-timers called "the smell of hot sulfur on his coat tails." His sermons were tirades against the evils of drink; he saw a demon behind every bush. He'd even hinted at a history of snake handling during his ministry in the mountains, and that was way too weird for the good citizens of Graham, Oklahoma, in the spring of 1963.

"What was Ralph supposed to do this afternoon that you're trying to sucker me into doing for him?"

"He was scheduled to see Emily Prentiss, the woman we're executing Friday. The law says we have to provide her a minister in her last days. She's never asked for one before but she's asking now, and Ralph's out of commission, got the gout, can't get out of bed. Can you cover it, Mac?"

Mac groaned and then caught himself, hoped Blackburn didn't hear him.

"Listen, Oran, I'm swamped. Can't you get—"

"Hey, I've tried, looked into everybody I could think of, 'cause I know you're ..." embarrassingly pregnant pause "... that you haven't gotten all the way back up to speed yet."

Blackburn was a member of Mac's congregation and there couldn't have been a man, woman, child, or pet gerbil among his 250-member flock who wasn't aware that their pastor was not doing well. No, sirree, not doing well at all.

"Says she's Protestant, so that leaves out Father Liam and that new guy—what's his name?—the Eastern Orthodox minister. And I called ..."

Mac tuned out as Blackburn rattled off the member list of the Durango County Ministerial Association. Each, for one good reason or another, was unavailable to offer spiritual comfort to a dying woman this afternoon at 2:30.

Of course, not a one of them was any more unavailable than the Reverend David McIntosh. Couldn't get more unavailable than Mac, but it appeared he was stuck with the job.

He could go on autopilot. It wasn't like it was the first time he'd faked it.

"Okay, okay, Oran," Mac interrupted. "Point made. Looks like I'm your man. How about I meet you in your office at a quarter after two. That suit?"

"Make it 1:30." Mac caught an odd undercurrent in his voice. "It'll take awhile to brief you about the inmate and the protocol."

"What's to brief? You think I don't know who Emily Prentiss is and what she did?"

Emily Prentiss's crime was the kind of gruesome horror folks would have remembered even if she wasn't about to become the first woman executed in Oklahoma in more than half a century. And even if she hadn't been related to the controversial Amos Jackson Prentiss, a foaming-at-the-mouth opponent of the growing movement to desegregate schools and businesses in the South. The local newspaper had carried stories over the years about the various appeals in Prentiss's case, and the state press would be on this story like sour on pickles, sending in the big guns. The protesters would likely be out in force, too. If the execution of Elizabeth Duncan last August in California was any indication, Graham was in store for quite a circus by Friday.

"Not briefed about her story, just warned about her ... peculiarities. She's real different, Mac. You need to know that going in."

"Fine, Oran. See you at half past one."

Mac replaced the receiver, leaned back in his chair and stared up at the ceiling. What could he possibly find to say to a woman who was about to die?

5

Joy had art class right before study hall/activity period, the forty-five-minute time slot before lunch when students could remain in their classrooms and study or attend one of the various clubs that met in different locations all over the school.

All the "futures" met in designated areas in the cafeteria. FFA, Future Farmers of America; FTA, Future Teachers of America; FHA, Future Homemakers of America. The Rodeo Club met in the animal show barn by the bus shed. The Thespians Club met on the stage in the auditorium. The Beta Club met in the library.

Most of the 500 or so students of Durango County High School went to some club meeting rather than twiddle their thumbs for forty-five minutes waiting to be dismissed for lunch. Joy was a member of several different organizations, was the fourth vice president of FHA, though she wouldn't be for long unless she memorized the purpose statement she was supposed to recite from memory in two weeks at the end-of-school banquet.

When the bell rang, the other students started gathering up their things, but she continued to paint. She'd worked all period on a new watercolor. It was an expressionistic piece. Or impressionistic. One or the other. At the top of the page she'd painted a big colorful circle with a little tail, like a tadpole, and fitting spoon fashion beneath it, she'd painted a smaller one. She'd named the painting "Momma Comma."

She'd been so intent on the piece that Mrs. Stevenson, the sweet, dithered art teacher, had noticed her interest and commented on it. She hadn't even stopped long enough to cut up with the other girls at her table, Sherry and Rhonda Jo, who'd only taken art as an elective and couldn't have drawn a stick figure without tracing it from a coloring book.

"Aren't you coming?" Sherry asked when she noticed Joy was still working. Sherry was wearing her new Ben Casey blouse. Joy had been dying to have one, back when she had a life and cared about such things.

"Can't," Joy said, stepped back and looked at her work. "I'm right in the middle now and I can't just leave it." Even Sherry knew you had to keep working in watercolors or they'd dry.

"What'll we tell Mr. Moore?" Rhonda Jo adjusted the pink bow in her ratted hair above her bangs and then gathered up her books. "He said he'd have some scripts for us to look at." She popped her gum as she spoke. "You know he'll want to know what you think."

Mr. Moore was the speech and drama teacher and the sponsor of the Thespians Club. Joy loved to act and had been in every play he'd directed since her freshman year, when she'd landed the lead in *Annie Get Your Gun*. She was one of his favorites. Everyone knew it. She had played Eulalie Mackechnie Shinn, the mayor's wife, in *The Music Man*, the junior class play last fall, even though she was only a sophomore. At the cast party, she'd pleaded with Mr. Moore to do *The Wizard of Oz* as the Thespian Club's summer production this year, had started practicing "Somewhere Over the Rainbow" and "Ding Dong The Witch Is Dead" with her mom, before …

"Just tell him the truth, that I had an art project to finish." She hadn't meant to sound snappish, but that's how it came out.

Gritting her teeth, she put down her brush and faced Rhonda Jo. "Sorry, I'm a little tense. It's drying faster than I thought, and I don't want to ruin it. Tell him I'll come by after school and pick up the books, if that's okay with him."

"Fine by me." Rhonda Jo was mad. She turned in a huff and flounced out in a cloud of Blue Waltz perfume.

Joy looked around. The classroom studio was emptying. Just as she knew it would. Mrs. Stevenson would have to leave in a minute, too, because she was directing the work on the decorations for the prom in the gym.

The little bird of a woman in her paint-splattered smock flitted over to her and smiled approvingly, then saw the title and giggled.

"You're going to be alright working by yourself now, aren't you?" she asked.

Without waiting for an answer, she fluttered toward the door, tossing absentmindedly over her shoulder, "You're going to be fine, too, aren't you Phoebe, dear?"

Phoebe Elrod was such a complete loser that even Mrs. Stevenson blew by her like she wasn't there.

"Yes ma'am," Phoebe said, without lifting her head from her own artwork—something that looked like the floor after a tribe of monkeys had a paint fight. Phoebe wasn't staying to finish her painting before the watercolors dried—she was working in oils. No, Phoebe was staying because she had nowhere to go, didn't belong to a club, wasn't involved in a single extracurricular activity.

Phoebe had been consigned to the bottom rung on the teen-age social ladder. She had a bad reputation, had been branded a skag because she put out, slept around. Joy was popular, not glitzy-cheerleader popular, but wholesome, preacher's-daughter popular. Those two social classes were separated by a cavern vast and deep. Joy had never before tried to cross it.

But Phoebe was the reason Joy had stayed behind, the reason she'd started the un-finishable watercolor—so she'd be stuck here, alone with Phoebe. For weeks last year, Joy had heard the talk in the girls' locker room about Phoebe, how she kept throwing up in her first-period class. Morning sickness, the girls had giggled; Phoebe had gotten herself knocked up! When Phoebe's bouts with nausea stopped abruptly, the locker room was abuzz with speculation. Could she possibly have "gotten rid" of the baby?

Joy had to find out, and if Phoebe had, how she'd managed it. And she had exactly forty-five minutes to do it.

Her heart was a lunatic woodpecker in her chest, her palms wet, her mouth dry. But she had no time for nerves, had not the luxury of giving in to anxiety and embarrassment.

As soon as the door closed behind Mrs. Stevenson, Joy pretended she needed more water for her brush from the sink in the back of the room. She had to pass by the easel where Phoebe was working to get it.

She walked slowly by, her heart hammering. But she couldn't make herself stop, just continued to the sink and filled the glass, her hands trembling.

What am I going to say?

Turning resolutely, she headed back toward the front of the room, slowed as she passed where Phoebe was working and acted like she'd just noticed the painting.

"That's nice," she said.

Phoebe jumped like she'd poked her with a cattle prod.

"Thanks."

She didn't look up, just kept painting—well, smearing the paint around, mixing the colors, doing exactly what Mrs. Stevenson had warned them *not* to do when working with oils.

"If you just keep picking at it, the colors will all smear together," she'd told the class probably a hundred times. "Be confident with your stroke, put the color where you want it and then leave it alone."

"You like to work with oils better than watercolors?" Joy heaved the question out into the dead air just to have something to say, to have some reason to keep standing there.

Phoebe turned and looked up at her then, and Joy was struck by a couple of things. One, she'd never seen that much mascara on a human eyelash in all her life and wondered how the girl could keep her eyelids open under the weight of it. And two, her eyes were a pure, pale blue—Mama would have called it cornflower blue—that was really pretty.

The rest of her face was a train wreck, though. Nose too big, with blackheads so thick some of them stuck out. Her oily forehead was a forest of yellow pimples, as was her chin. And the white lipstick she wore gave her the look of a three-days-dead corpse. Her hair was ratted out in a big bubble held rigid by the contents of the Revlon Hair Spray can Joy could see in her purse, and she wore her straight skirt rolled up at the waist. School policy dictated that girls' skirts had to be long enough to cover their knees, and the principal wasn't the least bit shy about singling a girl out and instructing her to kneel. If her skirt didn't touch the floor when she did, she'd be sent home. So all the skags rolled their skirts up at the waist and then pulled them back down when they feared they might get caught, up and down all day long like window shades.

Joy tried to concentrate on Phoebe's eyes, wondering as she did what she must look like to Phoebe. She'd taken her bath and dressed quickly and quietly this morning so she could get out of the house before Daddy woke up. But she'd studied her face in the mirror as she removed the bristled, black-mesh rollers she slept in to tame the natural curl in her long, burgundy hair.

A foggy reflection had stared back at her with wide, almond-shaped eyes the same light brown as her mother's. The image had looked…tired. She'd used a Cover Girl vanishing stick to hide the dark circles, rubbed it back and forth, but you could still see the smudges on her fair complexion. No, not fair, pale. So pasty-faced the dusting of freckles on her nose stood out like polka dots. Even so, with her full lips and heart-shaped mouth, and her hair teased and sprayed to turn up at her shoulders in a single, neat row like Annette Funicello's, Joy McIntosh was pretty. She recognized that, and with the same objectivity acknowledged that she wasn't beautiful. Mostly, she looked whole-some, like her picture belonged on a front of a Wheaties cereal box.

Yeah, right. Wholesome!

"I don't like to paint at all, with oils or watercolors or anything else," Phoebe told her. "Why do you care?"

"I was just making conversation, that's all."

Phoebe picked up her brush and turned toward the painting, dismissing her.

"I like your picture!" Joy blurted out and Phoebe looked back over her shoulder. "I like the colors. And I like—"

"No you don't." Phoebe cut her off and turned to face her again. "It's uglier than fresh road kill and you know it. I keep smearing this oil around and eventually the whole dern thing's gonna be the same color."

She put her brush down, sat back, and studied Joy. "What do you want?"

"Nothing, I just ..."

"Yeah, you do. You want something. What is it?" She gave a short, mirthless laugh. "You want to bum a fag, that it? You taken up the habit, a PK like you?"

Joy was certain if she took even one drag off a cigarette she'd cough for a week.

"Well, as a matter of fact, yeah, I do smoke. I started when I was a freshman."

"You gotta be kidding me. You smoke?" Phoebe cocked her head to one side. "No you don't."

"Yes, I do. I—"

Phoebe grabbed Joy's hand, turned it over and looked at her fingers. "No nicotine stains. This ..." she held up her own fingers, with distinct yellow marks on her index finger and the one next to it "... is what your hand looks like when you smoke."

"Well, I ..." Joy stammered and felt her face flush a deep red.

"Why would you tell me you smoke when you don't? Trying to be all friendly like. And how come you're shaking worse'n Barney Fife?" She was studying Joy, eyeing her up and down.

Joy hadn't counted on this, hadn't expected the girl to be astute enough to figure out the little game she was playing.

Light suddenly dawned on Phoebe's face.

"You're *in trouble*, aren't you!"

"What do you mean I'm in—"

Phoebe didn't let her finish. "That's it! You're in trouble and you came to me because ..." She stopped, her face darkened and she spat out the next words like the taste of them in her mouth made her nauseous. "... because everybody knows Phoebe Elrod's a slut and sluts know what to do when you're knocked up!"

All the color drained out of Joy's face, bleaching the crimson to chalky pale. She stood speechless. This wasn't how she'd imagined the conversation would go.

"No," she whispered, shaking her head in a denial both of them knew was a lie. "Listen, I …"

"Let me tell you something, Sweet Cheeks." Phoebe glared up at Joy, her words carried on a rush of decayed-teeth bad breath. "From one *slut* to another. You spread your legs and go ruttin' around in the backseat of some football player's new Ford—you deserve what it gets you."

"No, I didn't! I *wouldn't*. It was just the one time, right after Mama …" A sudden, fierce wave of nausea sucked the air out of her lungs before she could finish the sentence. She didn't need to, of course; everybody in town knew Joy's mother had died last fall.

Clamping her hand over her mouth, Joy dashed to the sink in the back of the room and barely made it before she vomited noisily. Then she stood there heaving, her eyes blurred with tears. There was only the little bit of cereal she'd been able to choke down for breakfast and after that just stomach bile. But she continued to dry heave until she was weak and breathless.

When it was finally over, she washed the foul smelling mess down the drain and turned around. Phoebe Elrod was gone.

Joy staggered back to the work table beside her easel and collapsed in the chair, struggling not to burst into tears. Then she noticed the piece of notebook paper folded on her stack of books. She opened it, her fingers trembling.

"Call me tonight, 272-5469. I'll tell you where to get help. Phoebe."

6

GRAHAM WAS LOCATED BEYOND WHERE ARKANSAS'S Ouachita Mountains edged into southeastern Oklahoma. The low range of mountains, blanketed with hardwood forests of red oak, white oak, and hickory trees, flattened out after it crossed the state line, left its trees behind and morphed into the featureless prairie that marched northwest toward Oklahoma City.

But the Indian Bluffs were an odd range of almost-a-mountain hills that somehow got cut off from their brothers and sisters to the east, dawdling ducklings that straggled behind the rest of the flock. The hills sat by themselves on the flat prairie, and the state of Oklahoma had seen fit to locate the Oklahoma State Penitentiary for Women just south of them, six miles northeast of Graham. You could see it from the highway, a collection of ugly gray buildings that nobody would mistake for any other structure than a prison.

When the first building in the complex was constructed in 1917, it was dubbed the Iron House because it was designed to house Oklahoma's worst offenders and the state's lone execution chamber. In 1941, the state added on to the state prison in McAlester and transferred all the male prisoners there, then consolidated the female inmate population from three other facilities and moved them to the Iron House. Since that time, it had become a run-down hellhole with precious little heat in winter and no air conditioning at all. Within five years, the 500-capacity facility was overcrowded. The current inmate population ranged between 750 and 800.

The electric chair in the Iron House had been the final earthly resting place between heaven and hell for the backsides of seventy-nine male inmates before a new execution chamber for men was built in McAlester. Not a single woman had been executed in the Iron House in the twenty-two years it had been a women's prison. In fact, not a single woman had been executed in Oklahoma since it became a state in 1907.

All that was about to change.

Mac stopped at the main gate security station on the east side of the building that granted admittance to a graceless gray tunnel, a road between two twenty-foot concrete block walls topped with razor wire that led to a second gate. Behind it was an open area in front of the administration building. Affixed to both ends of the tunnel were twenty-foot electrified fences also topped with razor wire that encircled the whole facility. The area between the two fences was a vacant space a hundred feet wide, a no-man's land, lit up bright as daylight at night.

As the guard called the warden's office to confirm his appointment, Mac tore the top off a roll of Rolaids and popped two into his mouth. The burning sensation in his gut had begun as soon as he hung up the phone from his conversation with Oran Blackburn and had been building in intensity ever since. It was a three-alarm fire now and if the pack of Rolaids he'd purchased at the 7-11 store on the way out of town didn't quench the blaze, he might have less time to live than the woman he'd come to comfort.

He'd been to the prison several times since he took over as pastor of New Hope when he and Melanie moved back to their hometown after he returned from Korea in 1953. But the place had never seemed quite as depressing as it did today, cold gray walls and gray slate roofs in the sparkling May sunshine.

The administration building was as run-down and dreary as the buildings that housed inmates. Hard to tell who was a prisoner here and who wasn't. After he was frisked and emptied his pockets into a metal basket at the security station in the check-in center, he followed a uniformed woman who could have snared gold for the Romanian women's wrestling team. She led him through a labyrinth of hallways, locked doors, checkpoints, and staircases to the warden's office on the fourth floor. The halls were poorly lit, probably painted institutional green, though it was hard to tell. They had the stale smell of old sweat and thrift store clothes, with the faint underlying aroma of sewage.

Mac barely had time to warm up the chair in the waiting area before a phone on the secretary's desk buzzed and she gestured down a short hallway to a large oak door at the end. The door opened as he reached for the knob.

"Good to see you, Mac," Warden Blackburn said and clasped Mac's hand in a firm handshake, lingering the extra beat or two that translated: I *really am* glad to see you.

Oran Blackburn was an odd-looking man. Taller than Mac by several inches, and Mac was six feet two. The warden was completely bald, with a red birthmark inconveniently placed on the top of his head so it always looked like he'd just whacked himself on some low-hanging beam. His shoulders were narrow and rounded, and the pronounced contour of his considerable paunch strained at the buttons on his white shirt. Mac was sure Oran hadn't been able to fasten a suit jacket around that belly in twenty years.

But he had a kind face and a surprisingly gentle manner for a man who'd spent his career with the dregs of society.

"Come in and have a seat." Oran gestured toward a matched set of high-backed leather arm chairs that faced a low table where a coffee pot and two cups rested on a silver tray. "Loraine just made the coffee, so it doesn't taste like road tar. You take cream or sugar?"

"Thanks, but I'll pass on the coffee." Mac seated himself in the nearest chair.

Blackburn raised an eyebrow at him.

"Indigestion." Mac fished the Rolaids out of his pocket as if to prove his point, then plucked the top one off the roll with his thumb and popped it into his mouth. "Lunch didn't agree with me."

Mac hadn't eaten lunch. Or breakfast. And he couldn't for the life of him remember what he'd had for supper last night. Surely to goodness he'd had something!

"Bless your heart," Blackburn said, and settled himself in the other chair. "You've got heartburn going *into* a meeting with Emily Prentiss. Most people don't have it until they're coming *out*."

"Swell."

But for a pile of mail on the desk and a stack of recent newspapers on a nearby chair, the office surely had not changed in any fundamental way since the building was constructed forty-plus years before. Bookcases sagged with dusty, unread tomes Mac would have bet his pension—if he'd had one—had all been published before either of them were born. The desk was utilitarian, the chair obviously uncomfortable. There was a Royal Electric typewriter on a stand in the corner.

"Like what you've done with the place, Oran," he said.

"Nobody likes a smart ass; you know that, don't you?"

Mac leaned forward and rested his forearms on his knees. "Okay, serious now. What have I gotten myself into?"

"You? Nothing at all. You'll go spend an hour with this woman—or five minutes or three hours, however long it takes. You'll leave and that's that. Now *me*? That's another story altogether. What *I'm* in is …" His voice trailed off.

"Is what?"

Blackburn let out a slow breath. "*Readers' Digest Condensed* version? At five o'clock this Friday afternoon, the Oklahoma State Penitentiary for Women will impose the death penalty on one Emily Gail Prentiss, age thirty-one, for the murder of her two-year-old sister. She'll be executed in an electric chair that hasn't even been turned on in twenty-five years." He paused for a beat. "If you had a toaster hadn't been turned on in a quarter of a century, you think it'd work?"

"That thing might not function? You're joking!"

"Serious as a heart attack."

"But how—?"

Blackburn held up his hand for silence. "Another story for another day."

Mac nodded. "Why five o'clock? I thought all executions were at midnight."

"Not midnight. Typically, they're held at 12:01 a.m. A death warrant is only good for one day. If the execution isn't carried out during that twenty-four-hour period, the state has to re-petition the court for another death warrant. Scheduling the execution for a minute after midnight gives the state time to deal with last-minute legal appeals and temporary stays. But this particular inmate has no pending appeals, doesn't even have a lawyer."

Blackburn grimaced. "And executions are also held in the middle of the night because the prison is in lock-down at that hour. But it doesn't really matter. The whole inmate population goes psycho after an execution no matter what time it's held, like they all got some low-powered electric shock themselves—just enough to make them mad, like slamming a thumb in a car door. Happens every time. At least it does in a men's prison and I'm assuming it'll be no different here. There are fights, stabbings. They throw feces at the guards."

Mac groaned.

"Yeah, its ugly. Only thing uglier is the protesters, who should start arriving sometime Thursday—the early birds'll probably show up the day before. And this facility sits out here on the prairie like a bump on a pickle with absolutely no way to contain them."

"And that's a problem because …?"

"Because protesters are nuts! Did you see what that woman did at Joe Polechek's execution in Alabama? Chained herself to the front gate. Handcuffed one arm to the gate, the other arm to the fence, then swallowed the handcuff key. Couldn't open the gate without tearing her apart. Which, in my opinion, was the only reasonable thing to do under the circumstances."

Mac chuckled.

"I fail to see the humor in that, Reverend McIntosh. Frankly, I've been thinking about saving up my own feces to throw at the protesters."

Mac let go then, a full belly laugh that finally ignited a smile on Blackburn's face.

The warden sat back in his chair with a sigh. "Hey, that's what the great state of Oklahoma pays me the big bucks for, right?"

He paused, looked hard at Mac, and shifted gears. "That's my story, so ... how are *you?*"

Oh, we most certainly are not going to go there*!*

"Gettin' by," Mac said.

Blackburn surely recognized that for what it was—a crock of the warm, sticky substance on the south side of a horse going north. The man was in Mac's congregation. He hadn't missed the signs in the past six months of ... of *what?* Mac had no idea what word to tack onto it, what label to give it. What *toe-tag* to attach to it—cause of death: "unknown." No, probably a simple "natural causes."

Since Melanie died, Mac had not performed any of a long list of ministerial duties that ranged from hospital visitation to preparing the church's annual budget. His sermons had gone from lackluster— and that was while he was still in shock or they wouldn't have been *that* good—to stumbling, to monosyllabic to ... non-existent. Got up three Sundays ago and couldn't speak, couldn't say a word. Just sat back down. After some very pregnant silence, the organist dutifully cranked out a few more songs, the song-leader led the congregation in a couple more hymns, they passed the offering plate, had a closing prayer, and everybody packed up and went home.

Last two weeks, they'd had "guest speakers."

Oh, but Mac was going to preach this Sunday. Yes sirree, he was going to deliver the sermon he'd been writing in his head for years!

"Listen, Mac, I, *we*, understand that—"

"Thanks, Oran. Really, I mean it, thanks. But I've got a killer day today and I had to squeeze this 'pastoral visit' in between appointments. So if we could just ... what am I doing here? I was a chaplain in the military but I'm not sure the same skills apply."

Oran gazed at him for a moment with the kind of sincere sympathy Mac had come to loathe in the past half year. Then he turned back to the business a hand.

"You're here because death row inmates are entitled to spiritual comfort in their final days. That's what the chaplain—and in our case, that's you—is here to provide to Emily Prentiss."

"So tell me about her. A *Readers' Digest Condensed* version; it's not like I'm getting into a long-term counseling relationship with the woman."

"She's epileptic, pretty severe grand mal seizures, but she refuses medication."

"How come?"

"Won't say."

"Can't you force—?"

"Nope. If she doesn't want to take medicine, the state can't make her."

"But why—"

Blackburn held up his hand. "Mac, you need to deep-six all questions that begin with 'why' because the answer to the whole bunch of them is 'I don't know.' Where Emily Prentiss is concerned, nobody knows much of anything."

Blackburn reached out, picked up the coffee pot, and looked a question at Mac. "You sure?"

Mac nodded and Blackburn poured himself a cup.

"Let me tell you what I do know," he said. "She was on the Long Dark when I—"

"The Long Dark?"

The warden rolled his eyes. "Don't look at me. I didn't name it. Death row in this prison's been called the Long Dark for as far back as anybody can remember."

"Spooky."

"In case it escaped your notice, this place's old, Mac. Outdated. And just last fall our esteemed representatives in the Oklahoma legislature voted down, yet again, a tax bill that would have provided the funds either to renovate it or, as I have recommended repeatedly and obnoxiously over the years, bulldoze the whole place off into a gully somewhere and start over. The Long Dark's in a wing on the west side, in the oldest building here. There's a covered walkway from the door on the end of it to the building where … well, come here, I'll show you."

Blackburn got up and crossed to the window behind his desk. It looked out into the quad, an area enclosed by the administration building on the east side and three other gray-stone buildings. The admin building was four stories tall, the other buildings three each, with no windows facing the quadrangle on any of the ground floors, bars on the two-by-three foot windows in the cell blocks and piles of razor wire on the rooftops. Guard towers stood sentinel at the four corners of the enclosed square, tall enough that in addition to the area encircled by the four buildings, the guards could see the open area between the buildings and the inner fence and the no-man's land between it and the fence that formed the outside perimeter of the prison. Though the quad's space was sectioned off into separated areas that contained space for volleyball and basketball courts, none of the inmates was playing a sport. The areas were mostly bare cages where human zoo animals stood grazing on the concrete, alone or in small herds.

Blackburn pointed to a one-story appendage that jutted out from the side of the building that formed the western wall of the quadrangle.

"That's the Long Dark, on the side of building two, which was the whole prison for the first fifteen years it operated. The other three buildings went up courtesy of FDR and the WPA. They built the Iron House for maximum security prisoners and then added on a death row as a separate cell block later on."

Blackburn sighed. "Don't know exactly when that was, but judging from the condition of the place, I'd say it was constructed shortly after the Ark went aground."

He leaned over and gestured toward the end of the Long Dark.

"See that building just beyond it, the one that looks like a Quonset hut?"

Mac nodded.

"That's where the chair's located." Blackburn looked pained. "It's got a name, too. They all do; every prison's electric chair is called something. Here it's Sizzlin' Suzie. Back when this was a men's prison, the guards would say a death row inmate, 'had a date with Suzie.' And when he was executed, they'd say he—" The warden caught himself. "'—*made it* with ole Suz.'"

Mac lifted an eyebrow to indicate he knew that probably wasn't the phrase they'd used.

"As you can see, there are gates in the fence in front of the Long Dark and a parking lot beside it, so folks who show up just for an execution have easy access." He gestured toward the open plains beyond the prison. "And if it weren't so *barren* out here—"

"You're not from Oklahoma, are you?" Mac interrupted.

"What was your first clue?" Blackburn pointed toward the gates. "If the topography were a little more cooperative, I wouldn't have so much trouble keeping the protesters at the front gate on the eastern side of the building and away from that entrance point. But I'm not holding out much hope for that, unless the highway patrol post in Durant sends more troopers. And they won't."

He turned and headed back to his chair. Mac sat back down and Blackburn picked up his coffee cup, took a sip, and made a face. "Cold." He replaced the cup and looked at Mac. "Emily Prentiss had already been here for six years when I became the warden here in 1955. Emily was seventeen, tried as an adult when she was convicted, and she's been in solitary confinement in the Long Dark for going on fourteen years now."

"Solitary! For fourteen years?"

"Death row inmates are segregated from the general population. That's why there's a separate cell block. But she'd have been in solitary or something like it for a couple of reasons even if she hadn't gotten the death penalty. You kill a kid and you don't last long in gen pop. Too many mothers in here. They won't tolerate a baby killer."

"I don't imagine the colored inmates have much use for Jackson Prentiss's daughter, either."

Blackburn nodded. "That's the second reason."

Jackson Prentiss. The Reverend Amos Jackson Prentiss, rumored to be the national Grand Poobah, or whatever they called it, of the Ku Klux Klan, he currently served as the chaplain of the Alabama State Legislature. Chummy with Gov. George Wallace, his "prayer" to open the legislature's spring session had been a vitriolic tirade against the "nigra communists" in the NAACP, and a plea that God would pour out righteous vengeance on the "growing black menace" plotting to mongrelize the races. Mac had seen an excerpt from the prayer on the *Huntley-Brinkley Report*.

In the past five or six years, Prentiss had emerged as the spokesman for religious bigots across the South who trolled the scriptures until they hooked some obscure verse they could pluck the scales off and fry up to justify their hatred of colored people. The man was slick, photographed well, and had a smooth, fatherly delivery. Almost understated.

It hadn't always been that way, though. Mac had been in Little Rock on the Fourth of July, 1954, and happened to catch one of Prentiss's campaign speeches at a rally in the park. A candidate for the local school board, Prentiss had outlined a one-plank platform: rabid opposition to the recent decision by the Supreme Court in *Brown v. the Board of Education of Topeka, Kansas*, the ruling that declared school segregation unconstitutional. The man had looked like a snake charmer, weaving back and forth, his voice a singsong rant, his eyes open too wide and little specks of white spittle in the corners of his mouth. Even then, before Prentiss had become the national mouthpiece for white segregationists, Mac had seen it. Jackson Prentiss was either crazy or evil. He now believed the man was both.

"Are there other inmates besides her on death row?" he asked. "She hasn't been in that whole wing by herself all this time, has she?"

"There have been times over the years she was the only one, I think. But even now she might as well be. Death row inmates don't share cells. There are ten cells in the Long Dark and right now five of them are occupied. Prentiss has been there the longest. The cells are arranged so there's no direct sightline into another cell, even through the slit in the door, and the prisoners are scattered—"

"Slit in the door? There aren't bars?"

"There are bars on the cells in the rest of the prison. Long Dark's got solid doors with a slit for food trays. Beginning to figure out why they call it the Long Dark?"

"Sheesh!"

"Death row inmates take a bath or shower in the bathroom at the end of the hall once a week and get an hour a day in the exercise yard—by themselves. That's it."

"Can you say 'cruel and unusual punishment'?"

"I don't make the rules, I just—"

"That was a cheap shot. Sorry."

"And you need to keep in mind how she landed in the Long Dark. Emily Prentiss *confessed* to decapitating her two-year-old sister. Described in graphic detail how she chopped the body into little pieces and threw the pieces in the river. The only remains they ever found of that child, if I recall, was her hair on the ax Prentiss used to—"

"Okay," Mac interrupted, "you made your point." He started to rise. "I think I know everything I need to know."

"Sit down, Mac. I haven't gotten to the good part yet."

Mac sat back down.

Blackburn looked uncomfortable. "Emily Prentiss is ... well, she's ... different." He ran his hand over his bald head, an unconscious gesture to smooth down hair that hadn't been there in twenty years. "She's ..."

"Come on, Oran, spit it out. She's *what*?"

"She knows things. Things she couldn't possibly know."

"Like?"

"Like a guard on the Long Dark was getting beat up by her boyfriend and Prentiss knew it."

"So she saw some bruises and a black eye."

"She never saw the guard's face. Couldn't. Slit in the door, remember?"

"Okay, she heard something and figured it out."

"She knew that another inmate, a woman in gen pop she'd never met, was dead in her cell. Brain hemorrhage. But Prentiss *knew*, talked a guard into going to check on her."

Mac said nothing, just listened.

"She knew that the guard, the one who was getting beat up, was in danger. Another guard overheard her begging the woman not to go home."

"And?"

"And she went home. Soon as she got there, her boyfriend beat her to death with a claw hammer."

Mac was beginning to feel very uncomfortable. "What's your point, Oran?"

"I'm just telling you what I know. A prison is the quintessential small town. Everybody knows everybody else's business. There are no secrets here. And among the residents of this small town, Emily Prentiss is known as a mystic, a psychic, a witch, Joan of Arc … *Something.*"

"Just because—"

"She sings songs in an incredible voice in the exercise yard and you can hear her all over the … I'm telling you, Mac, you need to be prepared for her voice. It's deep, almost like a man's, and odd-sounding."

"What does that have to do with anything?"

"The songs aren't … *songs.* No melody you can recognize and in a language nobody can identify. And, of course, she has fits and a lot of inmates don't understand what that is."

"I don't care what the inmates and guards understand. What do *you* have to say about her, Oran?"

The warden let out a long sigh, started to reach for the coffee cup, and remembered that it was cold. Then he reached for it anyway, turned it up, and took a couple of long gulps.

"I'm just going to tell you this, straight out. No commentary. You figure out for yourself what it means, if it means anything at all."

Blackburn described a day several years before when he was still new on the job. He'd been called to the Long Dark by a guard with an idea to convert a couple of unused cells there into badly needed storage space.

"When Prentiss heard my voice, she called out to me through the slot in her door."

Blackburn got up abruptly, walked over to the window, and looked out. Then he turned back to Mac.

"She kept hollering until I finally got a guard to unlock her cell and I went in to talk to her. She told me I needed to go home. Right then. That my wife needed me."

He turned back and faced the window.

"Did you go home, Oran?"

"Of course not; I blew her off," he said without turning around. "What was I going to do, dash out to my car and go barreling home because some crazy woman on death row said I should?"

Mac's voice was quiet. "What happened, Oran?"

Blackburn sighed, shoved his hands into his pockets and turned to face Mac. "When I got home that night I found out Joanie'd had a miscarriage that afternoon. She wasn't that far along—hadn't even told me she was pregnant because she wanted to surprise me. So she was there, all by herself, when it happened."

"And you think you should have ... what? Could you have done anything if you'd been there?"

"No." He forced a smile. "And since then, we've had Jacob and Joanie's pregnant again." He crossed back and sat down again with Mac. "I don't want you to go in there blind. You need to know what you're facing."

"Sounds like you'd be better off with some gypsy palm reader instead of me."

"She specifically asked for a minister, and you're the right man for the job, Mac."

"I wouldn't bet the rent money if I were you."

7

SHE SAW IT WHEN SHE OPENED the kitchen cabinet to get out a can of tomato soup for lunch. A tiny baby boy lay on his side just inside the cabinet. Very small, maybe six or seven inches long, but absolutely perfect. Had fingers and toes—long and skinny, like some tropical tree frog. There was a light fuzz of dark hair on his head, and a dusting of lanugo—the fine hair on premature babies—on his back and arms. He was breathing; you could just make out the tiny movement of his chest up and down.

Then he opened his eyes and looked at her.

Wanda Ingram stepped back with a strangled gasp and slammed the cabinet door shut.

Her breath hitched in and out of her throat; her heart beat a staccato rattle in her chest. Balling her hands into fists at her sides, she spoke aloud through gritted teeth.

"Not real! *It's. Not. Real!*"

It took every speck of strength she possessed, but Wanda forced her shaking hand to reach up and grab the handle on the cabinet door again. She squeezed her eyes shut as she slowly pulled it open. Then she peeked out one eye, through a slit and a forest of eyelashes.

Inside the cabinet was a collection of canned goods. Two cans of creamed corn, some green beans, a can of hominy, and three cans of soup. With a hand trembling so badly she could barely grasp with it, she selected the lone can of tomato soup, set it on the countertop and turned to the silverware drawer to get the can opener.

On the countertop above the silverware drawer was a puddle of bloody tissue.

"No!" she pleaded, shaking her head back and forth, her voice a pitiful whine. "Pleeease, no!" She rubbed her eyes, dug at them with her fists like a sleepy child. When she opened them, the countertop was vacant and clean. But she wasn't hungry anymore, didn't want any soup. Her appetite was gone.

She turned and walked slowly to the kitchen door, fumbling in the pocket of her dress for her cigarettes and lighter. She pushed open the screen and stepped out into the May sunshine, so bright it made her squint, crossed the small patio that looked out over Boundary Oak Lake, walked over to a battered lawn chair, and eased down into it like an old woman. Like she was seventy instead of forty-nine.

It was the lack of sleep, that's what it was. Hadn't slept since … she couldn't even remember when. How were you supposed to sleep with babies crying, *wailing* all night long?

Shaking a cigarette out of the crumbled pack, she held it between trembling fingers, lit it, and inhaled deeply. She sighed the smoke back out of her nose and mouth, leaned back in the chair, and closed her eyes, felt the sun hot on her eyelids.

Wanda Jean Ingram, you have got to get a hold of yourself!

She took another drag off the cigarette, tried to relax, to empty her mind and enjoy the feel of the sun in her face and the breeze in her hair.

Her mind bobbed on a deep, calm sea. And when his image surfaced there, it was as natural as bubbles popping to the surface out from under a rock. Wanda didn't fight it. She looked into his face, gazed into his liquid brown eyes, the color of maple syrup, and loved him as purely as any woman ever loved a man.

Dr. Paul Stephenson. Bayside Hospital, Houston, Texas, 1955. He was the *only* reason she took any interest in obstetrics and gynecology. She'd been an army nurse, made it into the military by covering up her family's history of mental illness and her own bouts with depression and … well, other things. She spent the first part of her career patching up boys who'd lost arms and legs, then switched to rehab. At the expense of everything else in life, dating, maybe even a family, she'd poured herself into helping the wounded.

But life handed her a whole new perspective on "wounded" during that last tour of duty in Korea. Seasoned OR nurses were in short supply in the front-line MASH units and she'd volunteered. She'd only been there three days, wasn't even completely unpacked, when it happened. They'd called it friendly fire, but it hadn't seemed very friendly when the operating room vaporized around her. Two patients, three surgeons, two nurses, and an OR tech died instantly. Wanda had thrown herself over the patient on the table and they were the only survivors. She was a hero, had the medals to prove it.

The doctors who stitched her back together told her she was lucky to be alive. But they looked down at their shoes or stared at some spot on the wall behind her when they said it.

Sometimes she'd indulge in fantasy, pretend Paul had fallen for her the way she'd fallen for him. That he hadn't cared she was ten years older and fifty pounds heavier than he was. That he could see deeper into her soul than her disfigured face, mangled jaw, and missing teeth, a visage that made little kids stare and point.

She'd switched specialties to be near him. Traded shifts to work when he worked. Studied nights to be the best OB/GYN nurse in the hospital so he'd notice her. He finally had. And they became … friends. So close he even asked her to help him pick out an engagement ring for his sweetheart. When he went into private practice, she was his right arm.

And when he started performing abortions on the side, well, he couldn't have done it without her. Together, they helped so many girls—frightened, desperate girls with nowhere to turn but to some butcher in a back alley. They offered a *safe* alternative. Sterile. Never had a single infection, not one! Never harmed *anybody!*

The girl who'd turned him in was crazy. Completely insane. Claimed she'd been pressured into it, said she'd tried to have a baby afterward and couldn't, that he'd made her sterile. Lies, all lies! But, of course it didn't matter. And after that, nothing ever mattered again.

The only light in all that darkness, what Wanda clung to like someone drowning to a piece of driftwood, was the indisputable proof that he *did* care about her, that she really did matter to him. Paul had shielded her, protected her, refused to name his assistant. And his crazy accuser couldn't identify her. She'd only seen Wanda wearing a surgical mask, and that nightmare day when the police came, the hysterical girl swore it couldn't have been Wanda, said she'd never have forgotten someone with a monster's face like that!

Paul had gone to prison; Wanda had gone free.

She suddenly jumped and dropped the cigarette that had burned down to her finger, grinding it out on the concrete with her houseshoe-clad foot. She shook her burned finger, blew on it to ease the pain, and her eyes filled with tears.

"Got to get a grip, Wanda Jean," she said out loud. "You got to calm down, that's all. Everything's going to be just fine."

She felt something warm brush up against her leg, looked down and there was Blackbeard, her calico cat, so named because the black patch around his left eye made him look like a pirate.

"Hey boy, where you been?"

She reached down to pick him up and something dropped out of his mouth onto the concrete beside her cigarette butt. It was a mouse, a dead mouse, bloody where Blackbeard had sunk his sharp teeth into its side.

And the limp gray creature looked just like …

Wanda lifted the cat into her arms, buried her face in his fur and cried. In the distance, she could hear the rumble of thunder. A storm was coming.

◆ ◆ ◆ ◆ ◆

Oran opened the door and Mac stepped in front of him into a cheerless room as empty and blank as the inside of a manila envelope. Walls, floor, ceiling—all featureless, some neutral color between cream and tan, graced by not a solitary picture, calendar, mirror, or rug. The attorney conference room's only furnishings were a plain wooden table and two equally neutered slat-back chairs.

The room was located on the third floor of the administration building, on the north end, with an entrance to the top floor cell block of building one down the hallway to the left, and access to the administration building's civilian areas to the right.

A lone, barred window offered an unobstructed view of the Indian Bluffs. This time of day, the sun should have brightened the dreariness. But during spring storm season, afternoon thunderheads stood daily sentinel in the western sky, dark behemoths poised to roar across the open plains and bludgeon a cotton crop with hail or rip the roof off a barn with a twister.

A bare bulb screwed into the fixtureless ceiling, strategically placed too high above their heads to reach without a ladder, cast a bilious light as lusterless as ashes.

But the thing was, the room didn't seem to need the bulb's illumination. It appeared to be filled with warm luminescence that came from the small woman seated with her back turned to the door. It was like she ... glowed.

Whoa there, Trigger. Steady boy. Let's not get spooked by Oran's overactive imagination.

When the woman turned and faced him, Mac almost gasped out loud. She looked so familiar! Profoundly, eerily *familiar.* Where could he possibly have seen her before?

His mind frantically thumbed through his mental Rolodex with her description: limp blond hair, severe acne scarring, eyes that, from here at least, looked to be a purple shade of blue, and teeth with the brown stain common to poor people who'd drunk high-fluoride well water as children.

But he couldn't place her, couldn't put his finger on who she reminded him of.

She sat as still as a windsock on a foggy morning, simply looked at him, her face benignly expressionless. The moment stretched out, elongated, didn't seem to be governed by the cranking of the earth on its axis. Then she spoke.

"Yes," she said.

Just the one word, an affirmation almost like an "ahhhh," a sigh, in the husky voice Oran had prepared him for, warned him about. Not unpleasant, just odd. It was deeper than sultry, with rounder, fuller tones. Still, in an alternate universe, she could have made a killing as the voice behind some perfume or lingerie commercial on television.

Made a killing. Freudian slip there, pal. Might need to bear in mind why she's sitting where she is in this *universe.*

Oran stepped into the room and hooked a professional smile on the front of his face like a surgeon's mask.

"Miss Prentiss, this is—"

"Oh, I know who this is! It's the Reverend David Allen McIntosh of Graham, Oklahoma, formerly of Seagram, Arkansas, who has come to see me on this stormy Monday afternoon 'cause ya'll are fixin' to fry me on Friday."

"Well ... yes," Oran said.

He cleared his throat and turned to Mac with a sympathetic look. "Whenever you're ready to leave, or if you need anything at all, just knock on the door. There's a guard right outside. He'll be watching."

Mac noticed the window in the door for the first time, filled with the face of a guard, like an eight-by-ten glossy suitable for framing.

Blackburn turned back to the woman seated at the table and nodded a farewell. "Afternoon, Miss Prentiss."

"Afternoon, Warden," she replied to his back as he rapped on the door; it opened and he closed it firmly behind him.

She turned to Mac. "You're welcome to sit, Reverend. Promise I won't bite."

Then she suddenly opened her arms in an expansive gesture. "Ain't this here the finest room you ever did see?" She hopped to her feet, the quick, abrupt movement of a squirrel, and rushed to the wall she'd been staring at. "But right over in this corner, there's a crack."

She pointed to it. Mac took her word for it; he could see no defect at all from where he stood.

"Don't know what in the world'd make a crack like that but it's plain's day. It's the only one, though. I checked, been over the whole room lots of times. And there's a hole in the baseboard over there, not a real big 'un, but it's new, didn't see it the last time I—" She stopped, seemed to catch herself and sighed.

"Sorry 'bout that." She offered a self-conscious laugh. "I don't spend a whole lot of time with people, as you can well imagine. Sometimes, I spend a whole afternoon a'wondering what folks talk about these days. When they're just sittin' around together, not doing nothing special, reckon what they say?"

She walked slowly back to the table and sat down and the absolute quiet and centeredness he'd noticed when he came into the room returned. Stillness gathered around her again, disturbed bees settling back on the hive.

"You *can* talk, right?" She leaned her head to the side and squinted up at him. "You being a preacher 'n all, you *can* speak?"

He found that the smile on his face was genuine. "Well, yes, if you'd give me a chance, I could probably string two or three words together to hold up my end of the conversation."

He crossed the room, pulled out the wooden chair, sat down in it, and looked across the table at her. Yeah, her eyes, framed in ridiculously long lashes, were almost purple. At least in the bare-bulb light they looked it, an arresting, disquieting color.

"What would you like to talk about?" He fervently hoped she didn't want to discuss anything spiritual.

"I dunno. How 'bout … weasels?"

"Weasels?"

"Yeah, you know what a weasel is, doncha?"

"Well, yes, I—"

"Them furry little critters used to get in our chicken house. Of a night, I'd hear the hens a'cacklin' and squawkin' all crazy like and I'd jump up and go runnin' out there. But it was always too late. There'd be a hen missin' sure, carried off into the night."

She stopped, and he watched emotions he couldn't identify play across her face. Her voice got quiet, her eyes large.

"How'd you like to be eat alive?" she whispered. "Sharp teeth in the dark a-chompin' down—with nobody to come save ya?"

Mac sat tongue-tied, looking at a face that might once have been pretty, before what must surely have been a hellacious case of acne sank sharp teeth into it and chomped down.

Maybe talking about something spiritual isn't such a bad idea after all.

It was like she'd read his mind.

"You think maybe we ought to talk about dyin' and God and Heaven and Hell and all that?" Her voice seemed to come from the bottom of an oil drum.

"If that's what you want to talk about. Do you?"

"Yeah—sometime. But not right now. I already know 'bout them things, anyway. I made my peace." She smiled then, a smile both innocent and as old as the earth. "When you're fixin' to get punished for the worst thing you ever done, it sets you free. Ain't no liberty quite like it!"

"Hard to argue that."

The silence again. Mac scrambled for something to say. "Look, is there something I can do for you? Is there anything that *is* troubling you?"

"Uh-huh. You."

"Me?"

"Oh, nothin' bad. Tryin' not to stare's all. I'm sure the warden told you 'bout the Long Dark. You gotta figure it's a joy I can't hardly hold onto just to sit in a room and talk to somebody 'bout anythin'—dying or cracks in the wall or weasels or the Second Coming."

"What do you know about the Second Coming?" In his head, the question was mere curiosity, but it came out sounding condescending.

"I was in church ever Sunday morning, Sunday night, and Wednesday night of my whole life!" She snapped. Then she shook her head. "That ain't how I know, though. I never listened to *none* of that. But I can *read*. I went to school through the sixth grade 'fore Jackson pulled me out." The word—*Jackson*. Somehow she managed to give an inflection to it, a sound almost like a growl.

"I read good and the Bible was the onliest book we had in the whole house. Bunch of it was too tangled up, but I got out what I needed. How God loves us." Her eyes suddenly puddled with tears and she added in a hushed, reverent whisper: "How Jesus *died* to save his children."

She looked out the window and didn't seem to be talking to Mac at all. "First off, when I read that part, I couldn't hardly keep all of it in my head. Seemed like I'd try to stuff it in and pieces'd be hang-ing out my ears. The whole of it seemed so big. But then after—"

She glanced at him, then dropped her eyes. "Well, I finally did understand how you could love that much."

She stopped. She sat so *still*, didn't fidget, he almost couldn't see her breathe. Her look was like that, too. Quiet and penetrating.

"You don't like that, do you?" she asked. "Me talking 'bout God and Jesus. Yore face got all closed-up like and squinty-eyed."

Geez, was he that transparent? His inner struggles so blatant a woman who hadn't been around another human being in more than a decade could read him?

Her hands suddenly flew to her mouth. "Oh, I'm sorry. Why, inside you're as cut up and bleedin' as a hand got stuck in a hay baler. I'm *sorry!*"

She looked stricken, like his emotional pain had somehow leapt across the space between them and attacked her heart, too.

"It's about yore wife dying, ain't it?"

"How do you know my wife died?" The hair on the back of Mac's neck began to rise like the hackles on a scared dog. Distant thunder rumbled in the west.

"But you ain't been left *alone*. You got a little girl, doncha?" Her voice carried the rumble of the thunder in it. "Her name's Joy and she's got red hair, just like you got red hair. Ain't it a wonderment that God done that, give you the child you asked for, a little girl to love who looks just like you, red hair and freckles!"

"Who told you about Joy?"

The air thickened, like the breath of a storm just before the rain hits. But the storm outside was still miles away.

"You don't have no other children, though. Just the one. The girl with long red hair."

In all his forty-three years, Mac had not the slightest experi-ence with the supernatural, nor did he ever expect to. Once, he would have said that God *could*, but seldom *did* the miraculous. And given the rarity of God's displays of power, actually seeing one was about as likely as seeing a fatal traffic accident. How many fatalities occurred every day? Every second? But did you ever *see* one? It's a big old world out there, he would have said, and an even bigger God.

And now? Right now, he couldn't have articulated a compelling case for the *existence* of God, let alone argued a Deity's ability—or desire—to dabble in the affairs of mortals.

"Was it Oran? Did he tell you about my family?" There was a tremor in his voice.

"I apologize, I sincerely do." Her eyes welled with tears again, became deep, shiny pools of purple light. "I truly did not mean to upset you and here I've gone and done the very thing I had in mind not to do."

He spoke slowly, enunciating each word carefully, struggling to keep his voice level. "How do you know these things about me?"

"Why, that new guard on the Long Dark, the Mex'can from Nogales, she told me. She visited your church once."

Mac let out a breath he didn't even realize he'd been holding. It came out in a rush as lightning flashed bright behind the Indian Bluffs. The roll of thunder that followed was closer now, louder.

"Well, yes, I do have a little girl." He managed a small smile, but it was real, more relief than anything else. "But she's not so little anymore, she's—"

"Sixteen."

"Yes." He was still uneasy. That Mexican guard must have taken a private-eye class from Stu Bailey on *77 Sunset Strip*. "She's sixteen and growing up fast."

"Can I tell you something? Please?" Her voice was earnest, pleading. She reached out her hand across the table as if to take his, then hesitated and pulled it back. "And you not get all flustered and in a tizzy about it? But you got to believe me. Can you do that?"

"What is it?"

She hesitated, seemed torn. "I'm scared when I say what I got to say, you're gonna jump up and go runnin' out of here and not never come back."

"I promise I won't do that."

"There's somethin' the matter with yore little girl, with Joy." Princess's voice was both soft and deep. It somehow managed to resonate even though it was barely a whisper. No, not resonate. *Hum.* The buzzing sound around high voltage wires, or a transformer box. "What it is ain't anythin' you can see on the outside. Somethin's wrong. Somethin's a'hurtin' her. I can feel it. She needs help. Will you help her?"

She reached out her hand again, but this time she touched him. Just barely. Her fingers felt like a butterfly had lit on his arm. "Promise me. Promise me you will."

It suddenly hit Mac all in a rush that the rail-thin woman with the haunting eyes and scarred face wasn't Joan of Arc, wasn't Rasputin, a gypsy fortune teller, or a witch. The explanation was a whole lot less dramatic. Emily Prentiss was simply insane. If she hadn't been crazy when she got here, the years of solitary confinement had driven her mad. Either way, the result was the same. He wasn't talking to a psychic; he was talking to a lunatic. She wasn't to be feared; she was to be pitied.

"I tell you what I'll do. I'll talk to her tonight, ask her if everything's all right. How's that?"

She tilted her head to the right and half smiled. "Why, Reverend David Allen McIntosh, I do believe you're humorin' me."

"Guilty as charged." *Bad choice of words.* "What did you expect me to do?"

"Just what you're doin.' Makin' nice. It'd be a hard man could tell a dyin' woman to butt out and shut up. You ain't a hard man."

"I'm a whole lot harder than you think."

"No you ain't. You ain't hard a'tall. Hard's all the way down, and you're just scabbed over on the outside from gettin' dragged through the rocks. Scabs fall off, though. When it's healed up underneath 'em, scabs fall off. Hard that's all the way to the bone don't never change."

A crack of lightning split the sky and thunder rumbled on its coattails. The light in the room flickered briefly. Princess looked up at the bare bulb. "Wiring's so old here, if there's a storm at five o'clock on Friday, they might not have enough juice to fry me."

Mac winced, remembering what Oran had said about the reliability of the electric chair. Then he looked at his watch.

Princess didn't miss a thing. "'Fore you go runnin' out of here … you asked if I needed anything and I do—two things."

"What might they be, Miss …?" He realized he didn't know how to address her. Emily? Miss Prentiss.

"That's it. See? That's the first thing, my name. You don't know what to call me. So … could you … would you call me Princess?"

"Princess?"

"Yeah. Emily *Prentiss* … somebody I used to know once, she couldn't say it right, so it come out *Princess.*"

"I'd be glad to call you Princess."

"I do truly thank you, but the next thing's harder."

"What's the next thing … Princess?"

"Would you come back and see me tomorrow?"

That caught him off guard and he started backpedaling quickly. "Well, I don't know." He didn't have time to … and besides, Ralph Beecher was the chaplain! Mac was just a fill-in. Maybe Ralph's gout would be better tomorrow. "I'd have to check my calendar."

"And the next day? And the next? Every day I got left!"

"Oh, I couldn't possibly—!"

"Yes, you can! If you want to, you can. You got *choices.* You're a free man and you get to decide what to do with all one thousand, four hundred and forty minutes, all eighty-six thousand, four hundred seconds of every single day!"

Lightning ripped a silver slash across the sky right outside the window and its clap of thunder was a hand grenade tossed into the room. It shook the walls and blinked the light and continued to rumble like the aftershocks of an earthquake.

Her voice was soft in the quiet that followed.

"Just four more days. After that, you get to go on with your life. You can go out and buy a new shirt or climb a tree, or swim in a creek or see a moving picture or watch that television thing I read about in a magazine once. You can do all those things next week 'cause I'll be dead. And you'll even get to sit there crunchin' popcorn in that moving picture and feel good 'bout yourself 'cause you done the right thing."

She leaned toward him, her body quivering. "Don't never underestimate the power of doin' the right thing, Reverend. Sometimes, it's the only gift life gives you. You comforted a dying woman in her last days. Ain't that worth a few hours out of your whole life? You so busy you ain't got time for that?"

Mac's response surprised him; he genuinely didn't know that's what he was going to say until he heard the words come out of his mouth. "No, Princess, I'm not that busy." He smiled at her. "I'll come back."

"Yes," she said with the same *ahhhh* tone as before. Like an amen.

Mac leaned back in the chair and stretched out his legs in front of him. "Okay. Let's talk. Why don't you tell me about—" She interrupted him before he could finish and he was glad she did because he had no idea where he was going with the question.

"About my life? You don't want to hear 'bout *my* life. But I surely do want to hear 'bout yours! Tell me about ... about *television*."

And so it went. The storm struck, lashed the building with rain, a centurion wielding a cat-o'-nine-tails. Lightning writhed in the sky, thunder hammered their eardrums. At times, it seemed like they were the only survivors of a shipwreck, set adrift in a storm at sea.

Eventually, the tumult blew itself out and gentle rain sighed down the windowpane. The guard whose face had never left the window in the door opened it and stepped inside. He was small and thin, but with a bit of a swagger, didn't look like he belonged in a prison.

"You done?" he asked and glanced down at his watch. "I'm supposed to get off early today. Got a gig in Tishomingo."

Princess's face was instantly stricken.

"I'll see you tomorrow," Mac said. "Okay?"

She relaxed.

"Okay by me, Rev. It ain't like I got plans."

8

The first time she tried, Joy's hands were shaking so badly she dialed the wrong number. The second time, the phone rang twice and then a man's voice answered.

"Hello." Gruff, annoyed.

"May I speak to Phoebe, please?" It was almost a whisper. She couldn't seem to find enough air to force the words out louder.

The phone clattered in her ear when he dropped the receiver on some hard surface.

"Phone's for you, Phoeb," she heard him yell. "And don't stay on it all day. It's a party line, ya know."

A party line! People could pick up the receiver and listen in to what other people said. How on earth could she have the conversation she needed to have when—?

"'Lo."

"Is this Phoebe?"

"Yeah, who's … oh, I know who this is."

"Your father—" Maybe it wasn't her father. "Or brother said—"

"It was my old man. What'd he say?"

"That this is a *party line*."

"Yeah, six people on it, all up and down this road. Only way we could get phone service."

"Oh. But how …?"

"Party line ain't no trouble. Most people got better things to do than listen to somebody else's boring conversations. People just pick up when they want to use the line, and you can hear it when they do."

"But what if … I mean …"

"Look, you called to ask who made that *pretty dress* for me, didn't ya? That *prom dress*. Right?"

It took Joy a moment to catch on. Then she blurted, "*Yes!* Yes, the prom dress."

"Well there's this woman, see. A *seamstress*. She lives out by the lake."

"Boundary Oak Lake? She's right here, in Durango County?" Joy had assumed she'd have to go to Oklahoma City, Tulsa at least.

"You go out Route 79 south, then turn right down Harrod's Creek Road and go about three miles. She lives in a little house on the right that backs up on the water. You can't see it from the road, but there's a big black mailbox out front that's got some kind of bird, a red one, a cardinal, I think, painted on it."

"Harrod's Creek Road, three miles, house with a black mailbox with a cardinal on it. Right?"

"Yeah, but there's a couple of things you need to know. One is, this seamstress, she's … funny lookin', scary lookin'. Her face, it got all messed up somehow, like in a wreck or something. And two, she ain't cheap."

"How much does she charge?"

"Two hundred dollars."

Joy gasped. She didn't have that much money, not even in her savings account.

"You still there?"

"Yes, I just … $200, that's a lot of money."

"Well, when a girl's gotta have a prom dress, she'll pay whatever she has to pay to get one. And if you're the only seamstress in town who makes prom dresses, you can charge whatever you want."

"I don't have any choice, do I?"

"Nope. But listen, you need to talk to the fella who … your date for the big night. Takes two people to go to the prom!"

Joy hadn't thought about that. But where would Gary get $200?

"Don't you get all nicey-nice about it neither. Your guy wants to do the dance, he needs to cough up some of the money to pay for the dress! It sounded to me like he was the one wantin' to two-step. Caught you at a ... weak moment or you'd have sat that dance out. That's the way it was, am I right?"

He'd been so kind and loving, holding her while she sobbed, rubbing her back and telling her how sorry he was. She didn't even remember how they'd gotten into the backseat of the car.

"Yes, that's the way it was."

"Then he needs to pay! And don't you let him weasel out of it."

"I won't!" There was steel sheathed in the softness of her voice. She drew in a shaky breath. "So how do I get in touch with this wo—"

There was a pronounced *click-click* on the line.

"Hey, I'm on the phone here, okay?" Phoebe barked. "I'll be done in five minutes."

Silence.

"Listen, you don't hang up and I'm just gonna keep talkin' and talkin' and—"

The line went *click-click* again.

"I need to get off here," Phoebe said.

"Ok, just tell me how to get in touch with this ... seamstress."

"You can't call her. I don't know if she's got a phone. I don't have her number if she does. You just have to drive out there. Knock on the door and explain what you want. And take half the money with you as a down payment. She'll tell you when to come ... for the *fitting* and you bring the rest of the money with you then. Now, I gotta go—"

"*Wait!* Does it ... is it—" She whispered the last word. "*Painful?*"

"Yeah," Phoebe said quietly. "I ain't gonna lie—it hurts like the devil! You know, when you're there, and she's *doing it*. And later, you're gonna feel like crap for a few days. Like the worst case of the cramps you ever had."

Phoebe paused.

"And just a little friendly advice. Don't put it off. Go now, soon's you can. The longer you wait, the worse it's gonna be. Even a few days matters."

"Okay. This week then. I'll go this week."

The empty line hummed in the silence that followed.

"I really gotta go."

"Phoebe! Don't … I just want to … Thank you. You don't know how much I—"

"Hey, don't start! Just 'cause I told you where to get a prom dress don't make you my new best friend. And don't you be all nice and friendly like in art class tomorrow."

"All right. I won't."

"You and me, we're members of the same club now, that's all. It ain't like those silly clubs at school, though. This is a life club, and ain't a single member in it wanted to join." She laughed mirthlessly. "It's called the Universal Sisterhood of Girls Who Had to Get Prom Dresses." Then she paused and added quietly. "Once you're in, you're in for life."

"Thank you, Phoebe."

There was a click and the phone went dead.

◆ ◆ ◆ ◆ ◆

Jonas blamed himself. He'd tried to learn Maggie's patterns so he could head off trouble before it started, and he should have seen this one coming. It was late Monday afternoon and Maggie'd got where she hated to see the sun go down. He figured maybe she was afraid it wouldn't come back up again.

He'd helped her shuffle into the living room after lunch. She was so unsteady on her feet he didn't trust her to take more than a few steps if he wasn't right there beside her. She'd spent the afternoon in the blue chair by the window that looked out on the fields out back. Rocking. Back and forth, back and forth. Fiddling with her hands, like she was endlessly rubbing lotion on them. She refused to talk to him, or even look at him when he spoke to her, and as the day wore on, her eyes grew more and more unfocused.

He'd gone to the bathroom upstairs, had barely got finished doing his business when he heard a crash in the living room. He dashed down the stairs, trying to button the straps of his overalls as he took the steps two at a time. Maggie was standing in front of her chair in her long, pink nightgown. A pale blue lamp with a matching silk shade lay broken on the floor at her feet. She was holding the black fire iron that rested on the hearth between the ash bin and the wood box. Holding it like a baseball bat.

"Maggie?"

Then she swung, raked the iron across the curio cabinet on the wall. The glass and knick-knacks—the Maid of the Mists replica from their Niagara Falls honeymoon, blown glass that looked like the white oak steamboat; and her porcelain angel collection—exploded in a colorful cloud of glass shards as she continued the swing, through a crystal lamp and the family pictures on the end table and into hand-painted plates displayed on a shelf by the fireplace. In one, sweeping arc of destruction, she'd shattered thirty years of memories. Jonas was rooted to the spot in surprise and horror. Then she started for the television screen.

"Maggie, no!"

She turned on him. Swung the pointed end of the iron at his head, a look of such hatred and rage contorting her face he was almost too shocked to duck.

The iron caught the very top of his head, tore a fiery scrape across his scalp before his feet finally came unglued from the floor and he dashed across the room. When he snatched the metal club out of her hand, she turned on him, attacked him with her fists, pummeled his chest as he tried to grab her hands. She managed to claw his left arm, five deep gouging wounds down the length of it. Maggie had fingernails thick as a tiger's claws. And when he got hold of her wrists, she tried to bite him!

Through it all, she was making this sound in her throat, almost a growl, and then she began to scream. She yelled horrible things, accused him of trying to kill her, of infidelities, specific acts with women they *knew*: awful, awful things.

He finally got behind her, wrapped his arms around her, and held her so tight she couldn't move. She struggled, kicked, hollered, and wrenched her head from side to side. That part didn't last but a couple of minutes, though. She didn't have much strength at all.

Slowly she stopped wiggling and relaxed in his arms, limp. All the air'd drained out of her and her head lolled on her neck. He reached down and picked her up then—she weighed next to nothing—carried her into the bedroom and lay her gently on the bed. She just rolled over and sighed, like a little kid you carry into the house and put to bed after they fell asleep in the car on the way home.

His heart was slugging away in his chest so hard he could see it moving his shirt. He wanted to examine her, to make sure she wasn't hurt somewhere. But he was afraid to touch her, to wake her up, afraid she'd go crazy again.

In the end, he backed quietly out of the room and staggered back into the bomb zone that a few minutes ago had been a living room. He caught sight of his reflection in the mirror above the mantle and almost jumped back in fright. Blood was dripping down onto his forehead from the cut on the top of his head. And his arm!

He rushed into the kitchen and ran water over the wounds on his arm to wash the blood away. She'd got him good! A couple of gouges were so deep he'd need stitches to close them. He wrapped a clean dish towel around his arm, then another dish towel around the first one. That'd hold him for a little while. With a third dish towel, he dabbed at the scrape on the top of his head, but it had already stopped bleeding.

He went back into the living room, but couldn't face it, turned, went out the front door instead and sat down in the porch swing. His hands were shaking.

He sat for a long time trying not to think of anything. He tried to banish the image of her face, how she'd looked when she swung that thing at him. She could have killed him. Certainly tried hard enough. If he'd been a second slower …

Back and forth. Just swinging back and forth, listening to the comforting *eech-eech, eech-eech* sound the swing made. The sun slowly sank below the western horizon. The symphony orchestra of crickets under the porch began to tune up for their nightly concert and the frogs started hollering at each other—*rhubbub, rhubbub*. Then he heard Maggie from inside the house chattering about something. He could tell from the tone of her voice that it was over, that whatever had possessed her had passed.

He stood and used the back of his uninjured hand to wipe his cheeks; they'd got all wet somehow. Then he went inside to tend to Maggie and to clean up the mess.

◆ ◆ ◆ ◆ ◆

Mac heard Joy's voice in the living room talking on the phone as he came in the front door. He walked into the room as she was hanging the receiver back on the hook.

"Who was that?" he asked.

"Nobody."

"It was obviously *somebody*. Who?"

The words came out harsher than he intended. Seems like every time he talked to Joy lately, he ended up saying the wrong thing, or saying the right thing the wrong way.

"I'm sorry, sweetheart. I didn't mean to be so gruff. Long day. Forgive me?"

"Sure, Daddy," she said, but she didn't look at him. And she didn't tell him who she'd been talking to.

"Honey, is there something wrong with you?"

Now that *was tactful!*

Mac's father often told him, "You have *two* ears and *one* mouth for a reason." His daughter needed him to listen to her, not interrogate her. It was clear something wasn't right, and he had to find a way to get her to open up and tell him what it was.

And no, he wasn't struggling to communicate with Joy simply because some deeply disturbed death row inmate had advised him to. He had to start building bridges back to her, come to grips with the new order of things and their relationship in that order.

"I'm fine," she said, still without looking at him. She got up and started for the kitchen.

"No you're not," he said, his voice kind and tender. "I don't believe you're fine at all. I want to help, if you'll let me."

"I'm not the only one who's not fine; you aren't doing so hot yourself!" she fired back at him, her voice thick with unshed tears. "And if you really want to help, just leave me alone right now."

She turned, raced upstairs to her room, and slammed the door shut behind her. A few moments later he heard her record player, harmonized voices wailing, "… let's go surfin' now, everybody's learnin' how, come on a safari with …"

Mac shook his head. Why were all the kids so taken with songs about *surfing*? This was Oklahoma, for Pete's sake; there wasn't a body of water with a wave you could stand on for over a thousand miles in any direction. When he was growing up here, he and his friends hadn't obsessed over songs about mountain climbing or scuba diving.

He sighed, chucked the mail he'd just gotten out of the mailbox by the door onto the coffee table, and went into the kitchen. It had become customary, here in the new normal of their lives, for the first one of them who got home to put a casserole into the oven for supper. There was never a shortage of casseroles. The good ladies of the church had seen to that, mobilized their troops with sign-up sheets in the fellowship hall. A couple of times a week, somebody'd show up with a box full of casseroles. They'd pick up the empty dishes from the week before and deposit the new ones in the big, white Amana refrigerator Mac had gotten Melanie a year ago for Christmas.

He'd figured the ladies would stop a long time ago. It had been six months now. How long did those women intend to keep cooking his dinner? A year? Two? Until Joy graduated from high school?

And what was he going to do when the dinners stopped? And they most definitely would stop after Sunday. When he had his say on Sunday, there wouldn't be a sweet little old lady left in that church who had any desire to cook for him.

He went to the refrigerator, opened the door, and peered in. There were three "covered dishes." That's what the ladies called them. He lifted the aluminum foil on each one in turn. Chicken and rice. Unidentifiable, but there was big tube pasta in it and he loved that kind of pasta. What was it called? Cannelloni? Rigatoni? Something that ended in "i." And the one left over from last night—tuna, with crumbled-up potato chips on the top.

He slid the Corningware dish containing the mystery pasta off the shelf and deposited it in the oven. Then he turned the dial to 350 degrees. He cooked them all at 350; didn't know if that was the right temperature or not, but at least he was consistent.

What *was* he going to do when the casserole manna no longer showed up fresh on the ground every morning? What would they eat? Sandwiches would get old real quick. So would canned soup. Would he have to learn to cook? And what about Joy? Could she cook? He'd seen her in the kitchen helping her mother so surely—

The image was so clear it was momentarily real. Two apron-clad females, chattering a blue streak as they chopped and stirred and tasted, the aroma of their delicacies wafting out of the kitchen to settle with a comforting warmth all around him. Then poof, the vision was gone, and he was standing in the vacant kitchen in the too-quiet house.

He groaned out loud. Nobody to hear him, why not? Then just stood there, feeling … what? Empty. Profoundly *empty*.

What was it that woman had said today, that Princess? Said he could go out and buy a new shirt or climb a tree or swim in the lake, do anything he wanted to do next week—but she'd be dead. She didn't get it. He already *was* dead.

Forty-five minutes later, he and Joy sat down to dinner. That's how long he cooked all the casseroles—forty-five minutes. Joy had come downstairs, mumbled that she was sorry—tough day, too—then set the table. They ate in the kitchen, in the "breakfast nook" instead of in the dining room. With just the two of them, the dining room felt like a football stadium.

They'd always used the little table set in the bay window in the kitchen for quickie meals. Lunch on a busy Saturday. Breakfast on a rushed morning. Just a place to park and eat, not a place for a proper meal. He and Joy ate there every night. And that said something. He wasn't sure what, but whatever it was, it wasn't good.

"You want iced tea, don't you?" he asked.

She nodded, he poured a glass for both of them, then picked up his fork and—

"Daddy …?"

"What?" He stopped before he speared one of the fat pastas.

"You didn't ... we didn't say the blessing yet."

He felt his stomach yank into a knot.

"I'm sorry, I forgot."

"You don't ever forget to say the blessing."

He heard something like fear in her voice, and instantly understood that the blessing was important. It was nothing more than empty words to him. But Joy needed order in the midst of all the chaos churning around her, and the blessing represented one of the pillars that stood firm, that kept the roof from tumbling down on top of them.

He bowed his head. "Thank you, Father, for this food, and for the kind hands that prepared it for us. In Jesus' name, amen."

He looked up and smiled. "Sorry, my mind was a million miles away. So, tell me about school. How was it today?"

"It was—"

"And don't tell me fine. We are no longer going to allow the use of the word fine in this house. Fine is no longer fine. In fact, you will be fined for the use of the word fine."

"Fine by me," she said, and grinned.

"How was it really?"

"It was ... okay."

Mac started to protest, but she held up her hand. "Look, you can't ban all the bland words. There's got to be some acceptable way to say 'it was so blah, if I had to paint it, the only suitable color would be something between tan and cream.'"

Like the room where he'd met with Princess today.

"Sounds like my day was a bit more interesting than yours. I went out to the Iron House and talked with a woman on death row." He took a bite of the pasta tube. Chewy. Maybe he cooked it too long. Or not long enough. "Only there they don't call it death row. They call it the Long Dark."

"The Long Dark. Cool! What was she like?"

Mac realized he had absolutely no idea how to answer that question.

"Well ... now, don't take this wrong; she mentioned you."

"Me? How on earth does—what's her name?"

"Princess."

"Princess?"

"Emily Prentiss. Princess."

He waited for recognition to dawn on her face, but she merely looked blank. Didn't teenagers read the paper or watch the news on TV?

"Prentiss … Princess. Some kid's mispronunciation of the word, probably." Her little sister's, maybe?

"So how does this Princess know me?"

"Obviously, she doesn't. Just heard about my family and … I think she's nuts. Been in solitary too long."

"What'd she do? To be on death row she must have killed somebody. Who'd she kill?"

"Her little sister." He considered before he continued. "Who was two years old at the time."

"That's awful, Daddy. And she talked about me? What'd she say?"

He chewed up the piece of pasta and swallowed before he spoke. "She said I ought to talk to you because there's something bothering you, said you're … hurting inside."

Joy's face froze. He watched shock bleach out all the color in her cheeks. Her eyes filled with tears and she sat transfixed for a moment. Then she scooted her chair back from the table, got up, and tossed her napkin into the chair.

"Joy, what's the matter?"

"I'm not hungry anymore." She whirled around to rush out, but Mac stood and grabbed her arm.

"Honey, I'm sorry. What is it?"

"What is it? What do you *think* it is? Of course I'm hurting inside. We both are. And I—" She pulled her arm free. "I don't want any dinner." She didn't run up the stairs this time. She walked slowly. And closed her door quietly behind her. He waited for loud music to follow but there was only silence.

Mac sat back down and looked at the chewy, under/over cooked pasta on his plate. He didn't want it either. But he had to eat something, so he stabbed another piece and put it into his mouth. It was tasteless but innocuous and as he chewed it, he remembered. Actually, Princess hadn't said Joy was hurting. She said *something was hurting Joy*. A subtle difference, but different nonetheless. Said something was wrong with her. That she needed help.

The pale teenager who'd sat across from him three minutes ago certainly looked like she needed help.

Tuesday

May 7, 1963

9

JONAS WAS UP EARLY TUESDAY MORNING. No sense lying there all buggy-eyed, staring at the ceiling. He hadn't slept well. His arm hurt something fierce, but he had to admit the timing on the injury was fortunate. He already had a doctor's appointment scheduled for today.

Yeah, the doctor's appointment. The thought of it caused goose-flesh to pop out on his arms, set the scratches to aching all over again. He'd already set and then cancelled two appointments, but he'd be keeping this one. It was time.

He had bandaged the wounds the best he could the night before with Band-Aids and some gauze out of the medicine cabinet. Now he dressed carefully in a long-sleeved shirt. The nurse in Dr. Bradford's office could put on proper bandages for him. The wound on the top of his head had stopped bleeding on its own.

When he changed and cleaned Maggie, she might as well have been a Raggedy Ann doll, limp and totally unresponsive. He shaved and just had the coffee brewing when he heard her stirring.

"Tommy? Tommy, where are you?" she called from the bedroom.

Oh, no.

"Mary Anne, where's your little brother? You didn't let him get in the chicken yard again, did you? Out there chasing chickens?

Those hens won't lay for a week! Mary Anne, answer me, now you answer your mother!"

Her voice had down-shifted from annoyed through concerned to mildly frantic. Jonas didn't need this. Not today!

He set down the cup he was about to fill with coffee and went to the room that used to be the downstairs parlor. It had been converted into a bedroom after Maggie got where she couldn't climb stairs.

"Mornin' Maggie," he said cheerily and crossed to the windows on the far wall. "I'm gonna raise these shades and let some sunlight in, bright May morning like this, you need to enjoy the sunshine."

"Jonas, where's Tommy and Mary Anne?"

Well, she knew who *he* was today. One out of three.

"What would you like for breakfast this morning? I've got some fresh-squeezed—"

"Why are you ignoring me?"

She was sitting up in bed, had both her pillow and his stuffed behind her, with what he called a "deceptively alert" look on her face. Alert because she was talking in complete sentences that seemed to make sense and responding appropriately to reality. And deceptive because hers was an alternate reality.

Her long white hair hung around her shoulders and it occurred to him to wonder why she never looked disheveled, never had bedhead. Maybe because most nights she didn't move, just closed her eyes when he kissed her goodnight and then opened them the next morning lying in exactly the same position. That, too, was new. Why, when they first got married, she used to flop around like—

"I've searched and searched for Tommy and Mary Anne. They're both gone!" She glanced around. "Where are they?" He could hear the beginning sharp edge of hysteria in her voice. She could go off any second.

Jonas knew where Tommy and Mary Anne were. They'd been side-by-side for years. In cemetery plots close to Melanie's fresh grave.

Tom, their only son, had made it clear even as a child that he wasn't about to live his life on some farm in Oklahoma. He had run off to join the navy when he was barely eighteen. Jonas smiled at how proud the boy had been of his first ship assignment. He'd written them all about it. He was in Hawaii—*Hawaii,* can you beat that! In Pearl Harbor. On the USS *Arizona.*

Tom's was one of the few bodies they were able to recover after the ship was sunk. His death liked to have killed Maggie, too. After Mary Anne was born, Maggie'd miscarried three times before she had Thomas. Two years after Tommy died, the war took Mary Anne, too. An army nurse, she'd been killed by a land mine in North Africa. Their only surviving child had been Melanie.

Jonas fiddled with the cord on the shade until he was sure he could speak without his voice breaking.

"Know what I think? I think we ought to go sit on the porch swing together and have us a cup of coffee? What do you say?"

"Jonas Nathaniel Cunningham, why won't you listen to me? I just told you two of our children are missing. And if you won't go find them, I will!"

Okay, time to lie.

"Simmer down, Maggie. They ain't missin'. They're just outside a'gatherin' eggs. They'll be in the house directly."

"Tommy's too little to gather eggs! Jonas, what were you thinking? Why that boy—"

The doorbell mercifully interrupted the conversation. That would be Mac, here to watch after Maggie while Jonas went to the doctor. Guadalupe Hernandez, the Mexican woman who took care of her a couple of days a week couldn't come today, so Jonas had asked his son-in-law to help out.

Mac looked tired, like maybe he hadn't been sleeping. Jonas supposed he probably looked tired himself. Hard to see tired, though, on a face as old and worn out as his. But the younger man looked to be a weary that was beyond losing a few nights' sleep.

"'Lo Mac." He reached out long arms and folded Mac into a brief man hug. "You doin' all right?"

"Can't complain, Jonas, 'n you?"

"'Bout the same, I guess."

Men were such liars.

"Listen, Maggie kinda had a hard evening yesterday." He gestured toward the living room and Mac stepped to the doorway. He'd cleaned up the mess real good but he could see Mac suck in a breath when he surveyed the room.

"What happened to the—?"

"She broke a bunch of stuff." He didn't tell Mac she had attacked him, though, tried to protect Maggie's dignity, best as he could. "And this mornin' she's seein' little pink bunnies, only they ain't bunnies. I could call the doctor's office and reschedule. It ain't nothing that can't wait. Just a checkup is all. "

"You go on ahead, Jonas. It's always good to see Maggie, no matter what frame of mind she's in."

Jonas reached over and plucked his Allis Chalmers cap off a peg and fit it snug on his head.

"Right now, her frame of mind is … oh, I'd say something like 1926, maybe '28. She's upset 'cause she can't find Mary Anne and Tommy."

"Oh."

"Of course, by the time you get in there, she may have leap-frogged to a whole new decade." He turned toward the door, then turned back. "You okay, Mac?"

He saw Mac's jaw tighten at the question and he understood. He got tired of people pokin' and proddin' too. He reached out wordlessly and patted Mac on the shoulder, then turned and headed out the door.

WHEN MAC STEPPED INTO MAGGIE'S BEDROOM, her face bloomed in a beautiful smile and he was struck by just how much her daughter had favored her. Mac was good at spotting that kind of thing, family resemblance, could pick out the shape of a chin, or the taper of an eyebrow—subtle things other people missed.

But there was nothing subtle about Melanie's resemblance to her mother. They both had a haunting beauty, finely chiseled features, a high forehead and big, brown eyes with long eyelashes.

If you want to know how well your wife will age, take a look at her mother.

Maggie Cunningham was still a beautiful woman. Melanie would have looked stunning with white hair.

"Why Mac, how wonderful to see you," she said. That was a good start. She knew who he was. He'd seen her many times when she didn't have a clue—once, in fact, she'd spent an entire evening calling him Bart. No one could figure out who Bart might once have been in her life.

"Come on over here and have a seat." She patted the bed beside her. He sat down in the chair next to the bed instead and took both her hands in his.

"You look lovely today, Maggie."

"Well, of course I do, silly. The mother of a beautiful bride is more or less obligated to look presentable, and my Melanie is a strikingly beautiful bride."

Mac swallowed hard. Maggie didn't know Melanie had died. What was the point in telling her?

"Now, don't you be trying to get a peek at Melanie before the ceremony." She shook her finger at him. "You know it's bad luck for the groom to see the bride in her wedding dress before—" She stopped in mid-sentence, looked confused for a moment, then gripped his hands tight in hers.

"Mac, where's Melanie?"

He had an answer all prepared, used the same one, with minor variations, whenever Maggie asked about Melanie. "She's at home, Mom. Joy's got strep throat, remember?"

"No, she's not. She's not home with Joy." Mac didn't like the look in her eye. She looked too ... *there*. Too much like the old Maggie, full of piss and vinegar. Folks used to say that when Maggie Cunningham's feet hit the floor in the morning, the devil groaned and said, "Oh, crap! She's up." She'd whipped two generations of high school freshmen into shape in her English classes, doted on her husband, adored her daughter and—

"Something's wrong with Melanie, isn't it? And you've all been keeping it from me. Tell me. Please, Mac. *Tell* me!"

The words leapt out before he could stop them. "Melanie's dead, Mom. Breast cancer."

Maggie looked like he'd back-handed her.

Why would you say a thing like that? What's wrong with you?

Maggie gasped, made a rasping sound in her throat as she tried to catch her breath, and then began to shake her head slowly back and forth. No. *No!* Mac ached to snatch the words back out of the air and erase the agony on the old woman's face. Her eyes grew wide and instantly brimmed with tears. Her chin and lip began to tremble.

"Oh, Maggie," he wailed, "I'm so sorry. I didn't mean …"

His voice trailed off as her expression began to change. Her features rearranged themselves before his eyes. All the tension and distress drained away and a slow, knowing smile crept onto her lips.

"I promise, I won't tell a soul," she said and patted his hand. "Cross my heart." And she did, lifted her hand from his and made an X motion with it on the front of her cotton nightgown. "But can I have just a little peak at the ring before you ask her?"

Mac's tongue was a cold stone in his mouth.

"Yeah, sure, Mom," he managed to say. "It's out in the car. You wait right here and I'll go get it."

He bolted out of the room, then out the front door, staggered over to the swing, and plopped down in it. He didn't swing, though, just sat stock still, inhaling great lungfuls of morning air perfumed by jonquils and day lilies and the honeysuckle that had threaded its way across the trellis by the steps.

What he wouldn't give to be crazy, too! To be able to blink and transport himself to a reality where Melanie was just outside the door waiting for him. All dressed up as a beautiful bride.

Of course, that's what his well-meaning congregants kept telling him. That Melanie *was* waiting for him. That she *was* just outside the door.

And that, sports fans, was lunacy. It was fantasy. Believing that was as sad and pathetic as …

Believing in miracles.

They'd all stood in a circle around her bed when she was hospitalized the first time, before the cancer had chewed her insides into ground meat. Bruce Daniels had driven through the night to get back home in time. Cigar-smoking Bill Tucker was there, absent his Havana Supreme. So was Howard Wilson, with his ridiculously bushy eyebrows; short, fat Andy Porter; Lee Davenport, his voice squeaking with laryngitis and bald-as-a-scrubbed-onion Will Hardesty. The entire elder board of New Hope Community Church had reached out as one, anointed Melanie with oil and "laid hands" on her to pray for healing. He'd prayed, too. Oh my goodness, yes, how hard he had prayed!

But the thing was—if he was totally honest, he had to admit it—he hadn't believed, even then. Oh, if you'd asked him, he'd have told you he did. Maybe he even had himself convinced he did. But deep down in the core of his being, David Allen McIntosh didn't believe God was going to heal his wife.

Why not? Because the good Reverend McIntosh didn't believe … well, he didn't believe a lot of things. First off, he didn't believe God would do what he asked him to do. And the thing was, Mac couldn't put his finger on the point in his life when he'd stopped believing that. During the war, maybe? Korea?

A lot of men found God in a foxhole. Maybe he'd lost God there. He'd spent most of the Great War in the South Pacific. Guam, Midway, Iwo Jima. He was a non-combatant, a chaplain fresh out of seminary. But he'd carried a gun and he'd used it, anyway. Had to. Platoons short-handed like they were, his buddies needed him. They all depended on each other for survival. And yeah, he'd killed a man. Several, probably. Not up close, but he'd shot and saw them fall.

Was that it? Did the act of killing separate him from God in some irreversible way?

And he'd buried so *many* good men, friends, watched them die horrible, agonizing deaths. Was that when he stopped believing?

Maybe. Or maybe it was in Korea, when nobody was even sure what they were fighting and dying for. When they'd lose five men taking a hill and the next day they'd be ordered to pack up and leave the ground to the enemy.

Was that when it happened?

He didn't know.

The problem was that he'd kept lying to himself about it for so long he'd missed it, that seminal moment, that train-switch instant when his life had suddenly veered off course, headed down another track altogether, one going in an entirely different direction. He'd missed that, missed the opportunity to face up to the reality of it when it happened. Maybe he could have done something about it then, before the train had gone so far down the track there was no possible way to get back to where he'd started.

And suddenly realizing you didn't believe God would help you at the precise moment in your life when you *most* needed his help, that was—

No, it had been more profound than that, more than just not believing God would help. Mac had been forced all at once to recognize the foundational truth of life: *God just flat didn't care, didn't give a rip about Mac or Melanie or anybody else.*

It had been true, all right. His precious wife lay there, gasping for air, in so much pain all over her body he couldn't touch her anywhere, couldn't hold her hand, couldn't even give her a little peck on the cheek. Day after agonizing day! But God decided to pass on helping. God could have healed her. Instead, the Almighty let Melanie Cunningham McIntosh lie there and suffer. And then die.

By the time she finally groaned her last, rasping breath, Mac was no longer shaking his fist at God. He'd figured out by then there was no God.

"Tommy! Tommy, where are you, child?"

Mac straightened at the sound of Maggie's voice.

"You come here to me this minute, do you hear me? Tommy!"

He'd best get in there and soothe her before she got all worked up. Tell her some lie to make her feel better. Mac was good at that, had been perfecting that skill from the pulpit for years.

10

"Havin' trouble sleeping, are you, Jonas?" George asked.

George Stovall was the pharmacist at the Graham Rexall Drug Store. He and Jonas had known each other for sixty years. Maybe longer.

"Yeah, just can't seem to drift off."

Jonas hoped he didn't look as uncomfortable as he felt. He knew it was paranoia, but it sure did *seem* like everybody in the whole store had turned and looked at him as soon as he opened his mouth and started talking.

He'd fiddled around, walked up and down the aisles for half an hour, working up his nerve to go collect the prescription he'd gotten Dr. Bradford to write for him. Stood looking at the shampoos for ten minutes. Why on earth did a body need two dozen different kinds of shampoo? For dry hair and oily hair, shampoo to cure dandruff, green shampoo, pink shampoo, and yellow shampoo.

He used bar soap—rubbed it on his head when he took a bath. And Maggie's hair always just smelled clean, that's all.

He'd wandered through the toothpastes and the cold medications, through the Ace bandages and insoles—anything to put off what he'd come here to do.

Trouble was, he just wasn't used to lying. He'd never been deceitful, couldn't ever remember doing that, even as a child. Oh, he had character flaws, that was a lead pipe cinch. Lying just didn't happen to be one of them. And he knew he wasn't any good at it, no good a'tall.

He'd stuttered and stumbled when he asked the doctor for something to help him sleep even though he'd rehearsed the speech in his head half a dozen times. All about how he was up most of the night some nights, how he needed his rest so he could look after Maggie. But when it came time to deliver the spiel, he couldn't remember none of it, got tongue-tied, barely able to choke out any words that made sense. Didn't seem to matter in the end. The doctor just scribbled something on the pad and handed it to him, easy as pie.

But then he had to get the prescription filled. And he got flummoxed all over again.

George didn't appear to notice a thing, though. He picked up the bottle of pills and taped the label snug on the outside of it. Then he dropped it down into a sack and handed the bag across the counter to Jonas.

"What'd you do to your hand? That's a nasty scratch. You put anything on it?"

George was a world-class busybody. Well-meaning, but nosey all the same. One of the claw marks from Maggie's fingernails extended out from under the cuff of his long-sleeve shirt and George had spotted it. The nurse had tended to Jonas's wounds in the doctor's office. Dr. Bradford said scratches like that from a human hand were more likely to get infected than if an animal had attacked him.

Before Jonas could stop him, George reached out and grabbed his hand.

"Want me to put something on that? You don't want to get blood poisoning."

Jonas extracted his hand from George's grasp. "Naw, it's all right. My granddaughter's cat got me, but I've already had it seen to. Guess I need to put some more mercurochrome on it."

"Iodine's better. Burns worse, but it's better."

"Iodine it is, then. Well, it was good to see you, George. I—"

"Whoa, hold up there, Jonas. I need to talk to you about these sleeping pills."

George had a tendency to speak too loud. Part of the problem was he was a little hard of hearing. But mostly, he was just a loudmouth. Right now, it seemed like he was near shouting and Jonas glanced from side to side. Nobody was paying any attention.

"What about the pills?" Jonas spoke in a quiet voice and hoped George would follow suit. He didn't.

"You need to be careful with them is all. They're a narcotic, you know. That's why you can't get them without a prescription. They'll knock you out all right, they're strong stuff. But they could be addictive."

"Oh, I'm not going to do a thing like that."

"Nobody ever is! Never met a man yet said, 'You know, I think I'll just go out and become a drug addict.' But it happens."

"Thanks for the warning, but I—"

"What I'm saying's you might get where you can't go to sleep *without* taking a pill. And that's a misery you don't need. These things are good for the short term—just be careful."

"I will, George, promise. Thanks for the advice."

Jonas turned and headed toward the front of the store to pay for his purchase. He was already three steps away from the counter when George called after him, hollered where everybody in the store could hear.

"And for Pete's sake, Jonas, don't take more than the prescribed dose! Take too many and those pills will *kill* you."

❖ ❖ ❖ ❖ ❖

Not getting to run made Mac irritable. He needed the physical release. And the psychological one, too, he supposed. He had planned to run after he got home from looking after Maggie, but there'd been a message on his answering machine informing him that he had an 11 o'clock appointment. That made him even more irritable.

This one was just the latest in a growing list of appointments his ever-vigilant secretary had made for him without his knowledge or consent. He knew she was trying to take up the slack of his inattention, but her practice of booking him to see someone—just a name, Sam Bartlett—with no further information was maddening. He needed to speak to her about it.

But why bother? It wouldn't matter after Sunday.

Mac slipped in the side door of the church where the administration offices were located and Lillian was sitting primly at her desk outside his office door. For some reason he couldn't quite nail down, the sixtyish woman had always reminded Mac of a robin. It was something about the black-rimmed glasses parked on a pointed nose, or her considerable bosom that extended in a solid mass from her neck to her waist. Or the fact that the back of her head was flat. Her mother must have let her sleep on her back too often as a baby. At least, Mac had read somewhere that's what caused such things. He had no actual experience with babies, of course. Joy had been a toddler when he and Melanie adopted her.

They'd discovered her sitting quietly on the front pew in the church sanctuary early one Sunday morning, thought at first she was a little boy. The child was contentedly marking up a hymnal with a pencil. Not a thing wrong with her except she was "thirssy," wanted a drink of water. Lying beside her was one of the Visitor's Cards from the rack on the back of the pew. Written on the blank side of the card in an odd, backward-slanted handwriting were the words: *Got no plase for her so plees giv her a gud hom.*

That was it.

In the beginning, they'd planned to tell her she was adopted. But the right time just never seemed to present itself. And to be honest, a lot of folks didn't hold with adoption back then and they didn't want people to look down on her, think she was any less their daughter just because she wasn't their flesh and blood. It had been easy to let the issue slide. Since Joy had brown eyes like Melanie and red hair like his, people automatically assumed they were her biological parents.

"Why, good morning to you, Pastor McIntosh," Lillian said.

No amount of coaxing could convince the woman to call him Mac.

"Morning, Lil."

"Your 11 o'clock appointment is waiting in your office."

Right. The mystery meat.

Mac opened the door and found a man reading a newspaper, his booted feet crossed atop the coffee table. He spotted Mac and hopped up off the sofa like burnt toast popping out of a toaster.

"I'm Sam Bartlett."

"David McIntosh." Mac extended his hand. "Call me Mac."

"Your secretary told me I could wait in here."

The crew-cut man in his early thirties gestured to the newspaper he'd dropped on the coffee table. "Hope you don't mind if I read your paper. Can't help being a news junkie."

"News junkie?"

"Well, yeah. Didn't your secretary tell you? I'm a reporter for the *Oklahoma City Daily News.*"

Mac crossed the room to his desk and sat down in the chair behind it. When he had counseling appointments, he always sat in the chair opposite the sofa. It was less formal. People were more willing to open up in a homey atmosphere, at least that's what Melanie said. She was the one who'd added the little touches that made his office comfortable. Even hung yellow curtains to match the yellow in the floral design of the chair. Mel thought of everything.

"What can I do for you, *Mr.* Bartlett?" Mac said from the back side of the wide expanse of oak desktop. He wasn't interested in making the newspaper reporter feel comfortable and chatty.

The man looked confused. "Did I say something wrong?"

"No, but I suspect I know why you're here. If I'm right, I could have saved you a long, boring drive."

"And you think I'm here to ask about …?"

"Emily Prentiss, the woman who's scheduled to be executed on Friday. Is she the reason you're here?"

"Yes, she is. I want—"

"I don't have anything to say about Emily Prentiss." Mac started to rise.

"Wow, that was quick! I haven't been here ninety seconds and you've already passed judgment on me. Can't you at least *hear* me out before you *kick* me out?"

Mac reluctantly settled back in the chair. "I'm listening."

The man crossed to the desk and sat down in the straight-backed chair next to it. He ran his fingers over his close-cropped hair and let out a long breath.

"I'm going to give it to you straight up. I've been writing classifieds and obits for almost a year now. Just got out of college—night school on the GI Bill—and this is my first story." He must have spotted the dubious look on Mac's face because he hurried on. "Hey, listen, you are looking at a walking encyclopedia on Emily Prentiss! I've read all the old clips, the trial transcripts—both sets—even dug up the original grand jury depositions. I've read the appeals briefs and—"

Mac cut him off.

"Why'd you go to all that trouble?"

"Lots of reasons," he said expansively. "I want to do better than a simple twenty column-inches on 'child-killer gets hers.' I want to do something more real, more personal, more—"

"And the other reasons?"

He'd been on a roll, but the bravado suddenly sighed out of him and he looked sheepish. "Truth?"

Mac nodded.

"It was the only way I could get them to give me the story." He looked at his shoes. "I'm not the lead reporter, either. Another guy's coming down the end of the week to cover the actual execution."

"You're freelancing." It wasn't a question.

The young man shrugged. "How else am I ever going to get a chance to show them what I can do?"

Mac said nothing.

"I've been requesting interviews with Emily Prentiss for months, but she won't talk to me. Then I came down yesterday, noticed on the prison log that'd you'd seen her, and I thought maybe you could help me."

"Help you how?"

"Ask her if she'll talk to me."

"She won't."

In truth, Mac wasn't sure of that. He wondered why she'd turned down the man's requests for an interview in the first place. Surely, even talking to a reporter was better than talking to the walls.

Fact was, Princess would probably come off sounding so crazy in a newspaper story somebody might just decide she wasn't mentally competent to be executed. If that even mattered at this stage of the game, and he didn't know if it did.

"Will you at least ask her to talk to me?"

"No."

"Then tell me about her, about your conversations with her."

"You know I can't do that! I'm her pastor. Anything she tells me is confidential. I couldn't tell you even if I wanted to."

The man took up the study of his own shoes again, looked so defeated Mac felt a little sorry for him.

"Look, you already know her better than I do. She asked for a minister yesterday and I drew the short straw. I've only had the one conversation with her."

Bartlett lifted his head. "Do you want to know more about her? Wouldn't it help you counsel her more effectively if you knew her better?"

"Yeah, I suppose."

"I'll make a deal with you. You ask her to talk to me." He held up his hand before Mac could protest. "Ask, that's all. And I'll tell you anything you want to know about her."

Mac hedged. "I'll ask, but just so you know—I'm going to advise her to say no."

Bartlett's laugh sounded genuine. "You sure don't polish it up before you say it, do you?" He let out a breath and squared his shoulders. "All right, I can live with that. It's not much, but it's more than I've got right now." He leaned back in his chair. "What do you know about her already?"

"The basics, what everybody knows, that she was convicted of murdering her little sister and she's been on death row for fourteen years." Mac didn't call it the Long Dark or mention that she'd been in solitary. The man might already know those things and he could certainly find out somewhere else. But it seemed to Mac that both tidbits reeked of yellow journalism.

"She didn't just kill her little sister. Emily *beheaded* her, then chopped her up with an ax."

Mac groaned.

"The child's name was Angela, by the way," Bartlett said. "Emily described how she had trouble chopping through the kid's bones, how she had to take the dress off the body because it made it harder to cut up. And that the head was—"

"Okay, I think we've covered that part."

"I'm just saying, this isn't a case where there's doubt about whether the defendant committed the crime. No circumstantial evidence or uncertain eye witnesses. Emily admitted it, described it in excruciating detail. Almost seemed … proud of it."

"Why'd she do it? What was her motive?"

"She never said and the prosecution never could come up with a reason. She confessed and then clammed right up, refused to answer any questions or talk about anything but the murder. That's why I want to talk to her. There are a bunch of things about this case that don't make any sense to me. I want to write a story that clears up all the mysteries. Right now, the only person who can is about to take the answers with her to the grave."

"For instance?"

"She ran away from home, was on the run for almost two weeks and she took Angela with her when she split. So, did she take her little sister because she was planning to kill her? Or did she kill her because of something that happened during those two weeks? What was it? And once she'd killed the child and disposed of the body—?"

"How?"

"Threw the pieces of it in the Three Forks River, never recovered anything for the family to bury. But after that, why didn't Emily at least *try* to get away with the crime?"

"How'd they catch her?"

"She went to a circus in Fisherville all covered in blood! The clips said she threw some kind of fit there."

"The warden told me she's an epileptic."

"So here's this blood-covered teenager flopping around on the ground in a crowd of people, foaming at the mouth. Of course, somebody's going to call the police! And when she came to, she told them the whole story."

"Never tried to deny anything?"

"Nope, pleaded guilty and the judge sentenced her to death, court proceedings didn't take but a couple of hours. Of course, that was before that female lawyer got into the act."

"How could Prin … Emily afford a lawyer and why'd she bother?"

"I don't think she had a whole lot to say about it one way or the other. Some East Coast law firm on a crusade against the death penalty somehow got hold of the case and they made major hay with it. Said the defendant didn't understand her rights before she confessed and hadn't been properly represented, claimed diminished capacity. Convinced an appellate judge to throw out Emily's confession and they had to take her to court and try her in front of a jury. Result was the same, though. There was plenty of physical evidence to convict her even without a confession. She'd kept the bloody dress Angela'd been wearing and the murder weapon, the ax. Had strands of her sister's hair, long curls, on it."

Bartlett paused. "You know, I could show you pictures of the evidence, the bloody ax and—"

"I'll pass, thanks."

The reporter shrugged and continued the narrative. "I remember reading some of the testimony of Emily's step-father at her trial. I swear, that's what got her the chair, what he said on the stand. Him being a preacher and all—" The reporter stopped, looked uncomfortable. "I'm just saying, he was very … convincing."

"I've heard Jackson Prentiss speak—not just on TV, live—and I know how persuasive he can be," Mac said. "But I didn't know he was Emily's stepfather."

"Angela's stepfather, too, but he adopted them, changed their names to Prentiss. Emily's parents joined his church in Texas when Emily was about ten. Then right after her mother got pregnant with Angela, her father ran off with another woman and they divorced—a *big* deal in the forties. So the reverend married the pregnant divorcée, said he wanted to 'help her raise her children.' At some point, he moved the church way back in the Ouachita Mountains in Arkansas. He called it a 'family' then." The reporter leaned close and whispered, "Shoot, we'd probably call it a 'commune' now."

He straightened and continued the story. "Emily's mother died in childbirth having Angela. Prentiss broke down sobbing on the stand talking about it. The baby wasn't his blood kin, but he said as soon as he saw her, he loved her like she was his flesh and bone. Said she was pure and … 'unsullied' was his word. His wife of only a couple of months had given her life to bring the baby into the world and then Emily took that innocent child and … It was genuinely heartbreaking."

There was a beat of silence before he continued.

"But even after Emily was convicted by a jury, that lawyer—her name was … Solomon, Gretchen Solomon. She absolutely would not let it go, filed appeal after appeal."

That explained Princess's fourteen years of solitary confinement. It would have been far more merciful to have executed her on the spot.

"Why'd the woman keep dragging it out?"

"She didn't think Emily did it."

"After she confessed? That's nuts."

"I'm with you, pastor, but there you have it. The lawyer was quoted in a story, saying something like, 'if you'd ever talked to Emily, you'd know she couldn't possibly have done this.' Said that no matter what the evidence 'appears to show,' Emily couldn't have harmed the kid, that she *loved* Angela."

A sudden chill ran down Mac's spine. There was a part of him that could understand why the woman felt that way, bizarre as it sounded. There was just something about Princess …

"So the lawyer finally ran out of appeals, huh?" he said.

"Nope. Died. I think she was killed, stepped in front of a bus or something in Boston about a year ago. And without somebody putting on the brakes, the wheels of justice finally ground around to Emily Prentiss."

Mac was quiet.

"What else do you want to know?"

"Not a thing. Truth is, I think I was better off before. All this information does is make me sick."

"Are you going to hold up your end of the bargain, be an honest man, and ask her if she'll see me?"

Be an honest man? A much more intriguing question than Sam Bartlett realized. Mac had been a minister his whole adult life and that afforded a code of conduct. Tracks to run your life on. Without the code, was Mac an honest man?

"I agreed to ask her and I will. And if she wants to talk to you, that's her business." After hearing her story, Mac didn't feel quite as inclined to protect her.

11

MAC DIDN'T KNOW IF HE WAS supposed to go by Oran's office every day when he went to visit Princess or if he could just process through security at the check-in center and be taken directly to the envelope room. When he showed up at the main gate at 3 o'clock, the guard looked in vain for his name on a list. Apparently prison visitors were required to give prior notice.

He was struck by a small burst of panic, thinking that because he hadn't called ahead, they wouldn't let him see her. And it surprised him that the thought of *not* seeing her now exceeded the angst he'd felt at the prospect of meeting her in the first place.

Finally, the guard placed a phone call, spoke for a few moments, then waved Mac through.

"You need to get a pass from the warden's office," he said. "I'm not supposed to let you in without your name being on the day sheet."

Mac drove directly to the administration building, where he was greeted at the check-in center by the unsmiling, Olympic wrestling team guard from before. She patted him down and told him to empty out his pockets into a metal basket. Unlike the guard working security the day before, she began to meticulously examine the contents of the basket, setting aside everything metal, sharp or pointed—his car keys and two ballpoint pens. She could be all day at this.

"Just keep it all, I'll pick it up when I come back later."

She shrugged, marked the basket and set it in a shelf unit of baskets. Then she led him wordlessly through the rabbit warren of hallways up to the fourth floor to the desk of Oran's secretary.

"Didn't know you'd be back today, Reverend McIntosh."

"I'm sorry. I should have said something before I left yesterday. I promised Miss Prentiss that I would come and talk to her every day this week."

She looked up, surprised.

"That's okay, isn't it? I thought Oran said she was entitled to see a minister."

"She is. Let me explain the protocol." Her voice lapsed into the sing-song rhythm of one who has repeated the same words hundreds of times. "Gen pop prisoners are allowed visitors once a week, on Thursdays, for one hour, if they have not had any infractions of the rules, not gotten any marks against their names. Those visits are in the visitation center on the first floor of building three." She paused in the recitation to add a commentary. "The center has glass walls between the inmates and visitors, to keep down the flow of contraband—or worse. Death row inmates get to use the lawyer conference room on the third floor of this building, which has no such restrictions."

Ah, but the room does have a crack in the wall. Princess found it.

The secretary took up the litany again. "On the last week, a death row inmate is allowed daily visits, up to a maximum of three people a day, between 9 a.m. and noon and from 1 to 5 p.m. On Friday, the day of the execution, no visitation is allowed before noon or after 4 p.m."

She reached into her desk drawer and pulled out a badge, the kind you pin to your lapel at a Shriner's convention, wrote his name on it, then signed and dated it herself.

"With this, the guard will let you in the front gate without you having to call first or have your name on the day sheet."

"Thanks."

She looked at the clock on the wall.

"Prentiss is outside for her hour in the exercise yard right now. I'll send somebody to get her."

She reached for the phone as she spoke to the guard. "Would you take Reverend McIntosh to the lawyer conference room, please? Take him through the yard and up the back stairs. Maintenance is replacing the cracked hinge on the security door."

He walked beside, instead of respectfully three steps behind, Godzilla as they headed down the hallway.

Wonder if she's a high enough order of primate that she can actually speak?

"So, your name's …?" He said as he glanced down at her name badge. Smooth move. It was some Polish or Russian name, all consonants, totally unpronounceable. "Uh, what is your name?"

She grunted something that sounded like, "Warsa-cowski-peder-inski-wasniak … ski."

Silence, just the sound of her black jackboots stomping on the concrete.

"Well … I hear there's a new guard on the Long Dark," he prattled on mindlessly, remembering what Princess had told him yesterday. "A Mexican woman from Nogales. Do you—?"

She stopped to unlock a door for them to cut across an empty corner of the quadrangle to the back stairs leading up to the third floor of the administration building.

"Don't know who you been talkin' to, Rev'rend," she grunted, the accent pure Oklahoma, regardless of the cultural heritage. "There ain't no Mexicans working on the Long Dark. Newest guard there's name is Bradley."

Her words shoved a tiny silver ice pick into his side just below his ribcage. He probably would have asked more questions, but the door swung open and the sound came then, not from anywhere so much as from everywhere, all around him.

Oran had been right about Princess's singing—surely that's who it was. Mac had never heard anything like it. The melody seemed vaguely hymnal, something she remembered from a church service perhaps, or a camp meeting, maybe even a funeral. No not a funeral, not dark and somber. This was light and airy, each note a cherry dipped in the warm chocolate of Princess's husky voice. It was almost … Gaelic! Yes, like the old songs his Irish grandfather used to sing when he got drunk.

The melody sparkled in the glistening May sunshine as they continued across the quad. Even the Neanderthal guard seemed to be walking more softly in response to it.

The words weren't English or any language he'd ever heard. They were merely a collection of sounds, backwards syllables, perhaps, their not-quite-ness haunting and tantalizing. Words spoken in a dream before the harsh light of waking dissolved them and they dissipated even as you grabbed at them, wisps of smoke from a dying campfire.

He vaguely remembered some myth—high school English class, he should have paid better attention. Was it the *Iliad* or the *Odyssey?* The story of a warrior rendered helpless by a siren's song.

Surely, this was a siren's song.

The singing ended abruptly. But the sound lingered somehow in the stillness, the air empty and vacant without it, as if the music was the flip side of silence in the same way that light was the flip side of darkness.

The guard unlocked the door into building one, locked it behind them, and led through more locked metal doors, narrow, dark hallways, and up a staircase until they arrived at the manila-envelope room from the other direction.

Princess was already there. Sitting quietly, her hands folded demurely on the table in front of her.

"'Lo, Princess."

"Reverend," she said, in the voice that didn't belong in the scrawny body with the scarred face and brown teeth.

He walked to the table, pulled out the chair, and sat. Then he opened his mouth to tell her he'd heard her singing, to ask her about the words, the melody.

And to tell her there was a reporter who wanted to talk to her. And to ask about the fictitious guard and how on earth she …

Instead, he said. "You do realize, don't you, that you have your dress on wrong-side out?"

Seams showed at the shoulders and on the sides of the shapeless brown shift; the buttons down the front were invisible; a tag dangled in the back.

"It's Tuesday."

Mac's mind stumbled, trying to catch the train of Princess's thought. "Is that something like, 'I'm sorry, I can't hear you, my shoe's untied'?"

Princess wrinkled her brow. "Rev, you ain't making a lick of sense."

Mac started over, his speech slow and measured. "Am I supposed to see some connection between Tuesday and wearing your dress wrong side out?"

"Tuesdays, Thursdays, and Saturdays is wrong-side-out days. Mondays, Wednesdays, and Fridays is right-side-out days. And Sundays they give out clean uniforms."

"You change it because it's dirty?"

"'Course it's dirty. You don't change clothes but once a week, what you got on's dirty on both sides! Ain't got nothing to do with dirt. I switch it back and forth so's I can keep track of what day it is."

"Oh, so you—"

"So I get up Monday morning with a clean uniform on—ain't ironed or nothing, all wrinkled like an old dishrag, but it's clean, smells like bleach. And I sleep in it Monday night and when I get up Tuesday morning, I take it off, stand there nekkid and splash water on me from the sink to clean up best as I can and I put my dress back on wrong side out. I wear it all day, sleep in it Tuesday night, and then Wednesday morning—"

"I get it."

"You don't do something to keep track, you lose time and you don't know where it went. A day, a week … you can lose months, years even. It's just slipping through your fingers 'thout you knowin' and one day you look up and it ain't the same old same old, day in, day out. It's all gone."

She was sitting perfectly still, her face animated, but the rest of her body motionless. Then she was up and across the room, gazing out the window.

A *ground* squirrel, Mac amended in his head. She didn't move herky-jerky like a squirrel—just quick, like the hot-dog-shaped chipmunks that lived in community burrows on the Texas and

Oklahoma plains, the ones that called out to each other at sundown with a plaintive, *chig-chig-chiggeree* cry.

"Only way not to lose days is to grab hold of the little bitty pieces of 'em and hold on tight as you can to ever' one."

"Like …?"

"Like … like scratchin' a itch!" She turned to him, a smile on her face brighter than her brown teeth. "Ain't that a fine thing, to scratch a itch? Do you know you can make yourself itch, just by thinking 'bout it hard?"

She crossed the room toward him, but at the last moment caught herself and stepped so the table was between them.

"You try it. You can do it. Just think of some place on you … like your elbow … no, the back of your neck. Think 'bout the back of your neck. Concentrate on it hard. Go on. You think on it, you can make it itch."

She paused, waited.

"When it commences to itchin' don't scratch it right away. You let it keep itching 'til you can't wait nairy another second and then you can go at it. Just with the tips of your fingers, though; even if you just bit your nails you don't want to scratch and draw blood. It'll get 'fected quick if it ain't clean. Go on, now. Try."

Mac tried. Concentrated. Nothing. He thought about faking it, almost reached up to scratch his neck, to pretend.

"Sorry," he said. "Didn't work for me."

"I ain't surprised. Shoot, your mind's all full up. You're a-thinking about puttin' jam on your toast this morning, ridin' out here in your car with the window down, the wind blowin' in your face so it's hard to breathe."

Her smile grew wider.

"I rode in a car like that once! The windows down, ever' last one of 'em, and the wind blowin' through, hair in our faces, ticklin' our noses, and we was laughin' …"

The smile drained slowly away.

She sat down, quiet again. "My mind ain't all full up with things like yours. That's why I can do it, make a itch. My mind's so empty if I was to sneeze in there you could hear it echo."

She stopped abruptly and looked down at her feet. They were bare. It was the first Mac had noticed she wasn't wearing shoes.

"I done it again," she said softly.

"What did you do?"

"Talked. Blabbered."

"What's wrong with talking?"

"See I ain't had much practice with conversation. You talk, then I talk, then you talk. It's kinda like playin' catch, ain't it?"

"Kind of."

"I musta stayed up most of last night thinkin' I'd see you today and what I'd say, and I ain't said none of that yet."

Mac hadn't said any of what he wanted to say yet, either.

"Okay, tell me what you wanted to say."

"What I mostly wanted wasn't to talk a'tall. I wanted to listen. I wanted you to talk, 'bout life. You know, out there."

"Can I ask you something?"

"What I got to say you'd want to hear?"

"Where did you learn to sing like that?"

She looked surprised, embarrassed. "When'd you ever hear me sing?"

"Today. You were in the exercise yard, I guess. Where did that song come from?"

"Just made up. Outa my head."

"But the words weren't … English. Were they? What language is it?"

She was suddenly shy. Her face reddened and she ducked her chin.

"Them's my words is all. Made-up words."

"So they're just sounds, not really words."

"That ain't what I said." She cocked her head to the left, a pleat stapled between her eyebrows, her lips pressed together. "Are you listening to me? You know, conversation's a whole lot harder'n I thought it'd be. I said what I sing's *words*, they're just *my* words."

"For instance?"

"Well … *bomba-layla.* That means 'little baby.' And *wee wurlin.* That's 'wind blowing.'"

Lewis Carroll leapt out of Mrs. Branscom's sophomore English class and landed feet-first in Mac's mind: "'Twas brillig, and the slithy toves did gyre and gimble in the wabe." Carroll didn't have anything on a death row inmate named Princess. Shoot, he didn't even set his nonsense to music.

"You made up a whole language?"

"No, not ever' word in it. Just the ones I used in songs."

"Why?"

Princess gave him a brown-toothed smile.

"When Angel was little, I usta sing her to sleep of a night. She liked that, would lay there real still, like she was really *listenin'*. I didn't know no proper songs to sing, so I just made some up. She was so little, she didn't know the difference 'tween real words and made-up words."

Mac had a sudden, sick feeling in the pit of his stomach.

"Angel?"

"I mean Angela. I's the only one called her Angel. My little sister."

Mac grabbed words an instant before they leapt out his mouth. Instead of *you mean the little girl you murdered?* he managed to say, "Tell me about her."

The stillness around Princess gathered, settled. The warm honey of her voice bubbled up out of its center.

"She was so beautiful she broke your heart."

That was it. Silence. Princess was wrapped tight in it. Then her head came up and her face was animated again.

"You got your own little girl, doncha? She pretty?"

The silver ice pick slid back in under Mac's ribcage.

"She's gorgeous. Which brings up something *I* want to talk about. You knew about her, about me. And yesterday when I asked how you knew, you said a new guard told you. That wasn't true, was it?"

"No." She ducked her head again. "But I had to say somethin', else you'd a got all skittish and maybe woulda left, and I didn't want you—"

"What is the truth, Princess? How did you know about me? About my family?"

"Honest answer?"

He nodded.

"I don't have no idea."

"You don't know how you know?"

"There's lots of things I know that I don't know how. It's just there, in my head. I didn't put it there. Been that way ever since I ..." She paused. "... started having fits."

She must have read the startled confusion on his face. Leaning toward him, she spoke in the same, measured tone he had used with her earlier.

"I don't fret over not understandin' the how and why of it. I figure ain't no gutter in the world knows where the rainwater comes from. All of a sudden it's just there, and it flows right through and out the other side. The knowin', it's like that."

She looked deep into his eyes. "You forgive me? For lyin' to you?"

"You won't do it again?"

She dropped her eyes, studied the edge of the table.

"That's hard. Truth is hard."

"Yeah, truth is hard." Hard and sharp. Give it enough time and its razor edge would eventually slice through whatever pretense you wrapped it in.

She looked up. "Okay, I won't never lie to you ever again. But you got to make me the same promise."

"Deal." The word popped out before he could grab it.

"Now I ain't sayin' I'm gonna tell you ever'thing there is to tell." Her brown teeth peeked out of a small smile. "You know it ain't lyin' if you just won't say."

He threw his head back and laughed out loud, a full, belly laugh.

"Princess, you would have made a good lawyer."

"Lawyer? Why most of what comes out of their mouths don't make no sense a'tall."

"You got that right," he said, still chuckling.

"You talk to that little girl of yours last night, find out what's wrong?"

Mac's laughter froze in his throat.

"I talked to her, yes."

"And?"

"And what's wrong with her is she just lost her mother!" He didn't intend to raise his voice, but Princess jumped. "I'm sorry. Look, I don't know how you see things or know things, but it doesn't take some psychic power to figure out that my daughter's in pain. So am I. She's hurt and bewildered and—"

"It's somethin' else. It ain't a simple pain, it ain't mourning. It's all tangled up and there's a whole lot of scared in it."

"How do you—?"

"I don't *know!*"

Now, it was Princess whose voice was raised, not in volume but intensity. She stopped, steadied herself.

"I don't know how I know," she said, quietly this time. "I always been ... different. Please, Rev, it don't matter if you think I'm battier'n a bedbug. Just sit that little girl of yours down and look her in the eye and ask her what's a'eatin' at her."

Mac sighed.

"Nothing wrong with having a heart-to-heart talk with my daughter, I guess. Truth is, we've been needing to have one for a long time. You happy now?"

"As a pig in a mud waller." She smiled. "She's a pretty little thing, your girl—that right? You said she was gorgeous."

"Absolutely! Of course, I'm her father, so I might just be a teeny bit biased."

"You got a picture?" Again the stillness, intensity and focus.

"Well yes, as a matter of fact, I do. Her school picture."

Mac reached into his pocket for his wallet. Princess's eyes followed his every movement, she sat tense, breathlessly expectant. Then Mac remembered. The guard who'd frisked him had kept it in the basket by the door.

"Oops, I'm sorry. I left my wallet with my car keys downstairs."

All the air whooshed out of her. She squeaked out a little "Oh!"—the iceberg tip of a wail.

"If you'd really like to see a picture, I'll bring it tomorrow when I come."

She looked up and smiled and he could see the shadow of tears in her eyes. "Wouldja?"

"Sure, no problem."

"I ain't got no pictures to show you. Just the one, well four of 'em, that we made in that machine at the circus that day."

The circus—maybe the one where she had a seizure and was arrested. No, she said "we," and she'd already killed Angel when she showed up at the circus covered in blood.

"Who's in the pictures?"

"Me 'n Angel."

"I'd love to see them."

"Can't." She pronounced the word so it rhymed with paint. "There ain't no faces to see no more. I musta rubbed all the paper off 'em a-pettin' 'em all the time."

She brightened. "But you're gonna bring me a picture of your little girl anyway, right? I would powerfully like to see your child."

"I'll bring it."

She nodded. That settled, she switched gears.

"I said I's up the night, thinkin' of things I needed to talk to you about, remember?"

Mac nodded, steeled himself. He'd just promised this woman he wouldn't lie to her. So what did he say when she asked about life, death and eternity? Well—*it ain't lyin' if you just don't say.*

She suddenly hopped out of her chair and hurried to the window.

"That there!" She pointed to a collection of structures on the Indian Bluffs to the north. From here, it looked like a small village with some stores, a church with a steeple, maybe some houses—hard to make out specifics at this distance.

"Years ago, when that lawyer'd come and talk about things I didn't understand, I usta sit here a'starin' at that pretty little town." She turned from the window and smiled at him. "I usta make up play-stories in my head 'bout it at night, you know, pretending I lived there an' all. What's its name? You ever been there?"

Mac relaxed and shook his head. "Sorry to disappoint you, Princess, but that town's not real."

"How can a town not be real?"

"It's a movie set."

"Oh, go on! Really?"

"Back in the '40s, MGM made a low-budget Western here—think it might have starred Audie Murphy but I'm not sure—and they built a set up there in the hills. All that you can see, it's just false fronts. There are walls on the end buildings to hold the whole thing up and enough internal walls to keep it stable, but when you open one of those doors, you step all the way through and out the back side. The Durango County Historical Society took it on as a project years ago and restored it, painted it and fixed it up. Gave it the name of the town in the movie—Laramie Junction. Little old ladies spend hours up there every week, planting flowers and keeping the grass neat."

"Well I never," she said in awe, staring out the window. "I usta pretend—now don't you laugh at me—that I got married in that little church up there."

She turned back from the window and looked at him.

"I's all the time in church when I's a kid. The building was right down the bottom of the hill from our house, on the far side of the creek, away from where the colored folk lived, and I used to sneak off and go there when Jackson wasn't home. Just sit where it was quiet."

The growl was in the word again—*Jackson.*

"There was a piano in the church. You ever look in the back of a piano, seen what's in there? What makes the noise is strings. You hit one of them keys and this hammer-lookin' doo-dad hits one of them strings. Did you know that all the high notes, they got these little bitty strings, pulled reeeal tight."

She turned back, rested her forehead on the bars in front of the glass, tracing the outline of them with her finger.

"All my life, my insides was piano keys that didn't play nothing but high notes."

"You want to tell me about it, Princess?"

"Maybe someday."

"You're running out of somedays."

"Sayin' things don't make 'em not so."

"No, but sometimes it helps to talk. Get things out in the open."

"What does it help? I ain't gonna live to see thirty. Rake up a bunch o' awful stuff and talk about it now—shoot, that'd just ruin the time I got left."

She pointed out the window to a sight inside the walls of the Iron House. A small cemetery lay in the corner of the fenced-in area, on the northeast side so it wasn't visible from the Quonset hut that housed Sizzlin' Suzie.

"That there's real, ain't no movie set. They're gonna plant me there on Friday, a hole in the ground inside a cage." She paused, then added wistfully, "Ain't even gonna be free when I'm dead."

Then she turned with a resolute smile. "Now's my turn and I want to know 'bout you. Was you in the army? Did you fight in the war? Mama told me all about how my daddy fought in the Philippines, dodged bullets for three years, then come home and got kilt in a car wreck. Was you in the Philippines?"

Her mother said her father'd been killed in a car accident? Guess that was easier than explaining he'd run off with another woman. But wouldn't Princess have been old enough to know? Before he had time to consider the mystery, Princess's litany of questions drowned out his curiosity.

"Have you seen a ocean? I only ever been in Texas, Arkansas, and Oklahoma. You been overseas? Did you—?"

"Whoa, that's enough. Let's start with 'Was I in the army?'"

And so they talked. Princess peppered him with questions. He told her about everything from JFK, and John Glenn orbiting the earth in Friendship 7, to skateboards, Barbie dolls, *American Bandstand*, and the twist. He didn't trouble her with Korea, the Cold War, or civil rights, but did take a stab at explaining the phenomenon that was Elvis Presley. He struggled to condense, to fill in the gaps the best he could for fourteen years of silence.

The door opened as he was singing "… you ain't nothing but a hound dog …" in an off-key baritone. The guard with the eight-by-ten-glossy-suitable-for-framing face stepped inside.

"It's five o'clock, time's up now," he said to Mac. Then he asked, "You coming back tomorrow?"

Mac saw Princess tense, and then relax when he said, "I'll be here every day this week."

"If you want to wait, I'll take her back to her cell first, and then show you the way out through the administration building," the guard said. "That way I won't have to escort you back to check-in every day."

Mac suddenly remembered the newspaper reporter and blurted out, "Princess, I forgot. There's a newspaper reporter who wants to talk to you. He asked me to ask if you'd see him."

"He the same one's been a'pesterin' me for a interview?"

Mac nodded.

"I don't never talk to them people 'cause all's they ever want to talk about is bad stuff." She gave Mac an innocent look. "But if you think I ought to, I will. Do you?"

He didn't even have to consider the question. "No."

"No it is, then."

The guard gestured for Princess to step over to him. The man reached behind him and unhooked the shackles and leg irons fastened to his belt. Princess docilely held out both arms.

Mac's stomach rolled. He turned for the door.

"Don't forget them pictures!" Princess cried.

"I won't," he said over his shoulder. He stepped outside into the hallway and pretended to be examining his fingernails when he heard her shuffle out the door and down the hall behind him.

He was driving home before it hit him.

Princess said she wouldn't live to see thirty.

That didn't add up. If she was sentenced at seventeen and had been in prison for fourteen years, she'd be thirty-one.

He drove straight to his office, found the business card Sam Bartlett had left with him, and called the motel room number that he'd scribbled on the back.

"Tell me something," Mac said without any preamble. "How old was Emily Prentiss when she was arrested?"

"Seventeen. Why?"

"How did they know that, how old she was?"

"The prosecutor wanted a birth certificate but Jackson Prentiss said he didn't have it. Said her mama was dirt poor, she and her husband had been sharecroppers in Texas and Emily was born at home."

"So how did they know her age?"

"Prentiss told them. Swore an oath. Said she was seventeen."

"And the part about her father running off with another woman, who said—?"

"Emily wouldn't answer any questions about anything. All the information they got about her came from Prentiss. Of course, the members of his congregation backed him up, said the same thing he did."

Mac gave Bartlett the bad news that Princess had again refused to talk to him, then sat for a long time with his hand on the receiver after he hung up the phone.

Jackson had said she was seventeen.

Maybe Princess had "lost" two years …

Or maybe she was only fifteen years old when a court sentenced her to die.

12

Joy had slipped Gary a note during third period sophomore English class, the one class they had together, that told him to meet her after school at her car, that it was important.

Now she sat waiting, wondering if he'd come, wondering what on earth she'd do if he didn't. And what she'd say if he did. Then she saw him, walking casually out to the parking lot, laughing and talking with the other boys on the track team. He was tall, with sandy blonde hair in a crew-cut, a wide smile and white teeth.

At that moment, she hated him.

He opened the passenger side door and slid in.

"What's up, Joy? Only got a few minutes, then I gotta split."

"Not here. Close the door."

She turned the key and the 1953 Buick rumbled to life. Daddy had gotten the car for her on her sixteenth birthday, an adorable dinosaur of a car she'd dubbed Mr. Wilson, after the grumpy old man on the *Dennis the Menace* television show. The car had no suspension system whatsoever, and at any speed above fifty miles per hour the steering wheel vibrated so badly you could barely hold onto it. The radio was random. Hit a bump in the road and it would suddenly turn on with the volume pegged all the way up. Sometimes you could control it, turn it off or on, by banging your fist on the dashboard in just the right spot, but the station dial didn't work at all. The car was basic transportation, nothing more, just so she didn't have to ride a bus to school.

"Whoa, wait a minute. I got track practice—"

She turned on him. "Yeah, you're just going on with life aren't you, not a care in the world. Nothing's changed for you, while my whole life's ruined!" She glared at him. "I said, *close the door*. Now! We've got things to talk about and you probably don't want the rest of the team to hear what I'm about to say to you."

Gary reached over wordlessly and slammed the door shut. Joy pulled out of the school lot, headed toward the park and drove to the secluded, tree-lined lane in the back corner of it. It was a buzzing piece of teenage real estate on Friday and Saturday nights. Cars full of necking teenagers parked just far enough apart for privacy. That's where it had happened. That's where she'd given her virginity to a horny boy who used her grief to seduce her.

She pulled to a stop in the very spot, the best she could remember, where they'd been parked that night, turned off the key, and sat for a moment, collecting herself, facing forward, her eyes fixed on a distant nothing.

"Look, Joy, I—"

"I didn't bring you out here for you to talk," she said, still not looking at him. "Nothing you say means squat. I brought you out here to listen." She turned and faced him. "I am pregnant. *Pregnant!* Do you have any idea what that *means?*"

Her voice broke then and she couldn't continue. She hadn't meant to cry, never dreamed she would. She fought it fiercely, but for a moment she was robbed of speech.

There was silence as she struggled for control. The hush that fell over the car felt like a giant had dropped a Mason jar down on top of it, sealing it off from every other thing, living or dead, in the universe.

"I'm sorry, Joy," Gary said. "I really am. But it doesn't do any good to go ape over it." He suddenly looked horror-struck. "You don't think I'm going to ... that we're going to get *married*, do you? 'Cause I'm telling you right now there is no way, you dig? *No way!* I'm looking at a basketball scholarship to OSU and I am not *about* to—"

She found her voice then, cut him off.

"Of course, I don't want to get married, you idiot," she growled. "Why would I want to marry *you*? You're immature and totally self-centered—don't care about anybody or anything but … oh never mind." She suddenly felt tired. Exhausted. Totally wrung out.

"Then … what?"

"I'm getting an abortion." *Abortion.* She hadn't used the word before, not even in her head when she thought about it. It was a harsh, ugly word that lingered with the whiff of a dead animal in the air between them.

"You are?" There was something like awe in his voice.

"Yes, I am. But it costs $200 and I don't have $200. You're going to have to pay half."

"*Me?*"

It was almost comical how pathetic he sounded.

"Yes, *you!* What? Do you think it's just going to be *my* problem and I'm going to handle it all by myself and not trouble you with any of the ugly details? This is your problem, too. Gary. It's just as much your problem as it is mine. And you're going to help me fix it!"

"But I don't have $100. Where am I going to get—?"

"You think *I've* got $100? Don't sit there like you're broke, penniless. All I heard last winter was about that stuff—glass packs or whatever you call them—you were going to get for your car. You've been saving for months. You've got *that* money."

"Well, yeah, but I'm not going to—"

"Oh, yes, you are!"

She thought about what Phoebe said: Don't let him squirm out of it. Phoebe. The class slut. Fury welled up in her, a white lava anger that fired her face red and made her hands shake. And turned her heart to stone.

"Let me see if I can make this clear enough for a first-grader to understand." She hissed the words at him. "You're going to get $100 somewhere—I don't care if you have to hold up a filling station—and you're going to have it ready for me *in cash* by tomorrow after school."

"I can't—!"

"Because if you *don't* …" She leaned toward him and whispered the words in a soft voice louder than a fire alarm. "I'm going to go to your house and tell your parents that *you knocked me up!* Do *you* dig?"

"You *wouldn't!*"

"Try me!"

Gary stared at her, stupefied. Emotions skittered across his face like leaves hurried along by an autumn wind.

"I can't believe *you* … a preacher's daughter … would—"

"Would what? Put out for a loser like you? Know what, Gary? I've been asking myself that same question for weeks. Now, get out of my car."

"What?"

"How many things can 'get out of my car' mean?"

"You gotta take me back to the school. I got track practice."

"Then the run will do you good. Out, now! I'll meet you at the gym door tomorrow at 3:30. And, pal, you better have that money. Or you're going to find out for yourself what it feels like to have your whole life fall apart."

His face curled in rage then. "Fine! Okay, fine. I'll have your blood money." He grabbed the door handle, jerked it open and leapt out. Then he leaned back in.

"We both know who's the loser here and it sure ain't me. You're a whore! A whore who spreads 'em for anybody's got a zipper to pull down. And trust me, sweetheart, it just became my civic responsibility to make sure there's not a kid in Durango County High School who doesn't know it!"

He slammed the door and disappeared.

She sat for a moment, stunned. Then she let herself be sick, opened the car door and threw up, splattering her lunch in chunks on the pavement. Her eyes watered, her skin went clammy, but she didn't cry. Hers was a hurt too deep for something as simple and freeing as tears.

❖ ❖ ❖ ❖ ❖

Princess stretched out on her back on the bunk in her cell and watched the light fade out of the little path of sky outlined in the high window.

She had lived the past fourteen years in a concrete box eight feet wide and fifteen feet long. It had a bed, like an army cot with a two-inch thick mattress, up against one of the long walls and a beat-up, two-by-three-foot wooden table against the other. The four legs of both were bolted to the floor. The bed had no sheets, just a scratchy wool blanket and no pillow. There was a small shelf above it for Princess's belongings, if she'd had any. A little wooden, slat-backed chair sat at one end of the table. Even using it as a ladder, it was impossible to see out the little window just below the ten-foot ceiling. Princess had tried.

At the far end of the cell was a commode and sink. In the summertime, the smell of raw sewage often leaked out of the toilet so strong Princess sometimes had to put her mattress over the top of it to close it off. At the other end of the cell was a solid metal door with a slot near the bottom just big enough for a food tray.

Princess knew the cell as intimately as she knew her own body, had examined every inch of it time and time again in the more than a decade it had been her home. She knew the number of lumps on the walls and the size, shape, and location of every scrape in the concrete floor.

There was a large crack in the wall behind the commode, big enough for bugs. Roaches squeezed through it into her cell from time to time. Once, a large brown spider had come to call. She didn't like the roaches, picked them up carefully and shoved them through the food slot in the door. The spider was another thing altogether. She hated spiders; they made her skin crawl. For the first few years she was in prison, she'd suffered terrible nightmares near every night and most of them had a hairy-legged spider in them somewhere. The problem was, she couldn't kill it, couldn't bring herself to smash it with one of the shoes she kept tucked under her bed and never wore. But at the same time, she couldn't just let it live there, couldn't go to sleep at night for fear she'd feel it crawling up her leg. Gratefully, the problem solved itself after three sleepless nights. The spider simply died. Natural causes.

Princess lay on the bunk grinning, her body all a-tingle, enjoying the prickly feeling on her skin, the images flitting around in her head like water bugs on a still pond. The Rev was ever' bit as nice as she knew he would be. Ever' bit! It was plain to see he was a good man, that he'd been a good husband, a good father. And he was going to bring pictures of his little girl tomorrow!

Princess thought her heart might just swell up and burst out of her chest for the joy in it. Pictures! She reached up to the shelf above her head and retrieved her pictures: a strip with four almost-blank frames that were as crisp and clear in her mind's eye as the day they'd been taken. These were the only photographs she'd ever held in her hand, though she'd seen plenty on walls, like in the courthouse. The big stone building where she'd been tried for murder had a great hall you passed through on your way to the courtroom and every past governor of Oklahoma had his picture up on the wall there.

She lovingly stroked the empty frame where Angel's face, all covered in chocolate ice cream, looked out at her with her wide, brown eyes. A slow smile spread over her face.

And as the light waned and night reached out dark arms to embrace the world outside, the inside of a cell on the Long Dark in the Oklahoma State Penitentiary for Women glowed golden. Princess had opened her little treasure box of memories and selected one so bright the light would quickly burn itself out. But that didn't matter anymore.

She and Angel fly through the purple night while the world sleeps, the warm breeze in their faces dabbed with honeysuckle perfume. The trees, fences, fields, and houses they pass are shrouded in cloaks of full-moon silver, their eyes closed. Now and then, damp tendrils of cool creek mist caress Princess's cheek with the scent of black mud and wet weeds and dead crawdads.

Angel uses both hands to push her long hair out of her face where the wind has set her curls dancing around her nose. She bats at her hair with her chubby hands and giggles.

"Tickles, Printhess!" she says and smiles. "Whee!"

"Whee!" Princess repeats with a joyous, bubbling laugh as the world flies by outside, silent, dark, and deep.

She drives for hours through the night, bouncing along the dirt roads, farm roads meandering through the Arkansas countryside. Angel laughs when the potholes spring her up above the leather seat. But as the child tires, she no longer notices the wind and the bouncing. She lies over on her side with her head snuggled up against Princess's leg, yawns, closes her eyes, and falls asleep.

Princess slows down then, watches for the biggest ruts and bumps, tries to smooth out the ride for the angel asleep beside her. She'd been driving aimlessly, with no idea where she was going, just away from Oklahoma, back into Arkansas. But in the deepest ditch of the night, in the silence there, the sleeping child speaks to her softly. Not in her ear. In her head.

Turn here, the child says. And Princess turns there.

This road, take this road, the child directs. Princess follows, winding between fields, splashing through shallow creeks, bumping over cattle guards. She presses on at the direction of the small, warm presence asleep on the seat beside her, a cherubic face obscured by rusty curls.

The morning sun is just beginning to bleach the inky darkness from the sky when they finally come to the river. Princess doesn't know its name, but she has seen it in her dreams. This is the place. Here she will have to do the unthinkable.

She pulls the car behind a thick hedge of bushes on the hillside above the riverbank across the road from a small building. She turns off the key and feels the sudden roar of silence in her ears. Then the loud silence is replaced by river sounds, water moving slowly, sluggishly.

It is damp here, with a chill in the air. She rolls up her window, eases Angel over in the seat, then clambers over it into the backseat. She moves her knapsack and sets it in the floorboard. Inside the knapsack is what she took with her when she ran off into the night with Angel by her side and all that she has gathered up along the way. It's everything she will need to do what she has to do—Angel's lacy, white, store-bought dress, a pair of scissors, and a shiny new ax, sharp as a razor.

Then she rolls up all the car windows except the back window on the driver's side. She leaves it down so she can hear the river lumber past, smell the damp air.

She reaches over the back of the front seat then and lifts the sleeping child. Angel is as limp as a broken doll and Princess knows she sleeps sound. She could drop her out of her arms onto the seat and it wouldn't rouse her.

But she is gentle, easy. She sits down in the backseat by the open window and cradles the little girl in her arms. She turns and stretches her legs out on the leather-covered bench and wiggles a little to get comfortable. Then she relaxes.

And with every breath, she concentrates on feeling Angel in her arms. The weight of her. Her warm, soft skin. The smell of her silky hair.

She pats her back softly and sings into her ear quiet, nonsense words borne on strange, haunting melodies. She kisses her forehead or her cheek or her nose between verses.

Angel stirs now and then, wiggles. Once she opens her hand and grasps Princess's finger and holds on, like she used to do when she was a newborn. Then she sighs and settles, the sweet scent of her warm breath a bouquet in Princess's face.

The sky grays, molts into pink and shades of pale yellow as it gives birth to the sun again and another day. The last day Princess will ever see or hold or touch or smell the precious child in her arms. She cries then, great heaving, silent sobs that shake her body like her strange fits. She cries until every muscle in her chest is a throbbing agony, until her face and Angel's hair are soaked in her tears, cries until her throat is raw, her nose is running, and her breath hitches in and out. Cries non-stop, hard, for a solid hour—without so much as a squeak of sound to wake the child, sleeping so soundly that Princess's shaking body doesn't rouse her.

She finally cries herself out, weak and empty. Then takes deep, cleansing breaths. That part's over. Done.

The birds in the nearby trees that started chirping long before the light warmed the sky sing out now in raucous abandon; the world begins to wake. Angel stirs. Her eyes flutter open. She closes them again and dozes off. Princess cradles her. Waiting. After a time, the child opens her eyes again and looks around. Her still groggy gaze finds Princess's face and she focuses and smiles. She sits up in Princess's lap and stretches.

"You need to go pee-pee?" Princess asks, and realizes she has cried herself hoarse. The still-sleepy child nods her head up and down, her curls bobbing on her shoulders.

Princess turns and opens the car door, lifts the child to the ground, then gets out of the car.

"Right here's fine, sugar." She pulls the child's pants down. "Squat, now." The child obediently squats. Princess makes sure her pants are out of the way. Silence. Then the sound of the stream landing in the dirt. It splashes on Princess's bare feet but she doesn't care.

She lifts the child up onto the running board of the car and pulls her pants back up. Then sets her on the car seat.

"Printhess go pee-pee?" Angel asks.

"Uh-huh. You sit right there while I do my business," she says, then steps away from the car and makes her own warm, yellow puddle.

She gets back into the car, in the backseat with Angel, carful not to cut her foot on the ax lying in the floorboard. And closes the door solidly behind her.

"I'm thirssy," Angel says, her voice a sing-song whine.

"Don't you worry 'bout that now. In just a little while, you won't be thirsty no more, promise."

Princess takes a deep breath. She knows the child will not understand what she's about to say, but she says it anyway. Because she has to.

"Sweetie, I'm 'bout to do somethin' I don't want to do and you're not gonna like. And I'm sorry, I am so very sorry." She thought she was cried out, but her hoarse voice is suddenly tear-thickened again. "I love you more than ... life. I love you too much to let .... Less'n I do somethin', evil's gonna happen, sure. That's the way of life—ain't no changing or fixin' it. I know, 'cause I tried. So I got to be strong. I got to do what's best even if it's hard. Hard and cold and hurtful. The pain of it won't last but a little while, though, sweetheart. I promise I'll make it quick. Then it'll be over and won't nothing hurt you no more and you can rest easy. You understand?"

Angel shakes her head no and Princess smiles sadly.

"Well, I didn't 'spect you to. Long's I do, that's all that matters."

She takes a deep, shaky breath. Then another. She suddenly grasps the child and crushes her to her chest with a strangled sob and then releases her.

"Come on, now," she says, with a sniffle and wipes away the tear that has escaped to slide down her cheek. She forces a shaky smile. "We got to go *now." She gestures toward the passenger side door. "Over there. Can't get out on this side else we'll step in a puddle of pee."*

She reaches past the child and opens the door. Angel scoots across the seat and hops out. Princess picks up the knapsack with the ax in it and follows her. Taking the child's hand, she leads her down the hillside toward the river.

THE MOVING PICTURE OF HER MEMORY stopped there. Because beyond that was the darkness. Her precious gems were only light. And this was one of the brightest of them, golden light. When she basked in the warm glow of that light she could feel the softness of Angel's skin, smell her sweet breath, and hear the night sounds of the slow, muddy river outside the car window.

As she lay on her back on the bunk, she wondered if everybody had gem memories like that, or if other people had so many memories, none of them were as powerful and special as hers. Or maybe other people hadn't been careful, as she had, to preserve the light of their memories, treat them like the treasure they were and not allow them to go dim.

She sighed. It was likely she'd never know the answer to that question, that it would be like countless other mysteries she'd carry to her grave. If that was the way of it, there was nothing to be gained by poutin' about it.

She closed her eyes again. And there was nothing to be lost by warming her fingers on the warmth of her gems, either. Nothing to save them for. She could burn them all completely out; it didn't matter anymore.

She reached down into her mind, and thought about the wind in her face and the moonlit sky. And the cell glowed warm and golden again.

Wednesday

May 8, 1963

13

W ANDA PARKED HER CAR NEXT TO a cottonwood tree and walked through the dew-sparkled grass beside the row of headstones. She hadn't been to the cemetery since the funeral, but she was certain she remembered where the grave had been. She'd marked the spot that day, when the casket was still sitting on the ground with the blanket of roses on top under the funeral home marquee.

She stumbled, but caught herself before she fell. A little unsteady on her feet. Just tired. Didn't have anything to do with the medications she was taking. Medicine that was supposed to make her sleep, only it didn't. Medications for depression, too. Wanda knew how to write prescriptions for what she needed. She also knew better than to mix the two—sleeping pills and depression meds. So she was careful, didn't do it very often.

She needed rest, that's all. No, that wasn't all she needed, but what she really needed she couldn't have.

She stumbled down the little stone path past platoons of headstones standing at attention, casting long shadows in the dawn light. She was headed to the back of the cemetery. That's where she remembered it, in the back corner under a cherry tree.

Then Wanda spotted it and gasped. It looked so eerily familiar, a distorted flashback that swam in the tears in her eyes.

The tree was awash in white blossoms and delicate white petals frosted the ground beneath it. When they'd buried her, the tree had been bare, but snow-covered, shedding pure white tears on the crowd of mourners around her grave.

There was a black granite headstone now, set at the base of the tree. Wanda walked slowly to it and read the inscription out loud. "Melanie Cunningham McIntosh. Born: June 16, 1923. Died: November 3, 1962. Beloved daughter, wife, mother."

"And friend," Wanda whispered. "Beloved *friend*."

A breeze sighed through the cherry tree and blossoms settled slowly out of it into Wanda's hair.

"Melanie, I need to talk to you."

But that wasn't really true. She didn't need to talk to Melanie. She needed to listen to her. To hear her soft voice, and that laugh of hers that made you feel so ... included.

Wanda'd been holding it together pretty well until Melanie died. She'd met the minister's wife almost five years ago. She'd come to Graham because one place was as good as another when you didn't care where you lived, and she'd inherited a small farm a few miles south of town when her aunt died.

She'd tried, in the beginning at least, to put her life back together: she'd gotten a job working in the emergency room at the local hospital. Melanie worked there, too, had been an OR nurse like Wanda, so they'd had something to talk about. Truth was, Melanie hadn't reacted at all to Wanda's face, and you couldn't say that about many people. That's what had jumpstarted the relationship.

But Wanda couldn't handle the pressure of a job. Her nerves were shot. She quit before she got fired and retreated to the old farmhouse on Harrod's Creek Road.

And then that girl had tracked her down, the little sister of one of the girls she and Paul had helped. Wouldn't say how she'd found Wanda, just started sobbing. Said she was pregnant. Please, could Wanda do something? She had nowhere else to turn!

Wanda hadn't wanted to do it, but the girl had the same desperate, hopeless look all those wounded soldiers had had. They'd all believed their lives were over, destroyed, but Wanda had patched them up, then helped them learn how to use artificial limbs, how to get around in the world again. She'd put hope back in their eyes. The pregnant fifteen-year-old sobbing on her front porch believed her life was over, too. There was no hope in her eyes.

So Wanda had helped her. And after her, another one. And then another. Word somehow got around, she didn't know how. Girls came to her from all over, were glad to go to a place in the middle of nowhere far from home to have their "problems" fixed.

Within a couple of years, Wanda was as busy as she and Paul had ever been. Had thousands of dollars stuffed in shoeboxes and in the backs of drawers all over the house. Not that she gave a rip about the money. In fact, she'd considered in the beginning performing the service for free, but quickly realized she needed to charge for it. Charge a lot! So the girls were serious, had thought it through and were sure this was what they wanted. She'd slowly accumulated the equipment she needed, set up a surgery in the basement. Over and over, her shiny silver pans filled with bloody remains. She had a pit out back where she burned the "tissue." That's all it was—*tissue!* She refused to acknowledge the presence of tiny limbs, arms and legs, and little faces.

But after awhile, the images began to dominate her thoughts, to haunt her, and her world started to fall apart.

She'd turned to Melanie then, when it got bad that first time.

It had started with a lone baby crying. She heard it one night as soon as she switched off her bedside lamp. It was a far-off cry, a wail carried on the wind. Wanda thought it was a real baby. She leapt out of the bed, ran out to the front porch, actually expected to find that somebody had left a newborn on her steps. But there was no child and the night was silent. The cry started up again, though, when she went back to bed, as soon as she turned out the light.

That scared her! She sat up the whole night, shaking. The next night, it happened again. After a week of no sleep, she was desperate.

She drove into town, looking to find a church. Looking for absolution. Looking for ... she didn't even know what she was looking for. Just somebody to talk to before she went stark, staring mad.

She lurched through the big oak front door of New Hope Community Church, sank down in a pew on the back row, and sat there shaking. Then someone called her name.

"Well, hello there, Wanda."

She looked around and at first couldn't locate who'd spoken to her. Then she saw Melanie McIntosh—her head, anyway. She was on her knees on the floor between the front two pews.

"Melanie?" Wanda hadn't seen Melanie since she'd quit her hospital job. "What are *you* doing here?"

"I'm trying to find the earring I lost Sunday. I was hoping it'd be right here on the floor, but I don't see it." She stood up and dusted off the knees of her jeans. "Can I help you with something?"

"I was … is there a minister here?"

Melanie came around the end of the pew and up the aisle. As soon as she got close, she could tell something was wrong.

"Are you all right, Wanda? No, of course you're not. Can I sit with you?"

Wanda nodded and she sat. When Melanie told her "Reverend McIntosh" wasn't in, that was the first Wanda knew Melanie was married to the preacher. Then they'd just talked. Wanda was vague about what had sent her running to the church, said she was having trouble sleeping. Melanie didn't probe or push.

Later, Melanie told Wanda to call her if she wanted to talk some more.

Wanda called. Often.

She never did tell Melanie specifically what was bothering her, though she suspected after awhile that Melanie had figured it out. She was a smart woman. Wasn't likely an accident Mel steered the conversation in that direction, sometimes. "Life's precious, you know—a gift from God," she'd said more than once. Melanie had gently urged Wanda to talk to Mac. And Wanda met the man once when he brought his wife out to her farm to pick strawberries. Seemed like a nice enough fellow, but by then, Wanda was feeling much better.

She was over the hump. Oh, she'd gotten a little stressed out before, but she'd learned to pace herself better since then. The blackness that had formed a picture frame around her vision had slowly receded as she spent time with Melanie. All she'd needed was perspective, some human interaction. She'd just needed a friend.

But Melanie got sick. And suddenly, she was gone. So quick.

Wanda's world grew steadily darker through the winter following Melanie's death and didn't brighten with the coming of spring. Then the light went out altogether on April Fool's Day.

The girl had been fat, so it was hard to tell how far long she really was. And she'd *lied.* Said she was only four months. Looking back, Wanda was certain Paul would have caught it. But she wasn't as good as Paul. Truth was, Wanda was no good at all without him.

The fat girl's baby plopped out into the shiny metal dish—crying.

And Wanda had silenced it. Put her fingers around his little neck and squeezed. Only for a few seconds, that's all it took, and he was quiet.

But he started crying again that night. And he brought his friends.

"Melanie," Wanda said softly, as the cherry tree sprinkled blossoms into her hair, "I need you, Mel. *Please!* I patched up those soldiers, hundreds of them, and what did it get me? A useless medal and a face that scares children. Turned me into a freak! I gave all those girls their lives back and now I'm the one whose life's falling apart and there's nobody here for me. I'm all alone." She tried to stifle the tears, but the pain and loneliness escaped in a wailing moan and then she was crying in deep, heaving sobs that wracked her body. "I swear, I never meant any harm!" she cried out in anguish to the wind. "You know that, don't you, Melanie? I was just trying to help." She paused. "Can you hear me? Melanie?"

She waited, listened. The breeze picked up, gently ruffled the tree leaves. Made a sound like a little baby's laughter.

14

Wʜᴇɴ Mᴀᴄ ᴡᴇɴᴛ ɪɴ ᴛᴏ ᴘᴀʏ for his gas at the Texaco station on his way to the Iron House to see Princess Wednesday afternoon, he bought three candy bars—a Butterfinger, a Baby Ruth and a Hershey bar. It had occurred to him the night before that Princess probably hadn't had a candy bar in years, if indeed she'd ever had one.

Yeah, he'd been thinking about her. Thinking way too much about her, as a matter of fact, found that he replayed his meetings with her in his head the way golf addicts replayed every shot on all eighteen holes when they got home from a game. He'd been totally preoccupied with what had developed into a certainty in his head that Princess's step-father had lied about her age. Probably because he was enraged at what she'd done, though he sensed from Princess's reaction to the mere mention of Jackson Prentiss's name that there was certainly no love lost on her part, either.

He'd considered—even had the receiver in his hand a time or two—calling Oran and talking to him about it. Being tried as an adult and sentenced to die at age fifteen would surely be grounds for all sorts of legal maneuverings, a stay of execution, certainly. Perhaps a whole new trial.

But how could he prove Princess was telling the truth and not just confused? He couldn't, not in three days.

And to be brutally honest, what would it accomplish if he could? She was still guilty. She'd still be convicted. Oh, she'd probably get a prison sentence this time instead of the death penalty. Though in Oklahoma, even that wasn't a foregone conclusion. Oklahoma handed down more death sentences than any other state.

But what if she did get a prison sentence? Oran said she could never go into "gen pop" because she was a baby killer and because she was Jackson Prentiss's daughter. So she'd have to remain in some form of isolation. Was it right to condemn the little bird of a woman to more years alone? She'd said she had made her peace, that she was ready to die. How humane would it be to interrupt that process after all this time?

He stepped up to the counter to pay for the candy and his gasoline, acknowledging as he did that he was probably just taking the candy along as a peace offering because Princess wasn't going to like the report he'd be giving her about his heart-to-heart talk with Joy.

It'd be short; there hadn't been one. The squalling alternator belt under the hood of his car had finally snapped on his way back to town from the Iron House yesterday and by the time he got it repaired, it was almost dark.

He could hear music playing in Joy's room, somebody wailing "… come on, baby, do the loco-mo-tion …" Whatever happened to Bing Crosby, Frank Sinatra, and Tommy Dorsey? Now *that* was music!

He knocked on her door to tell her there was a whole new selection of casseroles, but she called out that she didn't want any supper, that she had a migraine. It did occur to him to wonder how she could stand music that loud if her head hurt, though he said nothing.

She didn't come out of her room the rest of the night. Sitting at the kitchen table alone, he choked down what tasted like chili, clam chowder, and Italian wedding soup all stirred together under a layer of cheddar cheese. When he rapped gently on her door as he went to bed, there was only silence.

And no, he didn't need Princess or anybody else to tell him that his relationship with his daughter was drifting farther out to sea every day. How did other single parents do it? Mourn the love of their lives and comfort a child at the same time? On the rare occasions when he felt strong enough to talk to Joy about Melanie, she was distant, preoccupied. Whatever he said was wrong, made her cry and withdraw further. Sixteen years old with the rocket fuel of hormones in her veins, you never knew which Joy you'd encounter from one moment to the next.

Melanie had been so close to Joy, actually seemed to understand her and her world. She'd listen patiently as Joy gushed about Bobby Darren and Frankie Avalon. Or fix brownies when Joy's friends, Beth and Shirley, came over to watch *American Bandstand*, danced the mashed potato, the swim, and the watusi with the three girls in the living room while Mac listened to a football game on the radio in the den. Mel even understood Joy's teen-speak. She'd tried to translate some of it for Mac once, but he got so lost on the subtle differences between a jerk, a flake, and a nerd that she'd given up on him.

In Mac's eyes, his teenage daughter was a totally alien life form and he had absolutely no idea how to have that heart-to-heart conversation with her he'd promised he'd have—and knew he *needed* to have, regardless of Princess's phobias. He had to tell Joy he was resigning his pastorate. And why. That was not a conversation he was looking forward to.

The young man who checked him out had been in his confirmation class last year. His name was Joel. After he dropped the candy bars into the sack, Joel cast a quick glance from side to side.

"Pastor, can I ask you something?"

Mac missed the desperation in the boy's words.

"Sure, if I can answer you quick. I've got an appointment; somebody's waiting for me."

"Are you … are you *sure* there's a God?"

Mac felt like the ground had tilted up and left him staggering, trying to relocate his balance.

He stared at the boy, stupefied.

"'Cause, see, I look around, and there's war, starving babies in India …"

Ah, the standard starving-babies-in-India question.

A derivation of the starving-babies-in-China and the starving-babies-in-Africa questions. Usually followed by: Can God make a stone so heavy he can't lift it? There'd been a whole section in his apologetics class in seminary devoted to answering those.

He reached out, picked up the candy-bar sack and looked the boy sadly in the eye.

"There's only one thing in life I'm sure about, son. And that is there's no way to be sure about anything."

On the way to the Iron House, he saw storm clouds building in the southwest sky.

His escort through the hallways and staircases of the administration building to the envelope room today was a short, stocky colored man. Or was the correct term negro? Or black, or African American? Mac never knew anymore what he was supposed to say. Everything was shifting, changing. What was acceptable yesterday was offensive today. To keep from putting his foot in his mouth, he usually found some way not to mention race at all.

This guard wasn't nearly as meticulous as the Polish wrestler had been about his belongings, said he could keep his pen as long as he showed it to the guard when he went in and again when he left.

Mac was careful to keep his billfold in his pocket. Good thing, too, because that was the first thing Princess said when he saw her.

"Did you bring it? A picture of your little girl. Did you remember?"

She was so excited she was bouncing on the edge of the chair. Her brown inmate dress was on right side out, Mac noticed. Wednesday. But she was still barefoot.

"Of course, I remembered. Don't you have any shoes?"

"You think this prison could get away with not giving prisoners shoes? I ain't never liked shoes, they hurt my feet. Now, will you sit down and show me the picture 'fore I explode all over this here room!"

Mac sat down and reached into his pocket for his wallet. He pulled it out, along with the three candy bars.

Princess looked at the candy bars as if she'd never seen one before.

"These are for you," Mac said. "I asked, and they told me I could bring in food if it was in the original wrapper, something you could get out of a vending machine. You like candy?"

"These are for me?" The voice, deep and soft. Timid, like a small child, with laryngitis.

"Sure, they're for you. Which is your favorite—Butterfinger, Baby Ruth, or Hershey?"

"You brought these for *me*?" The incredulity finally registered.

"It's three candy bars, Princess. Not the Hope Diamond."

She looked up at him and her almost-purple eyes were brimming over with tears. "I do thank you kindly, sir," she whispered. She reached out her hand to take one, the nearest, the Butterfinger, but was unable to touch it.

Her hand began to tremble and she shook her head back and forth slowly.

"Princess, did I do something wrong?"

"No, no! It's not you. It's just ... I don't know if I can proper explain it."

"Try. Small words. Nothing fancy. I think you do very well at explaining things."

"You do?"

She smiled a little, sat up a little straighter. Took a breath.

"It's just I got this hole in me, right here." She looked down and patted her flat belly. "Sometimes it's a big hole, seems wide as the big river. An' I can feel wind blowing through it, whistling in the empty there. I think that hole's scared, bein' scared, but I don't know 'cause I never had nobody to ask." She lifted her head. "Is that hole scared? Is that what you feel like when you're scared, a hole like that?"

Mac read the sincerity in her eyes as she spoke, and the sense he'd had that first day—that she *glowed*—returned. The light in the room had dimmed as the storm clouds approached, but her glowing wasn't about light. It was more about energy, humming transformer-like from such a frail creature. He had a quick, semi-hysterical thought that when they turned on the juice to electrocute her there would be such a back-surge of power into the wires that the person who flipped the switch would fry instead.

What does scared feel like?

"What you described, that's a lot like I feel when I'm scared," he answered slowly, choosing his words carefully. "But that place, that hole in your gut, that's where I feel other emotions, too."

Suddenly, his own voice was thick. "That's where I miss Melanie."

He hadn't meant to say that, hadn't meant to get that personal. After all, he was here to comfort her, not to bare his soul.

"That hole ain't where I ache for people," she said. "That's right here." She patted her heart. "Like there's a ice pick, stabbin' in it and any minute the hurtin' will be so bad, it'll just stop beatin' altogether." She sighed. "It never does, though. It keeps on beatin' whether I'm hurtin' or laughin', scared or snug and safe. Your heart beatin' and air—that's all you gotta have to live, ain't it. And livin's what you got; it's all God gives you."

Mac's mind wasn't tracking well. When he thought of Melanie, the pain took his breath away. He always had trouble concentrating in the moments after he got hit by that.

Thunder rolled in the distance.

"But why do these three candy bars upset you so?"

"'Cause I ain't used to the hole *not* being there. Been there so long, I ain't used to it bein' gone, and it's almost scary, you know, for it to be different." She looked up at him through a forest of long, black eyelashes. "Here in this room with you, I'm solid, ain't no hole in my middle. And that's enough. That's the best gift I could ever have and I'm grateful for it and if I died right this second, I'd be happy." She paused. "Then, on top of all that, you bring me candy. Can you see how that'd be ... so much you just can't take it all in at once?"

He could see. He nodded, not trusting his voice to speak.

Instead of speaking, he just scooted the candy across the table toward her. She picked each piece up like it was a bar of pure gold and slid it into the pocket of her uniform.

"You mind if I save these for later?" She managed a teary smile. "Shoot, if I's to eat them now, I might just pop from the pure joy of it."

"Explosions, by and large, are not good things," he said, testing his voice to be sure it was stable. Outside the thunder rolled again. Either the storm was a long way off or it was not a particularly powerful one. Thunder didn't boom, just a gentle rumble.

Princess was wrapped in expectant stillness again, humming—maybe producing a sound that'd cause a dog to whine and scratch at its ears. Or glowing. He didn't know which anymore and didn't trust his senses to tell him. The moment he stepped into this room every day, the normal rules that governed the functioning of the universe were somehow suspended. Here, in this place, they didn't seem to have any effect on reality.

"The picture?" she said, her voice coming from the depths of a kettle drum. "You said you'd bring a picture of your pretty little girl. Can I see it, please?"

Mac had forgotten all about the picture. He opened his billfold to the plastic picture holders. The first one was of just him and Melanie. It had been taken for the church directory last year. He rubbed his thumb over it and thought about what Princess had said about the images on her pictures, how she'd rubbed the paper off them "petting them." He could understand that.

He turned the billfold so she could see.

"That's my wife, my late wife. Melanie."

"No wonder there's a ice pick in your heart, a-missin' her," she said quietly. "That there's a woman full up to overflowin' with love and kindness."

Princess knew things. She just *knew*.

"Yes," he said, his voice shaky again. "And this is Joy." He flipped to the next picture. It was this year's school picture. She sat smiling into the camera, her hair fixed all neat in what she called a "flip." Took her half a can of hair spray to get it to stay in that style, and she always gave him her oh-Daddy look when he dared to suggest that it was a lot prettier when it just hung in curls around her shoulders.

He looked from the picture to Princess. She was frozen, wasn't even breathing. Her purple eyes, open wide, were filled with tears. She just stared at the picture, looking deep into the soul of the person whose image was captured there.

Instinctively, he reached up with his thumb and started to extract the picture from its plastic folder. "Here, would you like to see it up closer?"

But the picture was jammed tight. He had not removed the other pictures of Joy that rested beneath it, previous school pictures that he'd merely "wallpapered over" each succeeding year. When he pulled the current picture out of the plastic, the other pictures came with it, sprayed out half a dozen little Joy faces on the table top.

"Oh!" Princess squeaked. She looked up at him with tear-filled eyes, but could say nothing more than, "Oh!"

Thunder rolled again outside and rain splashed against the lone window.

Mac reached out and picked up all the pictures, then dealt them out like cards in order.

"This one," he held a photo that said 1953–54 on the white space at the bottom of it, "is the first one, I think. Yeah, it's when she was in first grade."

A cute little munchkin smiled out of the black-and-white photo. She had freckles all over her face and a gap-toothed smile. Braids lay on her shoulders, tied at the ends with ribbons, and she wore a dress with tiny flowers on it, buttoned all the way up to her neck.

"And this one is—"

Princess suddenly covered her face with her hands and sat back in the chair. She was obviously crying. Mac could see her shoulders shaking, but she wasn't making a sound. Then she began to rock back and forth in the chair, her face covered.

"Princess …"

No response.

"Princess, I'm sorry. I don't know what I did but—"

"It's okay," she breathed out between her fingers. "Gimme a minute."

She continued to rock and cry for a little while longer. Then sat quietly, her hands still over her face. Finally, she lowered her hands slowly, leaned over and wiped her face on the hem of her dress.

"I'm shamed and embarrassed by my behavior and I do sincerely ask your forgiveness for it," she said, her voice quivering.

"No, I won't forgive you."

She looked startled and panicked, so he hurried on. "Because there's nothing to forgive. You didn't do anything wrong."

"Well, I shouldn't have got so crying-like over that cute little girl. I's 'spectin' a big girl, a teenager. I had myself all screwed up to see that." Her voice got quiet, breathy. "Not a little girl. I wasn't 'spectin' to see no little girl. She … she reminds me of somebody."

Understanding as real as a gust of wind traveled from Princess to Mac. This little girl reminded her of her sister. A sister who never lost her front teeth or started first grade. A little girl Princess had …

Mac suddenly couldn't do it. He couldn't connect in his head anymore that the thin woman before him with tears in her eyes had killed anybody, much less a child. It was unfathomable.

But it also was true.

Get a grip, pal! She confessed, remember?

"I'd forgotten I had all these pictures shoved in there together. I took some out over the years, but mostly I was too lazy to do anything but shove another picture down over the one before. Sort of the geological method of filing pictures—the oldest is on the bottom."

He realized too late that the analogy went right over her head. But she didn't appear to be listening to him anyway. She was rigid and still and moon-eyed, concentrating on the picture, her focus absolute.

In the hushed room, time derailed, ran completely off the tracks and rolled over on its side in the ditch. In the world outside, a gentle spring storm splashed water on vegetable gardens and crops, window boxes full of flowers, new-mown lawns and just-washed cars. In here, there was only the scar-faced woman and the photographs and the man who dealt them out, one by one onto the table top.

Mac was surprised that his hand was steady as he put down the next picture.

"This one says 1956–57. Joy'd have been in fourth grade then, about nine years old."

He said nothing more, just watched Princess wrench her gaze off the little girl with braids and clamp it just as tightly on a smiling child with a full set of front teeth—though the rabbit teeth were still prominent. Her curly hair was pulled into what Melanie called dog-ears, ponytails on both sides of her head. He remembered he used to grab the ends of her dog-ears at that age and hold them straight out. Then he'd holler, "Hey, Mel, come look, an Indian just shot an arrow through Joy's head."

He smiled at the memory and noticed that Princess was smiling, too. An odd, little half smile.

He dealt out another picture.

"Joy's twelve here, seventh grade. Right before puberty grabbed hold of her and hauled her away where Daddy couldn't find his little girl anymore."

And it was true. Somewhere between age twelve and now, the connection between them had been broken. Maybe it happened to all fathers and daughters. He didn't know. And maybe the connection could be re-established—perhaps even stronger than ever. He didn't know that either.

The child in the picture had the beginnings of the beauty she'd display as a teenager, but still in a little girl's round face. Her hair hung in abandon around her shoulders, a gentle tangle of natural curls.

Melanie never did cut her hair short, he suddenly thought. As soon as it grew out long, Melanie had kept it that way. The pixie style came and went on the heads of other little girls in Joy's class, but his daughter's hair was always long.

Princess had pried her eyes away from the dog-eared nine-year-old and sat gazing with something like surprise at the pre-pubescent child of twelve.

I'd love to get inside her head and hear what she's thinking!

No, that would probably be a bad idea, a very bad idea. He suspected that in the swirling purple dark of Princess's mind lurked indescribable demons no man would want to face.

He waited, let her stare. Then finally dealt his final card. This was the only picture not in black and white. They'd just this year started taking class photos in color.

"Here's this year's picture, taken last fall."

Princess gasped and her hand flew to her mouth. She spoke for the first time, though he wasn't entirely certain she was talking to him.

"Oh, my, but she is beautiful. I think she's the most beautiful little girl—no, she's not a little girl. She's a young woman, a beautiful young woman … with red hair just like her daddy."

She looked up at him then and smiled. Time moved forward on the track again, slowly, not quite up to speed yet, grinding a little but no longer suspended.

"I do not have words fine enough to thank you for what you've done for me today," her voice was a whisper on a breath, soft and earnest. "You need to know a woman's gonna die content because of your kindness."

"Well, I didn't do … it was noth—"

"Don't you go brushin' it aside like you ain't done something special. It was kind and noble of you to spend time with a stranger you know's done the terriblest thing a person can do. That kind of goodness don't come from a man's heart less'n he knows pure love—both give it and had it give to him."

Like so many things Princess said, that hit Mac between the eyes. But she wasn't finished with him.

"An' while I got your whole attention, I want to know what you and …" She reached for the picture of Joy, the recent one, in color. But she stopped before she touched it, drew her hand back and merely gestured toward it. "… and the beautiful young woman in that picture had to say to each other when you had your heart-to-heart talk last night."

Mac felt like he'd been hauled into the principal's office and was about to try to convince him the dog had eaten his homework.

"We didn't talk."

"Well, for Pete's sake, why not?"

"She was sick. She locked herself in her room with a headache and didn't come out all night."

"And you just let her stay in there like that?"

"What was I supposed to do? Kick the door down? She's sixteen years old, and that's old enough—"

"To get yourself in a powerful lot of grownup trouble." Her voice got quiet, humming with power. "It gets stronger every day, every hour, the knowin'. The knowin' that something's wrong and your little … your *daughter's* scared and torn up inside over it."

She reached across the pictures to Mac's hand on the table, took it in both of hers and squeezed it. Her hands were warm and surprisingly soft. Her grip was tight.

"You look at me."

Mac fixed his eyes on her purple eyes, an outlandish shade of color you could drown in.

"I don't know what's wrong with your Joy, but it's a bad thing and it's gettin' worse. She's scared plum to death of somethin', and her insides is all tore up with wantin' and wishin' and regrettin' and just hurtin'. She misses her mama, that's true. But this trouble's not 'bout that. You got to talk to her. You got to help her. Her mama can't help her now. You're all she's got."

Mac found that it took all his strength to wrench his gaze away from hers, far more than it took to pull his hand away and gather up the photos.

Without looking at her, he said, "You frighten me, you know that Princess? You really scare me."

"Good. If scarin's what it takes to get you to do what you need to do."

"Oh, it's not just about Joy. You aren't who you should be."

"And who's that?"

It slipped out before he could stop it. "A cold-hearted murderer."

She looked like he'd back-handed her. He felt her reel backwards from the force of the blow, felt the glow about her dim as she cloaked it protectively. And he realized he could only see the light because she had totally opened up to him, had been completely vulnerable. The room seemed suddenly darker, colder.

"I am a convicted murderer and that's a fact, and come Friday, they're gonna fry me for it. Sorry I ain't acted like what I am."

"See, Princess, that's the problem. There's no guile in you. You *have* acted like who you are. It's just that who you are doesn't fit at all with what you've done."

Princess smiled a little. "You know, that's 'xactly what that lawyer lady said to me. The one that didn't make hardly no sense a'tall."

15

GARY WAS AT THE GYM DOOR waiting for her when Joy got there at 3:30. He held out an envelope, then pulled it back when she reached for it.

"Say please."

"This isn't a game, Gary," she hissed and held out her hand palm up.

Gary's face bore a look she'd never seen before, because if she had, she'd never have been foolish enough to believe his fake comfort and phony sympathy. That look was cruelty, and it wasn't a mask. It was reality; the sweet smile was the mask.

"What this is costing *me* is a cherry set of glass-packs that I've been saving for since last fall," he said. "But what it's going to cost *you*, baby-cakes, is something money can't buy."

His words were so much more true than he had any idea. She'd felt it again and again in the past few days. It was absolutely undeniable. She had felt the life inside her move.

When she showed no response, he continued, ground out the words through clenched teeth. "I promise you, inside a week, I won't just damage your reputation. I'll destroy it! When I'm through with you, everyone will look right through you just like they do ..." He scratched around in his mind to find a suitable comparison. "Just like they do Phoebe Elrod!"

Phoebe, a far more decent human being than this crew-cut All-American boy in his button-down plaid shirt who had pretended sympathy just to get into her pants.

And in the utter other-worldliness of the moment, that struck her funny. She threw back her head and laughed out loud. Her laughter made Gary even angrier. He slapped the envelope into her palm.

"We'll see how funny you think it is when—"

"Save your threats for somebody who cares, Gary. My mother taught me a long time ago: 'Never explain. Your friends don't need it and your enemies won't believe it anyway.' Take your best shot."

She leaned closer and whispered. "But your little plan might just blow up in your face. Smear mud on me and it'll get all over you, too."

Then she turned and stalked away. She made it out to Mr. Wilson, got in behind the wheel, and turned on the key before she totally fell apart. Her tears were so sudden and intense, she spit all over the dashboard.

Reputations were issued one to a customer. Lose it and you never got it back. It wasn't the same for boys. Gary's tale of making it with the preacher's daughter wouldn't damage his reputation. It would probably improve it, make him look like a stud. But her life would be ruined. How could she function, go through two more years of high school with everybody staring at her and whispering behind her back?

"Oh, Mama," she sobbed out loud. "Mama, I *need* you!"

Then she cried all the harder, heaving sobs that instantly made the muscles in her chest sore.

A sudden rapping on her car window startled the tears to a halt.

Standing outside her door were her two best friends, Beth Cambron and Shirley Finch, looking sad and concerned. She rolled the window down with one hand and wiped her eyes with the other.

"Are you okay?" Beth asked. Even though it was at least eighty-five degrees outside, she was wearing a sweater, her boyfriend's letter sweater. He was a senior and his class rung hung on a chain around her neck. Joy had thrown Gary's ring at him the night she told him she was pregnant and he asked if she was sure it was his.

"Is there anything we can do to help?" Shirley chimed in. Sweet Shirley, chubby and loveable. Joy had known both girls since kindergarten, made Popsicle-stick crosses with them every summer in Vacation Bible School, even stood together in line at the health department three years ago, waiting for their doses of polio vaccine on Sabin Oral Sunday. They were family.

"Want to go get a cherry coke or a root beer float?" Beth offered.

Tweedle Dum and Tweedle Dee. The worst problem either one of them's ever faced is a zit on her nose on prom night.

"I'm fine, really. I just go on crying jags sometimes. It passes."

"Can't we do *something* to make you feel better?" Shirley begged.

For just a moment, Joy longed to tell them what was really wrong, unload on them her pain, share her fear. But the moment passed quickly. Shirley had never even had a steady boyfriend. Beth had confided that she and Jerry did some heavy petting when they went out parking on the weekend, but they hadn't gone all the way. She knew both girls were still virgins. They'd be shocked—horrified!— to find out Joy wasn't anymore. That she and Gary had …

"You did make me feel better." She clamped the iron fist of desperation down on her emotions and stopped sniffling. "Knowing you care means a lot."

"We're still on for Sunday afternoon, right?" Shirley asked. Joy looked blank. "Riding around. In Mr. Wilson. Remember?"

Riding around was the tribal dance of Graham teenagers. It consisted of cruising down Main Street to the Piggly Wiggly parking lot, out US 270 to the Corral Drive-In for a lime ice and french fries, then back to Main Street again, checking out the teenagers in the other cars who were doing the same thing. And giggling at Martin Avery and his three friends—Marty and the Mooners—who pressed their bare butts up against the backseat windows whenever a carload of girls drove by. Not all that long ago, Joy had loved to go riding around with her friends, thought the Chinese fire drills they

did at red lights were a riot. But not anymore. And a part of her suspected they never would be again, that all her pain had pushed her
through an invisible door into some kind of parallel universe, and no
matter what happened, she could never return, could never again be
a carefree kid.

"We'll spring for half the gas," Beth coaxed. Gasoline had re-
cently gone up from twenty-five to thirty cents a gallon.

"Oh, sure, I remember. Let's do it. Cool." Joy choked the words
out between lips pulled tight in a fake smile. "Now I have to run, I
have a dentist appointment. See you tomorrow."

Before they could say anything else, Joy rolled up the car window and backed out of the parking place on the last row of the
high school lot. Then she headed south on Route 79 toward Harrod's Creek Road. She had a vague idea about how far out of town it
was, but still had to slow down and read the markers on every road
she passed. That wasn't a problem though, given that Mr. Wilson
wouldn't go more than fifty miles per hour without throwing a complete vibration fit.

After what seemed like ten miles but was probably less than
five, she found the sign and turned sharply southwest on Harrod's
Creek Road. There was a bump right after the turn and when she
hit it, Mr. Wilson's radio suddenly came to life, blaring Little Peggy
March's voice, the volume pegged.

"I will follow him, follow him wherever heeee may go," the voice
wailed.

Joy slammed her fist down on the dashboard.

"…there isn't an ocean too deep, a mountain so high it can keep,
keep me a—"

Bam! She banged the dashboard again and the radio went dead.
Then she checked the odometer so she could measure three miles. At
two and a half she'd start looking for a mailbox with a cardinal on it.

The closer she got, the tighter she gripped the steering wheel.
After awhile, she couldn't tell if it was vibrating because she was driving too fast or because her hands were shaking so badly.

Then she spotted it on the left side of the road, a black mailbox
with a red bird on it—not a cardinal, a woodpecker, but there was

nothing else anywhere near so that had to be it. On the right side of the road there was nothing but open prairie, but the lane leading back from the mailbox disappeared in brush and trees. She knew Boundary Oak Lake was back there somewhere. It was a private fishing lake only a few acres wide. Her parents had taken her there on a picnic once years ago. Daddy had pointed out that the lake was only about five or six miles, as the crow flies, northeast of her grandparents' farm on Seminole Road.

She bumped down the dirt lane, sunlight mottled by the trees lacing the hood of the old Buick. Her heart was in full-on stampede, her hands suddenly so sweaty it was hard to grip the steering wheel. The place was certainly secluded enough for the activity that occurred here. Neither the house nor any cars parked there could be seen from the road.

Then she hit a little clearing. On the far side of it, backing up on the lake, a small old house with a wide porch hunkered down behind unruly vines that had braided the trellises on either side of the porch steps into tangled mats and then slithered upward to take the roof captive as well.

She turned off the engine and sat for a moment. When she glanced down, she fancied she could see her heart pounding, shaking the fabric of her button-down blouse. Her wardrobe was becoming more limited by the day. Her thickening waist had already expanded beyond her jeans and capri pants. Now, she wore shifts most of the time, or full skirts with the blouse untucked above them. It seemed so sloppy. Her mother would never have allowed her to leave the house without her blouse tucked in.

She took a deep breath, got out of the car, crossed the yard, and walked up the wooden steps to the porch. Up close, it was clear that the house had been allowed to run down. The paint was chipped and peeling, the porch steps uneven, with nails sticking up. She didn't like the closed-in feeling there, where the trellises blocked out the sun. She lifted her hand to knock when something brushed against her bare leg and she jumped back with a little squeak of a scream.

A calico cat sat looking up at her; it had a patch of black around one eye that looked like that dog on the Motorola commercials on television. She reached down and petted the cat. Then straightened, steeled herself, and knocked on the door.

Nothing.

She knocked again.

Again, nothing.

Oh please, let there be somebody home! Please.

It wasn't a prayer, exactly. Joy hadn't talked to God in a long, long time.

She knocked a third time, heard movement inside. A cool spray of relief doused the flickering flames of panic, and she suddenly realized how badly she needed to go to the bathroom. Then the door opened and a woman stood just inside.

"What do you—?"

Then the woman spotted the cat at Joy's feet and leaned down to pick it up, scolding it gently, "I been looking everywhere for you. Where've you been?"

The few moments of distraction were all Joy needed to reel in her shock and revulsion. Phoebe had warned her, but the face of the "seamstress" was way more than "funny-looking."

The woman stood with the cat in her arms and Joy looked her in the eye and didn't flinch.

"His name's Blackbeard," the woman said, nodding at the cat. Joy was amazed her speech was clear with her mouth so distorted. "I call him that because of the patch over his eye." She paused. "What can I do for you?"

"Uh … I came out here … because—"

"That's what I thought. Well, you're wasting your time, honey. I don't do that anymore." The woman made a move to close the door.

"No wait!" This couldn't be happening! "Please! You don't understand, I have to get an …" She couldn't say the word. "I can't have this … I can't be pregnant!"

She suddenly burst into tears. She hadn't meant to, the tears had just exploded out of her. What would she do if this woman turned her away?

The woman's eyes softened slightly; her determination remained rock-solid.

"I know it's hard. I understand." She paused, then enunciated every word carefully, individually. "But I don't do *that* anymore! Period." She stepped back. "Sorry I can't help you." Again, she tried to close the door.

"My father's a preacher!" Joy blurted out. It was the first thing that came to her mind. When the woman froze, she rushed ahead. "So you see, I can't be pregnant. I *can't*. I don't have anywhere else to go for help. You're my only hope. *Plea—!*"

"Who are you?" The woman stood very still, didn't even seem to be breathing.

"I'm …" For the life of her, Joy couldn't recall the fake identity she'd created.

"Your *real* name."

"Joy McIntosh."

The woman gasped and her hand flew to the ugly rip in her face that was her mouth.

"Are you … *Melanie* McIntosh's daughter?"

She knew Mama?

Joy was so shocked and ashamed she couldn't meet the woman's eyes, just nodded her head and looked down at the threshold of the door. And the woman's feet. She was wearing ratty blue house shoes, the fuzzy kind, that were stained like she'd spilled spaghetti sauce or catsup on them. Joy allowed her eyes to travel up the woman's body to her face and was repulsed by the journey. Her dress was as filthy as her shoes; the buttons weren't even buttoned right. Her greasy brown hair was tied in a ponytail at her neck. Her face was the color of cigarette ashes and her eyes looked out in something like wonder at Joy from deep pits of sagging dark flesh.

"You're Melanie's girl?"

"Yes." Joy had to fight the urge to turn away from the putrid stench of the woman's bad breath. How could somebody like *this* do …? She was so dirty Joy couldn't imagine letting the creature near her, let alone *touch* her. Then it occurred to her to ask. "How did you know my mother?"

The reply was a barely audible whisper. "She was the best friend I ever had."

Joy almost choked. It was unfathomable that her mother even *knew* this woman. How could they possibly have been *friends*? But she was quick enough to press the only advantage she had.

"Then you *have to* help me! My mother's not here. I'm all alone. She would have wanted her ..." She swallowed hard. "... *best friend* to help me—you know she would!"

Now, the woman was unsure. She stood in the doorway staring at Joy with emotions the teenager couldn't begin to identify playing across her deformed face.

"*Please!*" Joy begged. Then she remembered the money. She thrust the envelope into the woman's hand. "Here's $100 and I'll bring the other $100 when I come back for ... when I come back. That's what it costs, isn't it? Two hundred dollars?"

The woman didn't speak, just stood stock still, staring.

"It's not about the money," she finally said. "I just don't do *that* anymore. I quit. I did it before, but I can't now."

"Fine, *quit!* Don't ever do it again—*after* you help me. Let me be the last one. You can quit then, but please, please ... if my mother were here, she'd be begging you, too."

Joy didn't really believe that. In fact, she was certain that if her mother were alive, she wouldn't be standing on this creepy porch shoving $100 at a dirty old witch. She wasn't sure exactly what her mother would have done, but it wouldn't have been this.

The woman's eyes filled with tears and she gave Joy a look that would probably have been tender and kind on any other face.

"All right," she whispered.

Joy let out a huge breath she hadn't even realized she'd been holding. "Thank you! Oh, thank you so much!"

"Be back here at four o'clock Friday afternoon." The woman sounded like a sleepwalker, like she was in some kind of trance. "Wear a skirt, no pants. A dark color. And bring lots of pads. You got somebody to drive you home?"

"Drive me home?"

"Yeah. I'll use anesthesia; you can't drive afterwards. You'll have to bring somebody with you."

"Then don't use anesthetic!"

"You don't know what you're saying, it—"

"I don't have anybody." Joy looked at the woman's filthy shoes again. "Nobody knows about this. I don't care how bad it … hurts, I can take it."

The woman shook her head. "You have no idea what you're saying, child. Now, you find *somebody*—I don't care who—to come out here with you and drive you home. How about the boy that put you in a family way?"

Joy merely nodded, afraid to argue. The woman stepped back and started to shut the door.

"I'll bring the rest of the money Friday."

The woman said nothing, just shoved the door closed.

Joy walked slowly back to Mr. Wilson, her mind reeling. She couldn't bring anybody. There was nobody to bring. Certainly not *Gary*! And if she couldn't—?

She gritted her teeth and grabbed hold of the racing thoughts before they could send her into a panic. She'd find a way; she had no choice. She took a couple of breaths to calm herself and the resolve of desperation shoved steel down her spine.

I'll show up alone and convince her to do it anyway!

She opened the car door and leaned her head against the frame before she got in.

"Oh, Mama!" she whispered. "If only you …"

Everything in her life would be different if her mother hadn't died. Now, there was only Daddy, and he was too shattered by her mother's death to be any good to her at all.

The truth was, when her mother died, Joy lost both her parents. And never before in her life had she needed them more.

16

PRINCESS CAREFULLY PULLED THE THREE CANDY bars out of the pocket of her dress one at a time and placed them on the table in her tiny cell. Then she sat back in the wooden chair and looked at them.

She picked up the Butterfinger, held it to her nose and inhaled deeply. It smelled like peanuts! Why would it have a name like "Butter" but smell like peanuts?

She sniffed the Baby Ruth then. After that the Hershey bar. She'd had chocolate before, but not like this, in a candy bar.

Her face wreathed in a happy smile, she wrapped her arms around her shoulders and gave herself a big hug. My, weren't these fine! Weren't they fine, indeed!

Lifting the Butterfinger tenderly, she eased the silver foil tube out of the outside paper wrapper. Then she began to unwrap the foil, careful not to tear it, like someone opening a Christmas present so they could save the paper for next year.

Once the candy bar lay naked on its foil wrapper, she picked it up and took a tiny bite off the end.

"Oh!" she said out loud.

She took another bite, making sure the crumbles fell on the table so she could scoop them up and eat them, too. When she began to chew she giggled. Why, it stuck your teeth together it was so chewy.

She had just placed the bar back on the foil and lifted the Baby Ruth when—

Bam!

The seein' came on her that fast, with a force that literally knocked her backwards out of the chair and onto the cell floor. She lay there, panting, her eyes wide, but what she saw was not the walls of a cell on the Long Dark in the Oklahoma State Penitentiary for Women.

She was looking out of Joy's eyes!

A monster stood in a half-open door before her, a hideous creature! The whole bottom portion of the monster's face was a ruin, scarred and mangled, with the jaw caved in on the right side and no chin at all—just scarred flesh stretched tight back to her neck.

She lay on her back on the floor whimpering in terror and disgust, shaking her head back and forth, but it wasn't the ugliness on the outside of the monster that Princess was responding to.

❖ ❖ ❖ ❖ ❖

The guard named Talbot came around with Princess's dinner tray a little after five o'clock.

"Food's here," she called out, and slid the tray through the slot in the door. She waited and called out again. "Prentiss, here's your tray."

There was still no response.

"Emily?"

The large black woman took the tray out of the slot and set it down on the floor, bent down, and looked through the opening. She could see Princess's feet, sticking out beyond her bed, and the legs of the turned-over chair.

"She's pitched a fit!" the guard said, and hurried down to the end of the passageway lined with cells to the guard station at the end.

Minutes later, another guard returned with her. The second guard had the key that fit the ancient lock on Princess's cell. He inserted it, opened the door, and stood beside it while Talbot cautiously approached the body sprawled on the floor.

Talbot had been a guard on the Long Dark for more than seven years. She'd been present the day Princess had warned Rhonda Weatherby about her boyfriend, begged her not to go home. She wasn't one to believe all the wild rumors about the scrawny little death-row inmate, but she did believe that. Wasn't nothing to believe or not believe; she's seen it with her own eyes.

The guard with the key was a rookie just learning the ropes, a stocky man in his late thirties named Hank Bradley whose face was twisted in a permanent scowl that matched his nasty disposition.

"She's epileptic, ain't she?" Bradley said from the door as Talbot approached the body. "Musta had a fit. Maybe she's dead."

Talbot knelt beside her. "I've seen her after she's had a fit. She kinda foams at the mouth, if you know what I mean, and wets herself." She examined the body. "She's just lying here, staring at the ceiling."

The guard passed her hand back and forth in front of Princess's eyes.

"Prentiss," she said. "Emily Prentiss. Can you hear me? Emily!"

Princess suddenly blinked two or three times and gave Talbot a blank look that gradually resolved into focus and recognition. She looked around, then suddenly sat up and scooted on her butt to the far wall of her cell, whimpering.

"Prentiss, you all right?"

"No, no," Princess whined, shaking her head from side to side. "No, stay away!"

The guard stood, looked at the other guard and shrugged.

"Well, she ain't hurt." She sighed. "Just nuts. Guess I'd be nuts, too, if I knew I didn't have but two days to live." She gestured to the floor outside the cell. "Hand me that tray."

Bradley picked up the tray, stepped into the cell with it and saw the candy bars.

"Wonder where she got candy?" he said, picking up the Butterfinger she'd unwrapped and taking a big bite out of it. "Always did like Butterfingers." He dropped the remainder of the candy bar into his pocket and placed the tray on the table. Talbot stood looking at Princess for a moment longer, then shook her head and walked out.

The cell door banged shut, there was the grating sound of the key in the lock and then it was quiet. The only sound was Princess whimpering.

An hour later, the guards returned after Princess refused to hand the tray back out through the slot in the door. Princess was sitting just as they'd left her. They debated reporting the incident, but decided there was no point. They could see the inmate wasn't hurt. And the warden certainly wasn't going to delay her execution just because she'd lost it—or maybe was pretending to.

Before he left the cell, Bradley snitched the Baby Ruth bar as well. Shoot, Prentiss wasn't eating it.

◆ ◆ ◆ ◆ ◆

It was the deepest, darkest cavern of the night before Princess came back to herself. She was aware of the cold stone floor, aware that her butt was completely numb from sitting on it.

She got up slowly and carefully, looked down at her dress to see … no, she hadn't wet herself. She hadn't had no fit. But she already knew that. She knew what had happened.

After she went to the toilet in the corner of the cell and did her business, she came back and sat on the edge of her bed, her arms wrapped around her waist, rocking back and forth.

She'd *seen*. It had happened before, so she recognized it for what it was. She had looked at the world through the eyes of somebody else. This time it was the daughter of the preacher who had give her those candy bars.

She looked up, glanced at the table. It was already after lights-out, but there was enough moonlight coming in to see. Only the Hershey bar remained. She went to the table, picked it up, tore the paper off and ate it ravenously. She barely tasted the sticky sweetness as it went down.

How in the world was she going to tell the Rev 'bout that monster? And it was a monster, sure. Princess had seen more than the hideous exterior. She'd looked into those eyes. She'd seen the madness there.

She shuddered. What she'd seen defied description. There was piles of *dead babies* behind the monster's eyes. All of them bloody and tore up, missing arms and legs. Piles of them! Only the thing was, they was cryin'. Ever' last one of them was wailin', making the awfulest racket you ever did hear.

What had Joy McIntosh got herself into that she'd truck with a witch like that? How would she ever make the Rev believe that his pretty little red-haired girl was a'danglin' by a thread over a black hole and down at the bottom of it was all sharp rocks and moanin,' dyin' babies?

And that woman wasn't the only monster that had suddenly reared its ugly head in Princess's few remaining hours on this earth.

Jackson was coming tomorrow.

She shuddered again, the power of the revulsion wracking her body like she was throwin' a fit. She'd see him, all right. She'd look him square in the eye this time. 'Cause she'd won!

◆ ◆ ◆ ◆ ◆

Even after his father-in-law had finally given in and hired someone to stay with Maggie parts of the day, Jonas still wasn't able to give the farm the time and energy it needed. So Mac had volunteered to help. He was strong, but "agriculturally challenged." After he and Melanie married, he'd taken a little country church just outside Seagram, in the mountains of southwestern Arkansas, and had done some farm work there to make ends meet on his paltry pastor's salary. That had been before they called up his reserve unit and packed him off to Korea. But over the past couple of summers, Mac had learned a lot about farming. Given the plan he intended to outline for Jonas this afternoon, it was a good thing the older man had been a patient teacher.

Mac drove into Graham from the prison but didn't stop, just drove all the way through and west on US 270, then south on Seminole Road to Jonas and Maggie's farm about six miles southwest of town. His mind was still spinning, just as it had every day after he met with Princess.

Jonas was mending a fence where the sheep had broken out of the pen; Mac quickly slipped into work boots, overalls, and a John Deere cap and hurried out to help him. The rain earlier in the afternoon had been gentle and most of it had soaked in, so the ground was soft but not muddy.

The two men worked hard for over an hour, Mac slamming the posthole digger into the ground and pulling out moist dirt, Jonas lining up the posts and stringing the wire. When they were finished, Mac pointed to the puddle of shade under an apple tree and invited Jonas to "sit for a spell." Without any preamble, he dived right in.

"I've been meaning to say something about this for quite awhile now," he began.

"I's wonderin' when you was finally goin' to get to it."

Mac was startled.

Jonas smiled. "Son, you're easier to read than a large-print Bible." He reached over and patted his son-in-law on the knee. "I don't mean nothing by that. It's plain somethin's eatin' at you. What is it?"

"I'm done. I'm quitting."

"Quittin' the church?"

"I have a meeting with the elder board on Friday night and I'll tell the congregation Sunday. But I'm not just leaving the church. I'm leaving the ministry."

Jonas said nothing. Just watched a chicken hawk circle high in the sky above them.

"You're not going to ask why?"

"Do you know?"

"If I didn't know, I wouldn't be doing it."

"That ain't necessarily the case."

Mac pulled up a stem of grass and stuck it in his mouth. "I know I have to leave the ministry. I don't believe it anymore. Maybe I never did."

"Oh, you did. I imagine you still do," Jonas tapped Mac's chest, "somewhere way down in there."

"No, it's gone." He looked into Jonas's eyes. "It died with Melanie."

JONAS WAS ASHAMED THEN, AS HE had been repeatedly in the past twenty years, that he'd ever had misgivings about Mac. He'd even told Maggie once he didn't think Melanie ought to marry him.

Oh, he was a nice enough young man, and the way he'd been smitten with Mel, hanging around her like a puppy since the third grade, was downright comical to watch. But Jonas wasn't at all convinced it was a good idea for his daughter to marry a minister. It wasn't that he didn't hold with preaching; he just hadn't ever met a preacher he could stand. Meddlin', interfering, sanctimonious busybodies, ever' last one of them.

He'd never shared that sentiment with Maggie, of course. She'd have bopped him in the head with a frying pan if he had.

Jonas figured that a man's business with God was between the two of them. It was private. Preachers never saw it that way.

But Mac was different. He didn't concern himself a whole lot with folks' behavior. When he preached, he opened up the Bible and told stories about Jesus; said if you knew God, everything else would work itself out in the end.

Jonas's own grandfather would likely have agreed with that. He talked a lot about what he called "top-button truth." If you get the top button on your shirt right, the old man used to tell the boy, then all the rest of the buttons will fall into place behind it. But get the top button wrong, and no matter how hard you try, nothing will ever line up like it's supposed to.

Nothing had lined up right in Jonas's life in a long, long time. Hadn't in Mac's either. But Jonas didn't believe it had a thing to do with the top button. The problem was that there were buttons *missing*. Important buttons. Those buttons had been ripped off their shirts and it was a waste of time to try to get the rest of the buttons to line up without them.

He looked kindly at Mac, then shook his head, turned and squinted into the setting sun. "If you're looking to me to talk you out of quittin', son, you come to the wrong man."

The two sat without speaking, their shared pain a silent bond.

Mac suddenly realized that he'd been so self absorbed he hadn't even considered how hard things had been in the past months for Jonas.

"How are *you* doing?" He asked quietly.

"Not worth a diddly dang!" Jonas said, then looked uncomfortable, like he hadn't meant for that to slip out. He was a private man. Stoic. Mac respected that.

The older man cleared his throat and changed the subject. "You quit the church, what *are* you gonna do?"

Mac took the stem of grass out of his mouth and tossed it away. "Since Mel and I both worked, Bill down at the Farm Bureau Insurance office convinced us to take out mortgage insurance when we bought the house—the kind that pays it off if either one dies. With no house payment, I won't have to make much to live."

He reached down and plucked another stem of grass.

"So I was thinking I'd work as a farm hand this summer—for you and anybody else needs it."

"Summertime you won't have no trouble finding work."

"Shoveling manure is strenuous but mindless." Mac grinned. "That's the kind of work I need—for awhile."

"And then?"

"Maybe I could teach."

"Maggie sure loved it."

"I'd never aspire to be as good as she was. I was thinking history, maybe science, do a little coaching—baseball, track."

"You told Joy yet?"

"Nope."

"If you're plannin' to jump ship on Sunday, might be a plan to give her a heads-up beforehand."

Jonas was right, of course. But after her reaction when he forgot to say grace the other night, Mac had become concerned about what her response might be. The kid's life had been safe and predictable until the unthinkable happened. Her mother's death had devastated her; it had shattered her sense of security, too. Would her father leaving the ministry set her totally adrift, without anything solid to cling to?

Mac picked up a clod of dirt and pitched it at a stinkbug ambling by the tip of his boot.

"Been waiting for the weekend. I'm going to talk to her on Saturday so she'll have the whole day to … work through it. But I am *not* looking forward to the conversation. I can't talk to her about anything these days. She's all closed up. Princess keeps telling me there's something wrong with her—besides the obvious—and I'm beginning to think she may be right."

"Princess?"

"The woman at the prison I've been going to visit."

"You ain't talking about that Prentiss woman, are you? The one they're fixing to execute Friday? How does she know anything about Joy?"

"You just asked the $64,000 Question." He turned and looked at his father-in-law. "I don't know how Princess knows what she knows, but then, neither does she." He stopped, shrugged. Now he understood how Oran had felt trying to tell him about Princess. She was a phenomenon you had to experience to understand. "You want to meet her?"

Princess had acted like Mac had brought her bars of gold when he gave her candy. How might she respond if he brought her somebody else to talk to besides the boring Reverend McIntosh?

"Now, why in the world would I want to meet a murderer?"

Mac suddenly realized he didn't think of Princess as a murderer anymore. He'd called her attorney nuts for refusing to believe she'd committed the crime she'd confessed to; apparently he had contracted the same mental illness.

"She's not like you're imagining, Jonas, but if I told you about her, you wouldn't believe me." Truth was, Princess disturbed him, unsettled him on a gut level like nobody he'd ever met. He was losing all perspective about her, and his father-in-law's presence might just add a much-needed ballast. He wondered what affect she'd have on a man like Jonas, a man with both feet planted firmly on terra firma. "Guadalupe will be with Maggie tomorrow afternoon. Why don't you come see for yourself?"

"Think I'll pass. I don't fancy meeting a woman who took the life of somebody who couldn't defend …" He stopped abruptly and studied the apple tree leaf he'd been rolling and unrolling as he talked. Then he looked up and nodded. "Okay, guess I'll tag along, you don't mind."

When Mac got home, there was a note from Joy stuck to the refrigerator door with a magnet. "Daddy, I'm at Shirley's house. That American history project we're doing together, the one where we're building the Jamestown Colony out of sugar cubes, it's due in the morning, first period. If it's okay with you, I'm going to spend the night. We're going to be working LATE. See you tomorrow. Love, Joy."

Was she dodging him, deliberately staying away so they'd have no time to talk?

He picked up the note and added his own words in big print on the bottom.

"Sweetheart, we have a date tonight. You and me. A casserole dinner. NO EXCUSES."

He put it back on the refrigerator door where she couldn't miss it when she walked through the kitchen after school tomorrow. Then he opened the door and stared at the covered dishes inside, lined up like corpses in a morgue.

Thursday

May 9, 1963

17

Jonas parked his pickup truck in Mac's driveway right after lunch on Thursday, full of questions about Princess and her case. Mac told him everything he knew about it as they drove east on US 270 toward the Iron House.

"They never found anything for the family to bury? Nothing?"

"Nope, but you got to figure the Three Forks is a big river, runs through Arkansas, Oklahoma, and into Texas. How'd you ever drag a river that size looking for … well, I don't know if they dragged it or not. I just know what that reporter—"Mac had just turned off the highway onto the road leading to the prison. "Speaking of reporters …"

Like mushrooms after a summer rain, a crowd of seventy-five, maybe a hundred people had sprung up on the prairie in front of the prison gate. The media was out in force. He saw vehicles parked off the road with "Channel 11 News First," and "OKC's News Source— KOKA" emblazoned on their sides. The ABC, CBS, and NBC news affiliates had all shown up; looked like every radio and television station in Oklahoma City was there.

But the majority of the people standing on the prairie were protesters, held in check by a small army of Oklahoma Highway Patrol troopers.

"Where in the world did all these people come from?" Jonas wondered aloud.

"Don't go looking for familiar faces," Mac said. "These folks aren't local. I think they travel the country, protesting at executions in prisons all over. Least that's what Oran said."

Mac glanced to his left, to the side of the prison that faced the Indian Bluffs. "And it looks like he's managed to keep the multitudes congregated out front like he wanted." Mac decided not to tell Jonas what Oran said he'd like to save up and throw at the protesters.

Troopers had stretched out yellow "Police Line" tape on both sides of the road leading to the main gate and had corralled the crowd behind the lines. Mac hadn't realized there'd be people protesting both ways, but there was a group of anti-death penalty protesters on one side of the road and death penalty proponents on the other. The antis had the pros outnumbered three to one.

Both sides carried signs and they hurled slogans and insults across the road at each other as Mac drove slowly down between the opposing sides.

One very fat woman held a stop sign with the words "Stop Executions Now!" printed on it. She was in a shouting match with a man on the other side of the road who held a sign that proclaimed "Murder Victims Had No Choice!" There was a group of half a dozen nuns in habits on the anti side, holding a banner that read: "Thou Shalt Not Kill." And a small group of teenagers, likely the children of the older protesters, held a series of signs that, when read in order, said, "Kids. Against. Death. Penalty." Mac wondered if protesting at an execution was considered an excused absence from school. Beside them was a tall, thin man whose sign charged that the state of Oklahoma should be executed for murder.

The people on the pro–death penalty side held signs, too. One said: "How would you feel if she'd killed your sister?" Another charged: "Don't Do The Crime, If You Can't Do The Time."

Mac drove slowly through the crowd. Listening to the biggest group, the opponents of the death penalty chant: "No more killing! No more killing! No more killing."

A smaller group on the other side was yelling, "Murderers deserve to die. Murderers deserve to die."

Mac looked around for Sam Bartlett but didn't spot him. The guard at the main gate security station was tense and edgy. Mac showed him his Shriners' badge, but it took him a minute to find the two names on his day sheet. Mac had called Oran at home last night to secure clearance for Jonas.

"They just penciled in Jonas Cunningham this morning," the guard said. "Can I see some identification, please?"

He looked at their proffered drivers licenses, asked them their dates of birth, and checked to see if what they said matched what was printed on the licenses. It was a far more thorough examination than Mac had been given on any other visit.

The guard at the inner security gate at the other end of the razor-wired tunnel was just as vigilant.

"You know where to go, right?" the guard asked. Mac nodded and headed for the parking lot in front of the administration building.

Another man was being processed through security at the check-in center there when they entered. They stood waiting as he emptied his pockets into a plastic tray. Both Mac and Jonas recognized him instantly. Standing before them was the Reverend Amos Jackson Prentiss.

JACKSON LOOKED AT THE GUARD IN front of him and was filled with revulsion. A thick wad of snuff puffed out the guard's lower lip and he was as black as a burnt stump. He reached over, picked up a paper cup, and spit brown juice into it. Then he wiped his mouth on the back of his hand and raised his eyes to Jackson.

"I need you to hold your hands out to your sides," the black ape said, and stepped around the counter.

Jackson stood as rigid as a flagpole.

"You aren't planning on laying your hands on me, are you, *boy?*" he hissed softly, his lips pressed together in a tight line.

This is what it had come to, niggers telling white men what to do. Jackson had known America would end up like this the day he read that Supreme Court ruling back in 1954.

"Segregation of white and colored children in public schools has a detrimental effect upon the colored children," it had said, as if that was somehow a *bad* thing. The monkeys shouldn't have been in school in the first place, should never have been allowed an education.

That's why he'd run for the school board in Little Rock the next year, to fight for white rights! But the fools had elected a lily-livered coward and look what happened. Those nine nigger kids went waltzing into Central High School like they owned the place! Governor Faubus called up the National Guard to keep them out, but the President of the United States sent in the U.S. Army to *protect* them!

Jackson had orchestrated the opposition, stood out in front of the school every morning united with his white brothers and sisters, spitting on every one of those nigger brats as they walked past.

Just like he wanted to spit on this jigaboo, disrespecting a white man because some fool had let him out of his cage and taught him to read.

Jackson drew in a breath and stood tall and defiant. "There is no call for you to touch me," he said.

"Ain't but one way to get past me, *Mister* Prentiss," the guard said. "Either I pat you down, or your can turn yourself around and go right back out that door you come in."

"Well, well, well." The ice in Jackson's voice lowered the room temperature twenty degrees. "It appears to me we have ourselves an uppity nigger, here." He looked to the two men standing behind him for a show of white solidarity. He didn't get it.

"It appears to *me* you're not going anywhere until you let this man search you," said the red-headed, freckle-faced one.

Jackson turned back to the guard and growled, "We know what to do with your kind in Alabama."

Last week, they'd showed the niggers who was in charge! Those school kids marching in Birmingham—Jackson's good friend Bull Conner had turned on the fire hoses, set the dogs on them!

"Case you didn't notice, we in Oklahoma," the guard said. "You playin' in my patch, now."

Jackson *had* to see Princess today! He slowly lifted his arms, his face a stone mask, his eyes aflame with raw hatred. The guard frisked him, pummeled his body so thoroughly the act resembled a restrained beating. Jackson stood proud and silent through it all.

"Have a seat over there," the guard said with a gloating, black-toothed grin, and gestured to a row of chairs up against the wall. "I'll call you when it's your turn." He spit into the cup again. "Hope you don't mind waitin', though. There's two other visitors on the list 'head of you."

"I'm the only kin Emily has," Jackson said through clenched teeth. "Who else would want to see my Emmy?"

"I would," said the man behind him, the coward who wouldn't stand up to the black ape. The man stepped forward and extended his hand. "I'm David McIntosh and this is my father-in-law, Jonas Cunningham. I'm filling in for the prison chaplain."

Mac didn't really want to shake hands with Jackson Prentiss, but it was the polite thing to do under the circumstances. The man had aged considerably since the day Mac heard him speak in Little Rock, but time had been kind, had etched his face with distinguished lines and streaked white into his wine-colored hair at the temples. He was tall and thin, stood ramrod straight in an unwrinkled, three-piece suit. He had a presence now, too, but it was a calculated dignity—form, not substance.

Prentiss looked at Mac for a beat, then grasped his hand in an iron grip and shook it up and down, once—the bare minimum. He fastened a smile on his face that never reached his cold, vulture's eyes.

"Pastor McIntosh," he said, "I appreciate you coming to offer comfort to Emily in her final hours."

Mac opened his mouth to speak but Prentiss wasn't finished.

"... *but* I do hope you haven't been so foolish as to hold out to her a false hope of glory. Of redemption or salvation. Emily is damned, Pastor McIntosh. Utterly and irrevocably damned."

"Really? How do you figure that?"

"Our Lord himself passed down that judgment." His voice took on the sing-song cadence of a sermon. "Jesus warned that it would be better for a man to have a millstone tied around his neck and be cast into the depths of the sea than to hurt one of his precious little ones."

He leaned toward Mac, the aroma of his English Leather after-shave filling the air between them.

"Emily *murdered* a little child," he growled, his voice rising in intensity and volume as he continued until he was almost shouting. "She *beheaded* an innocent babe. She committed the unforgivable sin and there will be justice! There will be retribution! The wrath of Almighty God will descend upon her and she will burn for all time in the bowels of eternal hell!"

With that, he turned on his heel and marched off toward the row of chairs. Mac took a step after him before Jonas touched his arm and shook his head.

"But that's not what that verse means!" Mac sputtered.

"You think you're gonna convince him of that?"

Jonas was right, of course. Mac let it go, though it rankled to hear someone twist the scriptures he knew so well to fit a private agenda. But what was the point in confusing a hate-monger with the facts?

When the two men were ushered into the envelope room a short time later, Mac noticed two things instantly. One, Princess's dress *wasn't* on wrong side out, and it was Thursday. And two, the sense of calm, the centeredness and stillness about her was gone. It had been replaced by a humming tension he could feel all the way across the room. Princess was a bullet in a chamber. The slightest move would send her hurling out at something. Or somebody.

"Princess, I'd like you to meet my father-in-law, Jonas Cunningham," he said with as much cheer as he could muster. "It was kind of you to allow him to come along with me today."

"I do gladly make your acquaintance, sir," she said, and Mac saw Jonas was staring at Princess, a profoundly startled look on his face. He'd forgotten to warn him about her voice. She didn't rise or offer her hand so Jonas merely nodded.

"Pleasure's mine, ma'am."

Someone had added another chair to the fine décor of the room so Mac crossed and pulled it out for Jonas, then sat down across from Princess. She was literally bouncing on the edge of her seat like a little kid who needs to go to the bathroom.

"I see your dress is on right-side—"

"Ain't no need to swap it now. You think I'd forget what today is?"

"S'pose not." He opened his mouth to speak again, but the dam burst before he had a chance.

"I seen last night. Oh, Rev, I *seen!* It was the awfulest, terriblest thing I ever did see in all my days. Oh, Rev! Joy's having truck with a … a monster. A witch! I seen it!"

"Princess, slow down and calm down. I don't have any idea what you're talking about."

"'Course you don't. How you gonna know less'n I tell you? Joy's got herself mixed up with a terrible woman, a monster. I seen her face. You ain't never seen nothing so twisted up and ugly in your whole life!" She stood up, placed her palms on the table and leaned toward him. There was fire in her purple eyes. "It's only happened to me a handful of other times in my life, but it happened last night. I seen out somebody else's eyes, Joy's eyes. I was sittin' in my cell and then suddenly my eyes could see what Joy was a-lookin' at right at that moment. And it was a monster."

The power of her voice was astonishing. It was rumbling and hypnotic, filled up the room with its electric intensity.

"So you saw what Joy saw and what she saw was a monster? Am I getting this right?"

Princess sat back down abruptly. She didn't speak, just looked at her hands in her lap.

"You're humorin' me again. I ain't sayin' I blame you. But I can't help it if I sound all crazy like. I'm just tellin' you what I saw."

"And that was?"

"Joy was standin' on a porch and a woman was at the door, with it open just a little. Joy give her a envelope."

"Joy gave some woman an envelope?"

"It don't matter if your girl give her a brass spittoon!" Princess burst out. "What matters is she wasn't no plain old woman. She was a monster! And when you looked inside her …" Princess paused, gathered herself and continued. "Inside the monster was dead bodies."

She looked up at Mac, took notice of Jonas for the first time and included him in her look.

"Joy's just a child. She don't know 'bout the world. She hadn't ought to be havin' dealings with nobody like that. You're her people, all she's got. You got to protect her."

Mac reached out and took Princess's hand. It was cold and clammy. She was trembling.

"Princess, look at me."

She lifted her purple eyes and stared into his.

"I have a date for dinner tonight with my daughter. I'm going to sit her down and talk to her. Really *talk* to her. I'm going to get to the bottom of whatever it is that's bothering her. Whatever is going on with her, I'll find out tonight."

She continued to stare into his eyes. And his heart.

"Princess, I'll protect Joy. I won't let anything hurt her. I promise. Okay?"

She let go the hold she had on his eyes and relaxed back into the chair.

"You say so, I believe you. Man like you don't lie."

Mac sat for a moment, didn't quite know how to transition from such emotional intensity into normal conversation.

Normal *conversation. With a woman who's going to be dead in a little over twenty-four hours. Right.*

Jonas broke the silence.

"Mac tells me he brought you some candy yesterday. How'd you like it?"

She looked up with a bright smile. Mac thought it would have been such a pretty smile if her teeth hadn't been so stained.

"I worried it around in my head half the night tryin' to figure out why they called that one a *Butter*finger when it tasted like peanuts."

"I always wondered the same thing myself," Jonas said.

"And that Hershey bar, it was fine indeed." Princess was beaming. She looked at Mac. "This is what it's like! I finally found out."

"What what's like?"

"People just sittin' around, talkin'. Remember I said I always wondered what in the world they found to say? This is it. A'tossin' the ball one to the other. Conversation."

She smiled at Jonas.

"I surely do thank you for coming to see me today, Mr. Cunningham. Conversation ain't the same when there's more'n two people. It's harder, ain't it?"

"How about the other one, the Baby Ruth?" Mac asked.

"Well ..." she said. She ducked her head and looked up at him through her lashes. "You know, I knew I'd be sorry I promised I'd tell you the truth. Knew that was gonna come back to bite my backside."

"How's that?"

"Cause I got to tell you I didn't eat but one of them candies—the Hershey bar one."

"What happened to the others. Are you saving them?"

For what? She's going to be dead tomorrow!

Mac gritted his teeth and forced himself to stay in the moment.

"No, I ain't savin' them. They's just gone. They was on the table ... and then they wasn't. I don't know what in the world could have happened to 'em."

"Tell you what—how about I bring you some more tomorrow?"

"I don't reckon I'm gonna want candy tomorrow. They done asked me what I wanted for my last meal. I figure my stomach's gonna be tied in a knot so tight tomorrow I couldn't shove so much as a walnut down into it."

Mac sat up straight. "About tomorrow ..." This was a dying woman and he was a minister. As long as he held that title he was obligated to offer spiritual comfort, whether he personally believed what he was saying or not. If it came down to it, Mac would just have to break his promise not to lie.

"They're gonna cut all my hair off. You know that?"

"I didn't know that." It sounded positively barbaric.

All at once, Princess was off again. Like a flat rock skipping across the smooth surface of a lake, her mind somehow managed to remain above the deep, murky waters and the cold dark of the depths.

"Angel had the prettiest hair you ever did see—the color of a rusty nail. And long—oh, my goodness. I washed it when I'd give her a bath of a night." Her scarred face was alive; her purple eyes saw another reality.

"We had this washtub, see. And I'd heat up water on the stove and fill it 'bout half way up, then pour in cold well water the rest of the way—so's it'd just be warm. Oh, how she loved to sit in that water, splashed it all over the floor, had to take a mop to it to clean up the mess."

"I used to give my kids a bath in a washtub," Jonas said. Mac looked at him.

"You did? Melanie took a bath in a washtub?"

"No, by the time she came along, we had a proper bathtub. But the older kids, yeah. We used a washtub."

"A washtub's all we had," Princess said. "Angel would stand up in it and squeeze her eyes shut and I'd pour water over her head out of a cookin' pot. When her hair was wet, it hung down to her butt. All the way down to that birthmark."

Princess grinned. "Angel had this birthmark on her right butt cheek. It was a red spot with three lines comin' out from it. Looked just like a fallin' star. The last time I washed her hair ..." She paused, the animation drained out of her posture. Mac watched her face rearrange itself in cold, hard lines.

"Jackson come in the kitchen then and—" Now that he'd met the man face to face, Mac had no trouble understanding the undertone in her voice when she spoke of him.

She didn't continue, just sat there.

"And what?" Mac prodded.

"I got soap in Angel's eyes and she commenced to screamin' and carryin' on and I like to never got her to stop." She hopped up, darted to the window and looked out longingly.

"I would powerfully like to see that movie set, Laramie Junction, up there on that hill. It sure looks real, don't it?"

"Sometimes it's hard to tell what's real and what's not," Mac said.

Princess turned her back to the window and leaned against the sill.

"I know what's real. And I know you don't think I got any idea. It's real that you're going to come back and see me tomorrow. And after you leave …" She turned back and looked out the window again. "I'm going to die."

Jonas cleared his throat. He'd been sitting there for the past couple of minutes with an odd look on his face. Mac was suddenly sorry he'd brought the old man. This was pretty deep stuff here.

"Look, if you'd like to talk to Mac privately now, I'd be glad to—" Jonas started to rise.

"No, sit back down Mr. Cunningham. I don't have nothin' to say you can't hear."

"Do you want to talk about that—what happens tomorrow?" Mac asked. "Do you want to talk about dying?"

"I wonder if it'll hurt's all. But they all tell me it don't. That you don't feel nothin' a'tall." She looked at Jonas. "Don't seem much sense in askin' questions today when they'll all get answered tomorrow."

"Are you afraid?" Mac asked softly.

She laughed at that, a big, full rumbling laugh.

"Wouldn't *you* be? I ain't had a solid bowel movement in more'n a week! They're a-fixin' to fry me tomorrow. 'Course I'm scared."

Then she thought a moment. "Least I'm pretty sure now that's what I'm feeling. That hole-in-the-my-side thing, I'm fairly sure now it's scared. And if it is … shoot, I been feelin' *that* for years."

She crossed and sat back down.

"Thing is, what's gonna happen tomorrow … it's what's s'posed to happen. Like I said, I done made my peace."

Mac thought about Jackson Prentiss. He didn't want Princess anywhere near that sanctimonious, graceless ogre. No telling what he might say to her. But there was nothing Mac could do to prevent the meeting.

He suddenly realized she was looking at him again with that quiet, penetrating look. The stillness had settled around her and it was like she could see into his soul.

"Don't you trouble yourself 'bout me, Rev. I'm good. A body don't get to pick what happens. All's you gotta decide is what you do about it. I made my decisions that got me here a long time ago. It's all led to this. And I'm ready."

18

PRINCESS SAT AT THE TABLE IN the room with a window that looked
out on the Indian Bluffs. That looked out on a town the Rev said was
a fake. Imagine that, a whole da-gone town wasn't even real.

She rolled around in her mind the images of her visit with the
Rev and his father-in-law, the way you'd wallow a lemon drop in
your mouth, licking up every last little bit of the sweet. He was sure
enough in pain, that old man was, hurtin' somethin' fierce. She surely
would like to know what was sucking the life out of him. But that
wasn't to be. She was coming to the end of it now, the end of everything. It was all a-hurtlin' at her, fast as a freight train. Every breath
she took, it was one of the last ones. Had to *treasure* 'em. Had to
treasure ever' one.

She sat wrapped tight in stillness, snug in quiet. Waiting for
Jackson to come.

But inside her chest, her heart was bangin' away loud as a wood
spoon in a metal pot. So loud he'd surely hear it. He'd come in that
door and take one look at her, hear her heart thump-thump-thump-
ing and he'd know he still had power over her. That all these years
later, she was still scared to death of him.

Tomorrow she was going to die. And today would be the first
time she'd been alone with Jackson since that last night, him sittin'
drunk in the chair with the broken springs in their little house high

up in the hills of Arkansas. The night she left, took Angel and all the money in his wallet, flung her knapsack over her shoulder and disappeared into the darkness.

Ever' time after that when she seen him, there was other people around. The police or her lawyers, the different ones of them. She seen him in court, of course, when he got up there on the stand and told all them lies. But he'd never come to visit her a single time in all the years she'd been in prison. They'd never been alone, just him and her.

Until today.

It suddenly hit her, come clunking down into her mind so powerful and heavy it was like somebody dropped a big rock right on top of her head.

What you got to be scared of, fool? Tomorrow, they're gonna kill you? What can he do to you today's worse'n that?

She burst into a rumbling roar of laughter. And that's how he found her. When the guard opened the door and Jackson Prentiss come striding into the room, Princess was sittin' at the table, laughing her head off.

He just stood there, looking at her, his lip curled up in a snarl like it always done when he was 'bout to get mean. Couldn't get mean here, though! There was a guard right outside the door that'd come runnin' in here and lock Jackson up somewhere his own self.

The thought made her laugh even harder.

"You're crazier now than you ever were." He spit the words out like they tasted bad in his mouth.

She was laughing so hard tears ran down her cheeks. She reached up and wiped them away and felt the laughter dribble down to a little giggle and silence.

Then she studied him, like examining some strange bug crawling on a leaf in the woods. In her mind, Jackson Prentiss was a giant, huge, menacing and terrifying. This man was old and used-up looking. Oh, his outsides was all shined up slick and glassy like, better'n she'd ever seen him. But his insides was a ruin of evil and meanness and alcohol.

Drink charged a price Jackson Prentiss had been paying every day since he was twelve years old. The man had reached out soon as he opened his eyes of a morning and there by golly better be a cold beer there to grab or he'd come up side Princess's head with whatever he could lay his hands on—a piece of firewood, a hairbrush, an empty bottle. She learned quick to rise at dawn and fetch a cold brew out of the ice box to be waiting by his bedside.

There wasn't usually much else in the ice box besides Jackson's beer. Often, there was no food in the house a'tall, and Jackson'd just leave her there to figure out how she was going to feed herself and Angel. His pitiful little group of followers couldn't afford to pay him diddly squat, so he'd got his self a part-time job at the sawmill, wouldn't be home 'til he'd drunk up most of his pay at the tavern late that evening.

That's when Princess took to walking down to the bottom of the hill where the colored people lived. Angel was just a baby. She didn't understand there wasn't no milk to drink. When those folks in their little shacks by the creek heard the baby crying, somebody'd find milk for her. And they didn't have hardly enough food to feed their own young-uns. Princess never would take nothing to eat from 'em, said she wasn't hungry, thank you kindly. Lots of days, she didn't eat, even though the colored folks tried their dead level best to get her to.

They was good people. Like the Rev. Not like Jackson. And Jackson wasn't a good man that drink made into a monster, neither. Jackson Prentiss was a caged monster that drink set free.

"You're uglier than you ever were, too," he said. He made a *humph* sound in his throat. "Though I suppose scars all over your face are better than those bumps, full of pus, oozing all the time."

He talked smooth and proper-like now. Must have learnt that along the way as his preachin' made him famous. Oh, the man could preach, she'd give him that. When he was in the pulpit, he'd get all wound up and it was like people's eyes'd start to glaze over, and before long they's ready to follow the man down the barrel of a cannon. That was how Mama got hooked up with him. Princess remembered the look on her mother's face when they sat together on the hard bench in the little store-front church in Texas, 'fore Jackson moved the whole bunch of 'em to the hills of Arkansas. Mama'd looked … *dazed*. Shoot, they all had! Only one among 'em wasn't slack-jawed and droolin' was Princess, and she was just a little girl. Nothing Jackson Prentiss ever said moved her that way, had just the opposite effect, in fact. What she heard was nothing but meanness and spite and anger. Sometimes, it was like she could *see* it, his mouth was all full up with snakes and spiders, and she'd hide her head in her mother's skirt, scared plum to death.

"It used to make me sick just to look at you," he continued, his lip still curled in a snarl. "Turned my stomach so I felt like vomiting."

Princess looked at him from her quiet place and realized with a sudden thrill of joy that his words no longer hurt her. She didn't care anymore! He used to rail at her, call her all manner of hurtful things. And she hated that worse than the beatings. The things he said stabbed into her soul with a pain worse than his fist hittin' her face, smashing her lip or him kickin' her with his boot as she lay on the floor in front of him.

She didn't care now, though. The joy that filled her heart with that realization spilled out onto her face in a huge smile.

"What you grinning at? And what's the matter with you? Did the imps of hell steal that ugly, gruff voice of yours so you can't even cry out for mercy?"

"What are you doin' here, Jackson?" She had known he would come, knew it the way she knew so many other things. She just didn't know why. "What'd you come all this way for?"

"To watch you *die!*" He crossed the room in a rush then, as if he actually meant to attack her. But he stopped at the table, put his palms down on it and leaned toward her, his face twisted up in a mighty explosion of rage. "I came to watch them fry you, send you straight into the fires of hell on a bolt of lightning!"

But Jackson's rage broke over Princess like a wave crashing on a rock. It barely even got her wet.

"You ain't mad at me for killin' Angel," she said, her voice a velvet hammer. "You're mad 'cause I ran off, 'cause I *won.*"

"You call dying in the electric chair *winning?*"

A sudden fury filled Princess with a power so intense it might have hurled her right through the bars on the window and out into the world a free woman. Words spilled out her mouth in the overflow of it.

"Nobody ever told you no and got away with it, did they, Jackson? But *I* did. Nobody ever *left* you, did they? Nobody but *me!* Nobody ever took what was yours and never give it back. I took *Angel* from you. I *beat* you."

Jackson's face was a boiling black hailstorm. Temper stole his polish and left him sputtering the words of his raising.

"How you figure that, you dumb whore? You're the one *loved* that little'un. Snot-nosed brat didn't mean nothing to me but she did to *you*. You run off with her, then had one of your idiot fits, went nuts, and killed her. You're the one lost it *all!*"

"That what you think, it was a accident?"

"Even that Jew lawyer of yours knew you couldn't a'murdered that child. She might have figured out a way to prove it, too ..." He paused, then added softly, " ... but I *fixed her.*"

Gretchen Solomon had been tall and willowy, with coal black hair she kept in a tight bun low on the back of her head. She wore round, rimless glasses and had skin pale as death. She'd grabbed hold of Princess's case years ago and held on like a dog a'worryin' a chew rag—just would not let it *be*. Princess went along with whatever Miss Solomon wanted. If it made the woman feel good to fight so hard for her life, well, what was the harm in that? Princess had cried for days when she died.

"What do you mean you fixed her?" The dread swelled up in Princess's belly so quick she couldn't breathe. "She was kilt accidental, fell in front of—"

"A *bus!* In Boston. Long drive from Alabama to Boston. Danged hard to find where somebody's at in a big old city like that, too—least that's what I hear. 'Course, I never been there myself."

His voice got quiet, but so full of meanness and spite you could have used it as rat poison. "I also hear them sidewalks there get real slick when it rains. Not hard a'tall to fall right out into the street if you slip ..."

He whispered the final three words: "... or get *pushed!*"

Princess squeaked out a little scream. "She never hurt you! Why would you do such a awful thing?"

"The way this country's goin', that kike coulda fooled around 'til she finally got you off," he hissed. "And I am *done* watching the perverted ways of man fly in the face of the righteous will of Almighty God!"

Princess stared up at him, moon-eyed. That's what he'd wanted, that look on her face. He settled then, calmed, crawled back into the imposter he'd dressed in that fancy suit this morning.

"You didn't beat me," he purred, "any more than those nigger savages'll beat me." He leaned toward her again. "You're going to die for trying and *so are they!*"

A darkness gathered around Jackson as he spoke. Princess could see it and feel the chill from it and she shrank back in revulsion. Jackson fed on the look in her eyes the way a vulture feeds on rotting flesh. He smiled, a great gash that showed teeth he'd had fixed all shiny and white, and spoke with quiet intensity.

"That black monkey who put his hands on me today, he'll be sorry. I'll get to him. One day soon. I get to all the black monkeys that cross me." He put on a look of fake distress. "Being on death row and all, you probably don't watch a lot of television, do you? Pity. A couple of months ago it was all over the news. This nigger farmer outside Birmingham was trying to get all his neighbors to register to vote, and he up and got himself hung. I hear his two little girls watched him get strung up, cried and begged those white men to let him live."

He leaned closer and said softly. "Their daddy thought he beat me, too. Shame you're not going to live long enough to hear about all the others, the ones to come. We *will* stop them, you know. Those nigger savages are just looking to rape white women and they are sorely mistaken if they think white men are going to stand idle and let it happen. They will *not* take over this country. But before the stupid monkeys figure out we're smarter than they are, a whole bunch of them are going to die trying. And that's just fine with me."

Princess had no air to speak. She turned away from him and stared out the window at the town on the hillside. But it no longer looked charming and inviting. Just empty, like Jackson. All false front and phony. Open a door and step right through. Maybe the fake town wasn't empty at all, she thought, but full of false-front people just like Jackson.

He followed her gaze. "Wish you's free to walk down the street of that town instead of getting ready to die?"

"No, I don't wanna be there no more," she said in a hollow voice. "But you should go sometime. You probably got *family* up there."

"Oh, I got a family all right." He fairly leapt on the remark. "I have a wife and two children."

He'd aimed to surprise her and preened rooster-like when he did. "A boy and a girl, nine and seven." His speech lapsed into his sing-song preaching rhythm. "And I am raising them right. I am raising my children in the fear and admonition of Almighty God. I am preparing by son and daughter to be mighty warriors in the celestial war between good and evil, in the Armageddon that's coming, the final battle against the powers of darkness in America."

He seemed to tire of the game once he'd put her in her place and she was proper cowed. He straightened up and strode to the door, then turned and faced her before he walked out.

"I'm staying the night in a hotel and I'll be here tomorrow," he said. "I'll be sitting in the front row of the gallery so I can watch up close when they flip that switch and *fry you!*" He hurled the final words at her, a rock aimed at her head. "And the last thing you'll hear before you're damned forever, before your flesh is consumed in the sulfur flames of an eternal hell, will be my voice—*laughing!*"

The guard came into the room after Jackson left and put the manacles and leg irons on Princess. He led her down the hallway in the opposite direction, toward the Long Dark.

She wasn't aware of her surroundings, though, took no notice of the looks she got from the other prisoners as she passed their cells. Her mind was full of the images of two little girls begging for their daddy's life.

And of two other children, Jackson's private victims. A little boy and a little girl Princess couldn't rescue.

❖ ❖ ❖ ❖ ❖

Jonas was unusually quiet as they left the Iron House. He didn't comment at all on the even larger crowd of protesters that formed a gauntlet they had to drive through, waving their signs and shouting their slogans.

He finally spoke as they were nearing the highway back to town.

"Pull over," he said, pointing to the wide, sandy roadside. "Right here. Just pull off on the shoulder."

Mac did as Jonas directed.

"What's wrong? You sick?"

Jonas turned in the seat to face him. "Kill the engine. I want to talk."

"Can't we talk on the way into town? It's getting late and I've got a date for dinner tonight with Joy."

"You don't need to be driving when you hear what I've got to say."

Mac reached up and switched off the ignition. In the sudden silence that followed, they could hear the distant chanting of the protesters at the prison gate, though they couldn't make out the words. There was a rumble of thunder, too. Mac glanced past Jonas at the southwestern horizon. A storm front was moving in.

"Okay, I stopped. Now, what is it?"

"I got a confession to make," Jonas said. He must have seen the shocked look on Mac's face because he rushed ahead. "Oh, it's nothing like that, nothing bad. It's about Maggie and me—and Joy, when she was little."

Jonas settled back in the seat and looked sightlessly out the windshield.

"You was gone—almost right from the beginning—in Korea and it was just Melanie and Joy. You don't have no idea how she doted on that child!" He turned to look at Mac. "Dressed her up in lacy dresses every day like she was a doll. Now, it might have been 'cause Joy's hair was so short—remember? She looked like a little pixie."

Mac nodded.

"And maybe that was it, that Melanie didn't want folks to think Joy was a boy."

Mac smiled, thinking of Melanie, carefully dressing the little girl who had been a gift from God.

"But the trouble was …" Jonas paused. "And mind, I'm not criticizin'. It's just—she wouldn't *never* let that little girl get dirty! I'm serious. Joy dripped the littlest spot of catsup on her dress, or scuffed her shoes, and Melanie was a'cleanin' her up so fast it'd make your head swim."

Jonas turned and looked at Mac.

"You knew she left Joy with Maggie and me the two days a week she worked at the hospital. She'd a'stayed home and never left that child's side if it'd been up to her. But it was something about certification, keeping her skills up. And of course, the extra money helped."

"It was good of you and Maggie to keep her," Mac said, totally bewildered by where Jonas could possibly be going with all this.

"We never did tell Melanie about this part, it was just our secret. But when Joy was with us, we made it a special point to let that child get grubby as she wanted to! We let her play in the dirt! In the mud! We'd let her wallow around on the ground, a'wrestlin' with the dog, or wade through the puddles on the way to the barn to pet the calves. We went out and bought a couple of changes of clothes—pants and t-shirts, socks and shoes—and soon as Melanie pulled out of the driveway to go to work, we'd change Joy's clothes and let her have a good time."

Mac chuckled. "Jonas, that's a wonderful story! Why didn't you ever tell Melanie and me about it?"

"Oh, it just never come up right to say it without it sounding like we didn't think she was a good mama."

Mac started to reach for the ignition key, assuming Jonas had had his say, strange as it was.

"I'm not finished," Jonas said.

Mac settled back in the seat.

"About a hour before Melanie was supposed to come pick Joy up, we'd get her all cleaned back up again, of course. Fact is, sometimes she was so dirty, we had to hose her off 'fore we could even take her in the house! In the summertime, she used to love to run through the backyard sprinkler naked, and sometimes I'd chase her with the water hose, a'squirtin' her. Then we'd give her a bath, wash her hair, put her back in whatever pretty little get-up Melanie had her dressed in, and she'd be sittin' there neat as a pin when Melanie came through the door and give her a big hug."

"Like I said, Jonas, that's a wonderful story, or confession if that's what you want to call it. Sparked, I'm sure, by Princess's story about giving her little sister a bath in a washtub. But I don't get your point? Why did you have to tell me this right now? What's so urgent about it?"

"I told you the story so you'd know how I know what I'm about to tell you."

"Which is?"

Jonas took a deep breath. "Which is that Joy has a shooting-star birthmark on her right butt cheek."

"What?"

Jonas patiently repeated himself, speaking very slowly. "I said, Joy has a shooting-star birthmark on her right butt cheek. Exactly like the one Princess described. Maggie and I commented on it lots of times, only we thought it looked like fireworks. A red spot and a spray of red marks coming out from it."

"I don't understand what you're—"

"You probably never seen it, Mac. You shipped out so soon after you adopted her. And knowin' how shy Joy got when she was four or five years old, you didn't likely see her in the bathtub by the time you got back."

Mac suddenly felt like he was running through a knee-deep pond of molasses. He was struggling to get his mind around what Jonas was saying, but ....

"Well ... no, I didn't. I mean, Joy was a very private little girl, kept the bathroom door locked so—" He stopped, his mind spinning. "Jonas, what's your point? Or do you have a point, beyond the fact that Joy may have a birthmark similar to—?"

"Not similar, Mac. The same."

"Okay, the same. So?"

"Didn't you see it? You've been sittin' across the table from that woman every day this week—couldn't you tell?"

A wide hole opened up in Mac's belly, like the one Princess described, the one she called fear.

"Tell what?" He gasped out the words because he could *feel*—he couldn't see it yet, *wouldn't* see it yet—but he could feel the answer coming. The way you have a sense of something hurling toward you in the dark.

"How much Princess and Joy favor each other."

If Mac had been standing, he'd have staggered backward from the blow. As it was, he collapsed back against the car door, his eyes wide, a great roaring in his head.

That first day. The first time he ever saw Princess. She'd been facing the wall, and when she turned around toward him he'd been struck by how *familiar* she looked.

He couldn't place it then. Or wouldn't place it. Perhaps it was the scarred face and brown teeth that threw him off. But now it was undeniable. Joy was the image, a younger, red-haired version of Emily Prentiss.

He dragged in a ragged breath. After all, he'd always been good at spotting a *family resemblance.*

"Are you suggesting …?" He couldn't finish the sentence. So many thoughts were flitting around in his head he couldn't concentrate on any of them. "You don't think *Joy*—?"

"Is Angel, Princess's little sister?" Jonas finished for him. "Yeah, Mac. I do. The little sister she was supposed to have murdered." Jonas paused for a beat. "And from the look on your face, you think so, too."

No! His mind backed up from it, the way you instinctively draw your hand back when the dog you were about to pet snarls at you. No, it couldn't be!

"Jonas, that's insane. Why would Princess confess to a murder if she didn't do it?"

"Ain't that obvious? Not but one reason a person'd confess to murder. She owned up to killing that child because she believes she *did.*"

"Princess just *thinks* she killed Angel?"

"Mac, that woman's dipstick don't touch oil! Surely you can see that. She had a hallucination or something about killing her little sister, obviously really believes she done it. She's loony."

"You've only been around Princess for a little while, and I'll grant you she was more psycho today than usual, but—"

"There ain't no buts to it, Mac. She *is* psycho. We're talking about a woman who *lost* two candy bars in a sealed cell on death row."

Mac started to correct him. Tell him it was the Long Dark.

"And all that nutty talk 'bout a witch a'chasin' Joy. A *witch*, Mac. She's crazy. She's spent the past fourteen years believin' she murdered her little sister. If *that* ain't crazy, what is?"

Mac couldn't go there, wouldn't go there.

"Jonas, you're taking a little thing like a birthmark and some similarity ... you're not making good sense."

"That's where you're wrong, Mac. Good sense is exactly what I *am* makin'. You said she was arrested at a circus in Fisherville. That ain't but about forty miles from your church in Seagram, Arkansas. I bet if you looked it up and compared the dates—when she was supposed to have killed that child and when you found a child in your church the same age, with the same birthmark and the same red hair—I'm bettin' those dates'd match up snug as bookends. Shoot, Joy might even have mentioned Princess when she was little, and you just thought she was talkin' 'bout some storybook character."

"Okay ... okay," Mac stammered. "You're sayin' Princess left her little sister in my church, but she *thinks* she murdered her? So how'd she *think up* all that blood? She was covered in blood when they found her, and there was hair, her little sister's hair on—"

"You reckon anybody bothered to make sure that blood didn't come from Princess? That was 1949, Mac, in a little bitty Oklahoma town. Maybe Princess was hurt, in a car wreck, or had one of them seizures of hers and hit her head. Maybe that's what caused the hallucination in the first place."

Jonas sat back and shook his head. "I don't have all the answers here, Mac. But I'm tellin' you, if some woman all covered with blood come walking up to me and confessed that she'd just chopped somebody up with a ax—and that *somebody* was nowhere to be found—I don't think I'd be out there checking to make sure her story lined up."

"But the hair ...?" Mac's voice was shaking.

"I can't explain it all. But just because I don't understand exactly what *did* happen don't mean it *didn't* happen." Jonas thought for a moment. "I figure Princess must have cut all Angel's hair off for some reason. Joy's hair was short as a boy's when she was left in your church. Long as Princess said her little sister's hair was, you cut it off, there's gonna be hair all over *everything*."

Mac couldn't argue it. Couldn't argue any of it right now. His mind was in a blender set for puree.

But it did fit. God help him, it did *fit!* A giant puzzle dumped out of a box onto a table and all the pieces fell into place. And even if they hadn't, there was nothing, absolutely *nothing* that could explain away the uncanny resemblance between his beautiful red-haired daughter and the scar-faced woman who sat so profoundly still in a manila envelope room down the hall from the Long Dark.

And Princess knew it, too! Her instant fixation on Joy, her concern for Joy, her fear for Joy, the response she had to Joy's pictures. Somewhere deep in the poor woman's addled mind, she *knew* Joy was the beloved little sister she had lost.

"I understand all this is a shock, Mac," Jonas said kindly. "I don't blame you for being upset. But you see what I'm saying, don't you?"

Mac didn't speak, just stared straight ahead at nothing. A breeze kicked up and pushed fresh air with the smell of rain in it through the car. Mac's heart was thudding in his chest to the rhythm of the chanting in front of the prison. People protesting the execution of Emily Gail Prentiss for the murder of her little sister fourteen years ago.

The final piece. Chink! *Murder.* Deep in his soul Mac *knew*—just like that lawyer of hers had known—that Princess could never have murdered anyone.

"You do see it, don't you? Answer me, Mac."

Mac stopped breathing. The whole world and everything in it stopped, too. There was a pause, a beat, before it all cranked up and started moving again. During that shrapnel-sharp fragment of time between one heartbeat and the next, everything shifted. After it, nothing in Mac McIntosh's life was ever the same again.

"Yeah, Jonas." The words tore holes in his throat when he said them. "Yeah, I see."

Jonas let out a long breath. Then sucked in another one.

"I hate to be the caboose a'pushin' the train, but there's a lot at stake here. That poor woman is fixin' to *die*. We don't do somethin' quick, she's gonna get executed for killing somebody who ain't dead."

He stopped again, lowered his voice and said softly. "And there's Joy to think about, too. She don't even know she's adopted. What's all this gonna do to her?"

Another blow to the belly! Joy! What about *Joy*?

Mac groaned out loud. Jonas reached over and put his hand on Mac's shoulder.

"Look, why don't we just take this one step at a time?"

"Fine by me." Mac felt giddy, drunk. "So what's the first step?"

"I'd say we gotta verify that birthmark. Make sure I'm not just a old man with a bad memory."

"So what am I supposed to do? Walk up to my sixteen-year-old daughter and ask her to drop her drawers so I can check out her butt cheek?"

Jonas laughed, a strained laugh but it was genuine. Mac even smiled a little.

"I've got a better idea. Maggie and me, we took pictures of little Joy a'playing in the mud, running in the sprinkler. I can't imagine there's not a shot of that birthmark in one of them pictures."

"You've got *pictures?*"

"Whole rolls of 'em—dozens and dozens. 'Course we never showed 'em to you and Mel, but we kept 'em. They're in one of them boxes up in your attic." He paused. "*Somewhere* in your attic."

19

Mac pulled his car in beside Jonas's pickup truck in his driveway and the two men went into the house. Jonas called Guadalupe and asked about Maggie. Mac watched his face as he talked and knew things hadn't gone well on the home front while Jonas was at the Iron House talking to … his granddaughter's *sister*.

Mac and Melanie had spent hours wondering aloud about the child who'd been left marking up a hymnbook in the little church sanctuary. Did she have brothers and sisters? And what about her parents? What happened that they'd had to give her up, that they had no place for her? Now he knew the answers to those questions, at least some of them. Yes, Joy did have family, an older sister named Emily. Her mother had died bringing her into the world, so her older sister had had to raise her, loved her desperately, tried to do a good job, but she was just a child herself, an epileptic and … Okay, she was off in the head, too. And Mac believed Joy's father had been killed in a car wreck, Princess's version of what had happened to their father, not Jackson Prentiss's. Now that he'd seen the man up close, he had no trouble at all believing Prentiss lied about Princess's age, too, so she'd get the death penalty. The man was a monster in a human being suit.

It was absolutely horrifying that Jackson Prentiss had been Princess's and Joy's stepfather! It made him physically sick to think of the man anywhere near either one of them. He was profoundly grateful that Princess got her little sister away from Prentiss, gave her a home and a family.

Cold dread crawled into his belly, a lazy rat, and began to chew on his insides. How could he tell Joy all this? How could he tell her that the family she grew up in, the only family she'd ever known, wasn't her family at all, that the mother whose death she was grieving wasn't even the first mother she had lost? The poor kid's mother dies, then she finds out the woman wasn't really her mother in the first place, that—

Oh, Melanie, what have I done?

And what was he about to do?

Jonas hung up the phone, but sat with his hand on the receiver for a few seconds. Then he looked up at Mac.

"Maggie threw food all over Lupe," he said, his voice flat and toneless. "Called her awful names and splattered her with …" He couldn't finish.

"I'm sorry, Jonas."

"Now she's just sittin', though, wringin' her hands and shakin' her head and mumbling." He offered a little smile, then it drained off his face. "How pitiful is that! When you're thrilled your wife is sitting in a chair talkin' nonsense." He shook his head and stood up. "Never thought I'd see this day. You're young and in love—this ain't what you look forward to when you say you want to grow old together."

"Jonas, I—"

"Never mind, I'm just babblin' my own self. 'Fore long, it'll all be over."

Mac wasn't sure what he meant by that. Before he could ask, there was a rumble of thunder and the wind brushed the bushes up against the living room windows.

"It's stormed dang near ever' day this week," Jonas said, like he was glad to change the subject. "Lupe said she wasn't busy, didn't mind stayin' the evening." He looked at Mac. "Let's get to it, son."

Mac nodded.

"I'll get the boxes out of the attic and bring them down here," he said. "It's too hot to go through them up there and the light's not very good."

"That's a lot of boxes to haul down the stairs. I don't have no idea which ones those old pictures are in."

"We'll just keep looking until we find them."

Mac went upstairs to the hallway between Joy's room and the bathroom. A door in the ceiling there concealed the fold-out stairs to the attic. He climbed up into the dusty darkness, waved his arm around above his head until he connected with the string that turned on the only light, a bare bulb suspended from the high-pitched roof.

All manner of the family's flotsam and jetsam was assembled there, from old Christmas trees to ugly lamps and cast-off furniture. At one end were stacked eight to ten large cardboard boxes, way back in a corner with all manner of debris in front of them. They belonged to Jonas and Maggie, but had been moved to their daughter's house five or six years ago after a persistent leak in their own attic threatened to damage their contents.

Mac picked up the one box he could get to, hauled it to the stairs, and maneuvered his way down with it. Jonas was waiting at the bottom to take it from him. Before he headed up the stairs to start digging his way back to the other boxes, he heard Joy come in the front door.

"Hey, sweetheart, I'm up here," he called. She came to the bottom of the stairs and looked up at him.

"What are you and Grandpa doing up there?"

He stared down at her and didn't answer. He was fixated on her face, wondering how he could possibly have missed the resemblance to Princess. It was haunting.

"Daddy? You've got the funniest look on your face. What are you staring at? Do I have a zit on my nose?" She turned to her grandfather. "Will *you* tell me what you guys are doing?"

"We're looking for something your grandmother and I put in one of these boxes years ago," he said.

Mac stammered, "Why don't you go pick out a casserole and put it in the oven for dinner, okay?"

"Okay." She turned and disappeared.

Mac looked at Jonas.

"Yeah, I saw it," Jonas said softly. "Don't know why we need to find a picture. Her face alone ought to be proof enough."

He picked up the box and carried it down to the living room while Mac went back up into the attic to start moving things around. Getting the platform rocker and the antique sewing machine out of the way was going to take some doing.

By the time Mac and Jonas finally had all the boxes sitting at the far end of the living room, the casserole was ready to come out of the oven. Joy set the table and they all sat down to dinner. Mac would later remember that meal as the strangest one of his entire life.

They talked, but it was skating-on-the-surface-of-reality conversation while three gigantic elephants sat in the middle of the room. Each of them was preoccupied with something they weren't talking about; none was interested in anything the others had to say.

The storm hit halfway through dinner. Rain and wind pelted the house and the lights blinked on and off a couple of times. When the meal was over, Joy washed the dishes, Jonas dried them, and Mac put them away. Then Joy practically bolted up the stairs to her room, obviously grateful she's been spared the "date alone with Daddy" that had been planned for the evening. Within seconds, the voice of Neil Sedaka wailed, "They say that breaking up is hard to do. Now I know, I know that it's true …" from behind her closed door.

Something was wrong with her, all right. Mac wasn't so dense that he missed that. But whatever it was, it could wait. It wasn't a matter of life and death.

He and Jonas went into the living room and Jonas tore open the top of the first box. They searched it and the next one, went through box after box as the storm raged outside in the darkness.

They'd searched through five of the nine boxes when they came upon a box loaded with nothing but pictures. Hundreds of them! Pictures that dated back twenty-five years. There were shots of Jonas and Maggie right after they were married along with pictures of Melanie's older brother and sister who had been killed in the war. It seemed that perhaps a box of old pictures had been dumped into another box of more current shots because the oldest were on top. When they hit the strata of pictures of Melanie growing up, Mac took them tenderly and spread them out on the floor.

Then two things happened at the same time. They found their first picture of Joy as a child. And a clap of thunder banged harsh and loud and the electricity went off.

The men sat in the dark, startled. The house was silent; Joy's music had died in mid-wail. She hollered down from her room upstairs, "Daddy, what was that?"

"Lightning must have hit a utility pole, sugar," Mac called back. "You want me to come up and bring a candle?"

"Don't bother. I'm going to bed. 'Night Daddy, 'night Grandpa."

"Don't forget to turn off your hi-fi, or when the electricity comes back on, it's going to go off like an alarm clock."

So much for that heart-to-heart talk he'd been planning to have with Joy for three days now. It was only nine o'clock. Why was she going to bed so early? She'd been doing that a lot lately, seemed worn out all the time. But if she was sick, it obviously hadn't affected her appetite. She looked like she'd put on a little weight, too. Her cheeks were fuller.

"I s'pose all the batteries in your flashlights are dead, right?" Jonas said. "They're always dead in mine when I need 'em."

"Matter of fact, I think I might be able to find one that works." Mac stood and began to make his way across the dark living room. He returned in a few minutes with two flashlights and a handful of what Melanie called votive candles. He set them around on the coffee table and end tables, then went from one to the next, lighting them with wooden kitchen matches he struck on the gray stripe on the side of the box.

Soon, the room was aglow with flickering candlelight. Mac sat back down on the couch and reached for a handful of pictures that he would now have to look at one at a time with a flashlight.

Jonas reached over and touched his arm.

"Mac …"

Mac looked up. He sucked in his breath in a stifled gasp.

The floor of the room was a shimmering sea of shiny Melanie faces. The candlelight reflected off the glossy surfaces of the photographs Mac had set out of the box right before the electricity went out, creating a glimmering collage of images. Melanie as a little girl. As a teenager. At their wedding. Her senior picture. One image after another. Melanie. Melanie, Melanie. And the images fairly leapt off the floor every time lightning spilled into the room in a brief, blue-white glare.

Neither man spoke. They sat in silence, staring at a phenomenon they could never have created. Melanie was everywhere, all around them. Seemed so near Mac felt like he could reach out and touch her.

"You know what I used to do?" His voice was a ragged whisper. "I used to go out and sit in the car in the garage and scream. When Melanie was dying, I'd pound my fists on the steering wheel and yell until I was so hoarse I could barely talk. The car in the garage—that was the only place I could let go where nobody could hear me."

"Everybody suffers in their own way." Jonas sounded tired. And old. He'd always been so robust, so active that Mac never considered his age. But tonight, he looked and sounded every day of his seventy-four years.

"How do *you* deal with it, Jonas?"

"Well-meaning folks'll say to me, 'Oh, if that happened to me, I just couldn't *stand* it!' Or 'I could *never* lose a child.'" His voice suddenly had a bitter edge Mac had never heard before. "It ain't that you're stronger'n other people. It's just that when it happens to you, you ain't got no choice but to stand it."

He paused. "Princess understood that. She may be crazy, but she got that much. She talked 'bout how a body don't get to pick what life gives 'em, I figure that woman had a hard row to hoe, don't you?"

"She also said you *do* get to decide what you do about what life hands you." Mac shook his head sadly and looked out over the sea of shiny Melanie faces. "The poor woman thinks she *did* decide, that she's about to be punished for what she chose to do." Mac sighed. "And it's all illusion. I always wondered if crazy people knew they were crazy. I guess the answer's no, they don't."

The electricity came back on in a sudden, blinding light. In the instant, bright glare of it, the aura of Melanie in the room, the sense of her presence vanished. Mac felt a stab of pain, profound and real. She'd felt so close and now she was gone again.

The men sat stunned for a moment. Mac heard the compressor in the refrigerator kick on but didn't hear Joy's hi-fi. She must have turned it off.

"Don't guess we need these." He indicated his flashlight and held out his hand for Jonas's. "Give me yours and I'll—"

"Mac, look."

Jonas pointed into the box at a picture that now lay on the top of the pile, uncovered when Mac had grabbed a handful of pictures right before the electricity failed.

Mac reached into the box and took it out, and both men stared at it for a long time without speaking. The picture was a close-up shot of a naked child standing in a puddle of muddy water with her back to the camera. Clearly visible on her right butt cheek was a red spot with three red streaks spraying out above it. Like fireworks. Or a shooting star.

Mac looked from it to Jonas.

"You know, even with the uncanny resemblance between them, I might have been able to talk myself out of believing. Until now." He shook his head in awe and wonder. "Princess really didn't do it."

"The poor woman out there at the penitentiary needs to be in a nut house somewhere, not in a cell a-fixin' to die. You got to talk to that warden friend of yours, get him to put a stop to all this."

Mac hadn't processed the chain of events in his head that far out yet, and suddenly realized that Oran didn't have the authority to refuse to impose the death penalty!

"Jonas, only the governor can grant a stay of execution. And on what grounds? What proof do we have?"

"What about this picture?"

"This picture proves that my adopted daughter has a shooting star birthmark on her right butt cheek. So? Where could we possibly get proof that the little sister Princess supposedly killed had the same mark? And is that even proof—a birthmark? A birthmark's not the same as fingerprints."

Fingerprints. Mac froze.

He suddenly jumped up, ran out of the room and took the stairs two at a time to his upstairs bedroom. There was a cedar chest on the wall under the window. He moved the vase of artificial flowers off the top of it and the doily the vase had been sitting on, then lifted the heavy lid. The chest was made with partitioned drawer space in the top that swung out to reveal a big open area beneath.

Mac moved the drawers and shoved aside the "throws." That's what Melanie'd called them, hand-knit mini-blankets Maggie had made for her daughter over the years. He took out a stack of "for company" appliquéd pillowcases and sheets. Down in the very bottom of the chest was a small, wooden box. It was ornate, hand-carved. Mac had gotten it for Melanie in Korea and she'd always kept her greatest treasures there. He opened it slowly, reverently. There was a lock of curly hair the color of rust from Joy's first haircut, the child's first-grade report card, several small teeth the tooth fairy had purchased from the little girl for a dime slid under her pillow.

In the bottom of the box, enclosed in a layer of Saran Wrap, was a church visitor's card. On the back of it, scrawled in that strange backward-slanted handwriting, were the words: "Got no plase for her so plees giv her a gud hom."

Jonas spoke from the doorway. "Mac, what'd you come runnin' up here for?"

Mac got to his feet and held up the card for Jonas to see. "This is the note that was laying on the pew beside Joy when we found her in the church that morning. From the moment Melanie picked it up and read it, she treated it like it was gold, immediately wrapped it in a clean, white handkerchief. That note was the only proof we had that the child had been abandoned—because Melanie knew from the moment she saw Joy that God had given her to *us*, an answer to prayer."

"But what does that note—?"

"Melanie kept it wrapped in that handkerchief, then later wrapped it in plastic. Other than the judge during the adoption proceedings, nobody but Melanie ever touched it."

Jonas still looked blank.

"Don't you see—the person who wrote this note, her fingerprints could still be on it."

"Fingerprints last that long, do they? All these years?"

"Beats me, I don't know why they wouldn't." Mac looked hard at the note. "But there's something else I *know* lasts that long—handwriting."

He crossed to the doorway where Jonas was standing and switched on the bedside table lamp for better illumination. He held the note under the lamp.

"Have you ever seen stranger handwriting in your life?"

Jonas fished around in his pocket for his bifocals, parked them on his nose and held the note out at arm's length from his face.

"No, can't say as I have."

"Compare this handwriting to Princess's and—"

"How you goin' to get a sample of her handwriting to compare it to?"

"I guess I'll … well, I'll just have to figure out a way to get her to write something down for me."

Jonas straightened up.

"Mac, how you figure to get all this done in time? Come five o'clock tomorrow afternoon, they're going to strap that little woman in—what'd you call it? Sizzlin' Sadie?—and execute her."

The inside of Mac's head felt like a merry-go-round full of monkeys.

"I have to be *sure* before I get Oran involved in this! Have *proof.*" Mac didn't know he had a plan until he heard himself begin to describe it. "I'll go to him after my meeting with her tomorrow—"

"Morning?"

"On execution day, no visitors are allowed before noon or after 4 p.m."

Jonas groaned.

"And I'll explain it all and show him the handwriting samples. I'll make him understand that all we need is time to have fingerprints lifted off the note. A day, just *one day*, and we can prove that Princess left her little sister *alive* in my church, that she just *thinks* she killed her."

"Will he stop the execution if he believes you? I thought you just said he didn't have the authority."

Mac's face lit up. "He may not have the authority, but he has something even better. A malfunctioning electric chair! He told me

Monday the electric chair's so old, it might not even work. I'm sure he's got it up and running fine by now. But he could use that as an *excuse*. If he wanted to bad enough, he could delay the execution until after midnight. Then the state will have to ask the court for a new death warrant, which they can't do until Monday morning when court's in session. All we need's a few hours."

"Would Oran agree to that?"

Mac thought about it.

"For Princess, I think he might." His voice hardened. "But if he won't, I'll make him. I'll threaten him. I'll tell him I'm going to march out to all those protesters at the front gate and tell them the story—tell them I can produce *alive* the person Emily Prentiss is about to be executed for murdering. No telling what those people would do with that kind of information! I'll tell him I'm going to give a Pulitzer Prize-winning story to a reporter friend of mine, all about how the warden of the Oklahoma State Penitentiary for Women had *proof* a death row inmate was innocent and he executed her anyway." The acid in his next words would have burnt a hole in boot leather. "I'll tell him I will make it my life's work to see to it he lands in a cell on the Long Dark himself, for the *murder* of Emily Gail Prentiss."

"You'd do that?"

"Execution shouldn't be the penalty for lunacy."

Jonas put his hand on Mac's shoulder. "I'll go with you, son. We'll do this together."

Mac was so touched he didn't trust himself to speak, just nodded, turned and headed back downstairs. At the front door, he gave the old man a hug goodbye instead of a handshake.

"If all my circuits weren't so fried, I'd probably see some ironic humor in this," he said with a little laugh. "Tomorrow afternoon, I'm going to keep the state of Oklahoma from killing Emily Prentiss, and at the elders' meeting tomorrow night, I'm going to execute the *Reverend* David McIntosh."

Jonas just shook his head and stepped out into the night. A moment later he was back. "Joy parked that car, that 'Mr. Wilson,' behind my truck; she's got me blocked in."

Joy's purse was hanging by the front door. Melanie had gotten Mac to put up the "handbag hook" after Joy was late for school three times in one week because she couldn't find her purse.

"Keys are in there," Mac said and went into the living room to start cleaning up the mess of pictures and boxes. But when he looked up, Jonas was standing in the living room doorway.

"I didn't mean to be nosey," he said uncomfortably. "But this fell out when I pulled out the keys. Thought you might ought to see it."

He held out a savings account passbook with a piece of paper stuck in it. Mac took the book, opened it and read the paper. It was a withdrawal slip. Joy had emptied out her savings account that afternoon. What did Joy need $100 for?

◆ ◆ ◆ ◆ ◆

It didn't do any good to stick her fingers in her ears. She'd tried that. The sound was coming from inside her head. Intellectually, she knew it was an auditory hallucination. She could quote the definition right out of a medical textbook, but the knowing didn't change anything. The sound was still there. A baby was crying in the distance. A newborn, wailing pitifully.

Wanda Ingram slowly sat up, pulled the sheet back and turned to lower her feet to the floor. What was the point in staying in bed? The crying that had awakened her from her drug-induced stupor would keep her from going back to—

What was that? When her feet touched the floor, it was *wet*. There was water a couple of inches deep in her bedroom! Had the toilet overflowed? The water heater ruptured?

She reached for the bedside lamp, but had the presence of mind to lift her feet up off the floor before she touched the switch. She could be electrocuted touching a lamp with her feet in—

She flipped the switch.

And then she screamed. It was a horrified howl that ended in a little hiccup when she clamped her hand over her mouth.

Her floor wasn't covered in water. It was covered in *blood*. Bright red blood. She could suddenly smell the copper stench of it, the reek, like wet pennies, peculiar to large amounts of fresh blood. She froze, sat with her feet stretched out in the air in front of her, staring at the bloody floor in wide-eyed horror.

Her breath came in hitching gasps, her hands began to shake violently. She turned quickly and scooted her feet back onto the bed. They smeared blood all over her sheets and on the pale pink chenille bedspread, the only thing besides a disfigured face she'd brought back with her from in Korea.

She shook her head back and forth slowly. No. This couldn't be. It wasn't really … She scooted back up against the headboard and grabbed it, as if her bed were a raft set adrift, floating all by itself in a sea of blood that was growing deeper by the second.

"It's not *real* …" She whispered the words, then dragged in a ragged breath and chanted louder. "Not-real-not-real-not-real-not-*real!*"

She wanted to close her eyes, believed that if she'd just close her eyes and keep them closed for a few seconds, when she opened them again, the blood would be gone. But she couldn't even make herself blink, let alone close her eyes.

The level of blood on the floor slowly rose, inched its way up the side of the dresser, swallowed the legs of the nightstand.

And the babies cried louder. The sound that had awakened her was the distant wail of a lone child. But the crying was no longer coming from a single child. More than one baby was crying now, each with a unique voice. Like a nursery full of newborns, all startled awake at one time.

It grew louder and *louder!*

Wanda clamped her hands over her ears and finally managed to squeeze her eyes shut. She screamed out in a shrieking wail, "Noooooo!"

The sound stopped instantly; replaced by an eerie silence.

Then a single baby began to cry, the ragged bark of a first breath. It wasn't a distant sound, though. It was as if the baby were right there in the room with her, dragging air into its lungs for the first time and wailing its entrance into the world.

"There, there," somebody whispered. "It's Okay. Mamashere. Mamasgotcha. Shhhh."

The soothing voice sounded familiar. Calming. And it quickly hushed the crying infant.

Wanda carefully opened her eyes.

There was no blood on the floor anymore, but the room had grown chilled.

Melanie McIntosh stood beside Wanda's bed, cradling an infant in her arms. Wanda recognized the child. It was the little boy who had been born alive, the one who'd cried. The one whose neck she'd squeezed until he stopped crying, stopped breathing.

Melanie wore a white nightgown, with a high neck buttoned all the way up and long sleeves with lace on the cuffs. Her honey blond hair was longer than Wanda remembered it. It hung in curls on her shoulders.

She wasn't looking at Wanda but down at the little baby in her arms. She shook it gently, that special way mothers do, and hushed it with her whispered, "Shhhhhhh." The baby finally lay still in her arms and she lifted her eyes to Wanda.

"Don't you just love to look at a sleeping baby?" she said. "So quiet and peaceful."

Wanda stared at the woman who'd spoken to her, certain it was Melanie. And equally certain the apparition wasn't real. Another, more elaborate hallucination. But the image *seemed* so real, so … *Melanie*. Perfect. No, not perfect. Something was off, different. Wanda couldn't put her finger on exactly what it was, but something wasn't right.

The room grew colder and the chill seemed to be coming from Melanie. The way a space heater emanates warmth, Melanie gave off cold.

"Here," Melanie said. "Would you like to hold him? He's sleeping soundly now."

Wanda shrank back. She didn't want to offend Melanie, so she blurted out, "I might wake him up and he'd start crying again." She shook her head. "I can't stand that crying."

"He was only crying because he was alone. As soon as I picked him up and cuddled him, he went right off to sleep."

Melanie stepped closer and the cold moved with her.

"You do know that's why they're crying, don't you?" she said. "They're alone and frightened. They don't have any mommies to look after them, to pick them up and comfort them. So they cry. You did know that, didn't you?"

"No," Wanda stammered.

"And you do know that they're not going to stop crying until somebody holds them and soothes them?"

"But ... who's going to do that?"

"Right! Who's going to do that? You took them away from their mommies and now they're all alone."

Somewhere inside Wanda, the voice of the little reason she had left cried out that she had to stop talking to this figment of her imagination, had to stop participating in her own lunacy. But she ignored it. The illusion of Melanie was better than no Melanie at all.

"I didn't mean to leave them alone, Mel. I didn't *know*. I was just trying to help. Those girls, they were so desperate, so hopeless. What else could I do?"

"Wanda, honey, you should have sent their mommies with them, to take care of them," Melanie said.

And Wanda saw then part of what wasn't right about her. Melanie's tongue was black, solid black.

"I don't know what you mean."

"Yes, you do, Wanda. You know exactly what I mean. Those mothers got up and walked away from here and left *you* with *their* babies. Lonely, crying babies. You shouldn't have let all those mothers abandon their babies to cry, endlessly cry, inconsolable. You should have kept them *both* here, the mothers and their babies."

Melanie sighed. Her breath frosted in the cold air gathered around her.

"It's too late now, though. The mothers are gone and the babies are here and you're just going to have to listen to them cry."

"But I *can't* Melanie," Wanda wailed. And her breath frosted when she spoke, too. "I can't listen to them cry, night after night. And there's other things, too. Dead babies lying ... I came to talk to you about it, came to the—"

"I know you came to me. Why do you think I'm here?"

"Melanie, stay here with me. Please, don't go away again."

"I can't do that Wanda. But if you do what I tell you, we can be together."

"What do you want me to do?"

"My baby girl, Joy, she came to see you yesterday."

Wanda looked pleadingly into Melanie's eyes. "Did I do wrong? I promised myself after—" She indicated the baby sleeping in Melanie's arms. "—that I'd never do it again. Should I have said no?"

Melanie smiled a wide smile and Wanda saw it wasn't just her tongue that was black. Her lips were black, too.

"If my Joy wants to send her baby away, I'm glad you agreed to help her."

Wanda sighed, relaxed.

"The baby's a girl, a granddaughter, and you don't want her to cry, do you? Cry and cry so you never get any sleep?"

When Wanda looked stricken, Melanie leaned closer and whispered softly. "Then you can't leave the baby alone. You have to send her *mother* away with her."

Melanie reached out and placed her hand tenderly on Wanda's shoulder. It was as cold as a stone in the night. "I want my baby here with me. My baby Joy and my baby granddaughter. You could send them to me. Or …" She smiled broadly. "You could *bring* them. That way you and I could be together."

When Wanda didn't respond, Melanie continued in that calm, soothing voice of hers. "You're so tired, Wanda. Why don't you leave this place where you can't sleep? Come here with me and it will be peaceful and quiet. Forever."

"Forever," Wanda repeated.

"You know what you have to do, don't you, Wanda?" Melanie cooed.

Wanda looked up into her eyes. She remembered that they were a warm, amber shade of brown. But in this light, they were black holes in Melanie's face with shiny things way down in the depths of them, things Wanda didn't want to see.

Reason cried out in desperation, "Wanda Jean Ingram, this is not *real!* You know it's not! Get ahold of yourself! This is just a—" Then Wanda silenced reason. Just like she'd silenced that little baby. She put her fingers around the last slender thread of rationality inside her and squeezed. Held on tight while it struggled, until it stopped wiggling, stopped breathing. Squeezed until her sanity was stone cold dead.

"I know what I have to do," Wanda told Melanie. "Bring you Joy and the baby."

Wanda heard the soft thumping sound Blackbeard made when he jumped up onto the bed. He wasn't allowed on the bed, but this time she turned around, lifted him up and cuddled him in her arms. He felt warm in the bone-chilling cold.

When she turned back, Melanie was gone.

But it was quiet. So quiet Wanda could hear the ticking of the alarm clock on the night stand. She reached over and flipped the switch on the lamp and plunged the room into darkness. Then she snuggled up with Blackbeard, shivering under the warm chenille bedspread. The soft hum of his purring sent her quickly off to sleep.

20

PRINCESS SAT ON THE BUNK IN her cell and watched the light drain out of that little patch of sky held captive all these years by the barred window high on the wall. Thoughts started to steal over her mind as dark as the lengthening afternoon shadows. As blackness slowly filled the two-by-two-foot square above her, Princess struggled to keep it from filling her soul as well.

It was all moving so fast and her head was so full up with things. It'd been dang nigh empty for years. Day in, day out, the sun come up, the sun went down and nothing happened in between. Absolutely nothing. There'd been *years* of that.

But now! More had happened to her in the past four days than in all the days she'd spent in the Long Dark put together! It'd give her enough to think about for another fourteen years. But she didn't have another fourteen years. She didn't have another twenty-four hours. This time tomorrow, she'd be dead.

The realization hit her with such force she was suddenly sick. She jumped up and ran across the cell to the toilet on the far wall and vomited, gagging and heaving until she was weak and panting and tears slathered her cheeks.

She flushed the mess down but the odor lingered. She could smell it even after she sat heavily on the side of her bunk again. So much for the "last meal." It'd been good goin' down, a chocolate ice cream and a McDonald's hamburger and fries—though they was cold. But it had sure scalded her throat coming back up. She better not try to eat tomorrow.

But if she didn't, she'd never eat again.

Never.

Right now that was the terriblest word she knew. *Never* sucked all the air out of her lungs and left her gasping like a minnow on a flat rock.

What had she done? What had she got herself into?

Her heart slugged violently in her chest. She could smell the sticky-sweet odor of her own sweat and she drew breaths in hitches. The rip in her side was so huge right now she was about to come completely apart, the top of her not attached to the bottom of her at all.

Death crawled into her cell then to keep her company in her final hours, a bloated, hairy-legged spider lurking in the corner just out of sight, its fangs dripping, waiting to take her. Its putrid stench filled the air, the rank stink of a dead animal.

She whimpered, wrapped her arms around herself and rocked back and forth on the bed in the sudden chill, making sounds a baby rabbit might make if it got caught in a threshing machine.

For all the years she'd sat in this cell, she hadn't had no say about nothing. But she did now. Things had changed in the past few days. She might be able to alter the course of her future. If she chose to, she could take hold of it and maybe write a whole new ending. She might be able to save herself!

Save *herself.*

The thoughts in her whirling mind stopped spinning so abruptly they slammed into the back of one another like train cars crashing into a stalled engine.

This wasn't about *her!* It never had been.

"That's just scared talkin'," she said aloud. Her husky voice sounded shaky, but she kept speaking and it grew stronger with each word. "Just fear a-babblin', talkin' things it don't know nothin' about! Can't listen to scared. It *lies.* Scared lies and mad lies and hate lies. But love *don't* lie." She lifted her head and shouted into the shadows, "My last night on this earth, I ain't gonna listen to *lies!*"

Her *last* night. That's what it was. The shakes started to come back but she glared at 'em and they run off and hid.

Last night? Fine then—she'd fairly well better make the best of it!

She shook her head and sat up straight. The pounding of her heart slowed; she stopped panting. Now that she could think, she concentrated hard, tried to figure what she ought to do, how she should spend the precious currency of seconds and minutes she had left.

She already knew how she shouldn't spend them—thinkin' 'bout Jackson Prentiss!

She'd already wasted precious minutes—all right, *hours*—thinking about him when she come back to her cell from his visit. Was so tore up over what he'd said, she almost didn't want that last dinner Talbot brought her.

But she couldn't do nothing about Jackson. She couldn't help all those people he was hurtin' and was gonna hurt. She had to just ... let it go.

And concentrate on good things.

Like ... well, she had some goodbyes she needed to say. And she wanted to sing—if she could. Her mouth bein' so dry, she wasn't sure she could make much sound a'tall come out of it.

And she wanted to open the jewel box of memories and run her fingers through the piles of precious lighted stones, feel the warmth of their throbbing colors on her face. Live every one of those moments over again.

One more time.

She leaned back against the cold wall and breathed in the stillness and silence. Then she began to sing. At first her voice was raspy, but it soon smoothed out and she belted out the songs she'd made up in her head over the years, one after the other. She sang in a language nobody but she understood, the melodies odd and somehow Irish-sounding.

In her mind, she wasn't alone in the cell anymore. She sung every song to her precious Angel, pictured the child lying warm in her arms, snuggling close, looking up at her with those caramel-colored eyes.

Princess sang for hours until she was so hoarse she could sing no longer. Then she examined her jewels, picked up each precious one and squeezed all the light and love and joy out of it. She drank all her memories dry, and sat on her bed smiling and full.

When her joy vanished, it happened in an instant.

A huge, menacing darkness formed in her mind between one heartbeat and the next, a swirling, horrifying madness so enormous it wouldn't all fit into her head at one time. Her face frozen in a monstrous cramp of terror, she sucked in a breath to scream, but horror tore such a huge hole under her ribs the air whooshed out and she couldn't make a sound.

The madness was *coming*. Rumbling, roaring, thundering toward her in a freight-train rush of utter destruction. The Big Ugly was out there in the darkness somewhere. It would rip open the sky, chew up the world and *kill people*. She could see their mangled, unrecognizable bodies and hear their screams.

Princess was held captive by the vision, riveted by the hideous savagery of it. Only one power on earth was strong enough to grant release and finally it came for her. A jerking, flopping, foaming-at-the-mouth fit stole her mind away from the Big Ugly and left her unconscious on her bunk, soiled and sweating as the sun began to bleach the night out of the sky on the last day of Emily Gail Prentiss's life.

❖ ❖ ❖ ❖ ❖

As soon as Jonas opened the front door of his house, he heard Maggie. Her voice came from the bedroom, where she was screaming random obscenities, whatever filthy word happened to drop into her mind.

Even now, it still hit him like a fist in the belly.

He went into the kitchen where Lupe was putting the finishing touches on a pan of her homemade enchiladas. The woman was a saint, couldn't stand to "just sit," so for the price of a caretaker for Maggie, he also got a part-time housekeeper and cook.

"Mr. Cunningham," she said, and looked relieved to see him. "You can have these for supper *mañana*." She set the pan of enchiladas in the refrigerator. "Just heat them up in the oven."

Then she looked at him sadly, "Your wife, she has had a bad day, sí?"

"I'm sorry. You should have called me."

Lupe shook her head. "It is just hard to see her this way. I do not want to live so long, if this is what it will be like."

"She wouldn't have wanted to, either," Jonas said softly.

"Before I go, I need to warn you about something." She told him she'd found Maggie that afternoon in the bathroom about to take a handful of random pills. "I almost had to fight her to get them away from her. She said they were her *medicína*. You need to be very careful; she might try it again."

For a long time after Lupe left, Jonas sat at the kitchen table, stunned by the providential—or so it seemed—turn of events. If he gave Maggie the sleeping pills now, Lupe would be the first to point out that the poor woman had almost poisoned herself before. No one would ever suspect that Jonas had given her a lethal dose on purpose.

His heart began to pound and he broke out in a cold sweat.

Could he *really* poison his wife? Could he actually ... *kill* her?

As if she could hear him thinking about her, Maggie began to call his name, in a sing-song whine that sounded like a little girl.

"Joonas, oooh, Jooonas!"

He got up and headed toward the bedroom. As he got nearer, he smelled a rank, disgusting odor.

Maggie was sitting in bed with something ... *brown* smeared all over her.

Oh no!

"Maggie, what have you *done?*"

She didn't answer, just looked down and smeared more of the substance on her arm, like it was hand lotion!

"Maggie, don't!" He rushed across the room. The stench was horrible. She'd made a mess in her diaper and was *playing* in it like a two-year-old. He didn't even know where to begin to clean her up. It was everywhere. On her nightgown, in the bed. In her hair!

"Come on, sweetheart, let's go take a bath—what do you say?"

She looked at him sweetly and dropped the F-word, a word his sweet wife couldn't even bear to hear. But the reality of life was that this shell of a human being was no longer his sweet wife. She was somebody he didn't know, somebody she'd never have wanted to become.

He went into the bathroom and ran a bath of warm water and put her sweet-smelling bubble bath in it. Then he went back to the bedroom, where she was still entertaining herself with her own …

He took her by the arm and helped her out of bed, stripped the filthy nightgown off her and eased her down into the warm water. She splashed in it like a baby, sending water all over the floor. Then he took the sheets and covers into the laundry room, along with her nightgown. He had to rinse everything off in the big laundry sink before he put it in the washing machine. It'd take at least three loads to clean it all.

After he checked on Maggie, who was now sitting listlessly in the water, batting at the bubbles, he got cleaning materials out of the cabinet under the sink in the kitchen and cleaned up the bed frame, the nightstand, the headboard and the spots on the hardwood floor. He put clean sheets and pillowcases on the bed and got another blanket out of the hall linen closet.

Armed with a fresh nightgown, he went into the bathroom to clean her up. She still had big chunks in her hair, and she never liked for him to wash her hair. Lupe had gotten her ready for bed and had let her hair down. So the mess in her beautiful white locks was heartbreaking.

He poured water over her head out of a pitcher, shampooed and rinsed, over and over. She cried when he got water in her eyes, fought when he soaped her head. It must have taken close to an hour to get her cleaned up and back in bed.

Jonas was worn out; Maggie was wide awake.

"Jonas," she said softly. He was changing into his pajamas and had his back to her. Hearing his name like that sounded so "normal" his eyes flooded with tears. Oh, to be able to turn around and Maggie would be there, his Maggie, and they could talk about their day. He'd tell her about Princess and Joy and what he and Mac had to do tomorrow. He'd tell her about finding the savings account passbook in Joy's purse, and ask what she—

"Jonas, did you forget?"

He turned around and she was sitting on the side of the bed, her feet on the floor like she was about to get up. She had that deceptively lucid look on her face.

"Forget what, sweetheart?"

"You did, didn't you? You forgot that today's our anniversary!"

She put her head in her hands and started to cry.

He went around the bed and sat down beside her and put his arm around her shoulders.

"I didn't forget, sugar! Why, I sent you candy and flowers—don't you remember?"

She stopped crying and looked up at him, tears streaming down her cheeks. "You did?"

"Why, of course I *did!* I wouldn't forget something as important as the anniversary of when my best friend became my wife." He choked on the words, and she responded to the emotion in his voice.

"Oh, thank you, honey." She leaned over and kissed him on the cheek. "Five years—it's gone by so fast! But we've got the rest of our lives to spend together."

If she says she wants to grow old with me, I'll lose it! I will!

She didn't, just tried to get to her feet.

"Hey, where you going?"

"I've got to go check on the baby, silly. I'll be right back."

"Tell you what, why don't you just settle yourself in bed and I'll check on the baby."

"You're a sweetie," she said cheerily. He helped her back under the covers, then went to push the laundry through. He'd bought Maggie a clothes dryer Christmas before last. She'd got where she didn't like to walk on the grass, even with shoes on, to hang clothes on the line in the back yard. It had seemed like quite an extravagance at the time, but once he'd dried his face a time or two on towels that felt all fluffy like, he knew it wouldn't be long before dryers caught on, before most everybody had one.

He came back into the room quietly, thinking she might be asleep. He still had to clean up the mess in the bathroom before he could go to bed. She was still awake, and he'd only made it a few steps into the room when she started screaming.

"Who are you? What are you doing in my bedroom?" She shrieked, then started calling, "Jonas, help, Jonas! There's a man in here!" She had the sheet and blanket pulled up to her neck and she was looking at him with such abject terror that he couldn't stand it. He turned on his heel and left the room. She called and called for Jonas, but he didn't answer. He just sat at the kitchen table, staring at nothing, waiting for her to fall asleep.

It was after 2 a.m. before he finished the laundry and cleaning, and by then he was emotionally and physically exhausted. Lying in the dark, listening to his Maggie breathe, he pretended for a little while that she was normal, life was good and everything was going to be okay. But he'd crossed over, gone beyond some point and he couldn't return. His mind was set.

Tomorrow, Mac was going to set an innocent, crazy woman free.

And so was he.

Friday

May 10, 1963

21

I DON'T THINK WE'RE IN KANSAS ANYMORE, Toto.

The piece of dialogue popped into Andy Cook's head and he smiled. Yeah, he and Dorothy had a lot in common. They'd both been dropped into a whole new world by a twister. Except in his case, it was more than one twister.

As a weather forecaster on the 10 o'clock news at KLBK-TV in Lubbock, Texas, he'd predicted several tornadoes during the 1962 spring storm season using nothing more sophisticated than the data provided by surface and upper air weather balloons. KLBK didn't have a weather radar system.

And he'd been right on every one. That skill—which often was one part knowledge and nine parts instinct—had catapulted him out of the bush league.

Andy set down his small box of belongings on the desk in his brand-new office and tried not to look awed when he glanced around.

He'd sweated bullets trying to land this job. Only the best and the brightest meteorologists ended up in Oklahoma City or Kansas City. That's where the big National Weather Bureau offices were located, because those places were home to the country's most violent weather.

"How you liking Oklahoma so far?" said a coworker standing in the doorway. "And don't tell me it's just like West Texas or I'll come up side your head with a slide rule."

In fact, it was remarkably like West Texas. Same featureless prairie, flat and empty. Same horizon-to-horizon visibility, unobstructed by hills or trees. In both places, you could see the storms forming in the west by mid-morning, huge clouds building on top of each other in the sky, waiting to swoop down like invading hordes of barbarians on the unsuspecting and the ill-prepared.

It was the task of the National Weather Bureau to figure out which of the mighty super-cells that swept across the plains were likely to spawn killers so they could warn the public about the most dangerous storms on the planet.

And he'd seen thunderheads building in the southwestern sky as he drove in to work this morning. He didn't like the color of them, a sort of yellowish green. They were already up to 25,000, maybe 30,000 feet and looked ugly.

"I'll pass on the concussion if you don't mind," Andy said. "What I'd really like is to get a look at the WSR-57 radar. I've been dying to see one."

"Down the hall, first door on your right," the man said.

Andy sat down at his desk and began inspecting the daily surface weather balloon report, then dug around for the most recent upper-air balloon readings. He didn't like what he saw. Before he even unpacked the brass nameplate his co-workers in Lubbock had given him as a going-away present, Andy headed down the hall to the radar room.

◆ ◆ ◆ ◆ ◆

Princess didn't eat any breakfast. As soon as she came to, she went to the slit in the door and hollered until Talbot came to see what she wanted.

"I had me a fit last night," she said sheepishly. "I ... messed myself and I need to get cleaned up."

Talbot's voice was kind.

"I'll bring you a fresh uniform when I bring your breakfast."

"Just bring me the clean dress, you don't mind. I ain't sure I could eat nothing."

Talbot brought her a fresh shift that smelled of bleach. She unlocked the door and went to step inside, but Princess just extended her hand through the partially open door for the dress. She was embarrassed, always was when she made a mess.

Once she got herself cleaned up, she washed her soiled dress out in the sink, wrung it out best as she could, and hung it over the pipe that ran along the wall.

I ain't gonna live to see that dress dry.

She waited for the horror of the thought to crash into her chest, but felt nothing at all. Maybe she was in shock. More likely, though, she just had other things to think about now. She was going to see the Rev today, the last day, and she'd find out about his conversation with his baby girl.

And suddenly it was lunchtime. It had been breakfast, and then it was lunch, one minute and then the next. How could the time go by so fast like that? She didn't remember any of it, didn't know what she'd done with those precious minutes and seconds. They was just gone. That scared her almost more than what she'd be facing in a few hours.

Then Talbot was outside her door again.

"You gonna eat any lunch today, Prentiss?"

"Naw, I don't …"

This would be the *last* last meal.

"I guess I'd like me a little something." Meals were served in a rotation every prisoner knew. It had varied little over the course of her fourteen years of confinement. Fridays were beans-and-cornbread days.

"When I come back for your tray, it'll be time to cut your hair," Talbot said.

Princess knew they'd have to shave her head. She'd been told all about it a couple of other times, before some appeal put off her execution date. But they'd never even gotten close to the actual cutting and it had slipped her mind they'd have to. How could something like that slip your mind, like maybe she'd forget all about dying this afternoon!

The beans and cornbread tasted like rocks and sawdust. Her mouth was so dry, it was hard to swallow so she ate very little. But it settled her, got rid of the empty ache in her stomach.

She slid the tray out through the slit in the door and a few minutes later, Talbot and that other guard, the man Princess didn't like, Hank Bradley, came into her cell. Bradley carried a pair of scissors, a straight razor, and a shaving brush and soap, and Talbot carried a basin of water. They both set their loads down on the table.

"Put your hands behind your back," Bradley grunted. Princess obeyed and the guard whipped out the handcuffs clipped to his belt and fastened them around her thin wrists. Then he yanked her toward the chair.

"Hey!" Talbot said. "No need to get so rough. You scared she's gonna jump you or something?"

"I ain't afraid of a dead woman," he spat back.

But he was, too. Princess could feel it, the fear a comin' off him like heat off a wood stove. She wasn't what he was afraid of, though. Dying was what put the scared in his belly. He probably hadn't never been so close to somebody about to die and it give him the trembles.

"This won't take long," Talbot said. "You just sit still and it'll be over 'fore you know it."

"No need to rush," Princess said, and was surprised that her voice shook a little. "I ain't in no hurry to lose my hair."

Talbot picked up the scissors, reached out and lifted a lock of Princess's hair and snipped it off right at her scalp. She deposited the hunk of blonde hair on the table top and reached out for another.

Princess cringed back, but Talbot was all business. Not mean, just efficient. As she lifted Princess's hair by clumps and snipped them off, Princess remembered another time, the sound of running water and the feel of warm curls in her hand. Pretty curls, not limp hunks of blond hair like hers.

As Talbot cut off one piece of hair after another, she and Bradley chatted about their favorite television westerns. Talbot favored

Rawhide and *Wagon Train*. Bradley liked *Gunsmoke* best, said he didn't think that someone called Miss Kitty was ever going to land somebody else called Matt Dillon. Talbot was sure she was a'goin' to someday.

Snip. Snip. Snip.

With every snip, Princess felt more naked and exposed. And anonymous, like she wasn't a person at all anymore, just a doll like the big ones she saw in a store window when she and Angel were running free.

Angel. She tried hard to picture the child's face, to think about her and not the cold metal next to her scalp. But she couldn't manage to focus, couldn't hold onto a memory to sink into.

Then it was done. Talbot wrapped a towel around her neck, wet her hands and rubbed them over the stubble of hair on Princess's head.

"Now be still; I don't want to nick you."

She rubbed the wet shaving brush on the soap until she had a lather, then spread it on Princess's wet head. A dribble of cold water slid down the back of her almost-bare scalp, under the towel and down between her shoulder blades. Water began to run down her forehead and she squeezed her eyes shut.

Then she felt the cold razor on her head. She jumped, couldn't help it, and felt it dig into her scalp.

"Be still!" Bradley said, reached out and grabbed her shoulders to hold her.

Soap in the cut stung, but Princess didn't move, just sat there, trembling inside. Three swipes on one side, one down the middle and three on the other. A couple of touch-up swipes and then Talbot removed the wet towel and wiped off Princess's head with it.

"That little cut'll stop bleeding in a minute or two," she said. She stopped then, bent down and looked into Princess's eyes. "You hold on now, hear?"

Princess nodded, but didn't speak. Then the guards gathered up their equipment, scooted the pile of hair on the table off into the soapy water in the pan, unfastened the handcuffs and left Princess alone in the cell.

She sat quietly in the chair for several minutes after they left, didn't move. Then she lifted her hand and ran it slowly over her bald head. Big tears filled her eyes as she felt the cold, clammy skin there and touched the spot where the razor had nicked her. She blinked and the tears spilled down her cheeks. But she didn't cry. What was the point? This certainly wasn't the worst thing that was going to happen to her today.

◆ ◆ ◆ ◆ ◆

Mac wasn't prepared for the sight of Princess bald. She'd looked fragile before, but there was a vulnerability to the frail, hairless woman sitting at the table that broke his heart.

He knew she saw his shock and he wanted to make light of it, but couldn't pull it off. Well, he'd promised he wouldn't lie to her. He'd keep that promise for a few more minutes anyway.

"You said they'd cut your hair but I didn't know they'd shave your head, too," he said from the door, where the sight of her had stopped him in his tracks so abruptly Jonas had bumped into him from behind. "I'm sorry."

"Aw, it ain't nothin'," she said. But he could tell it was, too. That it had upset her badly. She looked shyly at Jonas, embarrassed by her appearance. "It was kind of you to come today, sir."

The men crossed the room and sat down and Princess immediately riveted her attention on Mac's face.

"Tell me about the talk you had last night with your little girl," she said, her voice even deeper and raspier than usual.

Not just my little girl, your little sister!

"Princess, I promised you I'd protect her, didn't I?"

"Yes, you did. But you also said you'd talk to her. Did you?"

"I'll take care of Joy. I won't let anything bad happen to her."

"I know you love her, but do you understand how much trouble she's in? Did you ask—?"

Mac interrupted, leaned close and looked deep into Princess's purple eyes.

"Do you trust me, Princess?"

"Well, sure I—"

"Then you have to believe I'll handle it. I'll keep her safe."

She gazed deep into his eyes.

"Looks like I got to trust you," she said. "I s'pose if ever there was a man to trust, you're sure 'nough it."

Thunder rumbled in the distance and he tried to use it to change the subject.

"Sounds like it's going to storm again today. Jonas was saying just last night that it's rained almost every day this week," he turned to Jonas to pass him the conversational ball, but the older man didn't even try to catch it, just nodded. They'd driven to the prison separately and his father-in-law had seemed distracted when they met in front of the administration building. After Mac briefly outlined his plan, Jonas merely mumbled that it sounded "fine." Something was wrong. But Mac had bigger fish to fry right now than what was eating at Jonas, so he pressed ahead resolutely. "Guess the farmers need the rain, but it sure seems like it's been stormier this spring than it was last."

The small woman looked out the window fearfully and said something under her breath he didn't quite catch. Sounded like "ugly."

"What did you say?"

"Nothin.'"

Princess hadn't turned her dress wrong side out today; she'd turned her *self* wrong side out. She was closed up, veiled, all focus inward and contemplative. That's obviously what happened to a person who faced death with eyes wide open, knowing when it was coming.

But he was going to do something about that. He was going to keep this simple little woman alive, and deceit would just have to be the price of admission to life.

"I guess today's the day we need to talk about it, 'bout dying," she said. "I thought I's all ready for it. I mean, it ain't like it's a surprise, like I ain't been expecting it, waiting for it even, for years. Still, when it's right there in your face …"

"Princess, I need to—"

"Last night, I said my goodbyes. I said goodbye to the moon and the stars and when the sun come up, I said goodbye to the sunrise and the wind that brushes my face in the exercise yard. Only they didn't take me out there regular time today. That's when they shaved my head."

"I want to talk to you about your burial," Mac said.

She didn't seem to hear him.

"I won't never again stand in that yard, a'singin' my silly songs. I couldn't a-sung today anyway." She smiled a little half smile. "Got a frog in my throat and my mouth's dry as a sack of flour. That's the scared, the hole in my belly button. And that hole's so big right now, the wind a roarin' through it is so loud I can barely hear."

"Princess, about your burial. I have a plan—"

"I know there's a God. I been talkin' to him all day ever day the last fourteen years. And won't be long 'fore I get to see what he looks like. Won't that be a kick, meetin' him and Jesus, face up."

She cut her eyes at Mac.

"You gonna have to get over bein' mad at God eventually, Rev. You know that, doncha?"

She reached up self consciously and ran her hand over her bald head.

"I ain't looked in a mirror and I don't plan to neither! But I seen my reflection kinda in the window glass. All's you can see is scars and head! I'm gonna go to my grave a lookin' worse'n I ever looked when I was alive."

Mac leapt through the door she'd opened.

"You know how you said you didn't want to be buried here, in the prison cemetery, didn't want your body to stay a prisoner forever?"

"Yeah, I said that."

"Well, if you're in agreement, I can see to it that it doesn't."

Mac took a deep breath and turned his back on his promise never to lie to Princess.

"I talked to the warden. Oran said that with your permission I could claim your body after your death and bury it in the cemetery out behind my church." He paused, then added. "That's where my wife, Melanie, is buried."

Princess's eyes grew wide. "You'd *do* that? You'd put me in the same dirt as your wife?"

"Of course I would, Princess. She's buried near the back of the cemetery, under a cherry tree. I could have you buried near the cherry tree, too, if you'd like."

He glanced at Jonas, who added quietly, "This time of year, them white cherry blossoms rain down on Melanie's grave like snow."

Princess gasped. Her eyes filled so quickly the tears squirted down her face. "That's the kindest thing anybody ever done for me in my whole life."

Mac couldn't look at her. Instead, he reached into his jacket pocket and took out a pad of paper and a pen and placed them on the table in front of Princess. He'd had to jump through hoops to get the pen into the building, had to show it to the guard at the door when he entered, and would have to display it again when he left.

"All you have to do is write down that you give me permission to claim your body. And then sign it."

He shoved the pad and pen toward her.

She hesitated. "I ain't wrote nothing in a long time," she said, embarrassed again. "I ain't sure I still *can*."

"I'll tell you exactly what to say."

She took the pen in her hand and looked at it, then looked up at Mac. "How do you make this thing …?"

He took it back, punched the button on the top and the point popped out at the bottom.

"Look at that!" she said, and popped the point in and out. She smiled at Mac, then Jonas. "Ain't that grand!" Then she pulled the tablet toward her. "Okay, tell me what you want me to write, but you need to spell the words for me."

Mac had planned the script so Princess would have to write some of the same words that were in the note she'd left in the church: "Got no plase for her so plees giv her a gud hom."

"It doesn't matter how the words are spelled," he said. "Just write this down: 'Please' …"

She wrote "Plees."

He gave the rest of the words to her one at a time: "give Reverend McIntosh my body to take home. He's got a good place to bury it. Emily Prentiss." That construction provided eight words—*please, place, give, to, home, a, got* and *good*—that were also in the original note. He spelled "Reverend McIntosh" for her, but let her struggle with the other words. When she finally finished, she shoved the pen and notepad back across the table at him with an exhausted sigh.

"Whew! I'd forgot how hard writin' is. Will that do?"

Mac stared down at what she had written. Then he handed it wordlessly to Jonas. The old man didn't even bother to take out his glasses to examine it. He didn't need to.

Though the pen strokes were awkward from lack of practice, the backward-slanted letters were unmistakable. The misspellings were identical. You didn't have to be a handwriting analyst to see that the same person had written both the note Jonas was holding and the one in Mac's pocket.

He took the pad of paper back from Jonas and sat looking at Princess. He didn't know where to begin, how to tell her the good news that her sister was alive! And she wasn't going to die.

"You got the funniest look on your face," she said. "What's wrong?"

"Nothing's *wrong*. In fact, everything's …"

His voice trailed off. Then, because he didn't know what else to do, he just reached into his pocket and pulled out the sealed-in-plastic visitor's card. He placed it on the table beside what Princess had just written and scooted them both back across the table toward her.

"Princess, this is going to be really hard to explain. But please, just hear me out." He tapped the visitor's card and then the page she had written in his notebook. "You can see for yourself. It's obvious. The same person wrote both of these. And the person who wrote this one," he pointed to the visitor's card, "left her fingerprints on it, too. And they're still there."

She gawked at the plastic-wrapped card with wide, shocked eyes. Her gaze leapt to his face, then back down to the card. She suddenly sucked in a gasp, buried her head in her hands, and started to cry.

Mac looked a question at Jonas, who shrugged. This wasn't how either one expected the discussion to begin.

"Princess, stop crying and listen to me. I know you don't understand, you don't know—"

"I understand all right!" she gasped, her voice thick and tear-clotted. "It's *you* don't understand."

She cried hard, wrenching, heaving sobs. Mac tried repeatedly to get through to her, but she was too caught up in emotion to respond. Finally, he shouted at her.

"Princess!"

She stopped in mid-sob.

"Princess, look at me."

She lifted her head; tears streamed down her scarred face and dripped off her chin.

"I know you *think* you killed your little sister. But you didn't. She's alive. She's—"

"Of course she's alive! I know that. But please *don't tell nobody!*"

Mac stopped breathing, looked up and saw Jonas was as stunned and slack-jawed as he was.

"What did you say?"

"Why'd you do this? Why'd you butt in now, when it's almost—"

"Princess, I'm trying to save your life! You confessed to a murder you didn't commit. And you're about to be executed."

"I didn't ask you to save my life. You got to leave this be. You can't tell *nobody!*"

"Of course, I'm going to tell—"

"*No!*" she wailed. "You *can't!*"

"Why not?"

"Because you'll ruin everything! I worked so hard for all these years …" She shook her head and started to cry again, sobbing out, "You don't understand."

Mac sat back, stupefied. His ears were ringing, the way they'd buzzed deep inside when mortar shells had been exploding all around him in Pong Min Jong. He could barely hear Jonas' voice when he spoke.

"Miss Prentiss, you keep on sayin' we don't understand and you're da-gone right about that! You got to help us out here. You got to tell us what in the Sam Hill is goin' on."

Princess struggled to stop crying. She dragged in a sniffling breath and let it out in a slow, hiccupping stream. She took another breath and another.

"Okay," she finally whispered. "I'll tell. But the two of you—" She looked pointedly at Mac and then Jonas. "You're the onliest people on earth I *ever* told. And you got to promise me—"

"I'm not going to promise anything," Mac said. "Just tell me!" He realized he was practically shouting again. "I'm sorry. Look, I … just start at the beginning, when you ran away, and tell us what happened."

Princess reached up and wiped the tears off her cheeks, but her eyes still brimmed with unshed ones threatening to spill down her face.

Then she spoke, her husky voice ragged.

"It was the night I give Angel a bath, the time I told you and Mr. Cunningham about—and that was it, wasn't it?" She looked at Jonas. "Soon's I told about that birthmark, you wrinkled up your brow and I wanted to cut my tongue out. It's just I ain't used to doing that, having a conversation and knowing what not to say."

"You didn't do nothing wrong," Jonas said.

"Talk to us," Mac said.

Her lip quivered and when she pressed her lips tight together she blinked and splashed more tears onto her cheeks. She ignored them and took a deep, shaky breath. "All right. It was the night I got soap in Angel's eyes and she cried and cried."

22

*P*RINCESS RINSES AWAY THE SOAP AS *Angel screams. She pours glass after glass of well water into her squeezed-shut eyes and tries to soothe her.*

Jackson is furious.

"Shut her up, dang it!" he demands. "Make her stop that squallin'!" But even drunk as he already is, he understands there's no way to do that.

Muttering curses under his breath, he stumbles over to the icebox, takes out a beer bottle, opens it with his teeth, spits the bottle cap onto the floor and chugs the beer all the way down. He lets out a monstrous burp, gathers up two more cold ones, staggers to his chair, and plops down in it. He pops the top off one of them, sets the other on the floor beside his chair, and picks up the newspaper he brought home from the sawmill. Then he leans back and tries to read as he guzzles the beer.

Princess rinses and rinses Angel's eyes. Slowly the child stops sobbing. She has cried so hard for so long that she's worn out and her poor little eyes are blood-red from the lye in the soap.

Whispering comforting words, Princess dries Angel's hair with a ratty old towel and dresses her in the ragged t-shirt she sleeps in. Jackson's newspaper has fallen to the floor and his chin is resting on his chest, but he rouses up every now and then and takes a swig of his beer.

Easing open the back door, Princess takes Angel to the outhouse to do her business. She makes sure there's a fresh beer on the floor beside Jackson in case he reaches out his hand for one, then climbs up the ladder into the sleeping loft where she has made a flour-sack mattress stuffed with corn husks for Angel to sleep on. She rocks the child in her arms, singing nonsense songs to her softly. And after she goes to sleep, Princess stays there, holding her, kissing her forehead.

Her heart is pounding because she has formed a plan, a desperate plan.

Jackson is either asleep or has passed out in the chair. She waits until she has listened to him snore solidly for an hour before she makes her move. She gathers up a few belongings and puts them into a knapsack she'd sewed from flour sacks, like Angel's mattress. She packs a sundress she made for Angel, the white, store-bought dress Jackson got the child for Christmas, and a dress for herself, the only one she owns besides the one she's wearing. She slips quietly down the ladder and gathers up what little food is in the house—cold cornbread, a couple of apples, cheese, tomatoes and carrots from her little garden out back. Then she tiptoes over to Jackson. She's so scared she fears she's going to throw up, but she manages to pull Jackson's wallet out of his front overalls pocket, her hand trembling so violently she can barely hold onto it. She opens it and removes the only money inside—a twenty-dollar bill. She puts the bill snug into her zippered coin purse and drops it into the knapsack.

Back in the loft, she lifts Angel out of her bed and carries the sleeping child down the ladder. With Angel in one arm and the sack in the other, she has to scoot the back door of the shack open with her foot. As soon as she's outside, she wakes the child, because she can't carry her. They have to hurry.

Taking the sleepy child by the hand, Princess heads down the hill, the full moon casting a ghostly sheen on the dirt in the road. Angel whines, but Princess shushes her.

"We have to hurry! Shhhhh."

Past the collection of houses at the bottom of the hill where the colored people are fast asleep. Across the little stream, the water ice cold on their bare feet. Eventually, she leaves the road and travels through the woods. Angel is getting so tired she falls and Princess has to pick her up time and again. The little girl begins to cry softly but Princess presses on.

Finally, they break out of the trees and across a meadow she sees it. The water stop on the train line. Every night for years she has listened to the train whistle as it pulls into the stop. She knows what time it comes and has rushed through the night to get there while it is still filling up.

In the darkness, she steals along the side of the train, down from the engine at the water tank. Three cars from the caboose, she finds what she's been looking for: an empty cattle car with the door slightly ajar. She's able to push it open just a little farther, far enough for her to slip Angel inside and then follow her.

The air reeks of manure. But it's warm and dry in the dark cattle car and there's hay scattered on the floor. With the sliver of light shining through the open doorway, Princess gathers up hay and makes a pile against the far wall. She sits down there and cradles Angel in her arms.

Princess's feet hurt from walking barefoot through the fields and woods. Her heart is still pounding and her arms ache from carrying the heavy sack and often the child, too.

Then the cattle car suddenly lurches forward and stops. It lurches again and continues this time, moving slowly but gathering speed, going faster and faster. The train whistle wails and joins the song of triumph in Princess's heart. She's done it. She's escaped. She's free!

"We stayed hid in that cattle car for two days," Princess said. "Just goin' wherever the train was a-goin'. But we ran out of food on the third day, so when the train stopped for water, we hopped down out of it and walked into town."

Princess described the little Arkansas town, how she purchased the things she needed there—bread, lunch meat, a pair of scissors, an ax, and a quart of milk—in a small grocery store, and how the manager looked at her funny, "somebody like me havin' a whole twenty dollars an' all."

They walked along the road all that day, slept in a barn that night.

"Where were you going?" Mac asked. "Did you have some place special in mind or were you just wandering?" He wanted to ask about the ax, too, why she'd bought it, what she needed it for. But he'd hold that question for later.

"A little bit of both. I knew that train was headed west, and that's the way I wanted to go. West, across the state line into Oklahoma."

She smiled. "And part of it was just wanderin' 'cause we was *free*. For the first time in my life, I wasn't hunkered down, scared I's gonna get beat for sayin' somethin' wrong or not talkin' when I was s'posed to. Shoot, I was a kid on a holiday, and I sucked the juice out of every second of every day 'til it was bone dry."

She described eating in a diner one day at lunch, sitting right down with the paying customers and buying two bowls of soup and two sodas.

"And the next day ..." she looked down at her hands and spoke sheepishly. "The next day, I stole a car."

"You *what?*"

"Jackson, he had himself a motorcar when we first moved to Arkansas, 'fore it broke down and he couldn't 'ford to get it fixed. He'd go off now and again with one of the elders to preach somewhere and I'd get in that car and drive it 'round and 'round the yard."

She looked up and must have thought she saw disapproval in Mac's eyes.

"I'm ashamed and powerful sorry I done that, Rev, stole a car and all, and that's the honest truth," she said in a rush. "I never *planned* to do something sinful as that. The car was closed up in a shed I sneaked into to spend the night, wasn't nobody at home in the house next to the shed. Had an extra can of gasoline sittin' right there, so I just loaded up that can and drove away, kept moving all through the night. But I *had* to do it; I couldn't walk far enough 'fore all the money run out."

Princess talked about bumping along rutted back roads, waving at farmers not used to seeing a car where they lived. She followed the setting sun, hid the car in the woods and slept in the backseat at night.

"Then, we crossed a bridge over the Three Forks River and on the other side was this little town with a sign that said we was finally in Oklahoma. So I turned around and went back a ways and hid the car in the bushes."

She looked at Mac and her eyes shone.

"And the *circus* had come to that town! We didn't go into the big tent 'cause it was twenty-five cents more apiece to do that, but we walked around and seen the booths. That's where we had that picture took, the one I stared at so long I looked the faces clean off it!"

She smiled at the memory.

"They had lights there, blinkin' lights. And I had to be careful not to look at 'em, or I'd have a fit. I knew I'd found the place to come back to, where I knowed for sure I'd have one—because of the lights."

Mac wasn't sure what she was getting at, but he didn't interrupt, just let her talk.

"I took Angel back to the car, and we drove, going fast with all the windows down, through the night. Back east into Arkansas." She looked earnestly into Mac's eyes. "And it was Angel told me where to go. She was asleep on the front seat beside me, but she told me where to turn, how to get there. She led me to the proper place and we parked way back deep in the woods."

Princess leads Angel by the hand away from the hidden car down a steep slope to the bank of a slow-moving river. She sets the knapsack on the ground.

"I need you to sit right here on this rock and be real still, okay?"

Angel nods her head and sits. Princess pulls the little girl's t-shirt off over her head and lays it aside, then reaches into the knapsack and takes out the pair of scissors.

"I'm 'bout to give you a haircut!"

It's all she can do to force herself to lift up one of Angel's long, curly tresses and snip it off. A little half-sob escapes her lips, but when Angel looks up at her, she fastens a smile tight on her face.

"You're gonna look real pretty with short hair. It won't be all the time gettin' in your face, neither."

Princess carefully places the curl she has snipped off into the knapsack. Then she cuts off another lock, and another and another. When she is finished, the red curls that once hung all the way down the child's back are now lying on the ground all around her.

Princess picks them up, every one, and holds the mass of curls in her hand. She buries her face in them and feels their softness, inhales their sweet aroma. Then she resolutely walks to the bank of the river and tosses the hair into the water. She stands and watches it wash downstream until it is out of sight. Then she tosses the scissors into the water with a soft plunk sound.

She steps back to where Angel is waiting patiently on the rock and her heart catches in her throat at the sight of the child with her hair shorn off as short as a little boy's. Pulling Angel to her feet, she dusts all the stray hairs off her body before she puts the t-shirt back on her. With the knapsack in hand, she and Angel climb the steep grade back to the car. After she puts the knapsack in the backseat through the open window, she sets out with Angel toward the little building across the road from where she has hidden the car in the bushes. The building is a church.

She counts the steps as she walks, the last steps she will ever take with Angel at her side. She memorizes the warm feel of the child's plump hand in hers. The front door of the church is unlocked and they slip inside. There is a house behind the church and Princess "knows" the pastor and his wife live there, and that they'll be coming to the building in a few minutes to get it ready for Sunday services.

It's cool inside the building, the floor feels cold on Princess's bare feet. The sanctuary is darkened because the stained glass windows only allow a little of the early morning light to filter through. Princess leads Angel all the way down the center aisle to the front pew, lifts her up, and sets her on it.

She reaches into the rack on the back of the pew and pulls out the stub of a pencil and a lone visitor's card from the stack of them there. Sitting down beside Angel, she turns the visitor's card over and places it on a hymnal so she can write. It doesn't take long to inscribe the two sentences on the card. She puts the hymnal on the pew with the note and pencil on top of it and looks down at Angel.

She knows she must hurry now, that the pastor and his wife will be here any minute. She gets down on one knee in front of the little girl and says in a firm, cheerful voice.

"Okay now, sweetie pie. You said you was thirsty, right?"

Angel nods her head vigorously up and down. "Thirssy!"

"Well, I need you to wait right here for me while I go get you a drink of water. Can you do that?"

The child's brow wrinkles. "Go wid jew, Printhess!" she says, and tunes up to cry. Princess's heart stops. She looks around frantically, picks up the hymnal and opens it on Angel's lap. She hands the child the pencil. "Draw me a pretty picture while I'm gone," she says. "Okay?"

Angel smiles the most beautiful smile Princess has ever seen and nods her head vigorously.

"Uh-huh," she says, and begins to scrawl marks across the words of the song on the page: "... Lifted up was He to die; 'It is finished!' was His cry ..."

She gives the child a brief hug, doesn't dare hold her longer for fear Angel will feel how violently Princess's whole body is shaking.

"I'll be right back, sugar." She kisses the little girl tenderly on the forehead, lingers for a moment, then turns and bolts down the aisle and out the front door of the church. She makes it all the way outside before she bursts into tears, sobbing so hard she can barely stagger back across the road to the woods. She collapses there, crouches behind a tree trunk and peers through a bush at the building.

Her face twisted in a monstrous cramp of grief, her pimpled cheeks slathered in tears, she gulps out great heaving sobs without making a sound. She watches, bawling silently, until a man and woman burst out the front doors of the church. The man has Angel in his arms.

"YOU WERE *THERE*, WATCHING?" MAC WAS stunned. "Melanie and I found her and rushed out to see if we could catch whoever'd left her there. But there was nobody, not a car in the parking lot, nobody."

"I was hid good in the bushes," Princess said, her voice thick. "I seen you, the both of you, and I knew you'd take real good care of my Angel."

She put her head in her hands and cried, but just for a moment before she shook it off, looked up resolutely, and continued her story.

"After you went back inside, I got in the car and high-tailed it back the way I'd come, back toward that town on the other side of the Three Forks River, the one had a circus with flashing lights, the town in Oklahoma. I's about to get myself arrested and I wanted it to be in another state, so nobody'd ever even think to look for Angel in Arkansas."

Mac marveled that a young girl had figured all that out.

"And on the way back to that circus, I stopped and ..." She looked sheepish again. "I ... well, I stole a chicken." She looked stricken. "I'm *sorry* I done that Rev, I truly am, but I didn't have no choice. I prob'ly had enough money left to pay for it, but I didn't want no farmer to remember later that I bought it off'n him."

Jonas spoke gently. "I don't reckon the Good Lord was a-keepin' score on that one."

"I took the chicken out in the woods and chopped its head off and squirted the blood all over me and on that white, store-bought dress of Angel's. Made as big a mess as I could. I's careful not to let no chicken feathers get on nothin', though. Then I stuck that piece of Angel's hair to the bloody ax, put it and the dress in my knapsack, got back in the car and drove to that town where the circus was."

She described parking the car on a side street several blocks from the vacant lot where the tents were set up.

"You know, they never did figure out I's the one stole that car. Least they never said nothing to me 'bout it."

Then she gathered up her knapsack and headed toward the circus. Everyone who saw her gawked, poked their neighbors and pointed.

"I musta looked a sight! Them bumps on my face, my hair all tangley, goin' ever' which way from the wind a blowin' it and blood all over me!" Princess managed a small laugh. "Folks was probably talkin' 'bout it for years afterward."

She walked into the crowd waiting at the gate to buy tickets, stopped and stood staring up at the blinking lights.

"I knew they'd give me a fit, and they sure 'nough did. When I woke up, all those people was a-starin' down at me—includin' the sheriff. I looked up at him and said, 'I just killed Angela Marie Prentiss. I chopped her head off, cut her into little pieces with a ax and throwed the pieces in the Three Forks. She was two years old.' I made it sound terrible as I could so wouldn't nobody doubt what I said was true. And nobody ever did."

Princess stopped and sighed. "I didn't care what happened. I's hurtin' so bad in my heart I wouldn't a cared if they'd a strung me up and hanged me on the spot. I'd lost my precious Angel. I didn't have nothin' to live for."

Her purple eyes looked deep into Mac's. "When I run out of your church and left that little girl a'sittin' on a pew waitin' for me to bring her a drink of water—I *died* that day! My life was over."

23

JOY GRABBED HER BOOKS AND BOLTED out of American history class so fast she almost knocked down the teacher, a doddering old man whose memory was failing him. Just before class let out, the students had managed to convince him that he'd never assigned the homework he wanted them to turn in.

She hurried down the hall, not meeting anyone's eyes, rushing to get out of the building before Tweedle Dum and Tweedle Dee got out of their last class, home economics, down by the gym. She didn't have the time or the emotional energy to talk to her friends right now.

How could she stand there watching Beth blush when a cute boy said "hi" to her in the hall?

Or worse—listen to Shirley gush about what a "dreamboat" the President was, giggling that he and Jackie must still "do it" because she was pregnant. The First Lady was going to have a baby and the whole world was celebrating.

Well, nobody was celebrating Joy's pregnancy. It was so *not* a cause for celebration that Joy was about to …?

To what?

Kill her baby.

The words formed in her head as clear as a church bell on a cold morning. Joy literally staggered from the force of them, ducked into the girl's bathroom by the auditorium door and stood trembling in one of the stalls, sucking in great gasps of air to keep from being sick.

She hadn't let herself go there, had tackled any rebel thought, grabbed it by the scruff of the neck, stuffed it down into a trunk in a dark corridor of her mind, and then sat on the lid.

But there it was, right in front of her. Reality. She was about to drive out to a creepy house in the country where a filthy old woman was going to—

No! It's not a baby! It's just ... cells, a glob of cells, that's all!

You couldn't *kill* something that wasn't alive. It wasn't human, a person. Not yet. It was just ... potential life. An *it*. A *thing* that she had to get rid of or her life would be totally ruined. Facing her friends, the members of her church, her *father* pregnant was totally unthinkable. She would do absolutely *anything* to keep that from happening.

Determination calmed her. She would be strong. She had to be. There was only one way out. And once it was over, she could pick up her life where she'd left it and go on. Everything would be fine tomorrow. She just had to manage somehow to get through today.

She'd worn a skirt, a black one with a can-can slip, and she'd stopped by the drugstore on her way to school that morning and bought a whole box of Kotex. She'd done everything the woman had instructed her to do—*except* find someone to drive her home. As she pulled the big white car out of the school parking lot and headed toward Route 79, she actually prayed, the first time she'd prayed in ... since her mother died.

"God, *please* ... What will I do if that woman turns me away? Please help me!"

But she didn't really believe God would help her do what she was about to do. She was on her own.

As Joy drove south from town on Route 79, she took no notice of the ugly black storm clouds building in the sky ahead. Her hair was always encased in an Aqua Net Hair Spray suit of armor to maintain her Annette Funicello flip; on particularly windy days, she wore a headscarf. But she wasn't even thinking about her hair now. The day had turned off unseasonably hot and muggy and she rolled

Mr. Wilson's window down and let the wind blow in her face. Her hair broke free of the hair spray's hold on it and danced around, tickling her nose. She took deep breaths of warm air that smelled of rain and tried to wipe her mind completely clean, to blot out everything, to think no thought of any kind.

Into that emptiness, images formed, pale and dreamlike.

She is riding in a car at night, bouncing on the seat as wind blows her hair into her face. She is laughing and the woman driving the car laughs with her. But the woman is not her mother. It's someone she's never seen before, but who looks eerily familiar.

THOUGH INDISTINCT AND BLURRED, THE IMAGES seemed remarkably real. But when she concentrated, tried to get a better look at them, they dissolved, disappeared, puffs of smoke from the red embers of a dying fire.

By the time she pulled up in front of the house where honeysuckle trellises entombed the porch, she had a speech all mapped out in her head, knew exactly what she would say when the woman wanted to know who was going to drive her home. She'd tell the woman … Joy suddenly realized she didn't even know the woman's name, didn't know what to call her.

What difference did it make what her name was? It's not like they were going to exchange Christmas cards.

She sat for a few minutes, her fingers gripping the steering wheel so tight her knuckles were white, trying to control her breathing and stop her heart from pounding. She could feel every beat of it in the big vein in her neck. But she couldn't calm down and decided it didn't matter anyway. So she got out of the car, crossed the dirt yard, and stepped up onto the splintered boards of the porch. She didn't even have to knock. The woman opened the door before she had a chance and looked anxiously out over Joy's shoulder toward Mr. Wilson parked just outside the yard.

"You didn't bring anybody with you, did you?" she wanted to know. "Somebody to drive you home? You said you didn't have anybody, isn't that right?"

Joy launched into her speech.

"No, and I know you said I had to, but I couldn't find—"

The woman cut her off.

"It's all right," she said, and seemed to relax. She turned and fixed her eyes on Joy for the first time. When she spoke again, her voice was hollow-sounding. "I'm going to put you to sleep and then everything will be fine. You won't need anybody to drive you home."

Joy was puzzled, but so relieved that she wasn't going to be turned away, she didn't dare ask any questions.

The woman made no move to let her into the house, just stood there, like she was dazed. Her face was so distorted Joy couldn't read the look on it. The moment drew out until Joy finally remembered the money. She reached into her pocket and took out the envelope that contained the $100 she had withdrawn from her savings account yesterday.

"Here's the rest of the money, the final payment."

The woman took the envelope and tossed it carelessly onto a table by the door, then stepped back and gestured for Joy to come in.

"My name's Wanda," she said. "And I'm going to take very good care of you, just like your mama would want me to. In a little while, it will all be over. Over and done with. Forever."

Joy stepped into the house and the woman closed the door behind her.

❖ ❖ ❖ ❖ ❖

When Princess finished her account, she sat with her hands folded on the table in front of her. She was swaddled in stillness, but power and intensity throbbed beneath it, a hand grenade wrapped in a silk handkerchief.

Jonas was the first one to find his voice.

"How old was you, Missy, when all this happened?"

"When they arrested me, I just had turned fifteen years old. Jackson lied, told 'em I was seventeen, so I'd be tried as a adult. They couldn't give me the death penalty less'n I's a grownup."

Silence again.

"Why?" Mac asked tenderly. "Why'd you do it, Princess?"

She looked down at her hands folded on the table, then spoke one word with a thousand shades of loathing.

"Jackson."

The hair on the back of Mac's neck began to stand up. She still wouldn't look at him or Jonas, just stared at her hands. She pulled in a deep breath and held it. After a heartbeat of silence, her siren's voice spoke words crafted from razor blades and jagged glass. Words you couldn't even get near or they'd slice you open all the way to the bone.

"Angel ain't my little sister. She's my daughter. Mine ... and Jackson's."

Mac couldn't breathe. Every speck of air had been sucked out of the room by the nightmare horror, bald and almost smoking, a truth so unthinkable it lay beyond the drapes and furnishings of his simple, ordinary life.

Princess was Joy's *mother?*

And Jackson Prentiss was Joy's father!

"I'm sorry Rev. I know it's hard to hear a thing like that. But you asked to know the whole of it, and there it is."

Jonas was struggling, too. His face had turned gray and he was mumbling, "... red hair. That fella did have *red* hair."

"Jackson told on the stand how Mama died havin' Angel, said that's why she was so precious to him—'cause his wife give her own life for her little girl. Made the jury feel so *sorry* for him." Princess lifted her head and Mac fell back from the rage and loathing in her eyes. "Well, Mama never done no such a thing! She died of a fever, and 'fore she was even cold in the ground, Jackson up and says I got to *marry* him. He always had looked at me funny, made my skin crawl, but I never thought ... Shoot, it was just a couple of weeks after my birthday; I's only thirteen."

Thirteen years old!

"I said no, said I wasn't gonna do it! And he tore into me somethin' fierce. Come up side my head with a piece of firewood and I liked to a-died my own self. That's when I started havin' them fits, after he beat me that time."

Mac was filled with an inarticulate, maniacal rage so powerful it swept every other emotion out of his soul. For the first time in his life he knew without doubt that he could strangle the life out of another human being with his bare hands.

"One of the elders in the church performed the ceremony, said it was legal in Arkansas and maybe it was." She made a *humph* sound in her throat. "Guess Jackson finally come to his senses though, thought better of marryin' a little girl when I got … in a family way. He yanked me out of school and wouldn't let me set foot outside the house so's nobody'd see. Made me tell people Angel was my little sister, that he'd 'dopted us. Wouldn't let her call me Mommy, neither. She's the one turned Emily Prentiss into 'Printhess.'"

She sat back in the chair then and her eyes stared at a distant nothing.

"That shack we lived in didn't have no runnin' water and I had Angel there one day while Jackson was at work in the sawmill. I was just a kid myself, didn't have no idea what was happenin' to me or what to do. It's a miracle of God either one of us lived through it.

"Jackson come in that night, musta heard the baby crying outside. All he said to me was, 'It a boy or a girl?' When I told him it was a girl, he said we'd call her Angela, after his mother. I figured he could call her whatever he wanted; I'd already give her a name. 'Cause from the very first moment I held that squirmin' little'un in my arms, bloody and white stuff all over her, I knew who she was. She was a Angel."

Princess described how Jackson had gone back outside to the well and drawn a bucket of water. He brought it back to the house and warmed some up so Princess could clean herself and the baby while he scrubbed up the mess of the birth. He heated up a can beans for supper and brought Princess a plate while she lay in the bed with the baby.

"The next day, it was back to normal. He never paid no attention a'tall to that child. Oh, he got drunk and brought her home this lacy, white, store-bought dress one Christmas, but lots of times we didn't have no food to eat and I had to go a-beggin' from the coloreds at the bottom of the hill. He went back to … messin' with me, just like he always done, but right after Angel was born was when I got that stuff on my face, my chest and my back, them awful bumps. Jackson hated that, said it made him sick, that I's so ugly it made him want to puke when he looked at me."

Jonas spoke softly, the venom in his words as poisonous as a snake bite. "Somebody ought to of put a shotgun barrel down that man's pants and blown his privates out the back side of his long johns."

Princess actually smiled.

"I didn't care that he acted like Angel wasn't there. That just meant she was mine, all *mine*." She looked sunshine out her eyes at Mac and Jonas. "I don't have words fine enough to say what a gift she was to me, how my heart filled up to burstin' ever day with lovin' her. Ever' breath I took, I took for her; ever' thought was 'bout my Angel. She was everything good and beautiful and holy in the whole world, all wrapped up in a little girl with red curls."

The sunshine left Princess's eyes.

"Jackson never paid her no mind a'tall until that day when she was two, the day I's telling you about that I give her a bath in the washtub."

Angel's bubbling laughter is the most joyous sound Princess has ever heard. She's sitting on the floor with the child and reaches out to tickle her again when the front door suddenly bangs open and Jackson stomps in, looking meaner than a mason jar full of hornets.

He's obviously been drinking, but even with his speech muddy, Princess has no trouble understanding him.

"Heard about your little party this afternoon at the bottom of the hill," he roars at Princess, then turns on Angel. "I know what you done, too, Little Miss Priss."

Joe Dan had told Jackson! Princess had seen the man, one of the elders of Jackson's little church, drive by in his pickup truck, staring out the window at them. She should have known he'd go find Jackson at Shakey's Tavern and fill his ear full about it.

Princess and Angel had gone down the hill as soon as the child woke up from her afternoon nap. Bess Washington, the nice colored lady in the shack by the road, had told Princess a couple of weeks ago that her cat was about to have kittens and Princess wanted to show them to Angel.

The four little critters were adorable! Two of them had mostly white fur, one had white and brown spots and one was black as a lump of coal. Angel had fallen in love with that one. Wouldn't hardly put it down the whole time they were there.

Bess's youngest, Willie, a three-year-old with great big ears, was the only playmate Angel had ever had. They'd wandered over to the creek together with two of the kittens and sat petting them while they dangled their toes in the inch-deep water.

Princess was standing on Bess's porch, asking about her tomato plants, when she heard a truck coming. Didn't hardly have no traffic at all on that road, so she was surprised to see Joe Dan's pickup come around the corner. Wasn't no time to hide, so she made like she didn't care that he seen, just waved at him real big as he drove by.

But she saw how he was gawking at Angel and Willie. She looked over at them and the two children were sitting there holding hands!

"Joe Dan saw you with that little nigger boy!" Jackson yells at Angel and the tone of his voice terrifies the child. She jumps up off the floor and starts to run, but Jackson grabs her arm, like to of yanked it out of the socket.

Princess leaps to her defense.

"You leave her be!" she shrieks, but never even makes it to her feet before the back of Jackson's hand connects with the side of her face. The blow knocks her sideways into the wood stove, her head bangs into one of the metal legs and the world goes dark.

She hears Angel's sniffling beside her as she comes to. When she opens her eyes, the child's face swims blurry in front of her and the room spins. She closes her eyes for a few more moments and opens them again. Angel's face is clear. Her left cheek is an angry red, her left eye swelling. She's gonna have a shiner. And her bottom lip is split.

"*Printhess!*" *she squeals when she sees her mother's eyes are open, and throws her arms around her neck. Princess struggles to sit up with the child clinging to her, then cradles the trembling child in her lap, rocks back and forth, crooning, "Shhh now, hush. You're okay."*

"Oh, no she ain't," Jackson says from the doorway. Princess whirls around and he is leaning on the doorframe for support.

Princess sucks in a little gasp of terror, but instead of advancing on them, Jackson sneers, "It ain't okay for any kin of mine to truck with black savages!"

Princess wants to tell him that the "black savages" fed his kin when he'd left them to starve while he drank up all the food money. But she would never dare to say such a thing. Jackson spits on the porch, turns and marches off down the hill.

She holds Angel until the child stops trembling, then puts her down and starts supper. Jackson doesn't come back, so the two of them eat beans and cornbread and sing silly songs as Princess washes up the dishes.

Then she gets Angel's bath ready. She has just gotten the little girl's hair all soaped up when she hears Jackson's heavy boots on the front steps. She turns and he is standing in the open doorway. He has a beer in one hand and a little black kitten in the other.

"Kitty!" Angel squeals and reaches out her hands for it. Princess feels a cold stone in the pit of her stomach.

"What are you a-plannin' to do with that cat?" she asks fearfully. But she knows the answer.

Jackson doesn't reply, just finishes the beer, curls his lips up in a cruel smile and holds the animal out to Angel by the scruff of its neck.

"Gimme kitty," Angel pleads and tries to climb out of the washtub to get to the cat.

"You're gonna kill it, ain't ya?" Princess says.

"No, I ain't," he says. He pauses, then purrs quietly, "But she *is!"*

Princess gasps.

He steps to the cabinet where she set the bean pot to dry, drops the black kitten down into it and puts the lid on top.

"Get her dry," he commands Princess, "and I'm gonna show her how to treat a nigger *cat!"*

PRINCESS SHUDDERED AT THE MEMORY. MAC and Jonas were both so sickened they couldn't speak. Then she took a breath and continued the story.

"So I turned where he couldn't see, and I rubbed soap in Angel's eyes a-purpose! And she started screaming, yelling, and carryin' on. He waited, but she just kept a-cryin' and he couldn't do nothing with a squalling child so …" She stopped. "Truth is, I forgot all about that cat in the pot. Never give it another thought. Had too much else on my mind."

She turned in the chair toward the window and gazed out at the little town in the Indian Bluffs.

"I stood there pourin' water over Angel's head, her a-cryin' while I tried to figure out how I was gonna get her out of there. I knew then he was gonna hurt her. Beat her, sure. But hurt her worse than that. He was gonna turn her into a mean, miserable, spiteful monster just like he was, squeeze all the love and laughter out of that little girl and fill her plumb up to the top with meanness and hate. He was gonna steal her soul. And wasn't no way in the world I could protect her."

She turned back to the table, rested her hands on it and looked earnestly into Mac's face.

"Time we got off that train, Angel's face was just about healed up and I had me a plan. I done a lot of thinkin' as that cattle car bumped along the track. I figured out there was only one way to end it. I couldn't get away from him. Sooner or later the money'd a-run out and he'd a-found us. And if I'd of just left Angel someplace, Jackson woulda tore up the whole country 'til he found her. Not 'cause he cared anything about her, but because she was *his*. The onliest way in the world he'd a-give up on her was if she was dead."

She fell silent again, took in a shaky breath, and then the stillness settled over her. Princess was finished.

Mac shook his head in wonder at her incredible story, then reached out and placed his hands over hers. In the silence, he looked tenderly at the frail mother who'd willingly paid an incredible price to save her little girl in the only currency she had—sacrifice.

24

Andy Cook stopped breathing, waited for the green radar beam to circle the WSR-57 radar's black screen and return to the spot where he'd seen it. Yes, it was there!

"Take a look at this!" he called out, and the three other meteorologists who'd been huddled around the radar a few minutes earlier dropped the maps and weather balloon data they were studying and rushed to his side.

"See it?" They waited and the green beam swept around again and illuminated the massive storm system gobbling up the southeastern part of the state. "Right there!"

A shape had appeared in the cloud formation that showed up as a blob on the radar screen. A hook shape.

One of the other meteorologists cursed softly under his breath. "Look at the size of that thing."

A hook formation on the tail end of a cloud was the only visual sign radar could pick up of a tornado within a storm system. But that's all it could determine, just that a tornado was there. Radar could not detect whether the tornado was on the ground or a thousand feet up in the air.

Andy had only read about the hook-shaped formation of a tornado visible on radar. He'd never seen one until today. But the supervisor of the section had seen plenty and he began giving orders like a drill sergeant, instructing his team to issue a tornado watch for the area directly in the path of the fast-moving storm. Area radio and television stations would be notified immediately.

A tornado watch meant only that conditions existed in which a tornado could form. Spotters on the ground would have to confirm that a tornado had touched down. And that was a problem. Many twisters, shrouded by clouds or concealed inside rain storms, were hard to see, and spotters were scarce. Communication was an even bigger issue. Radio transmissions were always interrupted by severe storms; power and phone lines were usually among the first casualties of bad weather. In other words, the very thing the spotters were looking for often prevented them from reporting that they'd found it. But only after confirmation by a spotter would the National Weather Bureau issue a tornado warning, which meant a tornado was on the ground and headed in a particular direction. The warning would urge those in the tornado's projected path to take immediate shelter.

Though Andy knew the protocol as well as anybody else in the room, he wasn't satisfied with a mere tornado watch. There were so many of those during spring storm season on the plains; people ignored them, and he had a really bad feeling about this storm. Absent a single bit of concrete information, Andy's gut still told him this hook was a tornado on the ground. He trusted his gut. And gauging from the intensity of the storm that had formed the huge hook—the super-cell thunderstorm stretched up 45,000 feet!—the tornado could be massive.

Andy turned to the wall and studied the big map of Oklahoma, where the progress of the storm was plotted out with stick-pins. He knew West Texas intimately, could tell you every town in a 100-mile radius of Lubbock. But he wasn't that familiar with Oklahoma, and as he studied the area in front of the storm, he relaxed slightly. Nothing much out there but empty plains, cattle ranches, and a few oil rigs. The only town on the map directly in the storm's current path was Graham and it was sixty miles away. Only a handful of all the recorded tornadoes in history stayed on the ground more than ten or twenty miles.

Well, there was the Great Tri-State Tornado on March 18, 1925 ... It killed 695 people and injured 2,000 more on its three-and-a-half-hour, 219-mile rampage through Missouri, Illinois, and Indiana.

For just a moment, Andy considered chucking the protocol and calling city officials in Graham, just to give them a heads-up. But he didn't. He couldn't get all worked up over his first sighting of a tornado on radar or he'd get himself fired his first day on the job! That crotchety old weather forecaster in Lubbock had often warned him not to run ahead of his headlights. "When it comes to twisters, son, think horse, not zebra," he'd said. In truth, the vast majority of tornadoes that formed inside thunderstorms remained in the clouds and never touched down at all. And of the ones that did, the fastest forward speed ever documented was fifty miles per hour. So *if* this twister really was on the ground, and *if* it was a sprinter, it wouldn't strike Graham until well after five o'clock. That was more than an hour from now. There was still plenty of time.

◆ ◆ ◆ ◆ ◆

All the clocks in Dawson Station, Oklahoma, stopped at 3:59 p.m. The brutal rainstorm lashing the little cluster of buildings that wasn't even on the map had cut the power lines. Families in the five houses nestled beside the road between the gas station and the general store were plunged into semi-darkness as the rain grew more intense, became a solid wall of water, the wind screamed and wailed, and hail the size of golf balls pummeled the rooftops.

Cloaked in the massive rainstorm, no one saw the tornado coming before the dead center of the monster twister slammed into the town and erased it, wiped it off the face of the earth as if it had never been there at all. The boiling black wall at the bottom of an eight-mile-high rotating column generated winds 300 miles per hour at its core and seventy-five on the outer perimeter. It demolished every structure and then sucked up the debris. It scooped the vehicles off the ground, yanked the bark off the trees, and left nothing behind but the foundations of seven buildings and a mile-wide stretch of land scrubbed as featureless as if it had been bulldozed.

Fourteen people died instantly.

The savage twister had covered the nine miles between a field outside Tishomingo and Dawson Station in less than nine minutes.

◆ ◆ ◆ ◆ ◆

Mac picked up his notepad and the visitor's card encased in Saran Wrap and slid them both into his jacket pocket.

"I have to go talk to the warden," he said.

Princess's bald head snapped back like he'd slapped her face.

"Ain't you been listenin' to a word I said? You can't do that!"

"Earth to Princess!" he cried in frustration. "You've got a date with Sizzlin' Suzie in …" he looked at his watch "a little over an hour—for killing somebody who's not dead."

"I already told you, I made my peace. I'm ready."

"Princess, they're going to *execute you*."

"This ain't about *me*. It ain't never been about me. It's about Angel. Everything I done, I done for her. I got her away from that monster and she's safe now where he can't hurt her. She's got you …" She turned and nodded toward Jonas, who was sitting stock still, his eyes huge, "and Mr. Cunningham. I've give my little girl a good life. But if you tell the warden, you'll ruin everything. All those years a-sittin' by myself in that cell, that'll all a-been for nothin'."

Mac was so dumbfounded he could think of nothing to say; she kept at him, her siren's voice full of surging power.

"You ain't thought this through, Rev. You ain't thought what the truth of this is gonna do to your Joy!"

Joy!

"What's it gonna do to that child to find out the only mother she ever knowed wasn't really her mama a'tall? That she was born to a thirteen-year-old kid in a filthy shack, and her real mama's a scar-faced woman with brown teeth who's got a fifth-grade education and spent the last fourteen years all alone in a cage on the Long Dark?"

Her voice was the rumble of thunder.

"What's it gonna do to her to find out her father ain't the good Reverend McIntosh, neither? That her *real* daddy's Jackson Prentiss, maybe the most hated man, and for sure the most *hate-filled* man in the whole country?" She stopped, then whispered in horror. "He's done things you don't know about ... *killed* people."

She leaned across the table and hissed at him, "And you best re-member that *Angela Marie Prentiss* ain't but 16 years old! You thought 'bout what you're gonna do when Jackson comes to *claim* her?"

Mac gasped.

"Don't you think for a minute he won't. She's *his!* Him all fa-mous, got them powerful friends, ain't no way you could stop him. You promised me you wouldn't never let nothing bad happen to her. That man blacked her eye when she was just two years old, what do you think he'll do to her *now*? This secret comes out, Jackson will *destroy* the whole rest of that child's life. I done all this to get my Angel away from him. You *can't* give her back!"

Mac's head was spinning. He was dizzy, nauseous. She was right, of course. The truth about her parents would shatter the child. And what about her future? What would Jackson Prentiss do to her if he *took* her?

But if Mac *didn't* tell, Princess would be—

"Princess, do you realize that my silence will *kill* you?"

She said absolutely nothing, sat stock still, studying him. Then she shook her head in wonder.

"I swan, I never dreamed conversation—just talkin'—was this hard. You're the one that don't understand, Rev. You still don't get it, do you? *You* ain't killing me. The state of Oklahoma ain't killing me. Ain't nobody *killing* Emily Gail Prentiss. Nobody's *taking* my life; I'm *giving* my life. Of my own free will. For my little girl."

Suddenly, Princess froze. Literally stopped moving, stopped breathing. She'd been looking at Mac and her eyes were still pointed at him. But it was plain she didn't see him anymore. She saw some-thing else entirely.

"She's 'bout to throw a fit," Jonas said.

Mac had never seen an epileptic seizure and had no idea what to expect. But Princess didn't fall out of the chair to the floor. She didn't shake and foam at the mouth. She sat frozen where she was, looked like she was viewing a movie he and Jonas couldn't see. A horror movie, from the look on her face.

It was eerie to watch her, her bald head shining in the dull light of the bulb high up in the ceiling. Her eyes moved, like people's eyes moved when they dreamed, except she was awake. Or he assumed she was awake. He shot a glance at Jonas, who didn't look good at all. His face was ashen.

Then, as abruptly as she froze, she gasped for a breath and then another. She slumped back into the chair, her eyes closed, her head fell forward and hung limp on her neck, and she sat there panting.

"Princess?" Mac said softly. "Are you all right?"

Her head came up and she looked confused, seemed to have trouble focusing, then understanding and comprehension lit her face and her hand flew to her mouth.

"Oh, Rev, she's there again! Angel's there right now with that monster woman!"

Angel. It was jarring to realize she was talking about Joy. And the monster woman again. Oh, boy.

"Princess, I don't think—"

"Now you listen here to me, Rev!" The full force of that rumbling voice pinned him back in the chair the way John Glenn had been slammed into his seat when that rocket took off for space. "I know you don't believe me, but you *got* to believe me. You got to! Sometimes … sometimes I can see out Angel's eyes. It's happened to me a time or two over the years. One time, she was ridin' a bicycle. It was a blue bicycle and it had them, oh, I don't know what you call them things, little strings, colored strings on the ends of the handle bars."

Mac stopped breathing and looked at Princess with wide, uncomprehending eyes. Joy had had a blue bicycle when she was a little girl, and it had streamers, red—

"Red, white and blue strings. I could see 'em a-flappin' in the wind. And then she hit something in the sidewalk. It was where a tree root had growed and kinda broke up the concrete, and she went flying off the bike and landed in the dirt and she was hurt, her arm hurt and she was crying and—do you know when I'm talking about? Do you remember?"

"She was seven years old," Mac said, his voice airless.

"Little Joy broke her arm a-fallin' off that bike," Jonas said, so soft Mac barely heard him.

"And another time, she was in the back floorboard of a car and you musta had a wreck or something 'cause she was all squished-up down there and then you picked her up and … that's how come I knew you was a good man, 'cause you were smiling and crying at the same time that day. I seen you through her eyes."

"When Joy was eleven, we were in a fender-bender. She flew into the back of the front seat and I was scared she was hurt. I jumped out of the car, opened the back door and lifted her …" his voice trailed off. He sat staring wide-eyed at Princess, stupefied.

"*See!* I ain't lying, Rev! I ain't makin' this stuff up! I ain't crazy." She stopped. "Well, maybe I am crazy, I can't speak to that. All's I know is sometimes I can see what Angel sees. And I *just did!* Rev, it was awful, the terriblest thing. It was … I …"

She struggled for words.

Mac reached over and placed his trembling hand on top of hers. Her hand was soft and warm.

"Look at me," he said. She turned her purple eyes on him and he fell into the depths of them. "Now tell me what you saw. Describe it to me, everything you saw."

"Angel was a'lookin' at that monster woman."

"What do you mean by 'monster woman'?" Jonas asked, sounding as shaken as Mac felt.

"The top part of her face, her eyes and nose, was normal. But the whole bottom part, it was all twisted up and smashed. Her jaw was caved in on one side, didn't have no teeth there, and—"

"Wanda Ingram!" Mac bleated. "That's … you just described Wanda Ingram!"

"You *know* the monster woman?" Princess gasped.

"No, she was a friend, well not a *friend*, she was somebody Melanie knew, was trying to help. I only saw her a couple of times."

"Why would Angel be—?"

"No! Oh … no," Mac gasped. His heart hammered in his chest so hard it hurt. It couldn't be. But it was. It explained everything. He turned to Jonas. "The $100 from her savings, that's why …"

"What're you sayin', son?"

Mac leaned back in the chair, looked up at the ceiling and pulled in gasps of air, trying hard not to sob.

"That woman, Wanda Ingram. Melanie thought, Melanie was sure she'd been … performing abortions."

Princess squeaked out a little scream, covered her mouth with both hands and sat shaking her head no for a moment. Then she leaned across the table and spoke earnestly.

"That's why I could see … dead babies in the monster woman's eyes!"

Mac did sob then, just one bleat before he sucked in a breath and regained control.

"Rev, it's worse'n you think. That woman's crazy."

"Melanie said she was losing it. Mel thought she was psychotic. She wanted to get her admitted to—"

"She's gonna *kill* Angel." Princess's voice hummed with a deeper power than Mac had ever heard. "I seen it in her eyes. She ain't gonna take her baby. She's got it all planned out, all thought through. Rev, she's gonna kill Angel! And then she's gonna kill herself!"

Terror dumped a bucket of adrenaline into Mac's veins. There was no hint of doubt anymore. He couldn't explain *how* Princess knew, but that didn't matter anymore. She *knew!*

"You got to stop her! You got to go right now!"

But he couldn't. If he left now …

"The warden, Princess. I have to show him the handwriting … in a little over an hour, you're going to—"

"Die. That's right, I'm gonna die. Just like I been a-fixin' to do for fourteen years. But if you don't go now, that woman's gonna kill Angel! You only got time to save one of us. You promised you'd protect her!"

Mac glanced at Jonas, but knew before he even formed the words that the old farmer would never be able to convince Oran to postpone the execution. He put his elbows on the wooden table and his head into his hands. Then he lifted his head and looked at

Princess, pleaded with her to make it different, to change reality somehow with her strange power. To do *something*.

"You're that little girl's daddy. There ain't no decidin' to be done here, and you and me both know it!" She reached out and took his hand. "You got to let me do this, Rev. You got to let me go."

His eyes filled with tears. He couldn't speak. Time dragged out; dangling lives by a sewing thread.

"All right," he gasped.

"Yes," she said, her voice hushed.

Then the concentrated intensity returned, a power surge hummed around her and she turned to include Jonas in what she said.

"I know a big part of you still thinks I'm off in the head. But I'm 'bout to say somethin' and you got to just *trust* me. You *got to* believe me and do what I say."

"What is it?" Jonas asked.

"You got to *run*, both of you. Run fast as you can. *South!*" She glanced out the window at the black clouds bubbling over the Iron House, and her deep voice was hushed. "The Big Ugly's a-comin'."

Both men were native Oklahomans; neither needed her to explain what she meant.

Jonas looked suddenly stricken.

"Maggie!" he said, his eyes huge, and he leapt to his feet. "She's at home, just her and Lupe."

"Go!" Mac told him. The old man turned without a backward glance and banged on the door. He almost knocked down the eight-by-ten-glossy guard and was gone.

"Hurry up," Princess said to Mac. "You gotta go, too!"

He got to his feet, then pleaded in a ragged voice, "Can't I do *something*?"

"Yeah, you can. You can give me them pictures of Joy." She paused and a bright smile lit her scarred face below her dark purple eyes. "Pictures of my Angel! They'll give 'em back to you. You know, after … I just want to hold 'em, so hers is the last face I see."

Mac jammed his hand down into his pocket, snatched out his billfold, opened it to the picture holder and emptied the contents onto the table. Four faces, the same yet different, smiled up at them.

"Anything else?" His voice was so thick he could barely speak.

"Just give me a hug, Rev. That's all. I ain't had a hug in years. Hug me goodbye."

Mac crossed to her side of the table, put his hands on her shoulders and pulled her to her feet. Then he put his arms around her and cradled her there, tight against his chest. She felt so fragile. He rocked slowly back and forth and patted her back. She made a sound, like a low moan in her throat. His tears fell onto the top of her bald head.

She suddenly pulled away from him, a look of terror on her face.

"You got to go *now*. Right now! Hurry, or it's gonna be too late!"

"But—"

"Just *go!*"

He turned toward the door and saw that the guard was already on his way in. Mac turned back to speak to Princess, but didn't. She was holding the pictures of her little girl in her hands, staring lovingly down at them.

"Bye, Princess," he whispered.

She looked up at him. "You won't never tell nobody—promise me that, Rev, and I'll die happy."

"I promise."

"Yes," she said. The hushed tone, the sighed amen.

25

THE GUARD STOOD IN THE DOORWAY for a moment after the preacher brushed past him and went tearing down the hallway like his pants were on fire. Then he backed out quickly, slammed the door shut behind him and leaned against it, breathing hard. He had broken a rule, an important rule, the kind that'd get you fired. Meetings between an inmate and a minister were strictly private. And Larry Patterson had been *listening*.

But it wasn't like he was a prison guard as a career choice. He was a twenty-eight-year-old country music singer who had to put food on the table until he could get a shot at the *Grand Ole Opry*. So he'd taken this job at the Iron House, drove here from Hansford, thirty miles away, and hated every day of it, felt like he was putting in his time same as the inmates, waiting to be set free.

As the low man in seniority, he'd been the one got picked to wait outside a door for hours every day staring in a little window while "the mystic" talked to the preacher. He'd been seriously ticked off about it, but come to find out, he'd hit the jackpot. Standing right here in this hallway yesterday afternoon, he got to meet Jackson Prentiss, *the* Jackson Prentiss. Larry had hero-worshiped the reverend for years, so smooth and polished, standing up tall and proud for a white man's rights.

Why, he'd seen the man on television just last week. It was such a big story they'd shown it at the beginning of the *CBS Evening News* and again at the end, right before Walter Cronkite said, "And that's the way it is, Friday, May 3, 1963."

A bunch of niggers in Birmingham—it looked to him like they were mostly teenagers—had been protesting something, marching down the street with signs, and the police had blasted them with fire hoses, set dogs on 'em, hit them with clubs. Larry had wanted to cheer! It was about time somebody grew a backbone and stopped letting the NAACP push 'em around! And when they'd interviewed the man done it—his first name was Bull, Larry remembered that—Jackson Prentiss was standing right next to him, smiling and nodding.

Prentiss had given Larry a good, firm handshake when he'd stammered a self-introduction. Looked him in the eye and told him, "Good job, son," then patted him on the shoulder before he walked away. Larry'd been so stoked about it he could hardly sleep last night. Meeting Jackson Prentiss was better than meeting the whole tribe of them Kennedys who'd taken over the whole da-gone country.

Now that he knew there was somebody as *important* as Jackson Prentiss's daughter in the room, Larry wanted to know all about her. So today—just for the entertainment value, mind you, he didn't mean nothin' by it—he'd cracked the door open just enough that he could listen in on the conversation. He couldn't hear it all, of course, had to close the door every time somebody walked down the hall, and the hall was full of people today, there being an execution and all. But he heard enough to piece it together, and the whole of it was more than a person could wrap his mind around.

That woman in there had only pretended to kill Jackson Prentiss's baby girl. Gave her to that preacher to raise instead. Kept Prentiss away from his own daughter for fourteen years with her lies! Larry was a divorced father so he knew what that was like, how a woman could twist things so you couldn't even spend time with your own flesh and blood. Prentiss had missed every minute of his little girl's growing up, and that woman in there was about to be executed for killing somebody who wasn't dead. Well, it served her right for what she did!

Larry had heard the mystic make that preacher swear he'd never tell a soul, but *he* was under no such obligation. And soon as they got the inmate back into her cell, he was going to go find Jackson Prentiss and tell him the whole story!

◆ ◆ ◆ ◆ ◆

Like wind through wheat, word spread in the prison complex that Princess was being taken from the lawyer conference room to the Long Dark for the last time. An eerie hush fell over buildings one and two, the cell blocks she would pass through on her way: an expectant silence, broken only by the rattling of keys in the ancient locks of the cell block doors, followed by the metal-on-metal clanging when the two guards escorting her banged the doors shut behind them.

The small, bald woman made no sound at all, just padded on bare feet on the cold concrete between the rows of cells. But the moment the first inmate caught sight of her, the whole building erupted in sound. Prisoners banged tin cups on the bars of their cells, yelled obscenities, and whistled. Some laughed and jeered; others applauded.

"You're gonna fry, baby killer!"

"Hope you suffer like that kid you chopped up with an ax."

"About time they give you what you got comin'."

A couple of inmates spat at her. One got her right in the face. Princess flinched reflexively but she didn't lift her handcuffed hands to wipe her cheek, just kept her head down and her eyes on the floor.

A number of the inmates refused to participate in the scorn and derision, though, the ones who believed she was special somehow, even if they didn't understand how. They watched her pass by in silence.

Once she reached the Long Dark, the four inmates locked behind solid cell doors there couldn't watch her pass, could only hear the guards' heavy tread and the little shuffling sound of Princess's manacle chain dragging on the floor. They didn't denounce and revile her, though. The next time the guards took Princess out of her cell, she wouldn't be coming back, and they knew they'd be taking that same walk themselves before long.

AFTER THE HEAVY METAL DOOR SLAMMED shut behind her with a loud clanking sound, Princess reached up and wiped the wet spot off her cheek with the hand not clutching her precious pictures. Then she rubbed her sticky fingers on the blanket on her bed, sat down at the table, and spread the pictures out on it so she could see them all at once.

It was profoundly quiet in her cell, but inside Princess's head, it was so noisy she wanted to stand up on a chair and holler "Stop!"

There was a big clock going, "Tick! Tick! Tick!" counting down the minutes she had left. It was four o'clock, they'd said. An hour: sixty minutes and it would be over.

And there was the rumbling deep in the darkest recesses, the hollow, scary places in her head where she wouldn't go. It was coming. The Big Ugly was coming to eat up the world.

On top of the ticking and the rumbling was a tangled jumble of thoughts. She had way too many things to think about and not nearly enough time to think them. Her mind was too full.

Trumping everything, of course, was her fear for Angel. Her child in danger sucked all the air out of her chest, blew a hole the size of Dallas in her belly. Angel was there—right now!—with the monster woman who meant to kill—

She cut the thought short; she had to let it go. She'd give it over to the Rev and he'd do everything any human being could do to save his baby girl. Couldn't do no better than that. She took a deep, shaky breath. She had to let that be.

But she didn't know at all how to think about her little girl bein' *pregnant*. There was nowhere in her mind to put an astonishing thing like that. How could it possibly have happened? A sudden, sickening thought pulled a little squeak of a scream from her lips. Had some man done to Angel what Jackson had done to her?

"No!" she cried out loud, shaking her head back and forth in horror. "Please, please no!" What if …?

Again, she cut the thought short; Princess didn't do what-ifs. Never had. Swore she never would. It was nothing but pure foolishness to go around second-guessing reality. Whatever happened,

happened, and that was the truth of it. It was just as likely Angel fell for a good-lookin' boy as it was that some man had fooled with her 'gainst her will. Wasn't nothing to be gained by fretting about how the girl come to be in a family way. The point was, Angel was pregnant. Angel was a-carryin' life inside her. A baby. Princess was gripped by a sudden wave of achingly tender longing. Why, she was going to be a grandmother. She giggled. A *granny* at twenty-nine years old!

But the Rev said Angel got tangled up with that witch woman 'cause she was trying to get rid of it! To kill the life in her belly. Princess's heart ached for her child. Why, the poor thing had just listened to scared, that was all. Can't never listen to scared. It'll lie to you ever' time. With the Rev all tore up over his wife and her having no mama, Angel didn't have nobody to talk to who'd set her right. When there ain't no lovin' voices in your ears, fear comes a' whisperin' and first thing you know, you start to listen and believe.

The Rev would love her through it once he found her. If Princess knew anything in the world, she knew that. Angel'd have a tough row to hoe, for sure, being pregnant and not married at sixteen. Whew! That was a powerful heavy load. Folks would judge her, scorn her, and whisper 'bout her. It broke Princess's heart to think of the pain all that would cause her precious daughter. But there was worse things than scorn. Angel come from tough stock; she'd make it. And then she'd have her own angel to love! Wasn't nothin' in life that even come close to the joy of lovin' a child!

Princess's own life would end; a new life would begin. There was somethin' right and fittin' about that.

She looked down at the pictures spread out on the table. How she longed to fall into them, spend a year just staring into the face of each one, imagining what Angel'd say and how she'd say it, what her hair smelled like when somebody brushed it and pulled it back in them dog-ears.

She picked up the final picture, the most recent shot of the pretty red-headed teenager, and let herself get lost for a few precious minutes in the face of the child—the young woman!—who was gonna have a good life. A good life with her own young 'un to love.

Princess had been strong as long as the Rev was around. But now that he was gone, she couldn't hold it together and she let fly, burst out crying. She wasn't immediately sure exactly what she was crying about, but knew it was about caring. It's not so hard to leave a life if you don't have nothing in it. All those years in solitary, it wasn't so awful to think of dying and not living like that no more.

But now!

Now, she knew the Rev and Mr. Cunningham and had had a little peek into Angel's life. And she so desperately didn't want to leave all that behind.

Why, she'd just got her first look at her little girl in fourteen years and now she wouldn't never get another one, wouldn't never hear about her again or see a picture of her precious grandchild—

Now, you wait just a minute, Emily Gail Prentiss!

A week ago she didn't have none of those wonderful things! Now, here she was a-whinin' about having to leave 'em instead of being grateful she had 'em in the first place. She was a blessed woman, for a fact, and she intended to go out of this world being grateful for what she had.

◆ ◆ ◆ ◆ ◆

There were eighteen metal folding chairs, three rows of six, set up for visitors in the windowless viewing area next to the execution room in the Quonset-hut looking building at the far end of the Long Dark. The six chairs on the back row were reserved for the press, the middle six for prison officials and any local or state politicians who wanted to make a statement one way or the other about the death penalty by their presence. The front six, the ones only fifteen feet away from the glass separating the spectators from the players, were reserved for the family of the victim.

Jackson Prentiss was the only man in the room. He had come an hour early and sat alone in the middle chair in the front row. The rain was making a racket on the roof of the building and the room had an unpleasant odor Jackson couldn't quite place. He glanced at the ends of the rows, where stacks of paper sacks had been set out for weaklings to puke in, and hoped it wouldn't stink worse later on.

He was seething. Things were not going as he'd planned and he was not a man accustomed to disappointment. His visit with Emily the day before had left him curiously unsettled. Oh, he'd put her in her place, all right. He'd hammered her with his words, bludgeoned her with the sheer force of his magnetic personality until she was a bloody heap, staring at him with those wide doe eyes he'd actually found attractive years ago. He'd cowed her!

Still …

There was a niggling itch in his soul about the woman. Something wasn't right. She was too smug, too … what was the word? Almost *serene*. She'd seemed at peace in such a profound way it left him disturbed, confused, and a little frightened. There was a power in her stillness he could neither understand nor tolerate. He'd done the best he could to crush it, but he had a sense that he'd never gotten to the core of her, that his blows had been flesh wounds, had not inflicted any real damage at all.

And her claim that she'd won! That she'd somehow beaten him! If she hadn't been under the protection of armed guards, he'd have leapt across the table and ripped her throat out with his bare hands. How *dare* she—a scar-faced little rat of a woman so skinny she probably wouldn't even generate a decent-sized puff of smoke when they fried her.

He took a deep breath and let it out slowly. There was something about Emily that touched a nerve deep inside him, reached down into the depths of him and released the man he used to be. Well, he wasn't that undisciplined, itinerant preacher anymore. He was in charge, kept company with the rich and powerful. His future looked bright and Emily didn't have any future at all. In less than an hour, she'd be dead.

That thought calmed him. He breathed deeply and looked around the room. What he saw pegged out his blood pressure all over again.

He'd assumed all execution chambers were alike, but this room was not constructed like the one in the Kilby State Prison in

Montgomery. He'd been there several times to watch niggers fry in Yellow Mama, the electric chair painted with left-over paint a prison road crew had used to mark no-passing zones. It was just one big room with the chair at one end and the visitors' gallery at the other. The folks on the front row weren't fifteen feet from the prisoner. You could hear him blubber like a baby and swear he didn't do it, the way that big buck did who'd murdered a white girl. That black ape heard the girl's family hurl obscenities at him and curse his soul. When they flipped the switch, you were close enough to smell his hair burn.

This building was different. It was divided into two separate rooms, with the electric chair in one and the visitors in another. Oh, there was a big picture window where you could see the whole thing. And they had a microphone in there so he could hear Emily's last words, listen to her cry and beg for mercy in that ugly, gruff voice of hers. But she couldn't hear him! And for months he'd been looking forward to his laughter ringing in her ears as she died.

He looked up when the door that led into the prison opened and in walked that suck-up guard, the skinny little guy who'd been outside Emily's door. He wasn't interested in chit-chat and opened his mouth to dismiss him, but the man started babbling before he had a chance. So he'd listened to the stupid guard stammer and stutter out his story. At first, Jackson scoffed, but his scorn slowly transformed through skepticism, doubt, and incredulity into belief.

Emily had lied! Angela wasn't dead at all! *That's* why she was so serene, so peaceful, so *smug*. It all made sense now. She'd kept a *live* Angela away from him for fourteen years. She *had* beaten him.

The flames of his fury licked at the base of his skull in such white-hot rage his brain threatened to explode out the top of his head. Sweat popped out on his forehead and upper lip, his hands began to shake, and he ground his teeth back and forth.

Well, she wasn't going to get away with it! He'd show *her*. He'd— What? What could he do about it? It was too late now. Emily *had* won.

No! There had to be *something*, some way to …

Wait a minute. Emily was willing to *die* to keep Angela away from him. But what if Emily knew he'd found out the kid was alive, that he was going to get her back from that preacher and keep her the rest of her life? What if he told Emily—

He couldn't tell Emily anything!

Jackson cut his eyes to the picture window, then turned and kicked the nearest folding chair, slammed his foot into it so hard it bounced off two other chairs and skidded across the floor into the wall. The mealy-mouthed guard stared at him in wide-eyed surprise.

The next time Jackson saw the scarred-up little woman she'd be strapped into that chair behind the glass and he couldn't tell her anything. She couldn't hear a word he said.

He suddenly stood very still, stopped breathing.

No, she couldn't *hear* him, but she could *see* him. What if the last thing she saw was Jackson and Angela—*together!* Oh, that would be rich. What if he showed her she was dying for *nothing*, that he had her precious Angel and wouldn't ever let her go. What if he was sitting there with his arm draped around Angela's shoulder, smiling as they turned on the juice and fried her. She wouldn't win then! He'd beat her, he'd have the last laugh after all.

He whirled around to the guard, his mind racing. The kid'd be home from school by now, and with a storm brewing, surely she'd stay there. He glanced at his watch—twenty minutes after four. He had forty minutes.

"Where does that preacher live?" he practically shouted.

"I don't know. I don't live in Graham." He must have seen the black fury on Jackson's face because he backed up like he'd spotted a rattler in the grass. "But ..." he sputtered. "I could find out. I mean, if you want to talk to him—he was going home. I heard him say he was going to see to Joy."

Suddenly, it hit Jackson, burst into his consciousness with a little sparkle, like a soap bubble popping. He *knew* where the preacher and his Angela lived.

Jackson turned without another word and rushed out into the pouring rain in the parking lot beside the Quonset hut. He spun out in the wet gravel, fishtailed almost all the way to the side gates in the fences that encircled the prison complex. The half-wit guard at the first one took interminably long to check him out of the facility. And

Jackson Prentiss was a man in a hurry; had not, in fact, ever in his life been in as big a hurry as he was in today.

❖ ❖ ❖ ❖ ❖

Oran Blackburn checked his watch and sighed. Half past four. Time to go prepare Emily Gail Prentiss to die.

Blackburn had been involved in several dozen executions in his twenty-three-year career in corrections. A couple had gone really bad. He tried not to think about them, but the images filled his mind every time a death-row inmate neared the end of the line, and Sizzlin' Suzie's sorry state of repair heightened his anxiety today.

He hadn't been in charge of the worst execution he ever witnessed, was grateful he wasn't the man who had to answer for what happened. An electric chair fires 2,000 volts of electricity through a prisoner's body. In theory, the shock should cause immediate unconsciousness, followed by nearly instantaneous death as the inmate's internal body temperature approaches 140 degrees.

That's not what happened that day in a gray stone room deep in the bowels of the Rockview State Correctional Institution in the mountains of central Pennsylvania. After they strapped the prisoner into Old Smokey, he'd refused a hood, and when they hit the switch, his eyes remained open, *aware*—until his eyeballs popped out onto his cheeks. He'd tried to scream, but his jaws had been locked down tight. Then his body literally burst into flames.

Blackburn later learned that botched executions that tortured prisoners to death or burned them alive were almost routine in Florida. That's when he made it his personal mission as a career corrections officer to be certain nothing like that ever happened on his watch. And it never had. Oh, some of the executions he'd performed had been … less than *tidy*, but in all of them death had been inflicted quickly and, he hoped, painlessly.

Most juries were reticent to sentence a woman to die in the electric chair unless her crime was particularly heinous. In more than two decades, Oklahoma juries had only handed down the death penalty to a handful of women. Prentiss would be the first among them to be executed. There had been no executions here since it became a women's prison in 1941, so the electric chair had sat idle for twenty-two years. Blackburn had had a crew go over the machine from top to bottom this week, but Sizzlin' Suzie was old as dirt. They'd tested her three times and she seemed to function fine. But there hadn't been a body in the seat during the tests, of course, and they certainly hadn't put through the full load of juice. No one could swear to what would happen when they did.

And the inmate who'd suffer whatever death Sizzlin' Suzie chose to deal out was the mystic, the seer, the little husky-voiced woman known as Princess.

Oran hated that. But it was his job to execute her and he sincerely believed ultimate retribution was necessary to the orderly functioning of a civilized society. He viewed dispensing final justice as a high calling, felt a certain gratification that a debt was owed the community and he collected it.

But there'd be no satisfaction in taking Princess's life.

◆ ◆ ◆ ◆ ◆

The old pickup made a wheezing noise that sounded like a horse ridden too hard as Jonas skidded to a stop in the dirt of the farm road in front of his house. The old man jumped down out of the cab and ran up the stone sidewalk to the front door in a limping gait, courtesy of the arthritis in his hips.

He was moving as fast as he could, but he couldn't shake the nagging sensation of trying to walk through deep water, of moving in a dream where no matter how fast you went your destination stayed out ahead of you.

He'd felt that way during the whole frantic dash home. The front edge of the storm had struck as he got into his truck at the prison. Raindrops fell from high in the blackening sky, big fat ones that went *splat* on the windshield and smacked the hood with a sound like a bongo drum. By the time he got to the front gate, the protesters were already scattering. Holding their protest signs above their heads as umbrellas, they ran helter-skelter to their cars parked along the road. He had to creep along to keep from hitting one of them.

When he pulled out on the highway, the real rain set in, a deluge pouring out of the brooding clouds. The wipers on his truck couldn't keep the windshield clear and he could barely see the road ahead of him. It had taken him dang nigh half an hour to drive twelve miles!

The half hour had seemed like three days. Because he was in such a desperate hurry and because his mind was in such chaos.

Princess knew … had *seen* …

How?

Joy was in danger!

Joy was *pregnant*. At sixteen? Why, when he was sixteen, he didn't even know where babies came from. All right, he did, too, but only because he lived on a farm around animals. He'd certainly never translated it into human terms. What was it with kids these days? He didn't understand none of it, the music, the dancing, not a bit of it made a lick of sense to him.

But he loved his granddaughter better than life and he would stand by Joy no matter what she did. No, not Joy. Angel. Princess's daughter.

How do you think about somebody like that? That woman had sacrificed her life; she'd loved *that* much. He didn't love his Maggie a speck less than she loved her baby girl. And he'd been planning to …

The rain had let up, the size of the drops shrinking until the clouds were just spitting them out in a fine spray, but the sky to the southwest was boiling and bubbling. He'd never seen clouds a deep, eggplant-purple color like that and he'd lived his whole life on the plains of Oklahoma.

Jonas burst through the front door and found Guadalupe folding laundry on the wide expanse of the dining room table. She looked up, startled.

"Where's Maggie?"

"She's asleep. About an hour ago, she—"

"We gotta get her up. Twister's a comin'!"

Lupe crossed herself and mumbled something in Spanish. "I've been listening to the radio," she said.

Jonas could hear it, turned up loud in the living room. He had a television set, but the least little bit of wind messed with the antenna on the roof and all he could get was snow.

"The weatherman said there was a tornado *watch*," she said. Tornado watches were as common in springtime Oklahoma as Catholics at a fish fry.

Jonas brushed past her and headed toward Maggie's bedroom. She trailed along behind, talking, "… but there hasn't been a *warning* yet. They didn't say—"

Jonas stopped, turned around and grabbed Lupe by the shoulders. He put his face close to hers and spoke slowly.

"A tornado's a-comin'. I don't care what the radio says, it's headed this way, and we got to git!"

Lupe turned instantly pale. "*Mís híjos!*" she cried.

"What about your kids?"

"They're home by themselves." Lupe lived four miles south of Jonas on Seminole Road. Her husband had just taken a job as a roughneck on an oil rig outside Oklahoma City and only came home on weekends. "The oldest, Juanita, is looking after the little ones, but she's only fourteen."

Jonas turned her body around and shoved her toward the front door. "I'll see to Maggie. You go get those kids and *run!*" Jonas had never put any stock in storm shelters or cellars. What was the point in hunkering down in a hole or cowering in a basement where a twister could drop the whole house on your head? He'd take his chances out in the open.

Lupe raced out the front door, didn't even close it behind her.

"And go *south!*" he called after her.

Princess had said to go south.

Jonas dashed to Maggie's darkened bedroom and flipped on the light.

She wasn't there.

26

Mac's heart was in more turmoil than the boiling black storm he caught sight of every now and then when the rain let up.

He had bolted out of the Iron House, jumped into his car, and gone barreling down the road in a near panic, only to be slowed almost to a standstill by a downpour so heavy he could only inch along with the stalled traffic. Precious minutes ticked away.

Straining to see the road ahead, which appeared and then disappeared in rhythm with his wipers' frantic effort to keep the windshield clear, he caught sight of twin red eyes through the onslaught of water. Brake lights. The car in front of him was slowing again.

Pounding his fists on the steering wheel in frustration, he roared out a cry of inarticulate rage, an animal noise: a growling howl that sounded feral and wild even to his own ears. It shocked him and somehow calmed him, allowed him to get a grip on his emotions so he could think.

Though his thoughts were tumbling around in his head the way clothes tumbled around in that dryer Jonas bought Maggie, he managed to grab one and hold on tight.

Joy's pregnant.

It was unthinkable, so unfathomable he couldn't seem to get his whole mind around it. It couldn't possibly be true and yet it so obviously was. Pregnant at sixteen.

"Why didn't she tell me?" he cried aloud, his voice anguished.

Reality settled into his belly, so stone-cold he shivered. How could she tell him when he wasn't there? Oh, the two of them had occupied the same geography, but in the past six months, he had been mentally, emotionally and spiritually AWOL. Poor Joy had been all alone. So scared! Trying to figure it out on her own. So desperate she was even willing to …

He let go of his grip on the thought then, and it sailed away in the maelstrom inside his head. But its emotional wallop lingered in his chest and tears sprang to his eyes, blurring his vision just as the rain started to let up. The traffic began to move ahead and pain was replaced by panic, the same urgent desperation he'd felt when Princess—

Princess!

He glanced at his watch. The fragile woman with purple eyes and a haunting voice had less than half an hour to live. The reality of it struck him with the blunt force of a runaway train. Princess was going to *die*—to save Joy.

But Joy would die, too, if he didn't get to her in time.

With a recklessness spawned by terror, Mac pulled out around the creeping car ahead and held his breath. He couldn't see oncoming traffic; if there was another vehicle in that lane, he would plow into it head-on. Fishtailing on the wet road, he passed the car and swerved back into his own lane seconds before headlights appeared to the left and a truck materialized out of the downpour. Mac sped away, going way too fast, playing Russian roulette again and again with oncoming traffic as he careened around everything that got in his way.

And the thing was, he wasn't even completely sure where Wanda Ingram lived. He'd only been there once when he dropped Mel off to pick strawberries. With his heart galloping in his chest, thudding in his ears, he slowed at each crossroads off Route 79, looking for Harrod's Creek Road.

When he finally turned southwest on it, the rain let up like he'd pulled out from under a waterfall. Then he could see what he was driving into—clouds so black they were purple, piled one on top of the other. Bubbling and boiling and writhing, they had swallowed the whole southwestern sky.

The Big Ugly's a-comin' ...

◆ ◆ ◆ ◆ ◆

Thunder rumbled as the guard named Talbot unlocked the passageway door and ushered Blackburn into the Long Dark. Even inside the stone walls, you could hear the wind and rain savagely pummeling the building. The warden smiled.

The storm had solved his protester problem more efficiently than a whole regiment of Oklahoma Highway Patrol troopers. There'd be nobody out front mournfully playing "Amazing Grace" to set the other inmates' teeth on edge. No chants, no hysterics. All the protesters were huddled in their cars, and it hadn't looked to Blackburn like the storm would be over in time for the hundred or so people to do anything more than mourn the passing of Emily Gail Prentiss after she was already dead.

Flanked by guards, Blackburn walked between the solid metal doors toward a cell halfway down on the right. As Talbot fit a key into the ancient lock, he steeled himself to face Princess. Dang it, he *liked* the woman. Okay, there it was, truth. He cared about her, with an affection born of more than long association. Though over time he had grudgingly developed a respect for how she conducted herself, it was more than that. He'd actually thought about it quite a lot, tried to puzzle it out, and came to the conclusion that his caring merely mirrored hers. People mattered to Princess, whoever they were. She'd certainly demonstrated that the day she'd told him to go home to his wife.

When he'd told Mac about the experience, he'd made light of it, passed it off as no big deal. But it had been huge. Princess hadn't just *urged* him to go home; she had *pleaded* with him, huge tears streaming down her scarred face. When he went into her cell, she'd fallen to her knees in front of him, begging him to go, saying his wife *needed* him. When he finally did go home that night, he'd found Joanie sobbing on the couch. She'd already had two miscarriages, so she hadn't even told him she was pregnant this time. As he'd cradled her in his arms, she'd whispered brokenly over and over again, "I wish you'd been here. I *needed* you."

He squared his round shoulders as the door swung open. Princess was sitting at the table staring into the face of a beautiful red-haired teenager—Joy McIntosh. What was Princess doing with a picture of Joy McIntosh?

PRINCESS LOOKED UP WHEN THE WARDEN stepped into her cell, but she was so focused on the picture of Angel that she had trouble shifting her attention to the warden.

"Miss Prentiss, I—"

"Princess, please, Warden Blackburn." Her voice resonated in the stone room, seemed almost to echo in the small space.

"All right, *Princess*," he said in a kind voice. "I'm here to talk about what's about to happen, to prepare you so you know what to expect."

"I 'spect I'm gonna die, ain't that right? I reckon I been preparin' to do that for fourteen years."

She was going to die. It was really going to happen this time. Today. In just a few minutes.

For a moment she was seized by such raw terror she feared she'd be sick again, but was certain she wouldn't make it to the toilet to vomit. Knew there was no way she'd be able to stand up on her rubber legs and move. And the horror was so intense she couldn't breathe at all. It was a physical pain in her belly so ragged and powerful that she recognized this must be real fear, the kind every human being could identify.

But as quickly as the terror grabbed hold of her, a calm took its place. The agonizing sensation in her belly, like a giant fist squeezing it, loosened. Her heart stopped pounding. She could breathe.

She didn't know if the whirlwind of emotions within her had been evident on the outside. The warden and the guards just stood there, looking at her. She saw compassion in the warden's eyes and in Talbot's. There was only fear in Bradley's.

"Well, go ahead then," she said, and her voice was firm, didn't tremble. "Tell me whatever it is you're—"

There was a *crack* as lightning split the sky and an instantaneous *boom* as the thunder rumbled in on its coattails. The lights in the cell and the hall flickered and went out. Then came back on again.

The warden looked around. "One thing you need to know is that there's a generator in the room next to the chamber that powers the … equipment. So a power outage won't—"

"Save me? I ain't lookin' to get saved."

She glanced at the pictures on the table in front of her. They instantly seized her attention and she fell into the images as the warden talked and the fury of the storm beat against the prison walls.

Princess grabbed hold of her thoughts and refused to allow them to wander from the faces smiling up at her. But she could feel it, the boiling, black rumble. The darkness.

The Big Ugly was coming fast.

◆ ◆ ◆ ◆ ◆

Even in the pouring rain, Jackson Prentiss had no trouble finding the road that would take him to the preacher's house.

Emily thought she was so clever, but she had given it away. She'd smarted off that he probably "had family" up there in that town on the hillside you could see from the prison. Looked like a little bitty town; the road to it wasn't even paved. Anybody he asked there would know where the preacher lived.

He'd planned to go roaring up to the town, grab the kid, and speed back to the prison in his brand new black and silver 1962 Pontiac Grand Prix. But right now he was only inching along in the downpour. The rain was falling in such a torrent that Prentiss could only see a few feet in front of the grill of the car.

He let fly a string of expletives and when he looked at his watch, he spewed out even more obscenities. It was 4:40 and he wasn't even to the town where the preacher lived yet, much less on his way back to the prison with Angela in tow, ready to sit smirking at Emily as she died.

Jackson had no doubt he could convince the preacher to make the girl go with him. His pitch would be short and sweet, a perfect one-two punch: *Here's the deal, Preach. You get your girl to go to the prison with me, or I'll tell her the whole story.*

He'd reassure the preacher that she didn't have to stay through the actual execution, just long enough for Emily to see her and then she could leave. In fact, the preacher could go along with her if he wanted to.

While the preacher was still reeling from the first punch, he'd land an uppercut to the jaw: *If you don't get her to go, my lawyers will be in court when the courthouse opens Monday morning with papers demanding full custody of* my daughter.

Then he'd purr: *But if you do, you'll never see me again.*

All he was asking was a half an hour of the girl's time in exchange for the rest of her life, and Jackson wouldn't give the preacher time to think it through and realize the whole thing was a gigantic bluff.

After all, Jackson had not a shred of proof that the preacher's girl was his Angela. If Emily had gotten cold feet and told the truth to save her hide, that would have been all over the news; the whole world would have known about it. And then he'd have fought to the death for custody of Angela—just to spite Emily! But with Emily dead, the *last* thing Jackson needed was for the press to get wind of all this, some nigger-loving reporter to start digging around in his past and find out about his "marriage" to a thirteen-year-old girl. No, he'd never tell a soul that he knew Angela was alive. But the preacher didn't know that.

The plan was sound; the preacher would cave in. Jackson only had to find him first! And right now he was puttering down a rain-slick road at ten miles an hour, racing a clock that was ticking away the final minutes of Emily's life.

Rage filled his chest like dragon's breath and he shoved his foot down on the accelerator. The big car leaped forward, though he could barely see twenty feet in front of him. That's why he missed the curve.

He was going way too fast when the turn materialized out of the downpour. He tried to stop, locked up his brakes, and the car skidded on the muddy road. Jackson watched, like seeing the scene in a movie, as his beautiful new Grand Prix slid sideways across the road, spun all the way around so it was facing the opposite direction, and then toppled off the edge of the road on its side in a ditch.

Though the impact wasn't severe, he was thrown out of the driver's seat into the bucket seat on the passenger side and banged his head on the door frame. He sat there stunned for a few moments, his heart thumping hard in his chest, until he got his bearings. Then fury burning blue-flame hot consumed him. He'd never be able to get his car out of the ditch by himself. And no telling how long it would be before the storm let up and he could make it into town to call a tow truck.

There was no way he'd be able to get Angela and take her back to the prison in time to see the execution. Worse, he wouldn't make it back there himself. Jackson pounded his fists on the dashboard, the sound drowned out by the huge hailstones that were now knocking dents in the metal of his new car.

◆ ◆ ◆ ◆ ◆

"Maggie!" Jonas yelled and ran to the bathroom.

Empty.

He raced from one room to the next in the downstairs portion of the house, hollering his wife's name as the radio squalled out, "The National Weather Bureau has issued a tornado watch for an area along and thirty miles either side of a line stretching from Atoka to Konawa, including the following counties: Atoka, Co—"

Jonas switched the radio off as he passed it on his way up the stairs. Graham was squatted smack in the middle of that line.

Maggie wasn't upstairs either. He opened every door, expecting to see her there. In the bedroom, the guestroom, the upstairs bath ... But each room was empty and silent. Where could she have gone? She'd never run away before. Then Jonas remembered what that Oklahoma City doctor, the one with the Hitler mustache, had said about old timer's disease: "Every morning you wake up in a whole new world."

Jonas came back down the stairs and stood helpless in the living room, staring at the spot on the wall where there once had been a curio cabinet, until Maggie'd smashed it the other night with the fireplace iron. His heart hammered in his chest so hard that for the first time in his seventy-four years, he sincerely feared he was going to have a heart attack. His whole body was slathered in fear sweat. He could smell it, feel it trickle down between his shoulder blades. He could feel panic down deep in his guts, too, scratching like a caged bobcat, struggling to get free.

If she wasn't in the house, she had to be outside. But *where?* Surely, she hadn't gotten as far as the barn. She wouldn't walk on grass, said it stabbed into her feet like needles.

The tool shed? The garage? He ran out the back door to search them and glanced southwest across the flat fields. The mammoth storm took up the whole sky, gray at the top, the color of a gun barrel, and soot-black at its pedestal base where lightning danced like shiny fishing lines cast into a lake.

The tool shed was dark and musty, built as a lean-to against the side of the garage. Something moved in the back corner and for a moment joy leaped in his heart. He'd found her! But he hadn't. It was just the calico cat Lupe kept setting milk out for, the one he'd almost run over when he came careening into the driveway … what? Five minutes ago? Ten?

"Maggie, where are you?" he wailed, but the only response was the whistle of the wind.

The rain hit hard again while he was in the garage, hammered the building so loud he thought for a moment the wind had torn the crab-apple tree out of the ground and dropped it on the roof. The wind did grab the single bay door he'd opened and slammed it shut, leaving him in the dark so that he had to feel along the wall to the side door.

As he raced toward the barn, sheets of torrential rain drenched him to the skin in seconds. Then the rain turned to hail, tiny pellets that attacked his head and arms like a swarm of bees. By the time he made it to the barn, the hail was the size of the doughnut holes Maggie used to fry up for him when she was making a dessert for a church social. The hunks of ice pummeled his bare head and beat down on his hands as he held them up to ward off the blows.

He tore open the side door of the barn and leapt inside, calling Maggie's name; went from horse stall to horse stall, looked behind the tractor, checked out the tack room. Hail beat on the roof of the barn like a dump truck load of gravel was falling out of the sky, making such a racket he feared he wouldn't hear Maggie's voice if she answered him.

But she wasn't there.

Before he finished searching the barn, he was sobbing in fear and frustration. He turned and raced through the hailstorm back to the house. The storm gobbling up the sky was now shrouded from view by the rain; rocks of hail hammered his head and shoulders and a savage wind tore at his clothes. He staggered through the pummeling to the gate and into the back yard.

Maggie was standing in the open back door in her white night gown, her hair loose and whipping in the wind. She was smiling like an excited child.

"Now it's your turn to hide," she called out above the roar of the gale.

And as he raced to her, Jonas had that sensation again, like he was running in mud, like he had cranked down to thirty-three rpm and the rest of the world was on seventy-eight.

In one motion, he scooped her up into his arms, turned, and suddenly he was sprinting like a young man, like an athlete, *toward* the storm, across the yard to the back corner. To the cellar.

There was no time to run away now and no place to go. He set Maggie down long enough to pick up a rock and pound on the rusty padlock. It gave on the second try and he flung open the double doors.

As he reached down to pick up his wife, the faucet of rain switched off in an instant; the wind stopped so abruptly he staggered forward a step, off balance from leaning into it. He smelled plowed dirt. Maggie quit struggling when they both heard a roar like the rocket that had launched John Glenn into space. They looked up as one across the field. A great maw of boiling darkness that extended down from the clouds and stretched out as far as they could see in both directions was hurtling at them in a freight-train rush.

Jonas didn't see a twister in it. Then he sucked in a ragged breath. *That* is *the twister!*

Frozen in terror, he only had time to think *Princess ain't the only one's gonna die today* before the roar ate up the world.

27

Even after everything that had happened, Mac groaned out loud when he saw Mr. Wilson parked beside the old house where the matted green trellis veiled the front porch. Some little part of him had held out, had not believed, had clung to the reasonable and explainable in the face of Princess's "knowing." Now there was no doubt, and his knees felt weak when he jumped out of the car and raced across the yard to the porch.

He was prepared to kick the front door in if he had to, but when he tried the knob, it wasn't locked. The living room was dark, the shades drawn, and it had a musty, unpleasant smell he couldn't place. Rotted food? A litter box? Sweaty, unwashed clothes? He forced himself to stand still just inside the door and listen for voices, but either nobody was talking or his heart was pounding so hard in his ears he couldn't hear the sound. The house was small and he dashed frantically from one empty room to the next, searching for his daughter. He longed to call out her name, but didn't dare. Princess said the "witch" was not just crazy, but homicidal, and he had no trouble whatsoever believing that. He didn't want to warn Wanda: he thought he might just need the element of surprise.

On the far side of the kitchen, beyond the pile of stinking, dirty dishes in the sink, he saw a small door ajar with a bright glow shining out through the crack. A basement door. He eased quickly down the creaking wooden steps, hurrying to the bottom before the noise alerted Wanda to his presence. When he stepped into the basement out of the stairwell, the bright light momentarily blinded him.

The room was as well lit as an operating room—which is exactly what it was; as clean and bright as the upstairs of the house had been filthy and dark. The white floor and walls were spotless; shiny silver instruments lay in clean trays on a white metal cabinet next to a raised examining-room table.

Wanda Ingram stood with her back to him beside the table; his beautiful red-haired daughter was stretched out on it with an IV tube in her arm. Her eyes were closed; her face was pasty. And as far as Mac could tell, Joy wasn't breathing.

◆ ◆ ◆ ◆ ◆

The warden repeated his question.

"Princess, do you understand what I've said to you?"

She looked up at him from the pictures on the table.

"I didn't hear a word you said, warden," she said sheepishly. "My insides is so tore up, I can't seem to make myself pay attention to nothing for very long."

"You want me to explain it again?"

"No need. I'll find out what's 'bout to happen soon's it happens. There's some things in life you're better off not knowin' and I 'spect the details of your own death is one of them things."

The warden nodded and the guard named Bradley, the one who was more scared than she was but hid it under gruffness, stepped forward with handcuffs and leg irons. Princess never could figure out why they trussed her up in those things every time they took her somewhere. Did they think she was going to try to run away? Or maybe fight them?

She didn't stand, just obediently held out both hands and Bradley fastened the cuffs on her wrists with a clicking sound. Then he knelt in front of where she sat.

"She ain't got no shoes on," he told his boss, as if the warden didn't have eyes in his own head to see. "Rules say a prisoner's supposed to be wearing shoes."

Blackburn looked at Princess.

"Shoes hurt my feet," she said.

The warden shifted his gaze to Bradley. "She can do this just as well barefoot as she can with shoes on. Let it go."

Bradley didn't like that much, but he turned back and clamped on the leg irons. The metal was cold and the irons and the chain between them were heavy. If she walked far in them, they wore a blister on …

But she wouldn't be walking very far. And a blister on the top of her ankle was the least of her worries right now.

"It's time to go," the warden said.

She picked up the pictures in her lap and tried to rise, but her legs didn't seem to want to hold her up; her knees were all rubbery-like. Talbot reached out and took her arm and pulled, and she made it to her feet.

The warden moved out of the cell. Talbot held Princess's elbow and the two of them stepped out into the hall together. Bradley came behind. Then the little procession formed for the walk through the Long Dark to the death chamber, with the warden in front and Princess walking along between the two guards, dragging her manacle chain.

The other four inmates on the Long Dark knew what was happening, though they couldn't see the hallway. A couple of them knelt on the floor and spoke out the food-tray slit in the door as she passed.

"You tell Ole Suzie I said hello, hear?"

Another simply called out in a mournful tone, "Dead man walkin'."

The words stole Princess's breath. But only for a moment. She hadn't been dead for the past fourteen years and she wasn't dead now, not yet. She still had moments, precious seconds. They hadn't all run out yet. She sucked in great gulps of air; she could still breathe. She was still alive. And she wasn't a man, neither. What'd they say a thing like that for?

Princess tried to grab hold of thoughts, but couldn't. She tried to savor sensations, but they skittered away too fast. The cold concrete floor on her feet. The feel of Talbot's hand on her elbow. Did she smell magnolia blossoms? Couldn't be, there wasn't no magnolias here. But that's what her nose told her brain—that she was smelling magnolias, so she savored the scent as if it were real. Funny what a person's senses do when their nerves are pulled so tight they're like the piano strings for high notes, so tight they almost sing.

Her other senses didn't seem to be working right either. Like all the signals in her head were scrambled. She saw bright flashes of light and color before her eyes and heard the rain on the roof of the building so clear it was like she was under a tin awning and it was hailing. She tasted metal in her mouth, too, like she was sucking on a penny, but that had happened before. Copper was the taste of fear.

This was it. This time she really was going to die, leave Angel and the Rev and the old man, Mr. Cunningham; leave them behind and go on to a new place. She didn't want to die! She wanted to live, to have a future. But she'd give that up, she reminded herself sternly. She'd traded her future for Angel's. She'd thought it was a good trade at the time and she still did.

The Long Dark was just that—long and dark. The hallway between the death row cells was lit only by bulbs in wire cages high up in the ceiling, and they cast a shadowy, circular glow on the floor, so you walked into a puddle of light, then out into the dark, then into the next puddle. There were six puddles of light between Princess's cell and the door that opened onto the covered walkway leading to the room where she would cease to be. She counted each one as she passed through it. Then the warden stopped and unlocked the door at the end of the hallway with a key he had in his pocket. The door opened outward, and as soon as he separated it from the jam, the wind tried to wrench it out of his grip.

The walkway might as well not have had a roof. When Princess stepped with a guard on each arm out into the tumult, a cold spray of rain came at them horizontally, liquid wind. The guards tried to hurry across the twenty feet of sidewalk to the next building. Princess couldn't move quickly with the manacles on her ankles, and she was certainly in no hurry. She loved the feel of the wind in her face and the rain on her skin. She stuck out her tongue, tried to taste individual raindrops, wiggled her toes in the little puddles on the concrete and felt momentarily breathless and exhilarated. Then the human convoy burst sputtering through the open door at the end of the walkway, and the little half-smile drained instantly off her face.

The room was cold and forbidding, with a light so bright it temporarily blinded her. But even with her eyes squeezed almost shut, Princess could see dark shadows in the corners of the room that no light could penetrate.

Talbot let go her hold on Princess's arm and Bradley shut and locked the door behind them. The others wiped at their clothing, shook the water off the best they could, but Princess stood still in that absolute way she had, a wet statue, with only her eyes moving, taking it all in.

A man in a white coat stood on the opposite side of the room. He had a stethoscope dangling around his neck and Princess recognized him as the prison doctor. He was a rheumy-eyed old man with a mass of white, tangly hair and looked like he'd spent way too much time snuggled up to a whiskey bottle. But she figured there probably wasn't no line of good doctors a-waitin' to go to work in a prison. She'd gone to him once when she tripped in the shower and busted her chin open, but now he wouldn't look at her, just stared at a spot on the floor about three feet out in front of him. There was another guard in the room, too. He wasn't anybody she'd ever seen before. He stood beside a small door on the side wall and he wouldn't meet her gaze either.

And sitting in the middle of the room, there it was. There *she* was. Sizzlin' Suzie. Ole Suz. Princess wondered how many prisoners her savage embrace had sucked the life out of over the years. They'd sat down right there, drew their last breaths and then she'd hurled them into eternity. But she looked almost ... ordinary. A sturdy, straight-backed wooden chair, oak probably, with thick arms and stubby legs. It sat on a raised black platform about six inches tall. There were straps on each arm rest and on the front two legs, and a big chest strap hung unfastened from the chair back.

Princess's knees suddenly felt weak again and she feared they'd dump her in a heap in the floor. She didn't want that, to go like that.

She hadn't done nothing wrong and had no reason to fear her death or what would come after. So she squared her shoulders, lifted her chin, and walked toward the chair, dragging the wet chain of the leg irons carefully between her feet. When she got to it, she stepped up on the platform, turned around slowly, and sat down on the big wooden seat. It was so tall, she had to raise up a little to get onto it. And when she scooted back in it, her feet dangled free, didn't even touch the floor.

◆ ◆ ◆ ◆ ◆

Jonas didn't know how he got down the fifteen-foot wooden staircase into the cellar. He was at the top and then he was at the bottom, and he had no memory of in between.

Then he dove through the fissure in the back wall of the cellar into the tunnels beyond, and ran bent over because the cave wasn't but about five feet tall. All he could do was drag Maggie along the smooth limestone floor behind him like a feed sack, holding onto the neck of her nightgown. Around one bend, another, and another, his eyes closed, reading the map of childhood memories inside his head in the utter darkness.

His ears began to pop and crackle.

Between one breath and the next the caverns went airless.

Suddenly yanked off his feet, he flew backward through the air and landed on his butt, and then he was sucked through the cold stone passage back the way he'd come. He still clutched a handful of Maggie's nightgown, but he wasn't sure anymore if she was still in it. The rumble of a thousand freight trains ate up his screams.

Light. Brighter. The stone beneath him turned to dirt as he slid across the cellar floor. Then he began to lift into the air.

◆ ◆ ◆ ◆ ◆

When Mac saw Joy lying like a corpse on the examining table in Wanda Ingram's basement, he let out a wild yell and leapt across the room in a couple of steps. Grabbing Wanda's arm, he jerked her backwards so abruptly she lost her balance and tumbled to the floor at his feet.

Mac didn't give the woman another thought. All his attention was focused on his daughter.

"Joy!" he cried. "Oh, baby, wake up!" He clutched her shoulders and shook her, but her head rolled on her neck like a broken doll.

"Joy!" No response.

So he slapped her. Hard. She sucked in a gasp and groaned and he knew she was alive! He ripped the IV needle out of her arm, picked her up off the table, threw her over his shoulder in a fireman-carry, and turned for the cellar steps.

Wanda stood between him and the staircase, a nightmare visage with her ruined face and wild eyes.

"You leave her alone," she growled, menace in her voice. "I'm taking her to her mother; Melanie told me to."

Advancing a step in his direction, she reached out for a razor-sharp scalpel lying on the tray of instruments.

Mac had no weapon to defend himself with, so he attacked the madwoman with the only thing he had—his daughter's body. He hurled Joy like a grain sack at Wanda. The weight and force of the body slammed Wanda into the wall and she slid down it into a heap with Joy on top of her.

Mac kicked the tray across the room in a clatter of scattered instruments, knelt, and lifted Joy up onto his shoulders again. As he did, there was a loud crack, followed by a rumble of thunder so close it shook the house above them and reverberated in the stone basement.

"Melanie didn't tell you to *murder* her daughter!" He tossed the words over his shoulder at Wanda as he stumbled up the stairs. "Melanie's *dead.* And you're crazy!"

Mac staggered through Wanda's house, squinting in the dark with illusory white orbs bobbing around in the air in front of him, courtesy of the basement's bright lights. Through the kitchen, bouncing off the side of the dining room table, into the living room where he banged his shin painfully on the coffee table, and out the front door onto the covered porch.

He'd made it two steps down off the porch before he looked up, and the world was all wrong. Then it came together in his head. The crack of thunder he'd heard—lightning had struck a tree on the fence line just beyond Wanda's yard. On the spot where the tree had stood was a smoldering stump. The trunk and limbs of the big oak had fallen toward the house and now lay across the crushed top of Mac's car.

He stood bewildered by the sight. Then he noticed that the rain had stopped altogether. In the sudden stillness, the leaves on the trees trembled, as if in fearful anticipation. He turned, dreamlike, and stared back across the lake at a great heaving darkness hurling toward them. It didn't look like a tornado, but Mac knew it was. Princess had said. The Big Ugly.

Terror and desperation launched him into a zone, a heightened state of awareness. He weighed his options carefully and decided what to do, without any sense of urgency—all between one heartbeat and the next.

Mr. Wilson!

Mac ran to Joy's car and yanked the door open. What if there was no key ... But it was there in the steering column. He tossed Joy into the passenger seat and was momentarily thrilled when the jolt shook a groan out of her.

Leaping behind the wheel, he cranked the engine. It turned over once, twice.

Please!

And then it caught and hummed. He shoved the car into drive to pull forward around the tree, then jerked the ancient transmission into reverse to turn around and head out the driveway. When he threw the car back into drive again, he saw her.

Wanda Ingram was standing on her porch. Just standing motionless, staring at nothing at all.

I can't. There's no time!

Mac pulled the steering wheel hard to the right, shoved his foot down on the accelerator and the old car leapt forward, the back tires spinning out a spray of gravel behind them.

28

Oran stepped back and tried to get a grip. His heart was beating the staccato rhythm of a snare drum in his chest, and his mouth had gone dry as a dust bunny. That frail little woman had walked over to Old Suzie and sat down in it like a little girl climbing into a too-big chair at Thanksgiving, her feet dangling, swinging back and forth beneath her. For some reason the sight totally unnerved him.

"Bradley, you can open the curtain now," he said, and was genuinely surprised that his voice was steady.

The execution chamber was an eighteen-by-eighteen-foot block room with a concrete floor that sloped slightly to a drain just inside the door—so guards could hose the place down to clean up any … mess an execution might make. A small window on the wall to the right of Suzie looked out over the prairie toward the Indian Bluffs, and the wall in front of the chair was completely covered, floor to ceiling, with heavy black drapes. The guard stepped to the draped wall, reached behind the fabric for a cord on a pulley, and slowly cranked the drapes open.

Oran watched Princess's eyes grow wide when she looked out through the window behind the drapes to a room full of folding chairs occupied by a handful of people, maybe ten of them, all men. Usually there were family members of the victims. He'd seen executions where as many as twenty or thirty relatives showed up, crying and screaming obscenities at the prisoner. He was enormously grateful that someone had had the foresight to design the execution chamber in this prison to grant some degree of privacy. In this case, it really didn't matter, though. The six chairs on the front row reserved for the victim's family were vacant. The crowd out front today was mostly newspaper reporters and elected officials who were determined to show their constituents by their presence that they supported giving murderers what they deserved.

Oran nodded to the other guard and he flipped a switch that turned on the intercom between the two rooms.

"Can you hear us alright?" he asked, looking out at the crowd. Several heads nodded. Then he turned to Princess and saw that she was peering out through the glass, searching for someone in the viewing room. She'd been sitting stiff and straight in the chair, her back rigid, but after a survey of the room, she slowly relaxed backward, not with an audible sigh, but with the posture that went along with one. Either she'd spotted the person she'd hoped would be there, or had confirmed that someone she didn't want to see hadn't shown up. Whichever it was, the result appeared to satisfy her.

"Miss Emily Gail Prentiss," he said, the formal tone an effort to distance himself from the emotional response he couldn't seem to get a handle on, "do you have any last words you would like to say before you die?"

◆ ◆ ◆ ◆ ◆

Jonas held tight to the handful of nightgown. He wanted them to be sucked up to their deaths together.

Suddenly, a jarring clunk blotted out the light above him and he plopped down into the dirt. The roar continued, but not as loud. Like he'd stuck his fingers in his ears. The sound slowly lessened, rumbled away, a mighty herd of buffalo stampeding the other direction.

It grew quiet. Still. Only a small shaft of gray light filtered down past whatever was jammed in the cellar doorway that had plugged up the opening where the doors had been ripped off. It was white. A chest freezer, maybe. Maggie was crying softly.

Maggie!

He was lying on his back, one arm stretched out above his head like he was trying to declare a touchdown. He pulled on the handful of fabric he still grasped in the other hand and there was weight on it. *In* it. Rolling over on his side, he tried to rise but nothing worked right, so he scooted in the dirt until he was lying beside her and could make out her face in the gloom. It was the first time he'd ever seen her hair tangled, a matted mess going every which way. There was a big scratch on her forehead and Lord only knew what else was wrong with her that he couldn't see. But she was alive!

"Don't cry, sweet pea." The words came out in a barking croak. Must have screamed his voice hoarse. Or injured his throat. Shoot, every bone in his body could be broke for all he knew! "Shhh, now. It's okay."

"Where are we?" Her voice was full of wonder. She eased up onto her elbow and looked around. "What are we doing in the cellar?"

She seemed so … *there.*

"Maggie?"

She turned and looked at him and he fell into the depths of her blue eyes, just like he did that first day when he'd stepped up on her father's porch with a bouquet of sunflowers in his hand. She reached out and brushed his hair up off his forehead like she always did, then touched his cheek tenderly.

And in that moment, just for that moment, she was his Maggie.

"It's all over, sugar," he whispered. "It's gone. You're safe now." And his heart swelled up with the joy of it. "I'll take care of you."

◆ ◆ ◆ ◆ ◆

Princess cleared her throat once, twice before she spoke.

"You'd think I'd a-thought of something important to say as my last words, studyin' on it like I have for fourteen years," she said. "But now it's come down to it, all my thoughts is running around on the top of my mind like water spiders and I can't grab hold of nary a one long enough to think it." She shrugged her narrow shoulders. "Besides, I ain't got no spit. Can't talk without spit."

Princess was quiet, in that profound way she had that made silence more than the absence of noise, made it a positive force, an aura wrapped tight around her. Oran had the crazy notion that if he reached out his hand, he could touch it, and the silence would feel like … warm smoke.

But he didn't reach his hand out. For a few moments he didn't move at all. No one did. They all seemed as frozen in place as he was. Time paused, then let out its breath in a slow, sad sigh and reluctantly moved on.

As one struggling through deep water, Oran lifted the paper in his sweating hand and prepared to read it aloud. It was Princess's death warrant, signed by the governor of Oklahoma in the presence of four witnesses, as was required by law. It had been issued for May 10, 1963, and was valid for another seven hours, until midnight.

"Whereas, Emily Gail Prentiss has—" he began, but that husky, disconcerting voice of hers interrupted him. It wasn't firm like it usually was. Though the people sitting out front wouldn't likely catch the tremor in it, Oran did. Because he was hearing it live instead of through a microphone. And because he was close, near her physically. But on a much deeper level he couldn't tack words onto, he was somehow close to her in a more profound sense as well.

"I ain't got nothin' to say sorry for, and nobody to ask forgiveness from. I done made my peace with Almighty God, and anybody else got somethin' against me, don't matter." She paused for a moment. "My slate's wiped clean. That's how I'm leaving this life. Guess that ain't a bad way to step into the next."

Oran cleared his throat and continued.

"… has been convicted of the crime of murder …"

❖ ❖ ❖ ❖ ❖

Mr. Wilson's front bumper clipped the side of the porch as Mac skidded to a stop in front of the house. Leaping out of the car, he raced up the steps for the woman who stood staring vacantly into space.

"Twister!" he cried.

Without another word, he grabbed Wanda Ingram by the wrist, dragged her down the steps, pushed the front seat forward, and literally threw her into the backseat. He jumped behind the wheel again and sped away, banging the door closed as he drove.

A glance in the rear-view mirror revealed that the bubbling black wall had made it to the far side of Boundary Oak Lake.

The world seemed to crank down into slow motion. Mac had his foot jammed to the floorboard and Mr. Wilson lumbered along the best it could, bouncing over the bumpy road, its steering wheel vibrating madly in Mac's white-knuckled grip, the radio blipping on and off so fast the music was unrecognizable.

With that same odd calm and clarity of thought, Mac analyzed the situation and weighed his options. The twister was so huge he couldn't even tell what direction it was headed. It might not even cross the lake at all, just rumble along the far side of it and away.

He tore his eyes from the road ahead and stole a quick look in the rear-view mirror. His mind almost refused to process what he saw. The lake was swirling upward in a gray wall of frothing water.

Is this what Moses saw when he crossed the bottom of the Red Sea?

But the wall of water behind Mac wasn't standing still. It was moving, *racing* toward him. Wanda sat up in the backseat, followed his gaze and saw the gigantic waterspout. She began to scream in terror, her wail mingling with the low rumble Mac could now hear, the sound of a stampede.

Calm reasoning again. All right, now he knew the trajectory of the storm—northeast—the same direction they were going on Harrod's Creek Road. And the twister that was gobbling up the world in a mountainous avalanche of water *was gaining on them.* Mr. Wilson couldn't possibly outrun it. Now what?

Go south! Princess said to go south.

Turning south would set them at right angles to the tornado. If they could go far enough, fast enough, it would pass them by. Unless it changed direction, of course. Or was so huge they couldn't get beyond it in time.

Problem: They were on the only road for miles. Nothing intersected it going south between here and Route 79. They'd never make it that far.

Well, road or no road, Mac intended to go south. That's what Princess had said to do, and right now he trusted that more than common sense, a good plan, or his own instincts.

Princess. She's going to die. Might already be dead.

He sucked in a strangled sob, then shook off the thought so he could concentrate. Easing the pressure on the accelerator, he jerked the steering wheel to the left, sending the lumbering white car into a sideways slide down the middle of the narrow asphalt road. He let the car skid for a couple of seconds, smelled the scent of burning rubber, then gave it the gas again. The old Buick fishtailed as the tires tried to grab, then leapt forward off the roadside into the ditch.

It was a shallow ditch, but the jolt sent Mac upward and his head banged painfully into the roof of the car. Joy bounced off the seat, hit the dashboard and landed with her legs in the floorboard and her torso on the front seat. Wanda flew upward, too, maybe hit the ceiling, Mac couldn't tell. But her screaming never missed a beat, it remained a continuous, wailing shriek. The radio turned on, blared out a single note from a trumpet, and turned back off again.

Mac held tight to the steering wheel as the old car bounced up out of the ditch on the other side, tossing everyone around again before it ripped into the barbed wire fence surrounding the vast expanse of pastureland. The wire didn't break and the car yanked out two old fence posts before the wire finally came loose from them. One strand of it remained tangled in the grill, flapping against the side of the car as they tore out across the open plains.

The prairie appeared deceptively smooth. Melanie used to say it was as flat as a Barbie Doll's belly. But in reality, it was as bumpy as trying to drive over a washboard. Mr. Wilson lurched up over yucca plants and banged down into prairie dog holes, filling the car with ancient dust expelled in wheezing gasps from the old seats.

A sandhill crane appeared in front of them in an explosion of gray wings as it tried to leap into the sky. But the car center-punched it, feathers flew, and the body bounced off the grill and collided with the windshield with a thunk that dented the glass and sent cracks racing out in all directions from the bloody smear.

Jackrabbits darted out of their path, bounding like midget kangaroos; they even scared up a coyote that dodged away and was gone.

Mac paid the animals no heed as he jammed his foot down so hard on the accelerator he feared he might shove it right through the rusted old floorboard. He could see the approaching monster to their left, could now see the cloud of dust that marked the edge of it. If they could just get beyond that point before it got to them ... so far away! The tornado was *huge*. The Big Ugly.

Time flew by, propelled by rocket fuel—and it also crept by like slogging through knee-deep mud in a swamp. Both at the same time. The world was a wild yell. Wanda was screaming. Mac realized he was shouting, too, an inarticulate yell of effort and determination, yearning and terror.

The monster drew closer every second. His ears began to pop and the car was filled with the scent of a freshly plowed field. The roar grew louder and louder; the dust cloud of its edge was just beyond them, achingly out of reach.

29

Durango County Deputy Sheriff Stan Oliver pulled to a stop and flipped on his blue lights. A downed tree was blocking Seminole Road. It was barely sprinkling now, so he got out of his vehicle to investigate, stepped over the tree trunk and froze. There was no road on the other side of the tree. The highway—asphalt, shoulder, *everything*—had been ripped right out of the ground. The officer stood stupefied for a moment, staring down the swath of devastation that extended as far as he could see in both directions. Judging from the direction the tree carcasses were leaning, the beast that killed them was traveling northeast. Toward Graham!

The deputy ran back to his cruiser, put the hand-held mic to his lips and pushed the transmit button with his thumb.

"Dispatch, this is Oliver, do you copy?"

When he released the button there was only static.

◆ ◆ ◆ ◆ ◆

For almost an hour now, Andy Cook had watched in growing horror as the massive storm swept across the Oklahoma plains, its image a green blob on the WSR-57 radar screen.

He hadn't ever observed the progress of a storm on radar, so he had nothing to use for comparison, but the other meteorologists had, and they said they'd never seen one move that fast. Andy had plotted coordinates, then used his slide rule to do the math, and if his calculations were correct, the storm was roaring northeast at a speed of sixty miles per hour. Most tornadoes tracked southwest to northeast.

The section supervisor had been on the phone almost non-stop for the past half hour, trying to get spotter confirmation of a twister on the ground. But the back-path of the storm was eerily quiet. Phone calls produced a busy signal; radio transmissions granted nothing but static. Out in front of the storm, no one he spoke to reported even a hint of a funnel cloud.

But the distinctive hook shape on the storm's radar image was unmistakable, and it had remained constant, without a sign of dissipating, for the past sixty-three minutes.

"Nobody's spotted a twister," the supervisor bleated in frustration. "And without a sighting, we can't—"

"What if they can't see it?" Every eye in the room turned to stare at the new guy.

"You're saying it's invisible?"

In theory, that was possible. A visible tornado was a combination of a condensation funnel—a rotating cloud on the ground—and a debris and dust swirl. A weak tornado traveling over wet soil it couldn't suck up, or over open countryside with no leaves or branches, could appear transparent.

But Andy Cook didn't believe for a second the huge hook on the radar screen was a weak tornado.

"No, not invisible. What if it just doesn't look like a tornado?" Andy spoke the thoughts as they suddenly formed in his head. "What if it's so big you can't see the funnel shape?"

The supervisor rolled his eyes. "If a big twister's right on top of you, maybe. But on those flat, empty plains, you can see a storm coming from miles away. Last guy I talked to said the base of the clouds was low to the ground. You could spot a funnel shape snaking down out on a low-ceiling storm like that—if there was one to see."

Not if it was huge, Andy thought. Monstrous. Not if it was ... a *mile* wide, if the cloud base the guy saw wasn't just low but *on* the ground. What if that *was* the tornado?

Andy turned back to the radar, watched the hooked menace bear down on Graham. And he couldn't stand it, couldn't ignore his gut any longer. He turned and walked quickly back to his desk, picked up the phone, dialed O and asked the operator to connect him to the courthouse in Graham, Oklahoma.

This is gonna get me fired.

"Durango County Courthouse," a cheery female voice said. "Betty Porter speaking. How can I help you?"

"This is the National Weather Bureau in Oklahoma City. A tornado—"

A clicking sound cracked in his ear and the phone went dead. Andy slowly lowered the receiver back into the cradle. He was too late.

◆ ◆ ◆ ◆ ◆

There was a great roaring in Princess's head, like a mighty, rushing wind was blowing inside it, the Big Ugly itself, a gale that swept through vast caverns between her ears, howling in hollow, empty halls. Those halls had been full once, jammed with people and impressions, sights, smells, laughter. And memories, gems of memory that glowed from the inside.

Now there was nothing there at all. She had consumed the memories, used them up, squeezed every sparkle of light out of them. And all the rest of the contents of her mind had been blown away by the wind, whisked up into the air like autumn leaves hurrying down a country lane.

Terror of the unknown had been gobbling up huge bites of her soul ever since the warden stepped into her cell, but she was beyond fear now. She had raced out ahead of it into the wind, felt the rushing air whip her hair back out of her face.

She couldn't think; had nothing to think about and no mind to think with. All she could do was feel. So she let go of thinking, let go of the reality of what was about to happen and filled her lungs with the sweet scent of a small child's breath, and the warmth of her chubby little hand.

Bradley and Talbot stepped forward then to strap her into the chair.

"I got to take these now," Talbot said, and tried to remove the pictures Princess clutched in her hand. She tried to speak, to tell the guard that she didn't want the pictures taken away, that she wanted to hold onto them until the very end. But she discovered she had no voice. All she could do was look at Talbot with mute pleading in her purple eyes.

◆ ◆ ◆ ◆ ◆

Mac gritted his teeth, leaned his body forward in the seat willing the car to go faster. The prairie in front of them was suddenly filled with jackrabbits. Dozens of them crossed in front of him, running from the monster. Mac mowed them down, their bodies stacking up like cordwood on the big grill on the front of the car.

Only another hundred feet or so and they'd be beyond the edge of the rumbling terror.

Please ... for Joy!

Mr. Wilson was suddenly engulfed in swirling dirt, a choking cloud of unbreathable air, and Mac knew his run for it was over. The car scooted sideways instead of forward, and he let go of the steering wheel—he wasn't driving anymore anyway—and threw his body over Joy to protect her. Then the real wind hit, knocked the car aside as carelessly as a child might kick a ball out of the way.

◆ ◆ ◆ ◆ ◆

At 4:55 p.m. the tornado warning siren began to wail from the bell tower of the old courthouse building in the center of the town square. Betty Porter had only heard "National Weather Bureau" and "tornado" but that was all she needed to hear. It took a few seconds for the siren to rev up to full blast, where it produced a warbling, high-pitched shriek like an air-raid warning. No one who heard it could mistake it for any other sound.

At that moment, normal life all over town stopped. From that moment forward, Graham, Oklahoma would never be the same again.

Mothers grabbed their children and shoved them into the basement if they had one, or into a bathtub under a mattress if they didn't. Plenty of people had bomb shelters in their back yards and they hunkered down in them, as frightened as they'd have been of a nuclear attack. The manager of the Piggly Wiggly grocery store herded all his customers into his big, walk-in freezer; Main Street shoppers huddled in back rooms, away from the plate-glass windows out front.

Still, some people wasted precious time wondering if this was the real thing or just a drill. Others didn't hear the warning at all, had their windows down, the fans whirring inside, and the mixer on making mashed potatoes for supper so they could eat in time to watch *77 Sunset Strip* at 7:30.

But most had a pretty good sense about such things, living as they did in Tornado Alley. They could usually spot the really bad storms and all afternoon they'd been eying the monstrous, eggplant-purple storm rumbling toward them across the prairie.

◆ ◆ ◆ ◆ ◆

"I'll just set the pictures right here in your lap," Talbot said, and pried Princess's fingers off the photographs. She placed them carefully on Princess's damp dress where she could see every one of them. Bradley unfastened her handcuffs and removed them, then took her arms and strapped them to the arms of the chair with worn leather straps that looked like the ends of a belt.

"Not so tight!" Talbot snapped, in a whisper only Bradley and Princess could hear. "She ain't going nowhere."

Bradley removed the leg irons and buckled down her right leg and then her left, fastening the straps affixed to the wooden legs of the chair around her skinny limbs. Then he picked up a wet sponge out of a bucket under the seat. A wire ran from it into an opening in the raised platform the chair rested on. Princess felt the cold of the sponge on her leg and jumped involuntarily, but she was trussed up so snug her body didn't move. She glanced down and saw him tape the wired sponge to her right calf.

Talbot then reached into the same bucket under the chair and withdrew a bigger sponge and placed it inside a leather helmet with an inner layer of copper mesh that she set like a crown on top of Princess's shaved head. The sponge was so wet it dripped, and rivulets of water streamed from it down her neck and into her face, but she gritted her teeth and didn't jerk away, just sat still while Talbot fastened the strap on the helmet under her chin.

But when the guard lifted a black hood and started to put it over her head, Princess found she still had a voice, after all.

"Don't you put that thing on me!" she cried. "I don't want no hood over my face." She gestured with her head toward the crowd of people in the viewing room. "I wonder they have any stomach for watching a woman fry, but if they can't take seeing my face when I die, they shouldn't a-come."

She turned to the warden then, standing several steps away from the chair by the window that looked out on the Indian Bluffs.

"Ain't no reason I got to wear that thing, is there?" she asked. "I don't want my last sight to be the inside of a black sack." She nodded toward the pictures in her lap. "That's what I want to see—them faces right there."

The warden paused for a beat, considering, then told Talbot to forget about the black hood. Talbot dropped it to the floor, then she and Bradley stepped back from the chair.

The loudest crack of thunder yet broke overhead at that moment, so loud it made the building's roof vibrate. Suddenly, the lights in the execution chamber and in the viewing room flickered once, twice and then went out. The windowless viewing room was plunged into total darkness, and the crowd assembled there was silent for a couple of beats, then there were murmurs and the sounds of chairs scooting around.

In the execution room, Oran froze. If the electricity failed, the generator was supposed to come on automatically. Why hadn't it? Thunder banged harsh and loud outside again.

Into the darkness, an otherworldly sound suddenly rang out, a voice as crisp and clear as a sleigh bell on a snowy morning. Princess sang! Her voice sailed high and free, trailing a haunting melody behind it like the tail on a kite. Her words were the shadow of language, its mirror image, sounds that communicated something achingly tender and remote that existed just a heartbeat or two beyond reality.

The song went on and on. Sometimes so soft it was barely audible, other times, loud, with pure, high notes an opera star would have been hard pressed to reach. Emotion filled every note. Fear. Grief. Loneliness. Serenity. But joy was laced throughout, the canvas on which all the music was painted, the thread that tied the errant pieces together into a whole that was somehow bigger and grander than the sum of its parts.

Oran stood transfixed in the darkness, hypnotized by the sound. No one else moved either. The sound transcended time, so later no one who heard it could say how long it lasted, or exactly what it had sounded like. But everyone who heard it knew it was unique, special, a sound they had never heard before and would never hear again.

The lights blinked again once, on and off. After another blink, they remained on. As soon as the light struck her, Princess fell instantly silent. But it took a moment or two before her song stopped reverberating in the room. The sound was replaced by a hum in the adjoining room, like an old refrigerator kicking on. The generator that was supposed to produce enough electricity to operate Sizzlin' Suzie was running.

◆ ◆ ◆ ◆ ◆

Mac heard a woman singing.

"Don't theeey know it's the end of the wooorld? It ended when—"

Skeeter Davis shut up abruptly and it was quiet again, no sound but a roaring echo in his ears.

He tried to open his eyes but the effort was too much. He'd had such a vivid dream! There'd been wind and running from it. Screaming and dirt. A nightmare.

Joy!

Mac's eyes popped open again. There was something sticky all over his face. He reached up and wiped it off so he could see. But what he saw was wrong, the horizon line was sideways. No, *he* was sideways.

When he tried to move, he heard a sound, a low moan beside him. Turning his head seemed to take forever, but when he did, he saw his daughter, slathered in mud, lying on the slanted seat next to him. She'd somehow got turned completely around, with her head next to the passenger side door and her feet almost in his lap.

It all came back to him in a rush and his heart stampeded in his chest in terror. The twister, racing toward the edge, and then …

But there was no wind now, just an eerie silence. He was lying up against the car door because the car was sitting sideways, not all the way over on its side, but not level.

He reached out a trembling hand.

"Joy?" He touched her leg. It was warm. "Joy!" She moved, her eyes fluttered open but didn't focus, then blinked shut again. "Joy, it's Daddy. Wake up."

"Daddy?" she mumbled, but didn't open her eyes.

That was enough, though. More than enough.

There was movement behind him. He turned and saw a mud-splattered Wanda Ingram lying in the backseat of the car, covered in something. Straw. She was breathing, he could see that, but when he called her name, she didn't answer, and her right arm appeared to be bent at an unnatural angle.

He might have broken bones as well. Joy might, too. But they were alive.

In a great rush, relief flooded over him, warm in his belly where he'd been tied in a knot in fear. He took a great gasp of air and let it out slowly. They'd made it!

He turned back toward the hole where the windshield had been, still unable to get his bearings. There was nothing in front of him but a stretch of empty, plowed dirt. His side of the car was lower than the other side. The car must be in a ditch or something. The view out the raised passenger window was clouds and a brooding, gray sky. He looked out his own side window and saw the same thing that filled the backseat—straw. No, hay.

The car was resting on a pile of hay in a field.

Mr. Wilson had been blown ... how far? Who knew? The outside edge of the storm had clipped the car, tossed it into the air and it had landed in a haystack. The absolute absurdity of that sent Mac into a gale of semi-hysterical laughter.

Maybe he better check to see if two black feet were sticking out ...

Hysteria overtook him and he laughed harder, howled, his eyes watering. The Big Ugly had ...

Big Ugly. Mac stopped laughing. *Princess!*

◆ ◆ ◆ ◆ ◆

As the siren began to wail in Graham, the tornado chucked Jonas Cunningham's orange Allis Chalmers tractor into a cherry orchard stripped bare of leaves and bark, gobbled up Joe Hanson's chicken-feeding barns and all 11,000 of his laying hens—left behind the straw nests, though, and most of the eggs, unbroken—and created an instant farm pond a quarter mile away with the water it had sucked out of Boundary Oak Lake. The twister covered the four miles between the shattered remains of Wanda Ingram's house and town in just less than four minutes.

Then it slammed into Graham, cut a swath of annihilation a mile wide through the southeast quadrant between South Main Street and US 270.

With debris as a battering ram, it ripped open the massive fifteen-story concrete grain elevator on the edge of town as easily as tearing into a Kleenex box and devoured hundreds of thousands of bushels of corn. The twister's color morphed like a chameleon from bubbling black to bright yellow before it plowed through the Ford dealership next to the elevator, tossing brand new Thunderbirds around like a drunken juggler while it sand-blasted their shiny paint down to bare metal with the corn pellets.

Hours after it sucked up clothing from the Pretty Woman manufacturing plant beside the dealership, skirts, blouses, and scarves rained out of the upper atmosphere onto rooftops, cars, and fields as much as thirty miles away. It hurled ladder trucks, pumper trucks, and ambulances into the air when it rumbled through the fire station, and heaved two smashed school buses onto the basketball court of what once had been the high school gymnasium. Its savage winds picked up an eighteen-ton road grader and chucked it onto the ninth green at the country club.

It set off bombs, too.

After it yanked the gasoline pumps out of the ground at the Texaco station, a tentacle of spilled gas ignited with a little *whump* sound, then followed the fuel fuse back to the underground storage tanks. The explosion could be heard for miles.

But the second explosion was even bigger, when the tornado hurled a propane tanker like a Molotov cocktail into the meatpacking plant.

Chewing its way through residential neighborhoods next, the writhing black wall swallowed houses with porch swings, bikes on the front lawn, and flower beds out back, and then vomited unrecognizable rubble, tangled heaps of shattered wood, twisted trees, mangled furniture, and the crushed remains of flattened vehicles.

And all the while it made a thunderous roaring sound. That's what the survivors remembered. Few of them saw the tornado; all of them heard it. When they talked about it later, when they relived the horror in dreams, woke up screaming in sweat-tangled sheets in the midnight dark, or suffered paralyzing daytime flashbacks, it was the sound that haunted them. They tried to tack words onto it, to describe it, but descriptions rely on comparisons and there was nothing to compare it to. A cement mixer full of rocks, a run-away train, a buffalo stampede, Niagara Falls, an avalanche, a rocket engine. It was a more terrifying sound than any of those, the pitted voice of death, destruction, and utter devastation, louder than all their descriptions combined. Those who lived to tell about it heard that roar as they huddled in basements or air raid shelters, a rumble that grew louder and louder until it vibrated the very earth, and when they pleaded with God to spare their lives, they screamed their prayers so God could hear them over the thunderous roar.

Any structure that took a direct hit from the twister's central vortex was vaporized. Mac's church disappeared in an instant; shrapnel from its stained glass windows sliced six inches deep into the brick wall of an elementary school on the other side of town. Farther out from the meteor crater of the twister's center, it slathered the lone remaining wall of an apartment complex with ice cream from the shattered dairy plant down the street and wadded up eleven mobile homes into smashed balls of tin. The two-mile wide backflow of the monster ripped off roofs, uprooted trees, and broke out windows all over Graham, even after it passed.

The devastation took less than three minutes; the dust had not yet settled from where it blasted its way into town before the tornado rumbled back out the other side. Its yellow color slowly fading, but its hunger unsated by its savage feeding frenzy, the twister shifted trajectory slightly and roared straight down US 270 toward the Oklahoma State Penitentiary for Women. The 761 inmates in the Iron House were not exactly innocents, but only one of them had been sentenced to die that day.

30

Jackson Prentiss looked at his watch. Emily would be frying any minute now. And he'd missed it! He'd missed the execution, missed the opportunity to laugh in her face, missed forever the chance to show her she hadn't beat him.

He didn't swear or pound his fists, though. His anger was deeper than a physical show of emotion. It was a burning down in his guts that consumed him from the inside out.

The scar-faced little tramp had surely looked for him in the audience. In her eyes, his absence was some kind of admission of defeat, an acknowledgement that she had won.

He'd wanted her to ride a lightning bolt into the bowels of hell with the sound of his laughter echoing in her ears and the sight of her precious Angel snuggled up next to him.

He shook his head in frustration and spoke aloud to the sound of the hail knocking dents in the hood of his car. "Long as that child lives, she's testimony to what that ugly little tramp did to me."

He suddenly stopped breathing. The thought burst full-blown in his head as his best ideas always did, and he leaned his head back and laughed out loud at the exquisite irony of it.

As long as that child lived ... well, that could be remedied. Oh, yes, it most surely could be fixed. Just like he fixed that Jew lawyer who got in his way. Emily stole Angela and gave her a whole new life.

Well, he'd take away from the kid what Emily had given. Emily's death would mean nothing if the child she died to save had … some kind of accident. Or maybe was outright murdered. Yes, a gruesome murder. Why not? Nobody in the world would make a connection between the famous Jackson Prentiss and some teenage girl in Oklahoma.

He smiled then; his plan put out the burning flame of rage in his belly and he was content. He would win. In the end, he always did.

◆ ◆ ◆ ◆ ◆

Princess's singing had almost unhinged Oran. He turned toward the wall and stared out the window until he could compose his face. What he saw in the next handful of seconds through that window would stalk the dark corridors of his nightmares for the rest of his life.

The golden orb of afternoon sun had just dropped below the leading edge of the storm system that formed a bubbling canopy over the Iron House and everything north and south of it stretching out fifty miles. The sunlight shining on the underside of the storm painted tattered wisps of clouds the pink and golden shades of a prairie sunset. The sun also backlit the monstrous *thing* heading north across the empty prairie, past the prison—toward the Indian Bluffs.

The thing was cast in stark relief, its form outlined by the slanted sunlight, a malevolent, swirling pillar that extended from the ground up through a gigantic hole in the boiling black overcast. It trailed a vast dust cloud in its wake like the plume of water behind a speedboat. Whipping silver strands of lightning flashed down from the bubbling caldron of black clouds above it, the spitting snakes of Medusa's hair; internal lightning flashed within the cloud bank, blinking on and off like Christmas lights behind a curtain. The thing's color boiled and changed as it roared past, a kaleidoscope of purplish black, gray, bruise-green and rust, all streaked with the bright yellow of a bug's guts on a car grill.

It suddenly hit Oran what he was looking at. He recognized the thing for what it was: a mammoth tornado, more immense and ferocious than anything he ever dared to envision, a black finger writing death in the dirt as it gobbled up the world.

All at once, he was afraid he was going to scream. He put his hands to his face, palms against his mouth to stifle the sound. But he couldn't tear his eyes away from the horror, stood transfixed as the nightmare twister hurled across the prairie three miles away, a stampeding elephant thundering toward the hills.

◆ ◆ ◆ ◆ ◆

It had stopped hailing. Jackson shoved open the car door and climbed out. It was still raining, though, so he took off his suit jacket to use as an umbrella and stood looking at the wreck. A brand new Pontiac, smashed on one side where it had hit the ditch, bunged up and dented all over by the hail.

With a disgusted sigh, he turned the direction he'd been traveling before the car spun around, peered through the rain and was relieved to see that the town he'd been trying so hard to get to was only another quarter mile or so down the road. He set out at a brisk walk to find somebody to haul his car out of the ditch, holding his coat out over his head and watching his step so he didn't slip in the mud.

It began to rain harder and he cranked up his walk to a jog. His suit jacket would be ruined! Then the rain became a torrential deluge; instantly soaked him to the skin. He could see nothing but the road a few feet in front of him. He hurried on, slogging through the mud, and finally the outline of the town appeared in the downpour.

Though he could barely see, when he drew nearer to the town he could tell it was a strange little burg. The buildings were all on the left side of the dirt street; none at all on the right overlooking the prairie and prison. At the far end of the block, he could just make out another row of buildings facing him.

He passed a sign that proclaimed "Welcome to Laramie Junction, Oklahoma," but there was no welcoming committee waiting there for him. The place was totally deserted; there wasn't a single car. And what he could see of the buildings looked odd, too, old fashioned. Squinting into the blowing rain, he could pick out what looked like a general store, a hotel and a … blacksmith shop? And were those *hitching posts* out front? It was like a town out of the old West! What in the …? Then he got it. This was a place like Williamsburg, Virginia, a tourist attraction, where people wandered around in period costumes to delight the visitors. Well, on some back street somewhere there'd better be a garage, one with a wrecker.

As he hurried toward the nearest business, the Laramie Junction General Store, the rain and wind stopped abruptly, like somebody'd turned off the faucet and unplugged the fan. The afternoon sun had dropped below the cloud bank overhead and sent shafts of light to cast the wet buildings in a sparkling, golden glow. Not a breath of wind disturbed the profusion of dripping red cannas and Indian paintbrushes in the flowerbeds beside the raised wooden sidewalks. It was so eerily quiet his footsteps echoed on the old wood as he hurried up the steps before it started to rain again. The slanting sunlight sent his shadow leaping out ahead of him, stretching it all the way to the door.

And for no reason at all, Jackson felt a chill ripple down his spine.

He crossed the sidewalk in long strides, eager to get inside where it was dry. Reaching out his hand, he turned the doorknob and it swung inward easily.

Jackson froze. In the open doorway was … a mound of dirt level with the sidewalk, brush, bushes, and the hillside beyond. If he stepped through the door he'd be right back outside again. It wasn't a building at all, just the false front of one, like a movie set.

He heard it then. A sound like a rushing train, a rocket engine, a cement mixer full of rocks. It was the pitted voice of mindless devastation. His ears popped and he smelled wet dirt.

He turned and looked down at the open prairie. A wall of bubbling, black destruction was hurling past the prison straight at him, so huge it ate up all the world.

Terror almost stopped his heart. He had time to know it was death, that it had come for him and there was no escape, nowhere to hide in this fake town where nothing was real.

He leapt through the doorway and out the back side of the wall in unrestrained panic, trailing behind him a wailing shriek. He raced across the muddy dirt pile and began to claw his way up the hillside. He slipped, fell, scrambled to his feet and kept climbing. As the roar grew louder, he screamed and wept at the same time, blubbering, "Please no, not *me!*"

THE MILE-WIDE LEVIATHAN RUMBLING ACROSS THE prairie lifted off the ground as it neared the Indian Bluffs, like a heron taking flight. The dust plume it had stirred behind it on the ground ended abruptly and the dirt began to settle out of the air.

It climbed higher and higher, still spinning savagely, still roaring forward, though slower now, its outside edges becoming less and less defined. It passed far above the top of the Indian Bluffs, but its downdraft toppled trees and exploded Laramie Junction in a swirling rumble of shattered walls and splintered boards. The whole general store section flew backward onto the hillside, slammed into Jackson as he fled in terror, knocked him to the ground and collapsed around him.

The twister continued to rise into the sky. As the speed of its whirling winds gradually decreased, it rained debris it had carried with it for miles—hunks of mangled metal, fence posts, barn doors, shingles, bricks, a fine mist of corn kernels and pieces of featherless chickens. The eight-mile-high rotating column above it slowly dissipated; the tip of the monster tornado finally reached the black ceiling of bubbling, boiling cloud, melded into it and was no more.

On the green screen of the WSR-57 radar in the National Weather Bureau office in Oklahoma City, the hook-shape in the blob of thunderstorm disappeared.

JACKSON LAY WITH HIS FACE IN the mud sobbing hysterically as a gentle rain sprinkled down on him. When his hysteria eventually calmed, he remained where he had fallen, panting, trying to get his breath as relief washed over him in a delicious, reassuring flood.

He'd made it; he'd even beat a tornado! A low chuckle bubbled up from his chest as he started to get to his feet. But he couldn't get up. He suddenly became aware of a heaviness, a weight on his back, pressing down so hard he couldn't catch his breath; he was beginning to have trouble breathing at all. Some piece of the shattered town, or set, or whatever it was, had obviously landed on top of him. Fear instantly traded places with relief in his gut, and the laughter died in his throat.

What if he wasn't strong enough to get out from under it by himself? How long would it be before somebody came along and found him?

With great effort, he managed to lift his face out of the mud, turn and peer fearfully over his shoulder to see what was pinning him to the ground.

Nothing was.

That was impossible! *Something* was holding him down, had him crushed to the ground so tight he couldn't move at all.

Raw terror gripped him. With his heart stampeding in his chest, he lifted his head up as far as he could and struggled frantically to get his arms under him so he could raise his body up on his elbows. But his arms refused to cooperate, lay limp, with the dull, numb sensation of a foot that had gone to sleep. Within seconds, he realized that he could not move any part of his body below his shoulders.

That's when he began to scream, the warbling, high-pitched screech of a terrified woman.

◆ ◆ ◆ ◆ ◆

Oran turned away from the window, his face ashen. He didn't say anything about what he had seen; he had no air to speak at all. And some part of him wondered if he'd really seen anything at all, if it was a hallucination brought on by the stress of this strange, heart-rending execution.

He shook his head to clear it, tore his scattered thoughts away from the nightmare vision and directed them to the remainder of the task at hand.

Princess was looking at him, her purple eyes huge. He stared at her sadly for a moment or two, then slowly nodded his head at the guard beside the small, white door. Princess gasped, then turned her gaze on her lap.

Her hammering heart banged so fast it might burst from the effort, but that open, airy feeling of a rip in her side below her ribs—it wasn't there. If that was fear, then she must not be afraid.

Good! She didn't want to spend her last seconds scared. She took a deep breath and focused on the pictures in her lap. And suddenly, they wasn't black-and-white pictures no more. They was real! Four *alive* faces a'lookin' up at her.

Angel at six, her hair in fat braids tied with blue ribbons ...

At nine, freckles on her nose and dog-ears ...

A twelve-year-old, her hair in a tangle of rusty curls on her shoulders ...

And the beautiful, red-haired teenager looked up at her mother with the big brown eyes of the toddler who'd whined, "I'm thirssy."

An indescribable joy filled Princess as golden and sweet as warm honey. Then they all *smiled* at her—the six-year-old didn't have no front teeth!

She smiled back. "Bye-bye, Angel," she whispered, so low not even Talbot could hear. "I love you."

The guard designated as executioner opened the white door, stepped inside, and flipped a single black switch to "on." When he did, 2,000 volts of electricity instantly completed the circuit from the wet sponge on the top of Princess's head to the one on the side of her leg. Her thin body went rigid, then jerked uncontrollably as the current sent her muscles into spasm, spilling the pictures in her lap out onto the floor. A smell like burned hair filled the room, but no sound of any kind escaped her lips.

Twenty agonizing seconds after Oran nodded his head the first time, he nodded it again. The executioner flipped the switch to "off" and Princess slumped down and was still.

Oran looked at the limp form held to the chair by leather straps and was profoundly grateful that she appeared to be dead. The machine had worked flawlessly, perhaps because Princess had been wet all over from the rain they'd run through. Old Suz had taken her life quickly and he hoped, painlessly. In fact, she wasn't even disfigured. Princess looked ... peaceful. Like she'd just fallen asleep in the chair.

"Check her out," he grunted at the doctor. "Make sure she's gone."

The doctor stepped closer, lifted his stethoscope and placed it on Princess's chest, taking great care not to touch the body. Often the skin of electrocuted prisoners was so hot it would burn.

He stood silent for a moment, listening.

The people in the viewing room were uncharacteristically quiet, sat unmoving, waiting for the doctor's verdict. They had not yet fully recovered from the sound of Princess's singing. None of them would ever forget it, and more than a few of them would someday long to get that haunting melody out of their heads.

Oran held his breath. He honestly didn't know if he *could* send another bolt of electricity through her.

The doctor stepped back and looked at his watch.

"Let the time on the death certificate of Emily Gail Prentiss read 5:02 p.m. May 10, 1963."

31

SUNDAY MORNING DAWNED SO CRISP AND clear the air itself must have been scrubbed with lye soap and hung out on the line to dry. Mac got up and dressed quietly, so as not to wake Joy. She'd had a rough couple of days. Then he drove as far as he could—only a few of the roads had been cleared of debris and tree limbs—parked the car, and walked the rest of the way. The symphony orchestra of chain saws was already tuning up before he even got near the church. He hadn't seen it, or what little must be left of it. Yesterday, he'd had to see to family and to Princess.

It had been late Saturday afternoon before he made it out to the Iron House to collect Princess's body. He'd spent the morning at the hospital with Jonas and Maggie—bunged up, couple of bones cracked was all. He'd have looked in on Wanda Ingram then, too, but she was already gone. After her broken arm was set in the emergency room, she'd been shipped off to the Oklahoma State Mental Hospital in Lawton. Then he'd had to borrow a car, a station wagon, and drive the long way around to get to the prison. US 270 was closed; three miles of it would have to be completely rebuilt before it could open again.

Mac had made arrangements for the warden's secretary to meet him when he arrived at the prison. Oran wouldn't be there, of course. The warden had lived on the southeast side of Graham. His house was gone. His family'd been in the basement when the twister hit. His wife was in the hospital; she'd make it. His little boy didn't. Jason Blackburn was one of the fifty-eight people the twister killed in its seventy-seven-mile journey of desolation that started outside Tishomingo and ended in the Indian Bluffs an hour and nineteen minutes later. Thirty-nine of those people had lived in Graham.

Everybody said it could have been a whole lot worse, though. Hundreds would have died if that siren hadn't blasted out a warning.

But the death toll would likely rise. There were people still unaccounted for; more than 150 had been injured, some of them seriously. And Mac had not been sorry to hear that Jackson Prentiss was one of them. An EMT friend told him that Prentiss had been found in the ruins of Laramie Junction, apparently had a broken back and was paralyzed. There was poetic justice in that. Princess had spent fourteen years in a cage on the Long Dark because of Jackson Prentiss; now he was the one who'd be locked up, a prisoner in his own body. And his would be a *life* sentence. Mac couldn't figure out why on earth the man had decided to go up to the movie set in the middle of a storm, why he hadn't stayed at the prison to watch the execution. Turns out the Iron House was the safest place in the whole county Friday afternoon … for everybody except Emily Gail Prentiss.

Two guards wheeled her body out on a stretcher and placed it in the back of Mac's station wagon. It was zipped up tight in a black bag and Mac didn't intend to unzip it. He'd already said his goodbyes. He'd called ahead to the funeral home—which was swamped—and said he wanted a simple casket and a quick burial.

There'd be no service. Who was there to mourn her passing?

He and Jonas would. Joy would, too. He'd told her the whole story, well, most of it. That Wanda Ingram meant to kill her and Princess knew it, sent him looking for her. That Princess had saved her life. They'd stayed up all night Friday, talking. It had felt like they were getting reacquainted. She'd been totally transparent, open and honest. He'd been open and honest, too—when he spoke of his own feelings. But he was neither when he told her the story of his meetings with Princess. He considered the promise he had made to the small, scar-faced woman a sacred vow; he would carry her secret to his grave.

Mac gawked at the devastation all around him as he picked his way through it. The utter destruction made it clear just how close he, Joy, and Wanda Ingram had come to dying. In a battle with a twister, survival was all about what you hit or what hit you in the monstrous swirling wind. A stray two-by-four could ruin your whole day. He was certain the debris that took out Mr. Wilson's windshield and windows would have taken them out, too, if all three of them hadn't been lying over in the seats. It was a miracle they were alive.

One of a herd of miracles he'd witnessed in the past week.

He stepped gingerly over a dead chicken. They were everywhere, hundreds—no, thousands—of them, littering the rubble.

The neighborhoods Mac knew so well were unrecognizable; the houses he'd run past every morning for much of his life had been reduced in seconds to tangled heaps of mangled debris, crushed under downed trees, flattened vehicles, or the roof of the house next door.

He passed an undamaged refrigerator sitting upright beneath a leafless tree, the door hanging ajar and the contents intact—a jug of milk, leftovers in Saran-wrapped bowls, something trussed up in aluminum foil, and bottles of catsup, mustard, and salad dressing. The vegetable and meat drawers on the bottom were missing. Pieces of tin and what looked like curtains were wound into the tree's bare limbs like tinsel around a Christmas tree. A bed and chest of drawers were the only two pieces of furniture that remained in the shattered brick house beside the tree. A hat hung from the bedpost and a church pew lay upside down in the middle of the unruffled bedspread.

The destruction all around him worsened the farther he went. The outside winds of the twister—still hurricane-force winds, he was sure—had struck here, like they'd slammed into Mr. Wilson and lifted it into the air. But he was walking toward where the epicenter of the tornado, the sweet spot, had mowed down everything it encountered.

He'd prepared himself for how damaged the church would be, for a huge pile of rubble where the building had once stood. But he wasn't prepared for … nothing. Mac looked around, trying to get his bearings in the desolate landscape. Then he spotted a handprint in concrete, Joy's handprint. Her name was scratched above it and the date, Sept. 4, 1953. She'd come with him the day builders had poured the concrete for the new porch on the building. Now that porch and the concrete slab behind it were all that remained of New Hope Community Church. There wasn't a brick or beam or piece of mortar. Mac walked in a daze around the slab, then noticed it wasn't completely bare. Up near where the pulpit had been there was a piece of colored glass from one of the stained glass windows. Mac squatted down and picked it up, turned it over and over in his hand, examining it.

He remained there for a long time, just staring at it. Then he heard a sound. He looked up, and picking her way through the nearby rubble was Maude Duffy. The president of the Women's Missionary Alliance, she was one of the little old ladies who'd been preparing covered dishes for him and Joy every day for the past six months.

"What are you doing here, Maude?"

She tucked her chin and looked at him over the top of her wire-rimmed glasses.

"It's Sunday morning," she said.

It was, wasn't it. Mac hadn't even considered what day it was.

Then Mac saw that Maude wasn't alone. Others were coming, too. A handful of people were making their way through the debris, coming from every direction, converging on the bare slab where the church had once stood. Will Hardesty, with a big bandage on top of his bald head, picked his way around downed tree limbs. Bruce Daniels limped along on a crutch, his leg from knee to toe encased in a plaster cast. Howard Wilson helped his wife step clear of a tangled pile of twisted metal that might once have been a chain link fence. Mac looked around, half expecting to see the other two members of the church's elder board that had never convened for its meeting Friday night, when Mac had intended to resign from the church, the ministry—and from God. Just like he'd resigned from life for the past six months. But Andy Porter and Lee Davenport weren't there. The last Mac had heard, both men were listed as missing.

Within a few minutes, there were probably two dozen people standing on the bare slab, talking quietly.

Mac wiped his eyes—must have gotten dust in them. He cleared his throat a time or two before he began to speak.

"When I announced last week that I'd be in the pulpit this Sunday, I planned to preach a sermon I'd been working on for months." He looked into all their earnest faces. "But I have something very different to say this morning than what I had planned." He gestured wide at the desolation. "I want to talk about rebuilding, redemption, and restoration."

His voice grew soft. "And about sacrifice."

Epilogue

Mᴀᴄ, Jᴏʏ, ᴀɴᴅ Jᴏɴᴀs ᴡᴀʟᴋᴇᴅ ᴅᴏᴡɴ the stone path between the headstones toward the cherry tree at the back of the cemetery. Joy moved slowly, ponderously, a week past her due date. It had been a very difficult pregnancy; Mac had watched his little girl become a young woman, a strong young woman, through the process. And in the past few weeks Joy had blossomed, smiled more and talked lovingly about the as-yet-unnamed child she was absolutely convinced would be a girl. Oh, the tears still came—often. And when they did, Mac comforted her, promised they would get through it together. And then he'd put his arm reassuringly around her shoulders and squeeze.

He did the same thing now as they walked along, the icy fingers of a cold wind reaching under his turned-up collar to tickle his neck. She gave him a grateful smile, but he could see her eyes were brimming. His probably were, too. Jonas's mouth was set in a thin, tight line. The three of them had come to the cemetery today with flowers for Melanie because it was the first anniversary of her death.

They stopped in front of her grave. Mac considered the black granite stone and decided it looked less foreboding and intimidating somehow than it once had. Now, it seemed … dignified, almost stately. It seemed to proclaim, "There is something very precious here."

The marker on the grave next to it was much simpler and plainer. On a small, white stone was inscribed a single, large word: "Princess." And beneath it: "Emily Gail Prentiss. Died May 10, 1963." Mac couldn't list her birth date because nobody knew what it was. But he had no trouble deciding what to put on the bottom of the stone. It was what she'd said to him that first day, the day they'd talked about weasels and she'd told him he was scabbed over from being dragged through the rocks. But scabs fall off, she'd said, her voice husky, her purple eyes sparkling. When you're healed, scabs fall off.

"Never underestimate the power of doing the right thing," Joy read off the bottom of the white headstone. She turned to her father, "You believe that, Daddy?"

Mac hesitated, but only briefly. "Yeah, I do, sweetheart."

"Good," she said, and let out a breath, "because I've got something to tell you." She must have seen the stricken, almost panicked look on his face because she smiled and patted his arm. "It's not *that* bad, Daddy." She turned to her grandfather. "I mean, it is bad … sad, really." She stopped sputtering and just said it, straight out. "I've decided to give the baby up for adoption."

Mac was so surprised he took a step backward. Give it up? He'd already come up with half a dozen girls' *and* boys' names, even if Joy hadn't. They'd already gotten a crib and the ladies of the church were preparing to give Joy a baby shower.

"Honey, you don't know what—"

"Yes, I do," she interrupted. "I have thought and thought about this, and no matter how much I want it to be different, I keep coming back to the same place: this baby deserves a mother like mine." She looked at the black headstone, then turned back and faced Mac. "And a father like you. A home and a family. I'm going to give my little girl a good life."

Mac couldn't speak, simply reached out and folded his daughter tenderly into his arms, the bulge in her belly making her hard to hug. An understanding that needed no words passed between him and Jonas. He struggled to get his voice under control as he looked over Joy's shoulder at the two graves under the cherry tree.

"Your mother would be so proud of you," he said.